THESE ARE THE WOMEN WHO LOVED SILAS TARKINGTON . . .

ALICE MARKHAM TARKINGTON: Si's first wife, she helped invent the Tarkington style . . . only to find herself cast aside.

CONSUELO BANNING TARKINGTON: The entrancing second wife who made marriage her career. Through years of Si's infidelities she'd hung on . . . determined to be his final wife. Now she knew nobody could take that away from her. . . .

MIRANDA TARKINGTON: Chauffeured to and from elite schools in her father's Rolls-Royce, she was the beautiful and pampered daughter who would grow to discover that nothing was as it seemed . . . not her father's past, or her own future.

ROSE TARCHER: A peppery matriarch hidden away in a Florida retirement home, she was the only one who knew the whole truth about the son she never stopped loving . . . even after he stole from her.

DIANA SMITH: The passionate, sexy mistress who loved Si Tarkington with the same hard, bright, uncompromising desire with which she coveted the diamonds she bought and sold for his store. But would her love exact too steep a price?

From an elegant Fifth Avenue salon to a manicured Long Island mansion . . . and from the Lower East Side to a mobster's lair . . . they had secrets to keep and a legacy to claim in the . . .

Carriage Trade

Carriage Trade

Stephen Birmingham

BANTAM BOOKS

New York·Toronto·London·Sydney·Auckland

CARRIAGE TRADE
A Bantam Book

PUBLISHING HISTORY
Bantam hardcover edition published August 1993
Bantam mass market edition / January 1995

ISBN: 0-553-56878-7

Published simultaneously in the United States and Canada

Bantam Books are published by Bantam Books, a division of Bantam Doubleday
Dell Publishing Group, Inc. Its trademark, consisting of the words "Bantam
Books" and the portrayal of a rooster, is registered in U.S. Patent and Trade-
mark Office and in other countries. Marca Registrada. Bantam Books, 1540
Broadway, New York, New York 10036.

PRINTED IN THE UNITED STATES OF AMERICA

RAD 0 9 8 7 6 5 4 3 2 1

For Beverley Gasner
And nobody but nobody else

Contents

Carriage Trade

Prologue

From *The New York Times,* August 12, 1991:

SILAS TARKINGTON, LEGENDARY RETAILING TYCOON, IS DEAD

Founder, Head of Tarkington's 5th Ave.

"He was to retailing as Carnegie was to steel, Ford to automobiles, Luce to publishing and Ruth to baseball." So said former New York City Mayor Edward Koch when notified of his old friend's sudden death. "His death not only constitutes a deep personal loss," the former mayor added, "it is a great loss to the City of New York and to the nation." He was Silas Rogers Tarkington, legendary founder and chief executive officer of Tarkington's, the famed Fifth Avenue specialty store that bears his name.

Death came to the tycoon on Saturday at his country estate, Flying Horse Farm, in Old Westbury, L.I., while swimming laps in his pool. When Mr. Tarkington failed to join his wife for lunch, she went to search for him in the pool area and found him floating face downward in the water. The family physician, Dr. Henry J. Arnstein, who flew immediately to the scene by private helicopter from his office in Manhattan, pronounced death by myocardial infarction resulting from coronary occlusion. Mr. Tarkington, a trim and athletic-looking man, though small in stature, had no previous history of heart illness. "But these things can catch up with a man without warning," Dr. Arnstein said. "He'd obviously been pushing himself harder than any of us realized."

An Innovative Merchant

Tarkington's became the favorite New York store of fashionable women around the world as a result of a number of merchandising innovations, most of them the result of the founder's lively imagination and retailing savvy. For instance, never in its history has Tarkington's had a sale or offered any merchandise that was marked down in price. "My kind of woman"—a phrase Mr. Tarkington often used—"is not interested in looking at merchandise that has been rejected by her peers, no matter how reduced the price," he said. As a result of this philosophy, it is the store's policy to keep no item in its inventory longer than three months. After that period, unsold merchandise, whether a $100,000 sable coat or a $100 pair of gloves, is stripped of its prestigious Tarkington's label and offered for resale to discount outlets around the country, usually at considerable financial loss to the store. At the same time, the Tarkington's shopper has always known that the goods she is buying are on the cutting edge of current high fashion.

"My kind of woman would not be pleased to buy an $800 pair of Maud Frizon shoes in May and come back in October and see the same shoes marked down to $450," Mr. Tarkington said.

"You would be astonished to learn how many retailers—and I mean highly respected retailers—offer sales and markdowns that are completely phony," he once told a group of Harvard Business School undergraduates in a retailing seminar. "Why do so many retailers use the words 'regularly' and 'usually' on price tags for marked-down merchandise? Simply because if they said 'formerly' or 'was,' they'd be lying. 'Regularly' and 'usually' are used to skirt around truth-in-advertising regulations. Beware also of merchandise tagged 'special price.' There is nothing special about the price, except that this is the price the retailer hopes to sell the item for. Every day in my newspaper, I see retail advertisements that use the phrase, You'd expect to pay. 'You'd expect to pay $300 for a thingamabob like this.' The words are meaningless and should fool no one, but many people are nonetheless taken in by this method of creating a fictitious comparative price."

Distinctive Advertising

As a part of its unique retailing philosophy, Tarkington's has never advertised a specific item. Instead, the store's small, discreet notices in newspapers like *The Times* and select fashion and shelter magazines say only "Tarkington's, Fifth Avenue," thereby steadily reinforcing the store's image of quality, costliness and high fashion for a select and wealthy clientele. It is typical of Tarkington's lofty approach to merchandising that when, during her 1972 state visit to New York, Queen Elizabeth II announced that the only retail establishment she wished to visit was Tarkington's, the store refused to capitalize on the publicity generated by the royal shopper. Instead, the store referred all inquiries about the Queen's visit to Buckingham Palace.

Generous Credit Policy

At the same time, Tarkington's has long been known for its generous credit policy. "Rich people always pay their bills," Mr. Tarkington said. "They may pay them more slowly than other people, but that is perfectly all right with us. My kind of woman travels extensively; she has homes throughout the world. She is not the sort of woman who sits down at her desk once a month and writes out checks. It's simply more convenient for her to do this once a year, or every two years, and our job is to cater to her convenience."

As a result, when, in the 1960's, retail stores began routinely adding finance charges to all accounts unpaid within 30 days, Mr. Tarkington refused to join this trend. "My kind of woman would be insulted if I ever tacked a finance charge on her bill," he once said. "I am in the business of serving clients, most of whom are also my friends. I am not in the habit of insulting my friends."

For most of its history, Tarkington's neither issued nor accepted a credit card. A customer's signature on a sales slip was sufficient. Then, in 1985, the store began issuing credit cards to customers who spent more than $10,000 annually in the store. These distinctive blue-and-pink cards have become something of an American status symbol—women have been known to place them conspicuously in their wallets and billfolds—and a woman with a Tarkington's card has no trouble establishing credit anywhere in the world.

In this way Silas Tarkington built a reputation for his store, and made himself a very rich man, by catering to the very rich. At the same time, he never made public the names of his famous clientele. Unlike other upscale retailers, such as Bijan and Giorgio, the walls of whose establishments are scattered with affectionately signed photographs of celebrity customers, Mr. Tarkington's office in the store contained only one photograph—of his wife. But the caliber of Tarkington's shoppers could be judged by the sight of Mrs. C. V. Whitney, Jacqueline Onassis, or Brooke Astor stepping out of a limousine and being escorted into the store by James, Tarkington's longtime doorman.

Not Without His Critics

Such personalized and idiosyncratic storekeeping earned Silas Tarkington his share of critics, however. "The so-called Tarkington philosophy is nothing but a gimmick," said a Fifth Avenue retailer who asked not to be identified.

"It's a gimmick to get women to buy on the basis of cost, not on the basis of quality or brand name. Since a lot of his suppliers, both on Seventh Avenue and in Europe, create special lines just for Si Tarkington, he gets his so-called 'Ours Alone' label. It's impossible to tell what his markup is, though I'm sure it's more than the normal 50 to 60 percent. I've seen merchandise in his store that seemed to me ridiculously overpriced. But he's created this mythical aura that if it's from Tarkington's it's got to be the best, and his customers have fallen for it. He's made it chic for a woman to be ripped off. It's a gimmick that worked in the spendthrift 80's, but it will be interesting to see how it works in the belt-tightening 90's. Also, it will be interesting to see what happens now that Si is gone."

Indeed, there is already much speculation in the fashion industry as to who will succeed the founder. "He *was* the store," one longtime employee told *The Times* today. "Nobody could do the things he did. His personal touch was everywhere." Often cited was his habit of telephon-

ing favorite customers to say, "Darling, I have something
new in from Paris that I want you to be absolutely the
first to see." There were customers who insisted on being
waited on by Mr. Tarkington personally and would accept help from no other salesperson. Though the store
never opened in the evenings, closing its doors promptly
at 5 P.M., an hour earlier than most New York retail
establishments, favored customers were given special
keys so they could enter the store after hours and shop
undisturbed. The late Greta Garbo was known to do
this; Miss Garbo was often seen leaving Tarkington's late
at night with an armload of garments to try on at home.
Those she decided against were picked up by a store
messenger the following morning. The store received
some unwanted publicity in 1987 when the *Daily News*
reported that Miami socialite Mrs. Curtis LeMosney
returned a $15,000 ball gown to Tarkington's a full two
years after she had purchased it, demanding a refund.
Mrs. LeMosney received credit for the cost of the
gown.

Specially favored female customers were also invited
to use Tarkington's sumptuously decorated fitting and
dressing rooms to change clothes for dinner and the theater. In these dressing rooms, cocktails and light snacks
were served by a maid in a black uniform with white
apron and cap. How many of these small personal
touches will be retained by whoever succeeds Mr. Tarkington is a much-discussed question. It has long been
assumed that Mr. Tarkington's hand-picked successor
was Thomas E. Bonham III, the store's executive vice
president and general manager, who has been with the
company since 1970. Mr. Bonham, 44, a neighbor of the
Tarkingtons on Long Island, reached at his home, was
asked whether he would be Tarkington's next president.
"That's an inappropriate question at this time," Mr.
Bonham told *The Times*. "No one can replace Si Tarkington." Mr. Bonham declined further comment, beyond
adding that the store will be closed today in the founder's
honor.

"Last of the Dinosaurs"

Others emphasized the unique role that Silas Tarkington played in New York retailing. "He was the last of the dinosaurs," said Eliza McCamber, president of the New York Fashion Group. "In my lifetime, I've seen the demise of any number of great specialty and department stores. Altman's is gone, Bonwit's is gone, Best's is gone, DePinna and Arnold Constable and Franklin Simon are all gone. I can remember when the Gimbel family owned Gimbels, the Strauses owned Macy's, and Andrew Goodman owned Bergdorf-Goodman. Now they're all parts of chains and not nearly as good as they once were. The personal touch is missing. And Saks, which was also run by the Gimbel family, now belongs to the Sultan of Dubai!"

Adding to the feeling that Tarkington's was run as a kind of paternalistic oligarchy was the fact that, in addition to their Long Island home, Mr. Tarkington and his wife maintained a 22-room duplex apartment on the top two floors of the Fifth Avenue store. Because New York building codes prohibit anyone other than a janitor to live in a building where dressmaking or manufacturing takes place, Mr. Tarkington and his wife are listed in the city registry as "janitor" and "janitress." "It made it such a cozy place to work," said one longtime employee, "with the boss and his wife living over the store."

Mysterious Origins

And yet, for all his fame and fortune, Silas Tarkington remained an elusive, even mysterious figure. Very little about his actual origins is known. In 1956 he seemed to appear from nowhere, full-blown, on the New York fashion scene. That was the year when, using capital from an unknown source, Silas Tarkington purchased the old

Truxton S. Van Degan mansion on Fifth Avenue and 59th Street, which was about to be razed. Initially, Mr. Tarkington used the various rooms in the mansion to lease small boutiques to other fashion retailers, retaining only the former foyer of the house for his own operations. Then, gradually, he took over these leases. Even today, the store's floor plan creates the feeling of walking from one small boutique to another.

In 1967, needing more selling space, Mr. Tarkington added considerably to his store by building an L-shaped addition to the mansion's northeast corner, an area that had originally contained the Van Degans' carriage house and gardens. This move aroused the ire of preservationists, who argued that the addition destroyed the mansion's setting and scale. However, since the mansion had never been given Landmark status, Mr. Tarkington was able to proceed with his plan.

"He was the most gracious and charming of men," said a former associate who asked not to be identified, "but at the same time he was a man of mystery. He never talked about his youth or early days. That was part of his fascination." Not even Mr. Tarkington's exact age at the time of his death is known, though he was assumed to be in his early to mid 70's. He studiously avoided the press and successfully resisted the efforts of a number of would-be biographers, sticking only to the scanty facts published in his company's 1975 "official" corporate history.

That corporate history, *Only the Best,* omits the founder's date and place of birth, his parents' names, and other vital statistics. The corporate history merely speaks of the founder's "Horatio Alger-like rise from poverty to fame and fortune."

Because so few hard facts are known, gossip and rumors about the man behind the facade have proliferated over the years. It has been said, for instance, that Silas Tarkington was not his original name. It has also been rumored that at some point in his career he had underworld connections, but no proof has been offered to back these allegations.

An Aloof Executive

As an executive, Mr. Tarkington was so aloof as to be almost invisible at times, making his presence known only through terse memoranda. "He was always very courtly and attentive with his special lady clients—and we were always to call them 'clients,' never 'customers'," said Mrs. Estelle Winfield, a longtime Tarkington's salesperson, "but when he walked through the store there was never much more than a polite nod to any of us. His office door was usually closed, and often no one was sure whether he was in there or not. Or we'd think he was there, and we'd find out he was actually in Paris or Rome or Tokyo, scouting new designers. One day he suddenly appeared with an armload of the most beautiful hand-knit sweaters I'd ever seen and plopped them on my counter. 'Where did these come from, Mr. Si?' I asked him. 'I brought them back with me from New Zealand last night,' he said. New Zealand! We didn't even know he'd been out of town.

"And the apartment! That was a really mysterious place. None of us was ever invited up there. I don't think even Mr. Bonham was ever there. The apartment was kind of a secret, sacred place, just for Mr. and Mrs. Tarkington."

"A Shy Man"

"I think my father was essentially a shy man," his daughter, Miranda, 24, told *The Times* today. "I think he enjoyed the perks that went with being rich and powerful, and having rich and powerful clients, but he never got used to being in the limelight. He hated it when flashbulbs went off."

Indeed, Mr. Tarkington was famously averse to being photographed. Though he often spoke in public, he did so only after being assured that no cameras would be allowed in the room. And when he and his wife appeared at social functions and cameras appeared, he frequently nudged his somewhat taller wife to the front, saying, "Photograph her, she's the beautiful one, not me." He once declared, "I see no value in personal publicity," and for news stories concerning him he usually insisted that one of a series of "official" photographs, taken in 1970, be used, rather than anything more recent. Similarly, Mr. Tarkington refused to be listed in *Who's Who in America* or other biographical volumes.

The Perfect Wife

Mrs. Tarkington was considered the perfect wife for a man in her husband's business. She is the former Consuelo Banning, one of a trio of sisters whom the press dubbed "The Beauteous Bannings," and who were belles of the Philadelphia social scene in the 1960's. The Banning sisters, Consuelo, Katharine and Lucinda, were the daughters of George F. Banning, a socially prominent Philadelphia attorney, and all three made socially auspicious marriages: Katharine to Andrew W. Mellon III; Lucinda to Nicholas de N. du Pont; and Consuelo, the youngest, to Mr. Tarkington.

With her porcelain skin, blond hair, pale blue eyes and model's size 8 figure, she became an ideal showcase for the designer fashions sold in her husband's store, and for a number of years her name has appeared high on lists of the world's best-dressed women. She has toiled for prominent charities, is a highly visible figure at New York's most fashionable restaurants, and when designers show their collections Mrs. Tarkington is always seated front and center.

"She's Tarkington's merchandise personified," says a friend who insisted on anonymity. "And having all those Mellons and du Ponts as in-laws didn't hurt Si's business either, in terms of attracting the kind of customers he wanted."

Mrs. Tarkington was in seclusion today and could not be reached for comment.

A Regal Life Style

Mr. and Mrs. Tarkington enjoyed a regal life style. In addition to Flying Horse Farm in Old Westbury and the New York apartment, the couple maintained homes in Lake Sunapee, N.H., and Palm Beach, Fla., and a pied-à-terre on the avenue Foch in Paris. Whenever Mr. Tarkington and his wife appeared in public, Mr. Tarkington, a man with an erect carriage and a full head of silvery hair, was always immaculately groomed and impeccably tailored.

Whatever his detractors may say about him, few would disagree that Silas Tarkington created and leaves behind him a retail establishment that is perhaps unique. In 1990 Mr. Tarkington received the Merchant of the Year award from the New York Retailers Association. In 1987 he received a special award from the Fifth Avenue Association for having done the most to maintain the tone of the street. Past recipients have been Pierre Cartier II, Dr. Aldo Gucci and Harry Winston.

Mr. Tarkington's interests, other than his company, included racehorses, which he bred and raced in Britain, Ireland and France. Though he declined to race any of his horses in the United States, one of his stallions, Flying Flame, won the Arc de Triomphe in Paris in 1971 and went on to win other important purses before being put out to stud in 1975. Flying Horse Farm, the Tarkington estate on Long Island, was named for this stallion.

Mr. Tarkington also amassed an important collection of Impressionist and Post-Impressionist paintings. It has long been understood that the Tarkington collection will be left to the Metropolitan Museum of Art. "That has been our informal understanding," Philippe de Montebello, the museum's director, told *The Times*. "But we shall have to see the terms of the will before we know whether the gift is a fact."

Shock Expressed

Friends today expressed shock at Mr. Tarkington's sudden death. "I saw him Friday at the Athletic Club," said one. "He looked to be in the peak of health and good spirits. He was always exercising. He'd never had heart trouble that any of us knew about. He must simply have overdone it, doing his daily laps in the pool."

Mr. Tarkington is survived by his wife and daughter. A previous marriage ended in divorce. Cremation took place Saturday under the auspices of Frank E. Campbell, and interment at Salem Fields Cemetery in Brooklyn will be private. There will be no funeral service, though the family suggested that a memorial service may be held at a later date.

Part One

MIRANDA'S WORLD

1

The Lincoln Building at 60 East 42nd Street is one of those solid, dependable New York office buildings, put up between the two world wars, which manages to confer upon its business tenants an aura of instant sobriety and respectability. No one flashy would ever lease space here, the building seems to say; no one who was the least bit sleazy would be comfortable. Stepping through the big bronze-and-glass doors into the marble elevator lobby, the visitor is immediately surrounded by a sense of probity. You are expected to be on your best behavior here, the vaulted ceilings of the lobby whisper almost audibly.

This is not a fashionable address; it is merely good. Forty-second Street isn't what it once was. Across the street, behind the imposing granite facade of Commodore Cornelius Vanderbilt's Grand Central Station, the homeless curl asleep in corners, looking like bunches of rags dropped from a great height. But from the twentieth-floor windows of the law offices of Mssrs. Kohlberg, Weiss, Griffen & McBurney, the blue-and-white flag of the Yale Club can be seen proudly flying above its Vanderbilt Avenue entrance, and it is from the Yale Club, and luncheon with his legal peers, that Mr. Jacob Kohlberg, senior partner of the firm, has just come for his two o'clock meeting. The *Times* obituary of Silas Tarkington is spread open on his desk.

"Very nice," Jake Kohlberg says, tapping the newspaper with the tip of his index finger. "He got the front page, and a full page inside the paper. Si couldn't have asked for a better sendoff."

"That was Tommy Bonham's doing," Miranda Tarkington says, almost proudly. "When Daddy died Saturday, Tommy pointed out that if we notified the papers then, the obituary would be lost in the Sunday paper. Tommy said, 'Wait till tomorrow morning. He'll get the front page on Monday.'"

"Of course one might have wished they hadn't mentioned that business about underworld connections," Jake Kohlberg says.

"Those rumors have been around forever," Miranda says. "No one pays attention to them anymore."

"And he received other awards that could have been mentioned."

"But those were the two that Daddy was proudest of."

"They might have mentioned that our father also had a son," Blazer Tarkington says. This is the first time Blazer has spoken. Blazer is Miranda's half brother, Silas Tarkington's son by his first wife. Blazer is twenty-eight, and he has chosen today to defy the law office's unwritten code of propriety. He is wearing a pair of faded Levi's, without a belt, and one leg of his jeans is out at the knee, revealing his own knobby knee, which, for some reason, is scabbed. Did Blazer fall and skin his knee on the way to this meeting? His posture, slouched in the leather office chair, legs spread apart, suggests no explanation. His sockless feet are in dirty Reeboks, one of them untied. Blazer's dark good looks are of a truculent variety. He is scowling now, his black eyebrows knitted over his black half-closed eyes and pleasantly off-center nose.

"Shit," Blazer says to no one in particular, and he removes a Camel cigarette from the pocket of his T-shirt, taps it against the heel of his untied sneaker, and lights it with a match.

In the brief silence that follows Blazer's comment—to which, of course, there is no real reply—Miranda wonders whether Blazer has been drinking. As Blazer sucks deeply on his cigarette, he shakes his head, and a thick shock of dark brown hair falls across his forehead. Miranda watches as her mother reaches out and touches Blazer's skinned knee with her gloved fingertips, a touch so gentle it would not ripple water. "You've skinned your knee," Miranda hears her mother say.

And Jacob Kohlberg presses a button on his desk. When his secretary appears at the doorway, he says, "Mildred, see if we can find an ashtray for Mr. Tarkington."

Needless to say, Blazer is not his real name. He was christened Silas Rogers Tarkington, Junior, but when he was just a little boy his father began saying of him, "This boy's career is going to blaze across the skies! Just wait and see. *He's going to blaze across the skies.*" It is perhaps unnecessary to add that this has not happened, but the nickname stuck.

When the ashtray has been delivered, Jake Kohlberg shuffles some papers on his desk and says, "Now, let's see. Are we all here? Is Miss O'Malley—"

"Pauline was going to try to make it," Miranda says, "but she telephoned me this morning to say that she's just too upset. She was afraid she'd break down. She's taken this whole thing very badly, I'm afraid." Pauline O'Malley was Silas Tarkington's private secretary for thirty-two years.

"I can understand that," Jake Kohlberg says. "We'll have to make do without her." He turns to the third man in the room. "And you, sir? Forgive me, but I've forgotten—"

"My name is David Hockaday," the fair young man says. "I represent Philippe de Montebello of the Metropolitan Museum."

"Ah, yes," Jake Kohlberg says. "Very good. Now, before we begin, let me explain that this is a somewhat

old-fashioned procedure, the reading of the late Silas Tarkington's last will and testament. It isn't strictly necessary
and is not legally required. I could easily have faxed copies to each of you. But I thought, considering the nature
of some of the bequests and the somewhat unusual contents of the instrument itself, that it might be a good idea
if we all met here this afternoon to go over the points
herein, so that I might answer any questions you might
have about the bequests or about the intent of the testator
in certain clauses—"

Consuelo Tarkington clears her throat and leans forward slightly in her chair. "Jake?" she says in her soft,
almost whispery voice. Miranda has noticed that her
mother, as always, is dressed perfectly for the occasion in
a navy blue Chanel suit with covered buttons, a blue Chanel over-the-shoulder bag with a gold chain, but with the
gold double-C logo removed, and navy pumps—all chosen to emphasize her pale blue eyes. Her fluff-cut ash-
blond hair is perfectly coifed, with two half-moon curls
perfectly framing her perfect forehead. Miranda knows
how much effort it takes to create perfect half-moon curls
like these, nestled just so, just off the face. On any other
woman, those curls might look too studied. But on her
mother they look, as always—well, just perfectly right,
the perfect touch. With a small frisson of jealousy, of
which she is not proud, Miranda thinks her mother has
the knack, the talent, the ability, call it whatever you
want, to make every other woman in the room look over-
dressed, or underdressed, or just plain put together
wrong. Even Miranda, in a simple black silk sheath, cut
to just above the knee, and a single strand of twelve-
millimeter pearls, her chestnut hair pulled back in a
ponytail and tied with a Hermès scarf, feels dressed all
wrong, compared with her mother. But then, she always
has.

"Yes, Connie?"

"I wonder if I could ask just one question before we
start," her mother says.

"Certainly."

"Jake, as I think you know, Si wanted to make some changes in his will before he died."

Jacob Kohlberg pinches the bridge of his nose between his thumb and forefinger. "That is true," he says.

"These were to be substantial changes," she says. "*I* know what they were to be, and I believe *you* know what they were to be."

"That is true," he says again, pulling a white manila envelope from his center drawer and placing it on his desk. "In fact, this office was in the process of preparing the new instrument for his signature when unfortunately he—"

"Died," Consuelo Tarkington says, a little sharply. "Please don't say 'he passed away,' or 'we lost him,' or, like my black maid says, 'he passed over.' He died, is what he did." She sits back in her chair. "I'm sorry. We've all been under a strain these last two days."

"I understand," Jake Kohlberg says. "But as I was saying, the new instrument was not yet ready for his signature when he—died."

"Well, what I'm asking you," she continues, "is whether, since you and I both know exactly what his final wishes really were, we can use that instrument—that draft, or whatever it was—whether we can use that as his last will and testament."

"Unfortunately, no. The new will was never executed. It was never signed or witnessed."

"But we both know he'd changed his mind about certain things—important things. So couldn't we consider—"

"Unfortunately—"

"—what my husband really wanted?"

"Legally, you see—"

"But couldn't we bend the law a little in this case, Jake? After all—"

"What you are suggesting constitutes fraud, Connie. And if it were even hinted that there was anything fraudulent about your late husband's will, it would open us up to lawsuits from all directions, since the size of the estate is, to say the least, extensive. I cannot suggest that you and I be parties to a fraud."

Mr. David Hockaday from the museum clears his throat. "I am afraid I shall have to divorce myself from these proceedings right now if anything like that is being considered," he says primly. "The Metropolitan Museum of Art would certainly not wish to be party to a fraud."

Miranda decides that she hates Mr. David Hockaday.

"And so," Jake Kohlberg continues, after a brief pause, "we must accept as the last will and testament of the late Silas Tarkington the one dated"—he places his glasses on his nose and removes the stapled document from its envelope—"dated June twenty-second, nineteen-ninety."

Miranda's mother sighs. "So we're about to hear read to us a last will and testament that wasn't his last will and testament at all." Her tone is bitter as she folds her gloved hands in her lap.

Jacob Kohlberg begins. " 'I, Silas Tarkington, being of sound mind and body, do declare this to be—' "

His voice drones on. Miranda fingers her pearls gingerly, and her mother, her head tilted slightly to one side, her chin resting on her fingertips, gazes absently into a middle distance somewhere between the lawyer's chair and her own, her beautiful legs crossed gracefully at the ankle, just so.

The residences are disposed of first. Flying Horse Farm in Old Westbury, the house on Jungle Road in Palm Beach, and the Paris apartment all go " 'to my beloved wife, Consuelo Banning Tarkington.' " Next comes the stable of horses, a small but distinguished one. This, " 'unless either party has an interest in maintaining same,' " is directed to " 'be sold at public auction, with the proceeds of such sale, less commissions, to be divided equally between my wife and my beloved daughter, Miranda.' " Miranda, knowing that her mother has little interest in horses, and also knowing that it costs $30,000 a year to stable a single animal, decides that probably this is what will be done.

Next come items of personal jewelry. Most of these

are bequeathed to longtime employees and old friends. A pre-Columbian gold tie clasp in the design of a man and a pre-Columbian gold frog go to the store's chief of security. An eighteen-carat gold signet ring goes to James, the store's doorman. A fourteen-carat yellow-gold gypsy-style ring containing a 1.78-carat emerald-cut emerald goes " 'to my old friend and associate, Thomas E. Bonham III.' "

"That should put an end to the rumor that there was any falling-out between Tommy and Daddy," Miranda whispers.

A pair of eighteen-carat gold cuff links set with cabochon rubies, and a matching set of studs, is left to Jacob Kohlberg himself, "with thanks for the years he has served as my principal legal counsel."

The list goes on and on, item by item, and Miranda tries to envision the pieces of jewelry her father liked the best, the cuff links she occasionally helped him fasten when he dressed for dinner, and the pieces he liked less and rarely took out of the drawer in the bank, and gradually a vision of her father appears before her, a small but commanding presence, and in her mind she dresses him, from top to bottom, the way she used to dress her paper dolls as a child, until he stands, elegantly and impeccably clad, as always, before her. And she realizes that there are tears in her eyes, though her mother's beautiful face is impassive.

Now comes the first small shocker. " 'To my faithful secretary, Miss Pauline O'Malley, I bequeath the sum of ten thousand dollars.' " There is a little collective gasp from the members of the family.

"Shit!" Blazer says. "She slaved for him for thirty-two years and that's all she gets, a lousy ten thousand bucks?"

Perhaps to change the subject, Miranda's mother interrupts. "Tell me," she asks quietly. "Does the name of Moses Minskoff appear in the will?"

"No, it does not," Jake Kohlberg answers.

"Well, thank God for small blessings," her mother says.

Jake Kohlberg hesitates, then nods, almost impercep-
tibly, in agreement.

Now comes the first mention of the art collection,
and David Hockaday sits forward in his chair and almost
visibly seems to prick up his ears. Miranda watches as he
opens his briefcase, removes a gold pen and a legal-size
pad of yellow paper, and makes a desk out of the briefcase on his lap. This is all he cares about, she thinks: the
art collection. It doesn't matter to him that a man has
died, and rather mysteriously at that. He doesn't care
about the troubled and divided family the dead man left
behind. He doesn't care about the uncertain future of Tarkington's, that rare and special store her father created,
the store that as a little girl she used to think of as her
own private castle, the store she used to dream of running
herself someday, if only her father would ever take her
seriously. Who *will* run the store now? Perhaps the will
offers an answer. . . .

As a little girl, Miranda used to come down from the
apartment at night and wander through the store after the
clients and the salespeople had gone, pressing her nose
into the minks and sables and lynxes and foxes in the Fur
Department on three to smell the pungent odor of the
pelts, each different; touching the skirts of the gowns in
the French Room, on four, and in the Bridal Salon next
door. Then down to Sportswear, on two, and then down
to the street floor, to Small Leather Goods and Shoes and
Accessories, the gleaming cosmetics counters, and all the
glittery contents of the locked glass cases of the Jewelry
Department. "That you, Miss Mandy?" Oliver, the
store's night watchman, would say to her as he made his
rounds with his time clock. "Just don't leave no finger-
prints on the glass or I'll catch hell from your daddy."
Sometimes, in the dressing rooms, she would encounter
some of her father's special ladies—the ones who had
been given their own keys—and sit and listen to them as
they gossiped and tried on clothes. Two slender dark-
haired women she got to know that way were Gloria

Vanderbilt and her friend, Oona O'Neill. Normally, dogs were not welcomed in the store—James kept them on their leashes outside while the ladies shopped—but an exception was made for the pair of borzois belonging to Doris Duke. And a small, angular, homely woman, who seemed to expect deferential treatment and the right to precede other women through doorways, turned out to be the Duchess of Windsor.

"I think we can dispense with the reading of the full inventory of the art collection," she hears Jake Kohlberg saying. "It is attached as Appendix A to the instrument. I've had a copy made for you, Mr. Hockaday, to review at your leisure. The entire collection, or rather the full list of items on this inventory, is bequeathed to the New York Metropolitan Museum of Art. However, there are some conditions."

Mr. Hockaday shifts the position of the briefcase on his lap and sits with his pen poised above his yellow pad.

Jacob Kohlberg reads: " 'Clause forty-six A: A gift in the sum of three million dollars is made to the Museum, to defray the costs of displaying and maintaining my collection, conditional upon the Museum's acceptance of the full collection and the terms under which it is given. Clause forty-six B: The collection shall be displayed in its entirety, in a special gallery to be designated the Silas Tarkington Collection in letters no less than twelve inches high. Clause forty-six C: My beloved wife shall be permitted to select as many as twenty items from the aforesaid collection and to retain them in her home or homes throughout her lifetime. Testator suggests that Monet's "Water Lilies," always a particular favorite, may be one of the works she may wish to retain. But upon her death, those works thusly retained shall be turned over to the Museum proper. Clause forty-six D: In addition to housing, displaying, and maintaining the Silas Tarkington Collection, the Museum shall designate Miss Diana Smith as Special Curator of this Collection and shall employ her in this capacity for as long as she may wish.' "

There is another small, collective gasp in the room.

"Your Honor," Mr. Hockaday begins.

"You don't have to call me Your Honor, sir. I am not a judge."

"Mr. Kohlberg, then. May I interrupt to ask, who is Miss Diana Smith? An art historian, I assume? A Ph.D.?"

"She's an old friend of my husband's," Consuelo Tarkington says softly. "And no, she never actually went to college."

"She's the jewelry buyer at Tarkington's," Miranda says.

"My husband always felt she had great taste in art."

Blazer sits forward, and as he does so the tear in his jeans splits wider, revealing more of his knee. "Goddammit, Mandy," he says, slamming his fist in his palm, "why don't you tell this fucker the fucking truth? She's our father's latest girlfriend, his latest mistress, our old man's latest piece of ass. She may be the fucking jewelry buyer, but she's also a thirty-four-year-old piece of old jade herself!"

Miranda shoots a quick look at her mother, whose face is a mask.

"Now, young man," Jacob Kohlberg begins, "this is neither the time nor the place—"

"Tell the truth, Mandy! You know who Smitty is as well as I do!"

"Blazer, I—"

"May I interrupt again?" David Hockaday asks. "Let me just say that the Museum cannot accept this gift without the approval of the board of directors. And so I must defer acceptance of the gift until the board has met and discussed these somewhat unusual terms and conditions, which may not, I should warn you, prove acceptable."

"I understand perfectly," Jake Kohlberg says.

"Our curatorial staff will also want to inspect the items in the collection. This has not yet happened."

"Perfectly understandable," Jake Kohlberg says. "So I think any further discussion of Miss Smith is irrelevant at this juncture. Meanwhile, clause forty-seven of the will provides that, should the Museum decline the bequest, the collection, with the exception of those items Mrs. Tarkington may wish to retain for her lifetime, is bequeathed to the aforementioned Miss Smith without further restrictions."

Blazer stamps out his cigarette in the ashtray and immediately lights another. "So either you get it or the old man's slut gets it. Take your pick, buddy-boy," Blazer says. Mr. Hockaday merely lowers his eyes beneath his blond lashes.

Once again Miranda looks at her mother, whose face remains smooth and impassive. How, she wonders, can her mother listen to things like this and register no emotion whatsoever? The stage, she sometimes thinks, lost a great actress when her mother opted for being a tycoon's wife.

Jacob Kohlberg clears his throat. "Shall we move along?" he says. "There are only a few more items." He reads: " 'As to my shares of stock in Tarkington's, Inc., which is located at'—et cetera, et cetera—'I direct that these be divided equally between my beloved wife and my beloved daughter, Miranda—' "

Once more Blazer interrupts. "Now wait a minute," Blazer says, "I've been sitting here for the better part of an hour listening to crap about his beloved this one and his beloved that one. What about his beloved *son*? Or don't I figure in this goddamn thing at all? Like I somehow didn't figure in his obituary?"

Miranda sees Jake Kohlberg's face redden. "I was just coming to that," he says. And he reads: " 'My son, Silas R. Tarkington, Junior, is to receive no bequests under this instrument, for reasons he will understand.' "

Blazer jumps to his feet and crushes out his cigarette in the ashtray, all in the same quick movement. "So what the hell?" he says. "Why come all the way up from the Village just to hear that I've been zapped in my old man's will? What a goddamn waste of time!"

"Blazer, that was one of the things he was going to change," Miranda's mother says. "I swear to you," and she reaches out to touch his hand but he pulls away from her.

"I'm not surprised," he says. "He was always threatening to cut me off without a goddamn penny, and now he's goddamn done it. But why the hell did you assholes have to drag me all the way up here to tell me he'd done it?"

"Jake, tell him this was one of the things his father was going to change!"

"It's true," Jake says. "He'd had a change of heart. Unfortunately—"

"Unfortunately, he changed his goddamn little heart too late!"

"I want to make it up to you, Blazer, out of my share, which is more than I need. I'll give you—"

"I don't want your money, Connie! And I don't want any of *his* goddamn money!"

"He wanted you to have it. He was angry when he wrote that will, but he forgave you later on. He loved you, Blazer. He loved you very much. He told me so."

"Well, I never wanted his goddamn love! And you— how can you sit there listening to crap about being his *beloved wife*? You weren't his beloved wife any more than my mother was his beloved wife! You were just— what? Just window dressing, no more important to him than one of the plaster mannequins in his Fifth Avenue windows! He didn't love you, he didn't love my mother, he didn't love me, and he didn't love Mandy. All he ever loved was his goddamn self!"

"Oh, Blazer, Blazer—"

"And meanwhile he was fucking every woman in New York, and you know it. You ought to know it, because he was fucking you while he was married to my mother. Well, you got what you were after, didn't you, Connie? You got his money."

"Blazer, don't say such terrible things about our father," Miranda says. "Or about my mother, for that matter."

"Why not? He was a fucking terrible man. He was a terrible father and a terrible husband. He fucked everybody over, and now he's fucking everybody over from the grave! Look! Look at how he's trying to fuck over the fucking Metropolitan Museum. Look how he's fucking you over, Connie, making you share the fucking art collection with Smitty, who was his last good fuck! Well, he's fucked me over for the last time, and all I can say is I'm glad somebody else killed him, because if somebody else hadn't killed him I'd probably have done it myself!" He strides toward the door of Jacob Kohlberg's office, nearly tripping on the untied shoelace. "Fuck you all!" he says. "I never want to see any of you fucking assholes again." And he pulls the door open, marches out, and slams the door behind him.

In the silence that follows, Miranda looks across at her mother again. Her mother has removed one of her gloves and is twisting it, twisting it, between her hands, but her pale face, framed by the ash-blond hair and the little crescent-moon curls, is still a mask.

"I think he's been drinking," Miranda says at last, though she knows it probably isn't true.

"I want to give him some of my stock, Jake," her mother says.

"He won't take it, Mother," Miranda says. "You know he won't take it. He'll never take anything from you. Or me."

And so, Miranda thinks, that is the way it will be. One half of Daddy's shares in the store will go to Mother, and the other half will go to me. Neither of us will have a clear majority, and together we can't possibly have even a consensus. If anything, this arrangement can only turn us into adversaries, even more bitter adversaries than we were before.

In the days since her father's death, she had dared to hope that things might have been left otherwise, even though she knew such a hope was unrealistic. He had never understood her feelings for the store, and neither had her mother, but to Miranda the store was home. It was the house she lived in. In her wanderings at night, after the store had closed, the racks and counters and fixtures and display cases became her furniture. In her mind, like a fastidious housewife, she changed and re-arranged her rooms, mentally experimenting with different groupings, different color schemes. One night, in the shoe department, she had actually rearranged the little gilt chairs and footstools, putting them at conversational angles rather than in a straight row. This gave that corner of the street floor a much more welcoming look, she thought, and surely the department head would notice this when he arrived at the store in the morning. He had indeed noticed, and everything had been quickly replaced exactly as it had been before.

In her fantasy house, she also had fantasy parents. Each of the mannequins, in all their languid poses, was her mother. They all had her mother's face. This was no accident, no coincidence. In 1985 her father had decided to update the store's stock of waxen ladies, and suppliers had submitted sketches. But none of their submissions had quite satisfied her father. "Not aristocratic-looking enough," he kept saying, "not classy enough for us," so the artists would tear at their hair and go back to their drawing boards. "Show us the kind of woman you have in mind, Mr. Si," they said at last, and on a sudden impulse he had pulled out some photographs of his wife. "Make them all look like her," he said. "That's what my kind of woman looks like." And so, though Tarkington's mannequins had been given various hairstyles and coloring, they all had Consuelo Tarkington's sculptured facial bones.

Consuelo herself had been amused by this. Miranda had found it unnerving, at first, to encounter her mother's face at every turn in the store, in every room of her house. But then she decided it was better to have dozens of beautiful mothers than no mother at all. These mothers were there whenever she needed one, and they all gazed at her with unerring approval and even curiosity.

After store hours, a new and tangible and approachable father could be found in this house too. He sat in his empty corner office, in an empty chair, behind an empty desk, waiting for her to visit him where, in real life she was not supposed to venture without an appointment or without being announced by Pauline O'Malley. Here was a perfect place to talk to him, where he could give her his undivided attention and listen to her ideas. At night, she would slip into her father's empty office, close the door behind her, and seat herself opposite the father who was sitting in the empty chair.

"Daddy, I have a plan," she would say to him. "It's about me and the store. Please listen to it. . . ."

And, even though he wasn't there, he would listen, listen, listen.

That way, he could become the most wonderful, caring father in the world while, downstairs on the selling floors, her mother, in a variety of welcoming gestures, greeted the guests who came to be treated to the wonders of Miranda Tarkington's store.

When a child isn't blessed with much in the way of parents, she thinks a little wryly now, the child becomes attached to *things*.

2

THE SCENE: *A drab stretch of West 23rd Street in Manhattan. Outside a nondescript office building, a sign reads:* MOSES L. MINSKOFF, DEVELOPER.

THE TIME: *A muggy morning in August 1991.*

The lights go up to reveal the interior of this establishment: a pair of offices, cheaply furnished. In the smaller of the two rooms, the reception area, MINSKOFF'S secretary, SMYRNA, sits reading a movie magazine and chewing gum. In the larger office, MINSKOFF sits in a swivel chair at his desk, talking on the phone. He is a large man in his shirt sleeves, with an unlighted cigar clamped between his teeth. He wears a yellow Ultrasuede vest, and a heavy gold watch on a gold chain is slung across his middle. In addition to his desk and chair, the principal features of his office are a big old-fashioned Mosler wall safe and a spavined sofa against one wall. The sofa's condition suggests that MINSKOFF often sleeps here.

MINSKOFF   *(on the phone):* I'm making a credit card call. *(He rattles off a fourteen-digit series of numbers. There is a pause.)* What? What do you *mean* that credit card has been canceled? This is an outrage! I shall most certainly report you to your supervisor, young woman!

He slams the receiver down and simultaneously draws a line through the top number in the list of numbers on the pad in front of him. Then he picks up the phone and dials again. Credit card call. . . . (More numbers.)

Thank *you*! Thank *you* for thanking me for using AT&T. I always use AT&T, and with the greatest pleasure, my good fellow!

While he waits for his call to go through, he consults his watch.

Milton? Moe Minskoff here. How's the weather out there? . . . Well, it's hot as hell here. Listen, Miltie, we got a little problem, you and I. You know that rock group you got booked into East St. Louis next Friday night, the Whatchamacallems? . . . Yeah, the Hot Jockers, that's them. Well, the fire chief's brother out there is a good buddy of mine, and it seems like their stadium has a capacity seating of seventy thou. And it looks like you've already sold ninety-five thousand tickets to that concert at fifteen bucks a pop. . . . Yeah, I know you gotta overbook for no-shows, Miltie, and who cares if a few hundred coked-out *shvartzers* have to sit in the aisles? . . . Yeah, I know all that.

But listen, Miltie, this fire chief's brother says the fire chief is real nervous. You've oversold by twenty-five thousand tickets! That's a hell of a lot of no-shows. This fire chief's brother says if the news got to the papers, the city council or whatever the hell it is would cancel the show and you'd have to fork back the entire gate. We're talkin' big bucks, Miltie. We're talkin' nearly a mil five, right? . . . Now wait a minute, Miltie, don't fly off the handle. All I called for is to try to help you out. No need to make a

federal case out of this. We're just talkin' fire laws,
Miltie, and this fire chief's brother says that for thirty
big ones this fire chief will forget about the whole
matter. . . . Yeah, I think I can get him down to
twenty-five. You happy with that figure? . . . Okay,
you Fed Ex the cash to me tonight, and I'll take care
of the whole thing. Plus my fifteen percent commission, naturally. . . . How's the wife? Slap her butt
for me, Miltie, and have a nice day.

He hangs up and immediately dials another call.

Credit card call . . . *(More numbers.)*

Hello, Chief Gomez? Moe Minskoff here. It's all
set, big buddy. I got your ten big ones for you.
They're Fed Exing the cash to me tonight from LA,
and I'll Fed Ex it on to you first thing in the morning,
minus my fifteen percent commission, naturally. . . .
Not at all. Don't thank me. That's what I'm here for.
Let me know if you have any more of these type of
problems, and have a nice day.

He hangs up and dials a third call.

Credit card call . . .

Sal? Moe Minskoff here. Listen, big buddy, we
got a little problem. You gotta lower your bid for
construction of that casino down in the islands by at
least five hundred big ones or you're outa the
ballpark, buddy. . . . Yeah, the prime minister
seems pretty adamant about that. . . . Well, maybe
I could talk him into it if you'd drop the price by
three-fifty. But if I do that, Sal, I'm gonna hafta ask
you a favor. I want you to put Irving Sentler in
charge of the construction down there. . . . You
know who Irving Sentler is. He's Honeychile's
brother. . . . Whaddaya *mean* who's Honeychile?
Honeychile is my *wife,* for Christ's sake! Irving needs
a job, and his wife wants to spend the winter in the
Caribbean, okay? . . . Well, I'll see what I can do.
Get back to you, Sal. Have a nice day.

Another credit card call.

Ah, Mr. Prime Minister. This is Moses L. Minskoff calling. How is the weather down there, sir?

Ah, how I envy you, basking in the tropical sun, the breezes rustling the palm fronds, those miles of sandy beaches, the blue crystalline waters of the sea. You truly live in paradise, sir. . . . Ah, but of course I have news for you. I wouldn't have called you, sir, if I didn't have news, and good news it is. Mr. Cortelli has lowered his bid by a quarter of a million dollars, just what you asked for. And the other good news is that he wants to place Mr. Irving Sentler in charge of construction down there. You're very lucky to be able to obtain Mr. Sentler, because he's the best in the business, the very best, and very much in demand. I couldn't believe you could be that fortunate when I learned Mr. Sentler might be available. But he's agreed, not without a certain amount of personal sacrifice, to take on your government's job. . . .

Yes, sir. . . . Yes, all financial arrangements will be handled through this office, to spare you personal involvement in any awkward money matters. . . . But, sir, I wouldn't consider asking for a commission from your government. . . . On the other hand, there was that little arrangement we discussed earlier. . . . Yes, once the casino is in full operation, we would each take a percentage—ten, I think, was the figure you mentioned—off the take from the tables and the slots. . . . No, I don't think of it as a skim, Mr. Prime Minister. I think it would just give us both a sense of having a partnership in your government's beautiful new casino. . . . Well, I do thank you, Mr. Prime Minister. It's a pleasure to do business with a man of your caliber, and I hope you have a wonderful day in your island paradise.

Hangs up the phone. With his hand still on the receiver, he frowns thoughtfully. Clearly, his next call will be of a somewhat trickier nature. His lips move as he formulates his thoughts, then he picks up the receiver and dials another credit card call.

Mrs. Van Degan? This is Moses L. Minskoff, the investment banker, calling from New York. You may remember me. I handled a number of real estate transactions for your late husband, which were, if I may venture to say so, very profitable to him. . . . Ah, you *do* remember me! How are you enjoying retirement in Arizona? . . . Good.

Well, the reason I am calling you is that I have a very unusual offer to make to you, an offer I am making only to a few close friends and relatives. I'm letting my mother go in on this, by the way. You see, I happen to have in my possession some promissory notes—IOU's, if you will—from the late Mr. Silas Tarkington. You may have read that Mr. Tarkington passed on recently. . . . Yes, I remember you were always a Tarkington's shopper, Mrs. Van Degan. Now, these markers of his—these promissory notes, I should say—are in fairly large denominations, representing funds I advanced to Mr. Tarkington over the years. I am looking at one, for example, for five hundred thousand dollars. These promissory notes are, in effect, undated checks. Now, obviously I wouldn't ask you to pay five hundred thousand dollars for a promissory note in that figure. On the other hand, I could offer you a fifty percent discount, the same discount I'm offering my mother, and let you have it for two hundred and fifty thousand. . . . What's in it for you? Ah, there's the beauty part, my dear Mrs. Van Degan.

You may have read in the financial press that Continental Stores has been for several months trying to take over Tarkington's. Si Tarkington was fighting the takeover. But now that the old ba—now that Mr. Tarkington has passed on, Continental is really going to pull out their big guns and up their offer to Tarkington's stockholders. In any takeover, these promissory notes become most valuable. Continental is going to have to buy them back, since they represent money Tarkington's owes. They will come to you with an offer, and I think I can promise you a thirty to thirty-five percent return on your investment within just a few months, Mrs. Van Degan. . . .

Is it legal? Would I offer a woman of your caliber

and social position anything that wasn't legal? Certainly it's legal. Here on Wall Street we call it factoring, the discounting of accounts receivable. You pay the discounted price, and I simply endorse the notes and turn them over to you. . . . Why don't I hold on to them myself? Well, here on Wall Street this is known as streamlining. My interest in Tarkington's is comparatively small in relation to the rest of my business, and managing these small matters just takes up too much of my time. Besides, I am in the business of serving my customers, and I thought of this as a way to repay your late husband for all the business he brought my way. He was a wonderful man, Truxton Van Degan, a truly wonderful man. . . . Yes, he did drink a bit, but never to excess, Mrs. Van Degan, never to excess, and I know he wanted you to be in comfortable circumstances after his untimely demise. . . .

Yes, you think about it, Mrs. Van Degan, but don't think about it too long. Remember, I can promise you a yield of between thirty and forty percent within a few short months, and these units of mine are being snapped up right and left. I only have a few more left, Mrs. Van Degan, so think about how many units you'll be wanting to buy. I'd recommend you get back to me no later than the end of the week. Let me give you my private, unpublished number. . . .

In the outer office, SMYRNA has been juggling some incoming calls on other lines, putting them on Hold. Seeing that her boss is briefly off the phone, she turns in her swivel chair and faces his door.

SMYRNA *(yelling):* I got the President of Mexico on line one, Moe. And the credit manager of Bergdorf's is on line two. It's something about Honeychile's charge account.

MINSKOFF: Tell the President of Mexico to go to hell. I can't do business with that spick. Tell him his Banco de Mexico isn't the only bank in the damn third world. I'll take the call from Bergdorf's.

He presses one of the blinking buttons on his phone and picks up the receiver.

Moses Minskoff speaking. *(a pause.)* What do you *mean* Mrs. Minskoff has exhausted the credit limit on her Visa card? That's quite impossible. Let me speak to your immediate superior, young woman. . . . You mean you *are* the credit manager? Then let me speak to the president of the store. . . . He's in Europe? Young woman, do you realize who the person is to whom you are speaking? I am Moses Minskoff the developer, and even as we speak I have the President of Mexico waiting on hold to speak to me. . . . What? . . . Then your computer must be malfunctioning, unless—unless—*(He strikes his forehead with the heel of his palm.)* Wait! Wait, please forgive me, but I had that Visa account closed last week. I just remembered, and I'm afraid I forgot to give Mrs. Minskoff the new account number. Surely that's the cause of this misunderstanding. Let me give you the new number. *(He paws through slips of paper scattered across his desktop.)* Here it is. *(He recites a thirteen-digit number.)* There. Does that satisfy your computer? . . . Of course it does. Now you let Mrs. Minskoff charge whatever she wants. She's a very good customer. I'm sorry about the mixup, but you were quite right to check. I'm going to commend you to the store's president when he gets back from Europe. . . . Thank you, and have a nice day.

Once more, he appears to be deep in thought before placing his next call. Then he yells to the outer office.

Smyrna! Get me the president of Continental Stores in Chicago. Name's Albert Martindale. Use the two-four-one credit card. See if you can get him on the line before you put me on the line; you know the routine. But if you can't, I'll go through his secretary.

We see SMYRNA placing the call and then, inaudibly, arguing with Martindale's secretary. Finally, she yells into the inner office.

SMYRNA: Won't work, Moe! She says put you on the line first, then she'll put Martindale on.

MINSKOFF *(sighs)*: Okay. *(He picks up the phone.)* Moses Minskoff here. . . . Yes, thank you. . . . Ah, Mr. Martindale! How are *you*? . . . Well, you may recall that you and I have been in correspondence about some shares of Tarkington stock which I own, and which you have made an offer to purchase in connection with your—ah—proposed acquisition—I dislike the term "hostile takeover"—of the Fifth Avenue store. As you may know, Mr. Martindale, I am something of an expert in the field of mergers and acquisitions, and, yes, I am considering selling my own small number of Tarkington shares to your investment group. . . .

Yes, but first let me tell you that, since the founder's sudden death, the situation has changed somewhat. . . . Yes, the situation has changed considerably, Mr. Martindale. But permit me, if you will, to move back in time a bit. To begin with, Silas Tarkington was my oldest and dearest friend. He helped me start in my business, and I helped him start in his. I was perhaps his closest confidant. Over the years, in addition to being permitted to purchase small amounts of stock in his company, I was able to advance him certain amounts of cash from time to time. These loans, in the form of informal IOU's, are still outstanding in my accounts receivable files.

Now, not long before his sudden death—just a couple weeks ago, in actual fact—Mr. Tarkington hinted to me that he felt his life might be in danger. He mentioned nothing that was actually specific, but as you and I know, any rich and successful man such as Si Tarkington—or even you yourself, or even I myself—is bound to acquire his share of enemies. In fact, when he mentioned his imminent death to me, I wasn't even sure whether or not he was contemplating suicide.

The real point is that, when I learned that he feared he didn't have long to live, I decided that it would be prudent if I were to call in these IOU's. Collecting debts from the estate of a deceased person can be damnably complicated, as I'm sure you know, so I approached him on that specific subject.

I said, "See here, old sport, I think it's time you settled my account and not leave your poor widow and children arguing with my lawyers."

What he told me then, frankly, shocked me. He told me that the store was experiencing severe cash-flow problems. He told me that Tarkington's had accounts receivable in the amount of many millions of dollars. He hinted that someone within his organization may have been embezzling from him, may have been cooking the books, may have had his hand in the till, and that he was on the verge of discovering who that person was.

In short, he was unable to repay the various debts he owed me.

Are you still with me, Mr. Martindale? . . . Why am I telling you all this? Because, Mr. Martindale, if you will let me broker this acquisition for your company, I would be willing to forgive those IOU's, or at least offer them to you at a seriously discounted rate, thus facilitating your purchase greatly.

Greatly, Mr. Martindale. Greatly. I think you can hear what I am saying. Sound good to you?

And that's not all I can offer you, Mr. Martindale. If the small matter of Si Tarkington's indebtedness to me were all I was telephoning you about, I would not be wasting yours and my valuable time, now, would I? As you know, Si Tarkington ran his business in a way that was unusual, not to say unique. Yes, unique is the right word. After all, Tarkington's is unique among American fashion retailers. Si Tarkington always kept the store's figures very close to his vest. It was never clear, for instance, what the store's markup was. As often as not, Si's markup was a matter of whim. His suppliers, those who created his "Ours Alone" line, were equally secretive about their prices. And it was never clear where, and how, he disposed of his unsold inventory, though it was obviously sold somewhere. Back in 'eighty-nine, when the F.T.C. boys came to review the store's operations, I remember Si chuckling—heh, heh, heh—about how the F.T.C. boys spent three weeks shuffling through piles of paper and went away scratching their heads.

But I am in a unique position, Mr. Martindale, to offer you the store's actual sales figures. I'm talking the day-to-day sales figures, department by department, for the last twenty-four months or longer —the full and complete set of the company's books. The person who controls these books is in my pocket, Mr. Martindale. And I can promise you that these figures will not amount to what you have been led to believe. Tarkington's has suffered from the recent recession as much as other retailers, if not more so, considering the upscale nature of the store's trade. I can supply you with the full list of accounts receivable. I can also supply you with an exact dollar figure for the store's current inventory, which, I can also assure you, is worth nowhere near what you have been told. . . .

What would you do with this information? Well, Mr. Martindale, under one scenario I'm thinking of, if the news were leaked to your competitors that you have these figures and that the property is being offered at an inflated price—well, if you're lucky, Mr. Martindale, your competitors will drop out of the picture, and the property will be yours. And you will have it at a distress-sale price, costing your company considerably less money. You'd have the advantage of knowing exactly what you're getting for your money, a not inconsiderable advantage, it seems to me. Of course, once you acquire the property, you can do whatever the damn hell you want with it. The Tarkington name—one of the top fashion names in the world—has some value, though it's hard to put a dollars-and-cents price on the value of a name. And the Fifth Avenue building has some value. But if your competitors were to learn that Continental has the precise operating figures. . . . Yes, I'd be happy to engineer that leak for you, Mr. Martindale, as part of our deal.

And I'd like to throw in one more offer, sir, while I have you on the line. In any proposal that is placed before Tarkington's stockholders, there is one important stockholder whose vote will be pivotal, and I have that particular stockholder in my pocket, Mr. Martindale. That particular stockholder will vote whichever way I tell he or she to vote. . . . No, I'm not at liberty to reveal that stockholder's name at this point in our negotiations, Mr. Martindale. . . . No, I can't tell you whether that stockholder is a family member at this point in time. I can only say that he or she will have the swing vote, and without that vote you're out of the ballpark, sir. . . .

Why am I making this offer to you? Well, let me put it this way. I've always admired the way you do business. And I understand that the other two serious bidders for the store are one of your arch-rival chains in the U.S. and a retail chain in Canada. Just say I'm enough of a red-blooded American to want to see Tarkington's stay in American hands, the *best* American hands. . . .

My fee? Well, let's say that would be negotiable, at the time you and I are ready to hammer out a contract. We wouldn't call it a finder's fee, exactly. I'd like to see it as a facilitator's fee. Some sort of percentage that we'd both agree on. . . . Well, you do that, Mr. Martindale. You think about it. But don't think about it too long. The heirs are anxious to get the estate settled. . . . No, there's nobody in the family gives a damn about running the store, except maybe the daughter, who works there. But she's just a kid. No experience. Too wet behind the ears. She'll be easy to handle. . . . So, nice talking with you, Mr. Martindale. Let me hear from you by—let's say Friday, latest. Thank you, sir, and you have a nice day, you hear?

He hangs up the phone, tilts back in his big chair, and rubs his belly. Then he makes another call, this time a local one.

Tommy Bonham, please, Moe Minskoff calling. . . . Well, if he's out, where is he? . . . See if you can locate him, sweetheart. Tell him I need to talk to him right away. Tell him it's urgent.

He hangs up again and dials another local call.

Eddie? Moe here. Listen, I need some new phone credit card numbers. Last ones you give me is turning into duds already. Get me corporate card numbers. They last the longest. Those individual numbers don't last shit. . . .

Whaddaya *mean* how do ya get 'em? Same way you always get 'em. Go out to the airport, hang around the pay phones, and when you hear some guy give his number, *write it down*—what're you, some kind of jerk? And if he starts punching in numbers, watch what numbers he punches. You got *eyes*, ain'tcha? Watch, and make a mental note. And re-member what I told you about delayed flights. Check the TV screens for delayed flights. That's when guys call their boss, or their wife or girlfriend, or who's meeting their plane, to say they'll be late. Just act like you're waitin' to use the phone. . . .

Whaddaya *mean* the price has went up? Listen to me, you little shmuck, there's about fifteen thousand other shmucks out there who can do what you do for me! You want this job or not? . . . Okay, that's more like it. The price stays the same, two bucks a pop. Now get out to La Guardia and start shlepping. I need fifty new numbers by five o'clock.

He slams down the receiver. Now he eases him-self out of his chair. He checks the wall safe, then walks into the outer office.

MINSKOFF *(to Smyrna):* Christ, I'm starving to death. I haven't had anything to eat all day. Doctor keeps telling me I gotta take off sixty pounds, but a man's gotta eat something, don't he? I'm going across the street to Harold's and grab a bite. If they locate Bonham, come get me.

Smyrna merely nods, not looking up from her magazine. He exits. Cut to: Interior, Harold's Diner, a seedy luncheonette with a counter and butt-sprung stools, most of which have been taped together with masking tape. HAROLD, in a dirty white apron, stands behind the counter.

MINSKOFF enters, takes a seat at the counter, experiencing some difficulty squeezing his large frame between the stool and countertop.

MINSKOFF: Harold, I keep tellin' ya, ya got these stools too close to the counter. I got a friend in the bar fixture business. He could get ya some stools—

HAROLD: Always sellin' somethin', ain'tcha, Moe?

MINSKOFF: Just trying to be of service. I'm in a service business, after all.

HAROLD: Well, what'll you have today?

MINSKOFF: Let's see. *(Studies the plastic-coated menu.)* Gimme a bowl of your chili, a double bacon cheeseburger heavy on the mayo, a large fries, a large onion rings, and a diet Pepsi.

HAROLD: Cash only, Moe. Remember my policy. Credit makes enemies. Let's be friends.

MINSKOFF: Cash, shmash.

He reaches in his back pocket and pulls out a large wad of bills. He waves this in front of Harold's face before replacing it in his pocket.

HAROLD   *(whistles)*: Comin' right up, Moe!

MINSKOFF   *(sighs, removes the unlighted cigar from between his clenched teeth, and balances it carefully on the counter's edge)*: Hit an Exacta in the sixth at Belmont. Yeah, it's been a pretty good week, all things considered. It ain't gonna be long now before Honeychile and me can hang it all up and retire to the Bahamas.

Blackout

3

As she steps from the bright summer sunshine of the street into the seductively lighted Cafe Pierre, it takes a few moments for Miranda Tarkington's eyes to grow accustomed to the gloom. She removes her sunglasses, and then she sees him. As usual, a tall, sleek, and expensively put-together woman has stopped at his banquette to talk to him, and Miranda watches the two of them in animated conversation. Tommy Bonham, she often thinks, must know every woman in New York, or at least every important woman in New York, and of course this is all a part of being vice president and general manager of Tarkington's. Even today, when the store is closed, Tommy is doing business. Miranda watches as Tommy rises and kisses the tall woman's outstretched hand to bid her adieu and the tall woman returns to her own table.

"Who dat?" Miranda whispers as she slides into the banquette beside him. "Me think-um big-time rich squaw, huh?"

"Rich Texas broad," he mutters out of the side of his mouth, still smiling in the direction of the departing woman's back. "Came over to complain about the store being closed today. Can you believe it? Not a word about your father's death. Just, When's the store going to open? She needs an evening bag for a party tomorrow night. 'Just a little clutch bag, but it's got to be silver.' "

"Not one of our latchkey ladies?"

"Are you kidding? Broad's a kleptomaniac. She likes it when I wait on her, but she doesn't know it's because I have to watch her like a hawk whenever she's in the store."

From across the room a redheaded woman in a red Ungaro suit and a pink blouse waves at them and blows an air kiss, mouthing the words, "Hello, darlings!"

Miranda blows an air kiss back, and Tommy smiles in the woman's direction. When he smiles, he has three dimples—one on each cheek, and one on his chin.

"Mona Potter," Miranda whispers. "This means we'll be in her column tomorrow morning."

"Bitch owes us fourteen thousand dollars," Tommy mutters. "She thinks she can pay her bill with column mentions."

"Poor Tommy," Miranda says. "I'd like a Lillet," she says to the waiter who has approached them.

"Certainly, Miss Tarkington," he says, "and may I tell you how saddened we all were by the news of your father's death? He often came in here, you know. We were all very fond of him."

"Thank you," Miranda says. "That's very kind of you to say."

"And of course everybody's wondering—will Tarkington's ever be the same? Can it ever be the same without him?"

"I think it's safe to say that Tarkington's will always be Tarkington's," she says. "Right, Tommy?"

"Absolutely." He nods his head in agreement. "Well," he says, after the waiter has departed, "how'd it go with the lawyers?"

"Oh, not very well, I'm afraid," she says. "Blazer made a terrible scene. I knew damn well he would. Because Daddy made good on his threat. He didn't leave Blazer a penny. I don't know why Blazer even came this afternoon. In fact, I called him this morning, and I said to him, 'Blaze, honey, please don't come to this meeting this afternoon, 'cause I don't think you're going to like what you're going to hear in Daddy's will.' But he said, 'No, I want to have the last word with the old son-of-a-bitch.' "

"And so he did."

"Of course, and he began shouting about—oh, you know, Daddy's girlfriends and all that. And about Smitty. And Mother just sat there, looking beautiful, saying nothing, as though she had ice water in her veins. Can you understand it? I know I could never put up with a husband who was flagrantly unfaithful to me, and *all the time*! Could you? Could you put up with a wife who was unfaithful to you all the time?"

He smiles. "Since I've never had a wife, I can't say," he says.

"That's probably why you've never had a wife. To spare yourself that aggravation."

He merely lowers his eyes and stirs the olive, on its toothpick, in his martini.

"But Mother—she seems just as unconcerned about Daddy's womanizing now that he's dead as she was when he was alive. Maybe someday you can explain my mother to me, Tomcat."

"I think," he says carefully, "that your mother's a very brave woman, Mandy."

"Very brave or very stupid. Or maybe brave and stupid are the same damn thing." She flips her chestnut ponytail with her left hand. "Anyway, I've stopped worrying about what my mother's feelings are. But poor Blazer, on the other hand—"

"Mandy," he says, "maybe I shouldn't say this, but don't you think Blazer had it coming to him? He treated his father like shit, and your father wasn't a man who liked to be treated like shit."

"Oh, I know, I know. And particularly after that last big row of theirs. But still—"

"He threatened your father, Mandy. He tried to—"

"I know, I know. But I think what hurt Blazer most

of all was not being mentioned in the obituary this morning. It was like reading that he didn't exist."

He shakes his head. "I don't know how that happened," he says. "I gave *The Times* all that information. Want me to see if I can get the paper to print a correction, mentioning that Silas R. Tarkington, Junior, was inadvertently omitted from the obit? They're pretty good at doing things like that for us."

"No. No, I don't think so. That would be like rubbing salt in his wounds. Like saying, 'Oh, and we forgot to mention that he also had this son.' No, the harm's been done."

"If Blazer had ever tried to make anything of himself, it might have been different. But face it, Mandy, your half brother's a bum."

She nods mutely, in agreement. "Still, he was always nice to me when I was growing up. And—in fact—it turns out that at the last minute Daddy was planning to rewrite his will."

"Really?" he says, looking at her, interested. "How do you know that?"

"Jake Kohlberg told us so. He was apparently planning to reinstate Blazer in some way and make some other major changes. But then he—died—and it was too late. . . . Thank you," she whispers to the waiter as he places her glass of Lillet in front of her.

"What sort of—major changes?"

"I don't know. After Blazer went storming out, I asked Jake if we could see a copy of the new will he'd been drafting, but he wouldn't show it to us. 'Lawyer-client confidentiality,' he said. 'But I'm his daughter!' I said. 'And I'm his lawyer,' he said. Stupid lawyers."

"Hmm," he says.

"Anyway, he left you his emerald pinky ring. I thought that was sweet of him. It's a good emerald, even though you-know-who picked it out for him."

"Smitty."

"Who else?"

"Smitty knows her stones. Anyway, I'm touched that he'd leave that to me, Mandy. Of course I could never wear it. It was like his signature. It was *his* ring. It will always be his ring."

"I suppose so, yes." She sips her Lillet.

"And what about the art collection?"

"That was something of a shocker, too. Mother gets to keep up to twenty paintings for her lifetime. The rest go to the museum—*but* only if you-know-who is made special curator of the collection."

"Smitty again."

"How'd you guess? That was a little callous of him, don't you think, putting Mother and Smitty in the same paragraph of the will? But again, Mother was cool as a cucumber when she heard. Didn't blink one mascaraed eyelash."

"Callous? I'm not so sure, Mandy. It could be his way of giving Smitty a new job. Getting her out of the store—for your sake."

"Really? You think so?"

"That's the way his mind worked. He's left you and your mother a major share of the store's ownership. And I don't think Smitty is one of your favorite people."

"Really? You noticed that? Well, aren't you smart, Mr. Tomcat. I *loathe* Smitty!"

"But you have to admit she's been a good jewelry buyer. Her department's figures have been among the best in the store."

"Unless he let her pad them—among her other special perks."

"No. She never padded any figures. No figures were ever padded."

"You mean those are her real boobs? Anyway, it's nice to hear you speak of her in the past tense."

He winks at her, and she smiles back at him.

"Actually," she says, "I don't know why I resent Smitty so. It's not as though she was the first of Daddy's girlfriends, and she probably wouldn't have been his last. It was just that—"

"That she was getting to be a little too important to him. In a way, it may be good that he died when he did, before he did something—foolish."

"You mean, like—"

"She told me she was going to marry him."

Miranda stares at him, but his eyes, as he sips his cocktail, wander away from hers.

Whenever Miranda looks at Tommy Bonham, she has never failed to be struck by his extraordinary good looks. "Heck, I was just a little Hoosier hick from Indiana," she has often heard him say. "Until Si Tarkington plucked me out of a cornfield when I was a kid of twenty-three, on a hunch that I might have some ability, brought me into the store, and taught me everything I know about retailing."

Well, that makes a charming story, but Miranda knows enough about Tommy's background to know that it isn't entirely true. What would her boulevardier father have been doing in Indiana? And in a cornfield, no less? No. Tommy may have come from Indiana, but after graduating from Bloomington, where he'd been a theater major, he'd brought himself to New York, hoping to find work as an actor. In New York, Miranda supposes, Tommy's good looks and—she imagines—his sexuality stood him in good stead. His first job at the store was as a salesman in the shoe department. But he rose fast, very fast—thanks, no doubt, to his good looks.

In his mid-forties, Tommy still has those good looks and that smoldering whiff of sexuality that is as lingering as his Giorgio cologne. But all traces of an Indiana cornfield have vanished, or been banished, by now, except perhaps in his slightly windblown blond hair, his deeply pigmented blue eyes, and that trio of dimples when he smiles. Otherwise, he suggests a cornfield about as much as a polished George III candlestick does. He has a burnished look, a finished look, the look of something designed and crafted with great care. She has heard Tommy Bonham described as "too good-looking," but if he gets away with such good looks it is mainly because he seems to be so utterly unaware of them.

Miranda Tarkington has known plenty of handsome

men—men who are handsome and know it—men whose eyes, when they enter a room, seem to travel on automatic pilot to the nearest mirror. But Tommy's eyes never do this. They travel to the nearest woman and seem to tell her immediately that she is looking her best. Tommy is not the *"Dah*ling, you look *mah*velous" type. His eyes say that for him. This is also the double secret of her mother's famous beauty. She appears to be completely unconscious of her looks. And when her azure eyes fix on the person she is talking to, that person suddenly feels that he or she is the most interesting, important, and desirable creature in the universe.

It is Tommy's good looks, Miranda often thinks, that have made him ideally suited for working in what is essentially a woman's store. Tommy's looks, she is certain, were what made her father elevate him to his second in command. In fact, all her father's employees were chosen for their looks, Smitty included. Form over substance, any day. Miranda herself would never have been allowed to work in the store if she hadn't been pretty. And it is interesting that Silas Tarkington should have chosen a man who could have been his wife's fraternal twin to be his right-hand man. "I have always loved to be surrounded by beautiful things," her father once said. Miranda sometimes wonders: What did—but it should be *what does,* since she is still alive—Alice Tarkington, who is Blazer's mother, look like? Miranda doesn't know. She has never met her, and naturally there are no pictures of her father's first wife. But Alice must be, or must have once been, a beauty, Miranda thinks.

Like her father, Tommy Bonham has his special ladies whom he always takes care of. When he spots one of Tommy's special ladies alighting in front of the store from a taxi or a limousine, James, the doorman, presses a special button by his station. This causes a buzzer to sound in Tommy's office. Then James steps forward, tips his cap, greets the woman by name—he is nearly as good at names as Tommy is—and offers her his hand to help her from her car. Meanwhile, Tommy is bounding down four flights of stairs—he doesn't wait for the elevator—to greet his client as she enters the store, rather like the concierge at a small, expensive European hotel greeting a longtime favored guest.

"Do you have anything to show me, Tommy?"

"As a matter of fact, we have several pretty new things," he says, taking her arm, not intimately but just so.

Other men occasionally feel uncomfortable with men as handsome as Tommy Bonham. Perhaps he stirs in them unwelcome feelings of homoerotic lust. But women fall in love with the Tommy Bonhams of this world. Most of Tommy's special ladies, Miranda long ago decided, are to some degree or other in love with him. Most rich men's wives, she also decided, must endure very boring husbands. And so Tommy, being unmarried, is able to perform, for his special ladies, all sorts of little tasks that their husbands have no interest in, or are unwilling or unable to take on. In addition to helping them select the perfect pair of sandals for the perfect ball gown, he takes them to lunch. He suggests new things they might do with their hair. He helps them decorate their apartments, escorts them to charity balls, to opening nights at the theater, to the shows at the galleries along Fifty-seventh Street and upper Madison. He listens to, and sympathizes with, their various tales of bitterness and woe. All this, of course, has been good for business and the store, and Miranda has often wondered how far these relationships have gone. But Tommy is too smart, she thinks, to have let any of these relationships progress through any bedroom doors. And he has been careful to spread the largesse of his attractive company around, so his name has never been attached to any of his special ladies as that lady's special walker or, as they say in England, laughing-man.

The comparison of Tarkington's to a small European hotel is an apt one, and in her father's monthly meetings with his staff he often said, "We must always remember to treat our clients as our guests." For the store's best clients, Tommy's office will make hotel, restaurant, and airline reservations. It will make massage and even dental appointments. It will suggest lawyers for divorces, doctors for plastic surgery. Last year, Tommy even escorted one of his special ladies as she toured New England, shopping for a boarding school for her son.

When Miranda first met Tommy—it was at the farm in 1980, when she was just thirteen—she fell in love with him herself. She was down from Ethel Walker for the weekend, and he came for the weekend too, and she thought he was simply the most gorgeous hunk of man she had ever met. Encountering him the next morning by the pool, clad only in his white bikini, she had been so embarrassed that she had run into the pool house, pretending to hear the telephone ring, rather than spend time with him in that nearly nude state. She carried fantasies of him with her back to school. Then, of course, she fell in love again with someone else, then out of love again. Then in love again, and out of love, with still another boy. Half of her life, she sometimes thinks, has been spent falling crazily in and out of love, each time harder and more cruelly than the last. There was even a time when she was convinced that she was in love with Blazer, her own half brother, rationalizing that, while sex with one's full brother was definitely taboo, sex with one's half brother would only be half bad—not that anything of the sort came close to happening.

Once she confessed to Kathy Williams, who had been her best friend at Walker, that there were times, when she was with a boy, that she had felt kind of an electric shock down *there.*

"You're obviously a nymphomaniac," Kathy had told her. Then Kathy had made a confession of her own. "I'm a lesbian," she whispered. After that, Miranda never felt quite the same way about Kathy Williams. And she had also stopped signing the entries in her secret diary "M.T.T.," which would become her stylish monogram when she married Blazer and became Miranda Tarkington Tarkington.

At school and college, she had taken her good grades

for granted. After all, good grades were what her parents expected of her. Then, when she was twenty-one, a senior at Sarah Lawrence, and was handed a gold Phi Beta Kappa key, she suddenly discovered she was smart. Smart women with Phi Beta Kappa keys didn't fall in love, she decided. They had careers.

She had always loved the store. It had been her private castle, and the precious items it displayed she pretended were her personal treasures. And so, though her father had initially disapproved, she had persuaded him to let her go to work at Tarkington's. She had started, at her father's insistence, in the mail room, at the bottom—"Where you'll discover that running a store like this isn't all glamour"—sorting and delivering the letters and memos, delivering the copies of *The Times, The Wall Street Journal,* and *Women's Wear Daily* to the men on the executive floor, men like her father and her old crush Tommy Bonham, whose offices were in the older part of the building that had been the Van Degan house—big, walnut-paneled offices with high ceilings and tall windows facing Fifth Avenue and the park, offices that smelled of old wood and wax and leather—and to the less high-ups, the merchandise managers and buyers, whose offices were in the new L-shaped addition where, though efforts had been made to replicate the grandeur of the old building on the selling floors, the offices were often small, low-ceilinged, and windowless—and smelled new.

Delivering interoffice mail might have sounded like a dull job, but Miranda discovered that it didn't have to be. She could read all the memos and learn what the buyers were buying and how much they were spending. She learned about the store's markup policy, which was nothing if not whimsical; buyers marked up their merchandise to what they thought the traffic would bear. She also learned a lot about the politics of storekeeping: who was in favor and who was not, which departments were in trouble, and why, and what was going to be done about it. She learned that, though her father officially made all the decisions, it was really Tommy Bonham who ran the store.

Then, after her stint in the mail room, she had worked as a secretary for the sportswear buyer. Then she had been made an assistant buyer, which was just a fancier term for secretary. Then her father had given her the title of Director of Advertising.

It was a flashy title, but it didn't mean a hell of a lot, and her father certainly knew that when he created the position for her six months ago. After all, the store's advertising was so-called institutional advertising—just advertising the store's presence, never any specific merchandise—and it was always the same, just a way of saying rather grandly to the public, "We're here." Mostly, her father had explained to her, her job would consist of ordering the ad space, making sure the store got the column inches it ordered, keeping the scrapbooks, and periodically being taken to lunch by space salesmen.

Still, right from the beginning, Miranda had tried to make the job into something more than that. She had designed a new, and snappier, company letterhead and bill head. "Our bills and letters look as though they were being sent out by a Wall Street law firm," she said to her father, showing him her new designs.

"That's what I like about them," he said with a smile.

Next, she had suggested colorful bill stuffers. The store had just opened a tiny new gift boutique with one-of-a-kind treasures, bibelots, and boxes, including a pair of rare Romanov Easter eggs designed by the court jeweler, Peter Carl Fabergé. Miranda proposed announcing the new boutique with a bill stuffer showing a color photograph of the eggs.

"Bill stuffers are just that," her father said. "Just stuff. They're an annoyance. They go straight into the wastebasket, like the renewal slips that keep falling out of the pages of magazines. My kind of woman wouldn't like them."

Her next campaign had been to have Tarkington's produce a catalogue.

"Catalogues are not our style," her father said.

"Saks does lovely catalogues. So does Bloomingdale's. So do—"

"My kind of woman would give a catalogue to her cook, who'd use it to wrap yesterday's fish. A catalogue would cheapen us, Miranda."

"But more and more people are shopping from catalogues. There was an article in yesterday's *Times*—"

"And where is yesterday's *Times*? Being used to wrap yesterday's fish. There are too many catalogues coming in the mail nowadays. People just toss them out. People come from all over the world to experience our *store*. Our store provides the Tarkington's experience. The Tarkington's experience cannot be conveyed through a catalogue, Miranda."

"Gucci has a catalogue, Tiffany has catalogues. So does Cartier. Of course ours would be the most beautif—"

"Does Harry Winston have a catalogue?" he asked her.

"No," she admitted.

"You see? I am in the Harry Winston league."

Try as she might, she had been unable to rock the boat or to change what had become "the Tarkington's way of doing things."

Under the mantle of Advertising came Publicity, but since the store eschewed most publicity and closely guarded the names of its celebrity clients, that side of her job hadn't yet amounted to much either. Frustrated, Miranda had often thought that any lackey could do what she did. She didn't even require a secretary. But she had decided to take her job seriously, nonetheless, to be patient and wait for the day when her father might take one of her ideas seriously and take *her* seriously—and pay her more than $30,000 a year.

"Retailing's a man's business," her father often said to her. "Women just don't take to it—except as buyers and salesgirls."

Which was a damned lie, and she could have told him so, but she didn't. What about Dorothy Shaver of Lord & Taylor, Geraldine Stutz of Bendel's, and Jo

Hughes of Bonwit's and Bergdorf's? Those were all legendary women—legends in their day—just as legendary as Silas Tarkington, for God's sake! Those legendary women were all dead now, or retired, and so wasn't the business ready for some new, young, talented female blood? But she had held her tongue.

Instead, she had enrolled in some weekday evening classes in marketing and business at N.Y.U. It would be years before she got an M.B.A., but what the hell? She was learning something. And, because she knew what her father would think of this particular endeavor, she had held her tongue about that, too.

Now, after a little more than three years with the store, she is still patiently waiting for something to do where she will be asked to make a decision or at least to offer an opinion. After three years with the store, Thomas E. Bonham III is just another properly aloof executive, her father's second in command, and his extraordinary good looks are just a familiar part of Tarkington's general landscape, no more remarkable than the six Baccarat chandeliers that light the center aisle of the street floor. Who must she get to take her seriously now? she wonders. Tommy Bonham, of course.

As though he had been reading her thoughts, he says, "One thing I wanted to ask you. When do you think we should reopen the store? With all due respect to your dad, do you think just being closed today in his memory is enough?"

"Absolutely," she says firmly. "I think we should open for business tomorrow morning at ten o'clock, business as usual. I think Daddy would have wanted that. And I certainly hope we're not going to drape the windows with black bunting, or have the salespeople wear black arm bands, or anything. Daddy would have hated that."

"I agree," he says. "So we reopen tomorrow and act as though nothing has happened, even though something monumental has."

"Yes," she says, and realizes, with a start, that she has just been asked for her opinion.

"Of course," he says, "I don't really know who's supposed to be running the store now that he's gone. I don't suppose there was anything said about that in his will."

"No, but obviously you are. You were always the heir apparent, Tommy."

"Well, I don't know," he says with a faint smile. "There's a board of directors and shareholders to consider."

"Well, you've obviously got my vote, Tomcat," she says, and immediately wishes she hadn't said that. Now that she finds herself a major shareholder, she mustn't start acting as though she thinks she's Tommy's boss or something, though, in a sense, she is.

"What about your mother?"

"Mother's never had that much interest in the store, as you know. But I'm sure she'd agree with me. You're the obvious man to take over."

"Well, suppose I serve as president pro tem," he says, "until the shareholders decide what course they want to take. You know there've been several outside offers to buy the business. Some of the shareholders may decide they'd like to sell."

"And let Tarkington's become part of a chain? I don't think any of us would like to see that happen."

"I guess there was no mention of that in your dad's will, either."

She shakes her head.

"So if it's okay with you I'll call a little meeting, before we open the doors in the morning, and explain that I'm assuming the title of president pro tem. After all, somebody's got to run the place."

"Absolutely," she says, thinking: *If it's okay with you!*

"Actually, I'm a little surprised your father made a will," he says. "With all due respect to your dad—he was my closest friend, you know—men like him sometimes begin to think they're immortal. They don't make wills, because making a will reminds them that they're not. Don't misunderstand. I don't mean to speak ill of your dad. I loved your dad."

"I understand."

"And if I do end up becoming the store's new president, I want to give you a position of real responsibility, Mandy. Your talents are being completely wasted in that advertising job, as I guess you know."

"Well, *I* think so," she says.

"And—you know—I was thinking before you got here, Tarkington's has always seemed like a kind of mom-and-pop operation, what with your mother and dad living in the apartment upstairs. A kind of cozy, family atmosphere. I think that's always been a part of Tarkington's special aura, its special charm."

"Daddy used to say he liked his clients to feel as though they'd been invited into Buckingham Palace. Or were staying at the Paris Ritz."

He laughs softly. "Well, you see? The Queen and Prince Philip live over the store, too. But I was thinking, what if you and I were to run the store as a partnership?"

"Partnership?"

"As co-presidents, perhaps."

"Co-*presidents*?"

"Why not? Another mom-and-pop operation."

"Oh, I don't think I'm quite ready for that," she says. "I don't know as much about the business as I need to know. I've never even been out into the market, for instance. I'd need—"

"I'd teach you everything you need to know," he says.

"But I don't have your experience, your—"

"You could be in charge of what I call the creative end of the operation. I could be in charge of the financial end. That's the way your father and I more or less divided things up for the past half dozen years or so."

"But as co-president?"

"Fifty-fifty partners. A team. Most of our clients are women, after all. I think they'd like the idea of knowing there was a woman at the top. And I know how much you love the store."

"That's true, but—"

"You see, I've always thought you had great retailing talent, Miranda. You've got the innate *feel* for it, the nose for it. Retailing's in your blood, and why shouldn't it be? You're your father's daughter."

She sips her wine thoughtfully. She would like to say, But in the two years I've been with the store, you hardly seemed to notice me. It was never more than a nod or a smile or a wave of your hand in my direction when we encountered each other in the hall. Months would go by, and you never seemed to know I was there. When did you notice this great retailing talent of mine—which, in fact, I do possess? But instead she says, "This is a big responsibility you're suggesting for me, Tommy."

"I know you're up to it. I know you'd do a superb job. You and me, in tandem, at the top."

"I'm certainly flattered, Tommy, but—why didn't you ever mention this to me before? That you thought I had some talent."

"I couldn't. Your father had some pretty old-fashioned ideas about women in top spots in retailing. And after all, your father was my boss. I'm just telling you now what I've always thought, what I've noticed about you all along. I'd just like to see you become the great retailing genius that your father was." He fixes his deep-blue eyes on her intensely. "I'm quite serious, Miranda," he says.

"Well, let me think about it," she says. "After all, all I'm doing at the moment is buying the same ad space, for the same ads, in the same publications, week after week."

"Pretty boring, isn't it?"

"True enough."

"And this idea of mine excites you, doesn't it? I can tell it does."

She nods and takes another sip of wine. "You're right, it does," she says. She stares deeply into her wine-glass. Co-president!

"Then do we have a deal?"

But at that moment, the maître d' approaches them with a white cellular phone in his hand. "Telephone for you, Mr. Bonham," he says.

Tommy holds up his left hand. "No calls, Jean," he says.

"It's a Mr. Minskoff calling, sir. He says it's urgent."

"Tell him I'm not here. Tell him I just left. Tell him anything you want. I'm taking no calls."

And now Mona Potter, in her red Ungaro suit, is also approaching their table. "When's Tarkington's going to open up again?" she demands in her loud voice. "I need to know for my column. And Miranda, sweetie, from you I need to know how it feels to've inherited a bundle of your old man's money."

4

As Connie Tarkington and Jake Kohlberg wait for the light to cross Forty-second Street, they hear a woman waiting next to them say to a friend, "Look, isn't that Consuelo Tarkington? It *is*! Jeez, I wish I had her money!" Jake responds by looking down at his feet, and Connie by removing an oversize pair of sunglasses from her purse and putting them on. The light changes, Jake takes her arm, and they cross the street together, heading north.

Jake chuckles. "Those shades aren't going to help you one damn bit," he says. "You're still one of the ten best-dressed women in the world. You're still a celebrity."

She sighs and says nothing, the heels of her Chanel pumps clicking on the sidewalk. Then she says, "Where are you taking me?"

"To the Yale Club, where we can have a quiet talk. Yale men are trained not to make noisy comments about their beautiful women guests." Ahead of them, the blue-and-white flag flutters in the breeze from its mast. They mount the short flight of steps to the club, and the uniformed guard at the reception desk says, "Good afternoon, Mr. Kohlberg," and nods politely to Connie.

They find a quiet corner of the east sitting room and settle themselves in a pair of large easy chairs. Connie crosses her legs and lets the heel of one blue pump dangle from the tip of her toe.

A waiter approaches them. "Tea, Mrs. Tarkington?" he asks.

"Yes, please. Lemon, no sugar."

"I'll have a brandy," Jake Kohlberg says. "Courvoisier."

"Well," she says after the waiter has departed, "maybe it will be nice not having to worry about being on the Best-Dressed List. Not having to worry about being a walking advertisement for Tarkington's."

"You've always been the best. The best there ever was."

Her lips part slightly to expose perfectly white and even teeth. "As Blazer said—like one of the mannequins in his Fifth Avenue windows."

"Ah, you've been more than that, Connie. Much more than that." To change the subject slightly, he chuckles softly again. "So many funny stories about Si," he says. "Is it true he once went up to the apartment and took some dresses out of your closet when he couldn't find anything in the store that a customer wanted?"

"Oh, that sort of thing happened all the time," she says. "I was always going into my closet to get out a particular dress, only to find that he'd taken it out and sold it to one of his ladies. I'd find other things in my closet, too. And in other places."

"Hmm? What sort of things?"

"Oh, like a pair of panties between the sheets when my maid went to turn down the bed. Or a box of tampons on the closet floor."

"Now, Connie, don't brood about those things."

"I'm not brooding, Jake. You asked me what sort of things I found, and I told you. There were other things. Worse things."

His brandy arrives, and her tea, and the waiter pours it for her.

"Let's talk business for a minute," she says when they are alone again. "Am I really going to be rich?"

"Oh, I think you're going to be very comfortably off," he says. "The houses, the other properties, the shares in the store—"

"How many shares will I own?"

"Well, Si owned about thirty percent of the shares outstanding. That, divided by two, would give you and Miranda each about a fifteen-percent additional position in the company."

"Plus the shares he gave us both from time to time—Christmases, birthdays, that sort of thing. But that wouldn't give us a majority position, would it?"

"Probably not. You'd each own roughly twenty percent."

"How much would these shares be worth, do you suppose?"

"That's hard to say until we've had a chance to examine the books. Inventory. Accounts receivable. That sort of thing."

"Of course."

"And I should warn you, Connie, that Moses Minskoff—whose name you mentioned this afternoon—has already resurfaced. He claims to be in possession of some IOU's of Si's, some promissory notes, representing loans he made to Si over the years. Of course until I've had a chance to examine these documents I've no way of knowing whether they'd stand up in a court of law. But I thought I should warn you that this Minskoff character has already started making sword-rattling noises."

She shivers. "How did Si ever get mixed up with a man like Moe Minskoff?"

He sighs. "Well, there were times in your husband's business when he needed ready cash, and needed it in a hurry. Minskoff was there to provide it."

She taps her lacquered fingertips on the tabletop. "He used my husband, and the store, to launder his filthy money—which came from God knows what crooked source!"

"Well," he says with a small smile, "when a man needs ready cash and someone else is on hand to supply it, he doesn't always question the source of the cash too closely."

"I suppose not. But still—Moe Minskoff. Of all the people in the world—"

"That's why I want to handle the Minskoff situation very carefully, Connie. I don't want anything about this to get into the press. I don't want anything to come out that would damage the store's reputation. Meanwhile, I think a more important question is, who's going to run the store now that Si is gone?"

"Well, I can't run it, and couldn't even if I wanted to, which I don't. Miranda's always said she'd like to run the store some day, but she hasn't had any real experience. Retailing is a—a *jungle*. Si often said so. And Miranda knows nothing about that jungle. Of course, that's Si's fault, too, in a way. He never wanted her to get any real retailing experience. He never even wanted her to work for the store."

"So I suppose it'll be Bonham."

She sips her tea thoughtfully. "I don't know," she says. "The *Times* story didn't mention it, but something happened between Si and Tommy a few months ago. I've no idea what it was. Si never discussed the business with me. But I got the distinct impression that Si had stopped trusting Tommy. I honestly think that if Si hadn't died when he did, he would have—I mean, I believe Si was thinking of getting rid of Tommy."

"Ah," he says. "That explains something I wondered about."

"You mean that in Si's revised will Tommy Bonham wasn't to be left the emerald ring."

"Now, you know I can't tell you that."

"You don't need to. You just did. And I think I know to whom, in the unfinished will, that ring was going to be left."

"Don't ask me that, Connie."

"I don't need to. I already know," she says.

"And so," he says, shifting the subject again, "I suppose the store will have to be sold."

She nods. "Yes, though it seems a shame, considering how hard Si worked to make Tarkington's what it's become. He built the business for Blazer, you know. It was all for that boy, but then Blazer—let him down."

"There've been several offers already. Some quite lucrative."

"Yes, I guess I'd say sell it. Sell it to the highest bidder. Because, frankly, there was something troubling Si those last few months before he died. Part of it was Tommy, but part of it was something else. I don't think business was as good as he pretended it was. He used to say, 'My kind of woman isn't affected by a recession. My kind of woman isn't even aware of an economic downturn.' But I think some of them were. I think a lot of them were. I think that was what was weighing on his mind. I think the store had begun losing money, perhaps was even hemorrhaging money. At times, these past six or eight months, I'd look at Si and see a very frightened look in his eyes, Jake—a terrified look."

"Of course, if the store were sold, it would become a very different sort of store."

"But perhaps that's inevitable. After all, that kind of store may not have any place in this city anymore—maybe not anywhere in the world. Think about it: all those famous little Tarkington's touches. Chanel Number Five in the ladies' room. Chaise longues in case a customer felt faint or wanted to get off her feet for a few minutes. Monogrammed hand towels. Maids running about serving tea or drinks or little watercress sandwiches—whatever the client asked for. Endless alterations to suit the client's whim, and never a charge for any of it. That sort of thing may have worked in the eighties, and even in the seventies. But this is the nineties, and people are tightening their belts, pulling in their horns. Tarkington's has become an anachronism. Specialty stores like ours are becoming a thing of the past. *The Times* was right—Si was the last of the dinosaurs. His breed's extinct, and so's his breed of store. I'm sorry, Jake. I didn't mean to launch into a long lecture on the state of the retailing business, a subject I assure you I know absolutely nothing about."

"I think you know more than you're willing to admit," he says.

They sit in silence for a moment or two, and she sips her tea. "This tea simply *will not cool,*" she says, setting down her cup.

"You know," he says, "when Blazer made his little—outburst back there at the office, he said something about wanting to kill his father but somebody else beat him to it."

She shakes her head. "I have no idea what he meant by that."

"You don't think there was any chance of foul play, do you?"

"I don't even want to think about it. What difference does it make? He's dead. Foul play or not, he's not coming back to life. Harry Arnstein said death was from a coronary, and that's good enough for me."

"But still—"

"The thing you have to remember about me, Jake, is that I loved the little son-of-a-bitch. In spite of the way he treated me, I still loved him. He may have treated me badly, but he treated other women badly, too. I wasn't singled out. Being unfaithful to me was part of his nature. I don't think it was possible for him to be faithful to any woman, much less a wife. And I miss him. Last night, I spent the night in town. I let myself into the apartment alone and realized he wouldn't be there. It's not that he was often there. In fact, most of the time he wasn't there. But I realized he was never going to be there again. I realized I'd never hear him say again that he was going out to walk Blackamoor, his big old Labrador. Even when there were times that he—and Blackamoor—were going to wind up in some girlfriend's apartment, I knew I was going to miss hearing him say that. I was going to miss him telling me his transparent little lies. Isn't it funny? I was even going to miss the bad things he did. Suddenly I felt terribly alone. I went from window to window, throughout that big, empty apartment, looking out into the street, thinking I'd see him walking Blackamoor, or see him stepping into a phone booth to call one of his girlfriends, even though I knew he was gone for good and was never coming back. And you know something? Even though I knew he was gone forever, and was never coming back, I was still jealous of him. Because I loved him. If anyone ever does decide to write his biography, I hope they'll put that in."

"As a matter of fact, I've already been approached on that subject," he says.

"Oh, I don't think so, Jake. I don't think we want anybody writing his biography, do we? No."

"The young man has good credentials. He's primarily a financial writer, and he understands retailing. He got some sort of an award for a piece he did in *Fortune* on Saks being taken over by the Arab consortium. His name is Peter Turner."

"No, I think not," she says. "Si didn't want anything written about him in his lifetime, and I think we should continue to honor those wishes. I hope you told him no."

"I told him I'd talk to him after I talked to you."

"And there are some things in Si's past that we wouldn't want—"

"I know what you mean, Connie. But just remember this one fact about journalists. If a journalist wants to write a story badly enough, he'll go ahead and write it anyway, whether you cooperate or not. And if you cooperate, you have a certain amount of leverage. You have a certain amount of control over the material, over what goes into the story, if you see what I mean."

She looks thoughtful. "Yes, you have a point."

"So you might consider cooperating with this Peter Turner—in order to have that degree of control."

She smiles faintly. "You're a very wise man, Jake," she says. "I've always thought so. How long have you and I known each other?"

"Twenty-seven years. I was best man in your wedding. Remember?"

"Of course. The day he died was my fiftieth birthday. Did you know that? Jake—am I getting old?"

"Oh, no," he says. "Not you."

"Whatever else could be said about my husband, you have to admit that Si Tarkington had balls." She sips her tea. "This tea is finally cool enough to drink," she says.

5

At the Beth-El Home for the Jewish Aged in Palm Beach Shores, Florida, it is time for Rose Tarcher's weekly bridge game. Rose Tarcher is ninety-six and, she likes to boast, she still has all her faculties, though her hearing has begun to fail her in recent years. "Which way is north?" she asks. "Which? Is this north?" Rose is superstitious, and likes to be seated on the north side of the bridge table.

No one really likes to play bridge with Rose Tarcher because she is notorious for being a bid hog. On the other hand, in the unwritten hierarchy of the Beth-El Home, Rose is what is known as "one of the higher-ups." Being one of the higher-ups means that Rose has money—some money, at least, though of course no one knows how much. In her room, number 17, she has substituted her own chintz curtains and bedspread for the ones provided by the home. She also has her own colored sheets, which she likes changed twice a week, though most residents get only one change a week, on Mondays. In her room she has a large-screen TV, with cable. She has her own Touch

Tone phone, with an extra line and a hold button, and a sterling silver mezuzah on her door.

Then there is her mink. It is a rather special mink, designed, she says, just for her. It can be worn at knee length. But then there is an eighteen-inch-deep panel of matched pelts that can be zipped onto the skirt of the coat, creating a floor-length garment. The coat has a high stand-up collar, and it also has a zip-on hood. Rose's mink may have seen better days, but it still has its Tarkington's label and Rose's monogram stitched into the lining, and on chilly evenings she often appears at the dinner table wrapped from head to toe in her mink.

In the draw for partners, Rose has drawn Ben Rosenthal, one of the few gentlemen living at Beth-El, and this draw is fine with him because, if Rose likes to hog the bids, Ben enjoys being dummy. The other players are Esther Pinkus and Lily Sachs. The bidding proceeds.

Rose opens. "Two clubs."

"Two spades," says Esther.

"Pass," says Ben.

"Four spades," says Lily.

"Two clubs," says Rose.

"Now, Rose, you know you can't do that," Esther says. "My partner said four spades."

"What?"

"My partner said four spades," Esther says, louder. "You can't go back to two clubs!"

"I didn't hear anybody say four spades," Rose says. "It's two clubs."

"Rose, you spoil everybody's fun when you play like this!"

"Let's see what you've got for me, partner," Rose says, and Ben lays down his hand. "Very pretty, partner," she says as Esther leads. Her opposing partners look glum. Rose often plays like this, using poor hearing as an excuse for not noticing intervening bids, and it is very irritating to the others. But another unwritten rule of the home is that arguments and quarrels among the residents are to be avoided at all costs, and any long-standing feuds would surely raise the hackles of Shirley Weinstein, the home's peppy redheaded Director of Activities.

Rose takes the first trick. Ben Rosenthal, as dummy, rises a little stiffly and slowly circles the table, examining the other hands. Then he moves toward the television set where, at low volume, a developer is extolling the wonders of time-share living at Delray Beach. At eighty-four, Ben is one of the youngsters at Beth-El, and several of the ladies consider him their special beau. On top of the set is a copy of today's *New York Times,* and Ben picks this up and idly glances at the headlines. "I see Silas Tarkington died," he says to no one in particular.

"What?" Rose asks.

"Silas Tarkington," he says.

"What about him?"

"He died."

Rose's cards tumble into her lap, and she fumbles to gather them up again. The color has drained from her face.

"Rose, are you all right?" Lily asks anxiously. Just the other day, old Mrs. Samuels suddenly turned pale like that and went to her Maker right at the dining room table.

"He didn't tell me," Rose whispers.

"How could he tell you?" Esther snaps. "He's dead."

"Didn't tell me he was sick."

"He wasn't sick. He drowned," Ben says.

"How could that be? He was a beautiful swimmer."

"What's he to you, anyway?" Esther asks.

"Only my son," she says. "Only my only son. You'd think someone would tell his only mother when her only son dies. Oh, Solly—" She reaches for the hanky in the bosom of her dress and dabs at her eyes.

"Silas Tarkington's your *son*?" Esther says. "How could that be? Your name's Tarcher."

"It was Solomon Tarcher before. Before he wanted to get fancy and changed it."

Esther snatches the newspaper from Ben and quickly scans the the obituary. "If you're his mother, how come you're not mentioned in his write-up?" she says. "They

list all the survivors. They don't mention any mother. I
don't believe you, Rose. How come he never came to see
you?" She is clearly still cross at losing a bid for game in a
major suit.

"I guess you would say we weren't close," Rose says.
She removes her glasses and wipes them with her hanky.
"But still—still, he was my son. My firstborn. I had my
feet in the stirrups on that table, and my doctor said,
'Push, Rose . . . push hard . . . push as hard as you
can . . . you're pushing life into your baby. If you push
hard enough, I won't have to spank his bottom when he
comes.' And then they handed him to me, and he smelled
—so sweet! Why did he have to die? Why is life so un-
fair?"

The others are silent now, and Rose, trying to collect
herself, replaces her glasses on her nose.

"We fought," she says. "But he was still my little
Solly."

"So that's where your money comes from," Esther
says at last, and Lily, from across the table, makes soft
hushing noises.

"That's what we fought about. After my late husband died, God rest his soul, and Solly needed money to
start his store, I loaned him some. It was called buying his
store's stock. I didn't get as much as I was supposed to
get. Not nearly as much. Simma was smarter. My daughter fought for her fair share and got it. Simma wouldn't
have anything to do with Solly either, after he tried to do
to her what he did to me. So you see I've had my share of
tsuris. Lots of trouble in the family. My life hasn't been
the bowl of cherries some of you seem to think it was, or
maybe I sometimes like to pretend it was. But what can
you do? Oh, my." She dabs at her eyes again. "Put one
foot after the other, like my late husband used to say,
God rest his soul. Funny, I always thought Simma was the
brainy one in the family. I always thought Simma was the
one who should have had all the success, not Solly. I can't
complain about Simma, can I? She's given me a wonderful son-in-law I love like my own son, three beautiful

grandchildren, and two greats. Simma visits me every week, come hell or high water, rain or shine."

"She's nice, too," Lily says.

Rose closes her eyes, and blinks twice, and takes a deep breath. "So Solly's dead," she says. "Well, I don't guess there's anything I can do about it now, is there? Solly lived in New York. Had fancy friends. Get on with your life, as my late husband used to say, God rest his soul. Pick up the pieces." With a sniffle, she slowly picks up her hand again, re-sorts the cards into suits, and fans them out between her fingers. Her hand trembles slightly. "Oh, dear," she says. "I've forgotten what our contract was."

"Four spades," Esther Pinkus says narrowly.

Rose studies the cards in her hand and then the cards arrayed before her on the board. "Partner, how could you have bid us up to four spades with that mess?" she says indignantly, and leads with her club ace.

Esther Pinkus promptly trumps it.

Ben Rosenthal crosses the room to Rose's chair and rests his hands gently on her shoulders. "I'm sorry, Rose," he says. "I just want to say that I'm truly, deeply sorry. I know how you feel. I lost one of mine, too. Car accident. It's not easy."

"Well, you should be sorry," she says. "We're definitely going to lose this one. Thank God we're not vulnerable."

Early that same evening, Diana Smith, thirty-four, lets herself into the side entrance of the store with her own key. Inside, she leans against the door for a moment, feeling dizzy. The last three days seem to have passed in a trance. Her doctor has prescribed Valium for her, and the pills turn time into a dreamlike haze, through which she feels she is moving silently and disconnectedly, like a swimmer under water, but going nowhere. She reaches in her purse to fish out a cigarette but then remembers where she is. She is here, in Si's store, where there is a no smoking policy. She closes the purse. She is not even entirely sure why she came here. What was it? Oh, yes. To check her department. To say goodbye to it, perhaps. Because, the way things stand now, this may be her last time inside these doors. Who knows, when Tommy Bonham takes over—as he surely will—what will become of her? She staggers forward, reaching out to steady herself against a display counter. *Did I take two of those dreamy little pills or one? I can't remember.*

Oliver, the security guard on duty tonight, nods to her. "Evening, Miss Smith."

"Good evening"—*his name?*—"Oliver."

"Sad day for all of us, ain't it, Miss Smith?"

"It surely is."

"Say, you feeling all right, Miss Smith? You look a little—shaky, sort of. A bit off your feed. Green around the gills, like the fella says."

"I'm fine. I'm just a little—upset. As we all are, Oliver."

Oliver nods again and continues on his rounds.

At the Hermès boutique, she pauses and lifts a sample flask of Equipage and sprays it behind her ears, on the backs of her wrists, in the cleavage of her breasts. Equipage is Diana Smith's signature fragrance, and the scent makes her feel more like herself. "I love the way you always smell," he used to say to her.

"When a woman finds a scent that suits her, she should always stick to it," she told him. He used to give her bottles.

She makes her way slowly down the center aisle, under the Baccarat chandeliers, toward the back of the store to where, under an archway of polished walnut, her own department is situated. There, in locked glass cases, her merchandise is displayed. On the store's books, this merchandise is valued at four million dollars, but she knows enough about retailing to know that the value of a store's inventory has little relationship to its real value, which is always considerably less. She moves slowly from case to case, earrings in one, rings in another, necklaces and bracelets in a third, pins and brooches and jeweled buttons in a fourth. Now she remembers why she came here tonight. She wanted to think about precious stones, and not about other things.

She has always had a special feeling for gems, and it is really only the precious ones that interest her. She has never been able to have much enthusiasm for semiprecious stones: the garnets, the tourmalines, the amethysts, turquoises, moonstones, opals, and the rest. But precious gemstones are quite another matter, and the sight of a nearly flawless, fiery diamond can induce in her an almost narcotic rush, a kind of adrenaline high.

Each stone—to her, at least—has its own distinct personality. An emerald, for instance, she sees as a man's stone. Rubies and diamonds look cheap and vulgar on a man, and there is a reason why Tiffany has never offered a man's diamond ring for sale. Tarkington's doesn't go quite that far, but when a man comes into the store looking for a diamond ring—or diamond studs or cuff links—Smitty's salespeople try, as politely as they can, to discourage him, to steer him toward emeralds or some lesser green stone such as aquamarine or malachite: masculine stones.

Rubies are tarts' stones, Smitty's least favorite of the big four. She's never met a woman wearing a ruby ring—or necklace, or ear clips—that she didn't instantly dislike and consider a tart. Tarkington's has its share of tart customers, of course—high-class tarts, to be sure, expensive tarts, but tarts just the same, or kept women. And when she sees such a woman sashay into her department, she will wink at her salesperson and slyly whisper, "Bring out the T.C."—the Tart Collection.

When a woman asks to look at emeralds, Smitty tends to think: Dyke.

Sapphires? Well, they are sort of a problem. Smitty has looked at some gorgeous sapphires in her time, but to her a sapphire has always been an old lady's stone. Old ladies with blue hair seem to be made for sapphires. There is a particularly lovely sapphire and diamond necklace in one of her cases right now, sold to her with documentation indicating that it once belonged to the Grand Duchess Tatiana of Russia—and it may have, though the vendor's price was almost suspiciously low—that Smitty has always admired. But she reminded herself that she is too young for sapphires. "You'll have plenty of time for sapphires, Smitty old girl," she told herself. "Puh-*len*-ty of time."

But diamonds—ah, diamonds are an altogether different story. They are ageless, forever young, pure, hard carbon, flash-formed in the volcanic bubbling of the young earth's crust. A good diamond is as beautiful on the ring finger of a teenage bride as on a dowager's lavaliere. In the glass case in front of her is the diamond he promised her: square-cut, 3.9 carats, finest gem quality, in a perfectly simple platinum setting. Using another key, she unlocks the cabinet, picks the ring out of its black velvet pocket, and slips it on the third finger of her left hand.

She could very easily turn, now, and walk out of the store wearing the ring. It was rightfully to have been hers. Oliver, even if he notices her walking out with an item from her own stock, would not question her. She has often borrowed items from stock before—for an important party, for instance, somewhere she might be recognized, photographed, written about. "Diana Smith, Tarkington's savvy jewelry buyer, wearing a diamond butterfly in her hair," Mona Potter might write. Si even encouraged this sort of thing. This sort of publicity did nothing but good for the store, and it cost Si absolutely nothing. He always encouraged his executives to look their absolute and most expensive best when they went out in public. It helped the store's image. Longtime salesladies, whom Si trusted, were even allowed to borrow designer apparel from the store's inventory. Smitty has done this too.

Right now, Smitty could go into her office and erase this item of her inventory from her computer's memory and that would be the end of it.

Except . . .

Except for Tommy Bonham, of course. Tommy Bonham's eyes always seem to be everywhere in the store. His memory itself is like a computer, and often even better, and if Tommy is about to take over, even temporarily, it is much too risky.

She has had her share of run-ins with Tommy Bonham in the past, and she is certain he doesn't like her. It was Tommy, for instance, who persuaded Si to open the two suburban outlets, in Westchester and Morris counties. Smitty opposed the idea from the beginning. "It won't work," she told Si.

"Why not? Why won't it work?"

"I'll give you two reasons why it won't work," she said. "For one thing, your salespeople. Here in Manhattan, you have a supply of bright, attractive, well-bred, and well-spoken men and women who, for one reason or another, need jobs. These are people who learn to respect and care about the merchandise they sell. These are the kind of salespeople our clients expect—people with good manners and good taste. These are people who know how to write thank-you notes and who know that when a woman buys a fifteen-thousand-dollar dress she appreciates a thank-you note from the person who sold it to her. But who are you going to find in Westchester County? Wives of bankers and stockbrokers and lawyers and advertising executives who play golf and paddle tennis. They don't need to work, and they're not going to want to work for us. People of the sort who work for us in Manhattan aren't going to want to commute to White Plains. We're going to end up having to hire former cleaning ladies from Tuckahoe.

"That's reason number one. Reason number two is that thirty percent of our clients are visitors from foreign countries. Is the wife of a Japanese businessman going to go to White Plains to shop? No way. Another thirty-five percent of our clients live in other parts of the country. Is a woman who's in town from San Francisco going to get on a bus and go to New Jersey to buy a dress?"

"But more and more of the city's money is moving to the suburbs," Tommy insisted, and he had charts and graphs and demographic studies to back him up, and Si decided to go along with him. Tarkington's would take Scarsdale and Morristown by storm. The suburban stores would each add a new department, called "Country Living," featuring more casual designer apparel.

Well, it hadn't worked, for the very reasons Smitty outlined, and after a while both suburban branches closed. Smitty had been right, and Lord knows how much money Si lost in that experiment. And the day the suburban closings were announced—meeting Tommy Bonham in the hall—she hadn't been able to resist saying sweetly, "I told you so!"

He had given her a look of purest hatred. Tommy the hagfish.

Prettyboy Bonham didn't like being told he was wrong. He liked it even less when that person was a mere buyer. He liked it less and less when that person was someone ten years younger than he, and even less than that when that person happened to be a woman.

She twists the ring slowly on her finger. A diamond of that size and importance looked smart when worn facing the palm of the hand. It would also look smart knotted in a scarf.

Suddenly, she is swept with an almost sexual longing for this stone. The feeling seizes at her very innards. She must have this stone and no other. It is hers. It was promised to her, and promises cannot be broken, can they? "A man is as good as his word." Si was always saying that, and so it must be hers, and now is the time to claim it. That's what she's doing: not stealing it, claiming it. Claiming her rightful property. She extends her left hand to the light. This stone excels in all four C's of gemology: color, clarity, cutting, and carat weight. It is ice blue. In the sunlight it will throw off prismatic flashes of red and lavender. In terms of clarity, it has been rated flawless. It has been cut in the full glory of fifty-eight facets, thirty-three above the girdle and twenty-five below. In the quaint language of gemology, this stone would be classified Extra River, from the early days of African mining when the finest diamonds were found in the alluvial wash of riverbeds. Yes, it is hers, it is hers.

She could write it up as a sale. There is a client in

Venezuela whose husband's bank pays all her charges. No bill has ever been challenged.

"Nice-looking ring, Miss Smith." It is Oliver, moving silently across the thick carpet, making his rounds, a witness.

She tries not to appear startled. "Yes, isn't it?" she says easily. "I have a client, in town from Caracas. I'm thinking of taking this over to her hotel and showing it to her."

"Caracas. Is that in Ohio?"

"Venezuela. South America." Her alibi.

Larceny, she thinks. Grand theft. Zip to ten years in the state pen. Prettyboy Bonham would like to see her in jail. Next to seeing her dead, he would like to see her in jail.

And yet, she thinks as Oliver moves away, would she ever feel the same about this ring as she would if he had actually slipped it on her finger, the way he had promised to do? That would always be missing, that one final gesture. Missing that final gesture means a lot. The promise cannot be real without that final gesture. And, worst of all, worse than knowing that the final gesture never came, will never come, is knowing that it was her own damn fault.

"Yes, you really blew it this time, Smitty old girl," she tells herself. "You really blew it this time, didn't you? You blew your last chance." Once again, she feels dizzy.

"Someday that Irish temper of yours is going to get you into big trouble, young lady—*big* trouble," her mother used to say when she was growing up, when she would sob and curse and kick the stairs whenever she didn't get her way. Locked in the kitchen as a result of some infraction she can't remember, she had hurled all her mother's best china out of the cabinets, smashing it, piece by piece, on the tile floor, and then stamping on it with her feet until the Wedgwood looked like drifts of snow. "Oh, you rotten, rotten little girl, you worthless little girl!" her mother had screamed, chasing her through the rooms with her younger brother's baseball bat.

"You're worthless! I'm going to kill you, you worthless little girl!"

And so, that day, their last time together, when she could have reasoned with him, could have tried to calm him down, instead she lost her Irish temper and then—

Slowly she removes the ring from her finger, places it back in its little pocket, slides the drawer closed, and locks the cabinet. For a moment, she rests her hands on the cabinet, and her reflection in the glass is moonlike, disembodied, unreal. Perhaps my mother should have killed me, she thinks. Perhaps that is what I deserved.

And so she makes her way out of the store, waves good night to Oliver as she passes him, and, ringless, leaves by the side door, knowing she will never be certain whether she left the ring behind because she is essentially an honest woman or was just afraid of getting caught.

On the street, she joins the crowd of pedestrians moving uptown. If you saw her, you would think this was just another attractive, well-dressed young woman with something weighing heavily on her mind. The Valiums are wearing off.

She makes a decision. Tomorrow morning, when the store opens, she will march into Prettyboy's office and resign. She will not give Prettyboy the satisfaction of firing her—or terminating her, as they say nowadays.

There are other good jobs in this city, she thinks. There are other nice places to live, and there are even other cities; she is sick of New York, sick to death of it, and New York didn't keep its promise to her.

There are also other men, men who will keep their promises. There are plenty of other men. You'd think Si Tarkington was the last man on earth, for God's sake! She's still young, still has her looks, her figure. She'll find someone.

Suddenly, instead of despair, her world is bright with expectation, hope, and a crimson thing called courage. She thinks of Scarlett O'Hara. Tomorrow is another day.

At the corner, she raises her arm to flag a taxi, just another bright young Manhattan career woman in a hurry.

"Hi, Smitty!" someone calls to her.

"Hi!"

She has always hated the name Smitty, which was given to her in high school, and has stuck, and now will probably never become unstuck. When they made love, he called her Diana, repeating it over and over, "Diana . . . Diana . . . my goddess of the hunt. . . ."

A taxi pulls over to the curb.

6

Peter Turner, struggling freelance writer, sits in his ninth-floor apartment at the Dakota, thinking.

The Dakota is considered a rather grand New York address, but Peter Turner's apartment is far from grand. The grand apartments are on the floors below, particularly those facing south, over the breadth of West 72nd Street, and those facing east, overlooking Central Park. The grand apartments of the Dakota are owned by celebrities of the magnitude of Lauren Bacall, Yoko Ono Lennon, and Roberta Flack. Peter's apartment is in the upper northwest corner of the building, tucked under a gabled, crenellated dormer window, and his only view is of the unadorned brick wall of the building next door.

The top two floors of the Dakota, on one of which Peter Turner lives, were once a warren of tiny servants' rooms, from the days when people kept servants. Out of these rooms, small apartments were patched together in somewhat haphazard fashion, like Peter's. The top two floors of the Dakota are where the gays live, and many little old ladies. Bicycles are parked outside apartment doors as often as wheelchairs, along the narrow corridors that link these residences in a pattern graspable only to those who live there. Peter Turner is not gay, though he lives alone, and though he has had admiring glances cast in his direction by certain neighbors. Not that Peter Turner is all that good-looking, though most would say he is not bad-looking, either. His face is composed of many planes and angles. "Your face is all corners," a former girlfriend once said to him. But he has one feature he is secretly very proud of: a thick, curly mop of black hair. Someone once told him that if a man can keep his hair past the age of twenty-five, he need never fear baldness. Peter Turner passed that watershed year three years ago, heaved a sigh of relief, and stopped worrying about it.

Now he is thinking about Blazer Tarkington. He would not be interested in Silas Tarkington's story if it hadn't been for Blazer. If it hadn't been for Blazer, he wouldn't have thought twice about it, wouldn't have given it the time of day.

Peter Turner and Blazer Tarkington were in the same class at Yale, and for a couple of years they both lived at Calhoun College. Peter had no idea why the guy was called Blazer. He assumed it might have something to do with the blazer jackets they all wore when they got dressed up. Every Yale man worth his salt owned a blazer, and it had to be dark blue, double-breasted, with solid brass buttons, preferably antique. The best blazers were custom made by Morty Sills. These jobs were made with real buttonholes on the sleeves that you could button and unbutton. So if you had a blue blazer with, say, a bright red silk lining, you could unbutton the sleeves and roll up the cuffs to show off the lining, and that was considered a real *Yale* look and you were ready for the tables down at Mory's. No breast-pocket insignia, please. That was taboo.

But the thing was, Peter doesn't think he ever saw Blazer Tarkington wearing a blazer. He was always kind of a scruffy dresser—T-shirts with hostile messages printed on them, torn jeans, dirty sneakers, that sort of thing. There was also a dirty old cap he sometimes wore, a duckbill type, and he always wore it backward. That was very un-Yale, that cap. Sometimes he also wore wire-rimmed granny glasses. Peter used to think Blazer was trying to look like John Lennon. He was built kind of like Lennon, tall and lanky. You'd never have guessed he was a rich man's son. For one thing, he never seemed to have any money. Sometimes Peter and his friends would ask Blazer to join them for a few beers, but he would just pull the insides of his pockets out, which was his nonverbal way of saying he was broke.

He wasn't unpopular at Yale, exactly. But he wasn't exactly popular, either. He was always kind of a loner, never seemed to want to be friendly, never seemed to want to get into a conversation. Blazer never had any real close friends at college. He wasn't *un*friendly, just aloof, as though he had some kind of private chip on his shoulder. He went out for boxing and made the team, which was unusual for a skinny guy, and Peter always thought boxing was a good choice. It helped him work off the hostilities he seemed to have.

He was into a lot of other things at New Haven. He worked on the *Record* as a photographer. He sang baritone in the glee club. He was a pretty good outfielder for the junior varsity baseball team. But you couldn't really call these *social* activities. Boxing, taking photos for the *Record,* singing baritone, playing outfielder—these weren't activities that required much social contact, or interaction, with other team members. At Yale, Peter tended to think of Blazer as an outfielder, always somewhere out in left field. Later on, after his classmates had all more or less gotten used to him and his antisocial ways, many of them decided that Blazer Tarkington was just a bit peculiar.

Peter was born and raised in Wisconsin, so he had never heard of Tarkington's store and the name meant nothing to him when he got to New Haven. Then, in the fall of their sophomore year, Blazer's stepmother arrived on campus. Peter never forgot that afternoon. It was the first hint he'd had that there was money in the picture.

He happened to be standing in the quad when Consuelo Tarkington's Rolls-Royce pulled up to the curb. Her driver, in a gray uniform and cap, hopped out of the car and opened the back door for her. First a long slender leg appeared. Then a gloved hand, holding a long cigarette holder with a lighted cigarette in it. Then the whole woman herself emerged and stood there. Just stood there.

It was not just that she was beautiful. She most certainly was—an icy blond beauty, with perfect white skin and cool blue eyes. Her hair, done in what in those days was called a bouffant style, was almost the color of her cigarette smoke. She was about Peter's own mother's age, so it would not be accurate to say that he found this woman beautiful in terms of being desirable or sexy. And it was not just that she was elegantly dressed, which she certainly was, though he can't really remember what she was wearing, except that it was something dark. It was simply the way she stood there. He'd never before seen a woman whose very posture could transmit such a sense of self-possession and self-command. She seemed to have complete authority over herself. Everything about this woman seemed so *sure.* Then she stepped from the curb onto the sidewalk, and there was certainty in the way she moved, too. Though he was standing at least fifty feet away from her, Peter swore he could smell her perfume in the autumn air. He recognized, for the first time, that hers was the assurance and self-confidence of money, and he knew all at once, with a pang of self-realization, that he would never be that rich.

"Come, Miranda," he heard her say, and even her voice was moneyed. Then her daughter stepped from the car.

None of his classmates had known that Blazer Tarkington had a sister—a half sister, as it turned out. She was no more than thirteen or fourteen at the time, and certainly no Yale man would expect himself to be magnetized by a fourteen-year-old kid. But this was no ordinary fourteen-year-old. She was not as tall as her mother, nor as fashionably thin, and she was darker. But everything about this girl seemed to glow. She shone. Her mother's beauty was snowy, alpine, but this girl's beauty was crackling, fiery. The sunlight caught her ponytailed chestnut hair and made it gleam like polished copper. She glanced in Peter's direction, registering no particular interest in the boy she saw, and her huge eyes were the color of apple cider warmed by a hot poker. Mrs. Tarkington took her daughter's arm, and they moved together across the grass under the few remaining English elms that still graced the campus, toward the entrance to Calhoun.

The Rolls alone would have been enough to attract its share of stares from bystanders. But as Peter looked around he saw that everyone in the vicinity—women with books spread out on the grass, men on their way to classes or the gym—had stopped what they were doing. Every pair of eyes, male and female, was following those breathtaking two. Then they disappeared inside the entrance, and the earth began turning on its axis once again.

It was in Blazer's sophomore year that he took up diving. Peter would see him exercising on the trampoline in the gym and practicing his dives at the pool. Soon he was developing the long, smooth arm and leg muscles of a diver, and by winter he had made the team. By junior year, he was something of a star. But, again, diving is something of a loner's sport, since one spends most of one's time beyond communication, in silent concentration on the board or under water. Blazer was maturing into a nice-looking fellow, who would have been better-looking if he smiled, which he rarely did. Everything he did he threw himself into with a kind of single-minded purposefulness and seriousness, humorlessly determined to be the best at whatever it was he undertook. He tackled his studies with the same furious determination and got excellent grades. But still he was not an easy person to get to know, and some of his classmates, having seen his younger sister —who went, they learned, to Ethel Walker, not that far away—would have liked to get to know him better.

So that was how he entered his junior year—always

polite but distant, a semi-hero of his class who refused to act like one or to join the gang.

Still, everyone expected that Blazer Tarkington would be tapped for one of the all-male senior societies, Scroll & Key, if not the big one, Skull & Bones. After all, coeducation notwithstanding, Yale was still a man's school. Males still called all the important shots at New Haven; women were merely tolerated. And Blazer certainly qualified for membership in one of the elite clubs. He'd won his letter in three sports: boxing, baseball, and as a diver on the swimming team. He'd been made photo editor of the *Record*. In his senior year, he'd gone out for the debating team—another lonely, pugilistic sort of activity—and made a name for himself there. He'd earned fine grades. All these considerations are supposedly given weight by the various tap committees in their top-secret deliberations. Then there was his father's money. That sort of thing wasn't supposed to be a factor in the selection process but it nearly always was, a big one. So Peter had assumed that Blazer would be a shoo-in for either Key or Bones, the perfect well-rounded Yale man.

But when Tap Day came, nobody tapped Blazer Tarkington.

People began saying that, where the senior societies were concerned, something was "wrong" with him, but nobody knew what it might be. Was his sexual orientation a little off? Not that anybody knew. As far as anybody knew, his romantic life at New Haven was nonexistent.

As far as Blazer himself was concerned, he didn't seem to care that the senior clubs had snubbed him. He was preoccupied with other matters. From his offhand attitude, he seemed to say that he hadn't come to Yale to get involved in that sort of thing, even though to be tapped by a senior society is considered the college's ultimate honor. He had other things on his mind, he seemed to say, though no one knew what they were. Perhaps he had come to Yale to exorcise some private demons, demons that only he knew about.

On the night before graduation, he got drunk—all by

himself, apparently—and around midnight who should come lurching into the Beta house, where a party was going on, but Blazer Tarkington. He hadn't been invited, and he wasn't a member of the house, so this was a serious breach of etiquette on his part, and quite unlike him. He stood there, swaying in the doorway, with an open beer can in one hand, and said, "Listen, you sons-of-bitches, there's something's been on my mind to tell you all for the last four years, and now I'm going to tell it!" Everyone grew silent. Then he leaned back out the door, vomited into a boxwood bush, and fell face forward into the bush, passed out. Peter and a friend carried him home and put him in bed. They never did find out what it was he'd had on his mind for four years and was finally going to tell them all.

After college, Peter pretty much lost track of Blazer. He was not the sort of person one tended to stay in touch with, after all, and the rest of his class were becoming too caught up in their new lives and careers in the outside world to take the time to look up old classmates. Occasionally, Peter would read something about the Tarkingtons in the newspapers. Mrs. Tarkington had been named number one on the International Best-Dressed List. Miranda Tarkington's coming-out party on Long Island was a big affair, and the gossip columnist Mona Potter anointed her Deb of the Year. There was no mention of whether Blazer was at that party or not. In fact, Peter read nothing in the papers about Blazer at all.

Then came today's obituary of his father on the front page of *The Times*. There were several things about this death notice that puzzled and intrigued Peter Turner. Why was the doctor flown in by helicopter from miles away in Manhattan? What were the reasons for the fact that no one knew Silas Tarkington's exact age, that his origins were "mysterious," that he disliked being photographed, avoided the press, and had "successfully resisted the efforts of a number of would-be biographers." Who was this guy, anyway? Peter wondered.

Blazer's name was not mentioned in the obituary. Had something happened to him? Peter looked him up in

the Yale Alumni Directory, and Blazer was listed as living
at an address in the East Village. The directory was a
couple of years old, so he consulted the Manhattan telephone book and there he was, at the same address.

There was still something about the obituary that
bothered Peter, and he couldn't put his finger on what it
was. Then it dawned on him. It was in the very last paragraph: *Interment at Salem Fields Cemetery in Brooklyn
will be private.* Salem Fields is a Jewish cemetery. Blazer
Tarkington was Jewish. That was why all the senior societies had snubbed him. Suddenly Peter was a little
ashamed of himself for not having worked harder, at
Yale, to make him a friend, for not having tried to get him
to remove that chip on his shoulder.

He suddenly remembered, after the snub, hearing a
Bones man say, "We just didn't think he'd be happy
here." And as far as Silas Tarkington's money was concerned, he supposed they just considered him another
Jewish shopkeeper. That was what was wrong with
Blazer. His Jewishness had given him a kind of birth de-
fect.

So Peter decided to call him. "I was sorry to hear
about your dad," he said, when he got him on the phone.

"Yeah."

"He must have been quite a guy."

"Yeah." It was the same old Blazer, taciturn as ever.

"I'm sorry I never knew him."

"Why?"

"Well, because, as you say, he was quite a guy."

There was a silence and, because this conversation
wasn't exactly moving right along, he decided to try a
different tack and get right to the point.

"Look," he said, "I'm thinking of doing an article
about your father. As you know, there's been very little
written about him, and he seems to have had an interesting life and career. I was wondering whether you and I
could get together."

There was another long silence, and for a moment
Peter thought they'd been disconnected. Then he heard
Blazer say, in an almost incredulous tone of voice, "You

want to write something about *him*? Why the hell would you want to do that?"

"Look," he said. "The obituary in *The Times* seems to raise more questions than it answers. Like, where was he born, and when? How did he get his start? I think there's a fascinating business story here, and a fascinating personal story too. After all, he created a specialty store like no other in the world. How did he actually *do* it? He was a kind of Horatio Alger hero, wasn't he? The American success story. Rags to riches—"

"Bullshit!"

"I'm serious. He seems to have been a completely self-made man. He—"

"Bullshit."

"Readers are always interested in finding out how a man, starting out with a single, rather specialized idea, can build—"

"You really want to dig up all that crap?" Blazer said.

"Maybe you're familiar with some of the business stories I've been writing for *Fortune,* Blazer," he said, moving right along, even though he wasn't getting much encouragement from the other end of the conversation. "I'm thinking of the corporate history of Tarkington's. The personal history of your father. Because the store *was* your father. There's even the question of who's going to succeed him—or if anybody *can* succeed him. Or if, in a business recession, when a lot of retailers are having problems, a store like yours—"

"Like mine? It ain't my store, buddy. Never was."

"Whether a store like Tarkington's can survive as the kind of store it's always been. There've been buy-out offers, I understand, and—"

"You're talking about opening up a real can of worms. I guess you know that."

"No," he said carefully, "I didn't know that."

"Or are you just one of those guys who come sniffing around my family because you've got the hots for my kid sister?"

"Nonsense," he said. "I've never met your sister."

Though he didn't add that he'd certainly like to talk to his sister too.

"All you Yale guys were only nice to me because I had a sister who looked like a hot piece of ass."

Peter decided not to comment on this, though it seemed a crude way for a man to speak of his sister. He continued with his pitch. "So what do you say, Blazer? Can we get together? Can I present my case to you in person?"

"Are you going to go into the funny way the old man died?" Blazer asked suddenly.

"What do you mean?" Peter said, all at once excited.

"Died of a coronary? There was nothing wrong with the old man's heart, except that it was made of industrial-grade concrete."

"You mean you think your father was—"

"Ha! They only put in the obituary what the family told them to put in. I'm just saying that something damned fishy happened that day at the pool, no pun intended."

"But who?"

"The old man had a lot of enemies," Blazer said. Then he said, "But what the hell. I don't really give a damn how the old man died. I hated the old bastard." Then, without skipping a beat, he said, "And loved him too. Hated him, and loved him too. After all, he was my father."

"Look," Peter said, "let me take you to lunch. We could go to the Yale Club—"

"Fuck the Yale Club! You won't catch me dead inside the fucking Yale Club!"

But even as he said these harsh things, Peter had the strange feeling that there were tears in Blazer's eyes. "Or wherever you say," he said quietly.

Blazer paused and seemed to consider this. "Well," he said at last, "if you're going to write all that garbage about the old man, I guess I can't stop you."

"It's not garbage, Blazer. It's hist—"

"Talk to Jake Kohlberg," Blazer said, interrupting. "Kohlberg was the old man's lawyer. Kohlberg knew him longer and better than I ever did. He'll tell you all the wonderful things the old man did. Then, maybe, if I talk to you, I can tell you some of the things that weren't quite so wonderful about him. Isn't that what you journalists like to get—a balanced view?"

A note of sarcasm had crept into his voice, particularly in the way he came down hard on the word "balanced," so Peter decided to change the subject. "Okay," he said pleasantly. "So—tell me what you've been up to, Blazer. It's been a while."

"Not much."

"Interesting job?"

"No."

Since that sort of left Peter hanging there, he said, "Well, look, I'll call Mr. Kohlberg, and after I've talked to him I'll give you a call, and maybe you and I can get together. It'd be great seeing you again, in any case."

There was another short silence. Then Blazer said, "Listen, Turner, none of you guys ever did shit for me at Yale. Everything I did at Yale I did for myself. What makes you think I should do shit for you?"

Peter took a deep breath. "Well, Blazer," he said, "I helped carry you home after you vomited and passed out drunk in a boxwood hedge in front of the Beta house. I held your head over a toilet bowl while you puked some more. Then I laid you on top of your bed, took off your shoes, loosened your belt, undid your collar, and wiped all the stinking puke off the front of your shirt. I took off your granny glasses and that dumb cap you always wore and put them on top of your dresser, laying the glasses neatly with the stems down. I wet a towel with cold water and put it on your forehead. Then I put a pillow under your head, my friend, and covered you with a blanket, and put a bucket beside your bed in case you needed to puke again. Remember any of that? Maybe not, because you were passed-out drunk. But I certainly never got any thank-you for that from you."

There was another little silence, followed by a short, humorless laugh. "Yeah," Blazer said. "Maybe you did do that. So give me a call after you've talked to Kohlberg." Then the line went dead.

But when Peter Turner called Jacob Kohlberg, he felt he had struck a dead end. The lawyer's tone was almost icily formal. "Silas Tarkington was a friend and client of mine throughout his entire business life," he said. "I'm afraid client confidentiality prevents me from discussing either his business or his personal life with you. In my book, client confidentiality extends even after the client's death. I'm sorry not to be able to help you, Mr. Turner."

Then, late in the afternoon, Jacob Kohlberg had called him back, and his tone was friendlier. "I mentioned your project to Mrs. Tarkington," he said, "and I believe she'd be willing to talk to you. She gave me permission to give you her private number. But give her a few days, while she adjusts to—the loss of her husband."

7

Miranda steps out from under the Pierre's marquee, turns south and walks a block, and there it is, her father's magical store, dark now in honor of his memory but still full of his life. As always, the sight of the grand old building, which appears to be nestled in its newer L-shaped addition, evokes a little inner gasp of wonder. How gracefully the elegant Nile-green awnings seem to reach out and embrace the avenue. She stands at the corner of 59th Street, waiting for the WALK light, admiring the sheer presence of Tarkington's as it manages to grace this corner of Manhattan.

Suddenly she turns, takes several rapid steps eastward down 59th, and steps into the recessed doorway of a religious bookstore, where she appears to be intensely interested in the titles displayed in its window. She has just seen Diana Smith emerging from Tarkington's side entrance, looking not quite her usual spiffed-up self, looking preoccupied. She has no wish to encounter her late father's mistress at this point, and out of the corner of her eye she watches as Smitty steps to the curb, raises her hand to flag a taxi, greets a passing friend, and finally steps into a cab and is borne away, southward, into the evening. This process, which takes mere minutes, seems to take hours. Then Miranda emerges from her hiding place, returns to the corner, and waits for the next WALK light.

Inside the store, she waves a greeting to Oliver, the watchman.

"Sad day, ain't it, Miss Tarkington," he says.

"Yes, it is."

"You have my deep condolences."

"Thank you, Oliver," she says.

"You just missed Miss Smith," he says. "She was just here."

"Oh, what a pity," she says.

"She was lookin' real bad, real green around the gills, like the fella says. She's takin' it real bad. We all are."

"What did she want, I wonder?"

"She took out a big ring she wanted to show to a customer from South America."

"Oh?" she says, making a mental note, thinking, Have the vultures already begun to descend? In a book about Barbara Hutton, she read how, after the heiress's death, all her jewelry was mysteriously missing by the time anyone from the family arrived. At least all of Smitty's merchandise is comfortably insured.

In the bank of three elevators, the southernmost car goes directly to the apartment, and Miranda enters it, using the magnetic card that will permit her to be carried, nonstop, to the upper two floors. The elevator glides upward, and she steps out into the mirrored foyer of the apartment. Milliken, her mother's major domo, greets her. "Mrs. Tarkington hasn't arrived yet, ma'am," he says. "She telephoned to say she'd be a few minutes late."

"Thank you, Milliken." She drops her bag on a chair and moves toward the green library.

"Mrs. Tarkington said it would just be the two of you for dinner tonight, ma'am."

"Yes."

"Mrs. Tarkington suggested something simple,

ma'am. Cook has made a crabmeat salad and a bread pudding for dessert. Will that be all right?"

"That sounds fine, Milliken."

"Shall I bring you a glass of wine in the library, ma'am?"

"Lovely, Milliken."

Milliken has just begun calling her ma'am, a title formerly reserved for her mother. Before her father's death, she was Miss Tarkington. Some subtle change in her status, a change apparent only to Milliken, has occurred in the last two days, and now she and her mother are both ma'ams. Should she feel pleased to be so elevated? Miranda is not sure.

The green library was always her father's favorite room. Of course it is really not a library at all. It is just a stage set for a library, just another of the stage sets her father created for his life. The walls and the bookshelves are covered in green leather, and so are the books themselves, but they are not real books. Behind these green leather bindings with their gold-lettered titles—*Views of Ancient Rome, Seventeenth-Century French Architecture, A History of Opera,* and so on—are blank pages. One whole wall of these *faux* books, for instance, swings open to reveal an enormous television screen. The people her father entertained here—his bankers, certain special clients, a few close friends—did not come here to read. They came to talk of money and merchandise or to play gin rummy at ten dollars a point. His "official" photograph, taken by Bachrach in 1970, half smiles at her from a low table.

Tonight the room seems strangely still and empty. The rack containing his collection of pipes sits on his green-leather-topped desk. The elephant-foot stand—*faux,* like the books—holding his collection of walking sticks is by the door, walking sticks topped with heads of eagles, sea gulls, lions, snakes, and horses, carved in teakwood, ivory, brass, silver, and baleen, some of them antiques but most of them copies. As she sits in her father's green leather chair by the empty fireplace, Miranda thinks she can still smell her father's pipe smoke in the air.

Milliken arrives with her wine on a silver tray. He places this on a low table beside her chair, along with a silver bowl of Cheese Doodles. Her father had a passion for Cheese Doodles and liked to nibble on them while he sipped his evening drink, which, of course, was never wine but Chivas Regal. His bar is still stocked with Chivas Regal, and the butler's pantry contains shelf after shelf of nothing but Cheese Doodles. The sight of the Cheese Doodles moves her strangely. "Thank you, Milliken," she says, and he withdraws.

She is sitting in the president's chair.

"Just think of the things you and I could do together," Tommy Bonham said to her.

"You mean I'd be your co-president?" she said.

"Partners," he said. "Full partners. Think about it, Miranda."

And of course she is thinking about it now. Carefully. Running the store. Running it with him. Fifty-fifty. Partners. Filling her father's shoes, in a real sense. Working with Tommy, the way her father did, as a team. Sitting at his big desk, in the corner office, pushing buttons, with Tommy's office right next door. Or, if they are to become co-presidents, will they both have corner offices?

Of course she has always dreamed of running the store. But it was just that, a hazy dream, with none of the specifics filled in. Now she must consider these specifics. To begin with, there is the possibility that she would be taking this big step too fast, that she is emotionally and occupationally unprepared for it, and that she will fall flat on her face. That could happen, of course, but Miranda has enough confidence in her ability and adaptability to feel sure it won't.

But one of the practical questions to be asked is this one: What will it be like to work with Tommy? One of the nice things about her present job, despite its boring aspects, has been her independence. She is really her own boss. She *is* the Advertising Department. Each month she is presented with an advertising budget, and as long as she doesn't exceed that budget the job virtually does itself, like a plane on automatic pilot. The only actually "creative" moments occur when she discovers a new publication, studies its demographics, and proposes that the store experiment by placing an ad in it. Otherwise, she reports to no one. Tommy Bonham and she have had no opportunities to clash, or disagree, or even to interact at all. He has always left her alone, treated her with distant but polite respect—after all, as he said, she was the boss's daughter—but now they will be interacting a great deal.

Miranda knows she is well liked by the store's personnel. That will not present a problem. On the other hand, she also knows that Tommy Bonham is less well liked. She has heard members of the staff complain that Tommy is overscrupulous in his attention to detail, that his eyes seem to be everywhere in the store at once, that he is too zealous in his criticism of the slightest oversight or shortcoming. Often, when an unpleasant chore had to be performed—the dismissal of an employee, for instance—her father delegated Tommy to perform that chore. She has heard Tommy referred to as her father's hatchet man. What will it be like with Tommy looking over her shoulder all the time, ready to catch her in her first mistake? In the beginning, at least, she is bound to make a mistake or two. Maybe even three. How will she react when Tommy, however gently, reprimands her in this process he calls "teaching her everything she needs to know"?

"No, Miranda," she can hear him say, "that's not the way we do it."

"But that's the way *I* want to do it," she can hear herself reply.

Stalemate. All at once, teamwork has ground to a halt.

Would the idea of co-presidents, where each had equal authority, really work? What would it be like? There are no ready answers to these questions, she thinks. We'd have to wait and see.

Then there is the question, What is Tommy Bonham really like? She doesn't really know. A complicated man, she thinks. A bachelor. Tommy Bonham's bachelorhood is by now an established fact of New York social life.

Only the adjectives used to describe that famous bachelorhood have changed over the years. In the 1970's, when
he first appeared on the scene, the word for Tommy was
eligible. "Handsome Thomas Bonham, one of New
York's most eligible young bachelors," Mona Potter
called him, and that description prompted a number of
eligible women to set about trying to correct the situation. They had not succeeded. By the 1980's, he had become a *perennial* bachelor. And now, in the 1990's, he is
a *confirmed* bachelor, with the word "confirmed" implying that he has taken his final solemn vows to remain in
an unmarried state. Women no longer bother offering
themselves to Tommy Bonham—not, at least, with marriage as their goal.

Of course there have been the usual number of sly
speculations about Tommy Bonham's sexual orientation.
Every single male past the age of thirty-five in this city is
accustomed to this sort of talk, and Tommy himself has
joked about it. "I know there are people who say I'm
gay," he once chuckled to Miranda's father. "Maybe I
should encourage those rumors. Maybe that would make
some of these broads who are trying to get me to the altar
leave me alone." Miranda has never taken any of these
innuendoes seriously. Many women Tommy has dated
have offered opposing testimony. "My dear, he's simply
the best swordsman in town," one woman gushed to her.
"I'm amazed he's never asked you out." But Miranda
knows why he never has. Because she was the boss's
daughter. Now, however, that situation has changed.

But this in itself raises another ticklish question. Remembering her wild, schoolgirl crush on Tommy, she asks
herself, What would happen if, working with him in such
close proximity, those old feelings should come surging
back? How would she react if he were to put his arm
around her or draw her to him? That would certainly
complicate things. Can she trust herself? She has often
found herself more than idly wondering—what woman
wouldn't, with a man as handsome as Tommy?—whether
he was just as handsomely constructed elsewhere. But no,
she decides. That crush was too long ago. She has long

since come to regard him as nothing more than her father's business adjunct, a store fixture. And he has never expressed any sexual interest in her. None whatever.

This afternoon, though, he said something that surprised her. "You know," he said, "I was the one who talked your father into giving you a job at the store in the first place."

"Really?"

"He was very much opposed to it. He wanted you to marry a man like David Belknap, and move to Westchester, and start having babies."

She made a wry face. "That's what David Belknap wanted."

"But I talked your father into hiring you," he said.

"So it's thanks to you that I'm working for the store at all?"

He winked at her. "That's right. You owe me one. You owe me one, Miranda."

Her father disapproved of many things about Tommy. He disapproved of his bachelor's lifestyle. He disapproved of his reputation as a womanizer and ladies' man and often said that Tommy should settle down with a Tarkington's-type woman. "He dates these Junior League girls," she had heard her father say. "Why doesn't he marry one of them? It would be better for our image." Her father said these things, despite the fact that his own reputation as a womanizer and ladies' man was becoming widespread and the women her father chose weren't all Junior Leaguers.

She had learned about her father's tastes in women firsthand when she was seventeen. It was the end of her first semester at Sarah Lawrence, and her name was posted at the top of the freshman honor roll. Excited, she wanted her father to be the first to know, so she hopped on a train to Manhattan and went straight to her father's office, feeling proud as punch, smart as paint. Looking up from her desk as Miranda marched toward her father's closed door, Pauline O'Malley sprang to her feet and tried to block her path. "You can't go in now, Miranda!" she cried. "He's in conf—"

"Nonsense," Miranda said, "this is important," and she pushed Pauline aside and tried the door. It was locked from the inside.

"Mr. Si!" Pauline screamed into the intercom. *"Your daughter is here!"*

Miranda pounded on the door. "Open up, Daddy!" she said. "I've got great news!"

It was a few minutes before the door opened, and Miranda was astonished by what she saw. His office was in disarray. Two lampshades by his sofa were crooked, there were sofa cushions on the floor, and a picture over the sofa hung askew. Her normally impeccable father looked similarly disheveled. He was in his shirt sleeves—he never worked in his shirt sleeves—and his collar and necktie were undone. His usually perfectly combed white hair was mussed, his shoelaces were untied, and he was perspiring heavily.

"What happened, Daddy?" she cried.

"I was just having a little nap."

But she had never known him to take naps and, from the way he was breathing, he looked as though he had been running, not sleeping. "You must have had a bad dream," she said. She knew that he sometimes did have bad dreams.

"Yes, that's it," he said. "I was having this really very bad dream, Miranda."

"Well," she said, taking charge, "you just march into your bathroom and clean yourself up. I'll straighten up this mess." Almost meekly, he obeyed her, and from his bathroom she heard water running. She gathered up the papers from the floor, put the desk lamp back on its base, straightened the pictures, and picked up the sofa cushions. Suddenly she heard sort of a scratching sound from inside his coat closet. She pulled open the closet door, and a naked woman was crouched there, looking up at her with frightened eyes, one arm crossed across her bare breasts and the other hand covering her crotch. She didn't know the young woman's name, but she recognized one of the models who paraded in designer dresses on the fashion floors. The woman was not much older than Miranda herself. "Well, *excuse me*!" Miranda said, and slammed the door closed. "I made the top of the honor roll, Daddy!" she shouted angrily in her father's direction as she marched out of the office, though she doubted he could hear her over the running water.

As she passed Pauline's desk in the outer office, the secretary gave her a worried I-told-you-so look.

Disgusted with him, she decided to punish her father and refused to speak to him for a solid month. When he called her at college, she refused to come to the phone.

When she got back to Bronxville, she told her roommate what had happened. "Should I tell my mother? Or not?" she asked.

"Not," her roommate said. "Don't make waves. Besides, all men are like that."

"Well, the man *I* marry is not going to be like that," Miranda said firmly.

Later, when they were back on speaking terms, her father had tried to offer her an explanation. "I know you found Miss Rosenthal hiding in my closet that day."

"I did indeed!"

"She was in somewhat of a state of *déshabille*," he said. "But let me explain. These things are something of an occupational hazard for men in my position. These girls, these little models, think they can advance their careers by literally throwing themselves at the chief executive. Sometimes, one has to literally fight these advances off, Miranda. That was what happened that afternoon. I was in the middle of fighting her off. Needless to say, I had words with her later, she apologized for her indiscretion, and I forgave her. Meanwhile, you should really telephone before just barging into the office. . . . I'm happy about the honor roll."

"Hmm," was all she said. She didn't believe a word of it.

"We have a lot of things we need to talk about, Miranda," her mother said to her this afternoon as they were leaving Jake Kohlberg's office. "Let's have dinner

together, just the two of us, tonight at the apartment."
Now Miranda is sipping her wine in the green library,
waiting for her mother.

Well, one of the things they will definitely *not* talk
about tonight is Tommy Bonham's proposition. Whatever
decision Miranda makes about that, she will make entirely on her own.

Still, she can't help wondering what her father would
have had to say about all this. "What do you think,
Daddy?" she asks him now.

"Do you really want to run the store?" the half-smil-
ing Bachrach portrait answers her.

"Yes!"

"Women can't run stores, Miranda."

"I'm taking night courses in marketing at N.Y.U. I
got an A on my first big test."

"You never told me that."

"I was saving it to tell you now."

"You don't learn marketing from textbooks. You
learn it from experience."

"What if I were to run the store with Tommy? He has
plenty of experience."

The portrait has no response to this. She has lost his
wavelength. *What did you say, Daddy? I can't hear you.*

Idly, and for no real reason, she picks up the green
telephone beside her chair and dials his private office
number. It rings once, twice, three times; she can even
hear it ringing faintly in the empty office on the floor
below. Then, all at once, he answers!

"Hello. You have reached the voice-mail number of
Silas Tarkington. I'm unable to take your call right now,
but, when you hear the tone, please leave your name,
telephone number, and any message, and I'll get back to
you as soon as possible. Your message can be of any
length. If there is any item in the store you're looking for,
or if there is any way I can be of service to you, please let
me know. Thank you for calling. Goodbye."

Miranda quickly replaces the receiver in its cradle.
No one has erased the tape on his machine.

If there is any way I can be of service to you. . . .

For the first time since her father died, Miranda allows herself the luxury of a good, noisy sob.

Then, outside the room, she hears the elevator door slide open and the brisk click of her mother's Chanel heels across the marble floor of the foyer.

"Miss Tarkington's waiting for you in the library, ma'am," she hears Milliken say.

"Be with you in a minute, darling!" her mother calls out, almost gaily. "I just want to slip into some more comfortable shoes."

How could her mother remain so composed? Of all the odd things that happened the day her father died, perhaps the oddest was her mother's behavior. Miranda had been in East Hampton for the weekend, visiting with friends, when her mother telephoned her. "Darling, something terrible has happened," she said, and then she told her.

Miranda, not even bothering to pack, had jumped into her blue BMW and driven directly to Old Westbury. But as she drove through the gates of Flying Horse Farm, everything there seemed as ordered and manicured as ever. She had expected to find the circular drive in front of the house filled with cars—police cars, an ambulance perhaps, reporters, television crews. She didn't know what she had expected to find, but when she parked her car at the foot of the steps leading up to the house, hers was the only car in the drive. Everyone, it seemed, had already come and gone. Dr. Arnstein had arrived by helicopter, signed the death certificate, and departed. The hearse had arrived from Campbell's, and her father's body was already on its way to New York and the crematorium. All this, it seemed, had happened before Miranda's mother telephoned her in East Hampton.

She ran up the steps to the house, where Milliken, who had obviously been weeping, greeted her. He squeezed her hand. "Your mother's in the sun room," he whispered.

She found her mother there, in the room decorated in

sunny garden colors—pinks, yellows, pale greens, and
blues—sitting in a wicker chair, looking as coolly beautiful as ever in a white silk blouse and white silk slacks,
working on her needlepoint. She was making a cover for
her tennis racket. Her mother rose when Miranda entered
the room, and they embraced, Miranda fighting back
tears.

"Darling, we won't have your father anymore," her
mother said simply. "He loved you so. He was so very
proud of you."

"What happened, Mother?"

"He was swimming his laps in the pool. He just decided to swim one more lap than his fine, strong heart
would let him—that's what Harry Arnstein said."

They sat, and Consuelo Tarkington picked up her
needlepoint and began listing the things she had done,
and the people she had notified, since she had found his
body floating earlier in the day.

"Did you call—"

"Smitty? Yes. Smitty has been notified."

"Tommy?"

"Yes. Tommy is coming by for a drink a little later."

"Blazer?"

"Of course."

"Pauline?"

"That's one call I thought I'd ask you to make, darling," her mother said. "Pauline tends to get so—emotional—and besides, you've worked more closely with her
at the store."

And so, feeling numb, Miranda had gone to the telephone and called Pauline O'Malley at her home in Kew
Gardens. Pauline had immediately become so hysterical
she had to hang up the phone.

Miranda returned to the sun room where her mother
was pulling a thread of golden wool through her canvas,
completing a flower in the pattern. She had tucked her
slippered feet underneath her in the chair. She spread the
canvas on her lap and examined it. Her pose was so se-
rene it seemed almost Oriental. She could have been
painted on a Chinese plate.

"What about the press?" Miranda asked her.

"Tommy's taking care of that," her mother said. "He pointed out, correctly, that if we report it to the press today, the news will be printed tomorrow, which is a Sunday. Obituaries just get lost in the Sunday papers. But if we wait a day, there's a good chance it will make the front page of *The Times* on Monday morning." She returned to her needlework.

Miranda sat opposite her mother. "Now tell me exactly what happened," she said.

"He told me he was going out to swim his laps," her mother said, without looking up from her work. "It was about eleven-thirty. I reminded him that lunch was being served at twelve-thirty. When he hadn't returned by then, I went out to the pool to look for him. That's when I found him . . . floating. I immediately telephoned Harry Arnstein."

Miranda glanced at her watch. It was nearly six-thirty, which meant that her father had been dead for at least six hours. "Why didn't you call nine-one-one?" she asked.

Her mother looked up at her briefly. "Nine-one-one is a *police* number, darling. There was no need to involve the police."

"But they would have sent the life squad. They might have—"

"You would have had police sirens—police ambulances—screaming down Heather Lane? Upsetting all the neighbors who were trying to enjoy a quiet Saturday afternoon? Really, Miranda. You know the thing your father loved best about the country was the peace and quiet here."

"But they might have saved his life!"

Her mother looped another stitch through her canvas. "Miranda, I assure you there was no life left to save," she said. "Harry Arnstein confirmed this."

"But still, that's what I'd have done!"

She spread her canvas on her lap again. "I'll tell you another reason why I didn't do that," she said. "If you get the police involved, they're required by law to perform an autopsy. Do you know what an autopsy involves? If you don't know, I'll leave it to your imagination, but it's horrible. I wouldn't dream of having such a thing done to your father."

"How long did it take Dr. Arnstein to get here?"

"He was here within the hour."

"You see? That hour could have been crucial. The life squad could have—"

"Miranda, *please*!" Her mother was beginning to show her first signs of impatience. "I did what I had to do. I don't think I even *thought* of calling nine-one-one. I'm not even sure I knew there was such a number. I wanted your father's life to end the way he would have wanted it to end—with dignity, and taste, and grace, and with just me and his old friend Harry Arnstein with him. Not with sirens screaming."

It seemed to Miranda that her mother was making a lot of different excuses that didn't quite hang together. She hadn't called 911 because the life squad would make too much noise and disturb the neighbors. The life squad would have meant an autopsy. She hadn't even thought about calling 911. She didn't even know there was such a number. She wanted the death to be dignified and private. "Why did you wait so long before calling me?" she asked. "You say he died at twelve-thirty. I didn't hear from you until after four."

"What would have been the point? I felt I had to do first things first."

"I might have liked to have seen him one last time. I might have liked to have said goodbye to him."

"I wanted to spare you that," her mother said.

"Spare me? That's what I'd have liked to *do*, Mother!"

She looked up from her needlework. "Death isn't pretty, Miranda," she said. "You don't know that. I do. It takes a certain amount of—practice—to be able to deal with death. You've had none. I've had a great deal. My mother, my father, my grandparents. Perhaps, the first time, I wasn't very good at it. But with practice I've gotten a lot better."

Suddenly Miranda was very angry. "How can you just *sit* there like that?" she had cried. "Just sit there like some goddamned female Buddha, as though nothing has happened! Sitting there with your goddamned needle-point—like Madame Defarge, stitching away while heads roll off the guillotine! Don't you have any human feelings, Mother? A man is dead. Your husband is dead. Maybe you didn't love him, but he was still your husband. And he was also my father! Whom I happened to love very much!"

Her mother rose slowly from her chair and folded the needlepoint canvas across her bosom. "This conversation isn't really getting us anywhere, is it?" she said. "I've asked people who want to pay their respects to come here for drinks at seven-thirty, and I need to freshen up. If you'd like to join us, you might want to freshen up too. You look a little windblown from your trip in from the Hamptons. Run a comb through your hair. Powder your nose." Then she was gone, leaving Miranda fuming.

That night at seven-thirty the guests started arriving —the old friends, some of the people from the store, the neighbors from up and down Heather Lane. Some people stayed for only a few minutes. Others stayed longer. Tommy Bonham was one of the first to appear, and Miranda watched as he took her mother in his arms, kissed her, and said, "Connie, I'm so sorry." Blazer arrived from the Village, looking more stunned than sullen, and Miranda was pleased to see that he had put on a dark suit and necktie. Harry Arnstein was there, looking solemn and professional, and Smitty had also come out from the city, looking red-eyed and a little frightened. She shouldn't be here, Miranda thought. And yet her mother had obviously asked her to come, and she watched as her mother made a special point of stepping over to Smitty, squeezing her hands, and kissing her lightly on both cheeks—kisses so light that flesh never touched flesh. Was this gesture done for the benefit of the audience, for the others in the room? "Isn't Connie re*mar*kable?" she heard someone whisper.

Moe Minskoff, who had had financial dealings with her father over the years, also appeared with his bleached-blond wife, who was called Honeychile—to her mother's almost visible displeasure.

"What are those people doing here?" she heard her mother whisper to Tommy Bonham. "Who invited them? I certainly didn't. How did they find out about this?"

Tommy Bonham merely rolled his eyes.

Meanwhile, both Minskoffs seemed to have decided to make an evening of it, not just a polite condolence call. They seemed to be settling in for the night.

By eight o'clock, there were perhaps twenty people in the formal living room. Milliken was serving drinks and passing trays of caviar on toast points, and Miranda's mother—now in a slender white silk jump suit with tiny silver bells at the belt—was moving about the room, try-ing to spend a little time with each guest, explaining how Si had had "a coronary accident" while swimming his laps—"Dr. Arnstein assured me it was very sudden, and there was no pain"—and soon the noise level in the room had risen, and it was clear that all the men in their sober suits and ties, and their wives in their demure little black dresses, were drinking and generally beginning to have a pretty good time.

"Si loved parties," Miranda heard someone say. "He would have approved of this."

But Miranda was not so sure.

Over the living room fireplace hung the large paint-ing of Flying Flame, her father's famous racehorse that had won the Arc de Triomphe in Paris in 1971, and, lean-ing against the mantel with a cigar in his fist, the portly Moses Minskoff was holding forth about the painting. "I remember when I came up with the name for that stallion for Si," he was saying. "I said to Si, 'Si, name him Flying Flame.'"

"Don't be ridiculous," she heard her mother say. "*I* named that horse."

"No," he said flatly. "In actual fact, I came up with

the name for that horse. I'm something of an expert on horseflesh, you know. It was the year of Comet Kohoutek, and I'd read in the paper that morning that the comet would appear like a flying flame across the sky. I said to Si, I said, 'Si, there's the name for your stallion—Flying Flame.'"

"I remember you telling me that story, Daddy," Honeychile Minskoff put in.

"Nonsense," Miranda's mother said. "I named him Flying Flame because his sire was named Fly By Night, and his dam was Torch Singer. You always try to do that —give a horse a name that will suggest the breeding line."

"No," Moe Minskoff said again. "I named him after Comet Kohoutek."

"I know you did, Daddy!"

"Comet Kohoutek didn't come until years later!" her mother said sharply.

With that, she saw Tommy Bonham's hand reach out and touch her mother's bare arm very gently. "I want to tell the story about the Queen's visit to the store," he said, changing the subject. "Si wouldn't admit he was nervous. But he was. . . ."

That was one of Tommy's great talents, avoiding unpleasantness, defusing a confrontation.

Miranda could understand the cocktail-party atmosphere that had overtaken the evening. Right after a death, there is a need for a certain release, and this was it —a release from the shock. But she wasn't feeling up to it, so she wandered from the party that was going on in the living room and out into the garden to the pool—where he died. It seemed as good a place as any to say goodbye to her father.

The pool was still as glass and inky black, though there were moonlight and starlight reflected in its glassy surface. She wondered briefly whether her mother would have the pool torn out and the excavation filled in, now that somebody had died there. She knelt by the edge and trailed her fingers in the still water. Then she put her fingertips to her lips, to taste the water in which her father had died. She stood up again.

The switch that turned on the underwater lights was mounted in a low stone wall that bordered the pool, and she walked to this and flipped it upward, but the lights did not come on. Then she realized why the surface of the pool was so still. The filter, which normally ran twenty-four hours a day, rippling the pool with its jets, was not working. She flipped the filter switch, but nothing happened. A third switch controlled the outdoor garden lights, but these were not working either.

She ran up the short flight of steps to the pool house and began flipping switches there. No lights were working in this part of the farm at all, and suddenly a shiver ran down her back, and she thought, *electricity*, the television set. Even without lights, she could see that the television set was not sitting where it usually sat, on a shelf against the far wall of the room, in its Lucite case. In the moonlight semidarkness, she searched for the television set, but she could not find it.

This was no ordinary television. In 1976, her father had made a special trip to Washington to show some designer dresses to Mrs. Betty Ford at the White House. To thank her for her purchases, Si had sent Mrs. Ford two silk Hermès scarves. The Fords responded by sending Silas Tarkington videotapes of all President Ford's speeches, along with a portable television set to play them on. An engraved brass plaque on the top of the set read:

FOR SILAS TARKINGTON,
A GREAT MERCHANT,
WITH WARMEST THANKS FROM
PRESIDENT AND MRS. GERALD R. FORD
1976

Miranda doubted that her father had ever played the tapes of the President's speeches, but he had the Lucite case made to display the set. And when he swam his laps, he plugged the set, tuned to the cable news network, into one of the outdoor outlets, and a red digital clock on the face of the set kept track of the time for him. He claimed that counting his laps was boring. Instead, he timed himself, swimming for half an hour, forty-five minutes, or sometimes for a full hour, whenever he was in the country.

The sight of that television set at the edge of the pool always made Miranda nervous. "What if it fell into the pool while you're swimming, Daddy? You could be electrocuted."

"How could it fall into the pool? It must weigh twenty pounds."

Blackamoor, his big Lab, often ran up and down the length of the pool as he swam and sometimes got excited enough to leap into the water and swim alongside, yipping with pleasure.

"What if Blackie tripped on the cord and knocked it in?"

"Nonsense. Blackie knows our routine."

Two years ago, for his birthday, she had bought him a scuba diver's underwater wrist chronometer. "It's guaranteed for depths up to a hundred feet," she told him.

"Great, but why do I need it?"

"It's to use instead of the clock on the TV set," she said.

He laughed. "It would break my rhythm if I had to keep looking at a watch all the time," he said. "I prefer my TV clock."

Then, as a joke, she had bought him an ordinary kitchen timer, with a bell.

He had looked at it. "Will this also give me my cable TV news?" he said with a smile.

And now the set was gone, and all the power in that corner of the farm was out, and her father was dead.

In the distance, from the main house, she could hear the sound of laughter. "Oh, he was a wonderful man, a wonderful man," she heard Moe Minskoff saying. "Sucha sense-a yuma. . . ."

Behind the pool house was Blackamoor's kennel, and she went to look for him. There were no lights there either, but Blackie bounded up from his bed, wagging his tail, and seemed pleased to see her. But when she offered him a milk bone, he didn't want it and just dropped it back into her hand.

And so she sat with the big dog for a while, stroking his ears, with his big head resting on her lap. He seemed sad, as sad as she was, and perhaps even sadder because there was no way for him to express his sadness. From the main house, farther up the hill, the party sounds continued, and she could even hear her mother's tinkly, polished laugh. From Blackamoor now came soft whimpering sounds, whether of pleasure or sorrow she had no way of knowing.

Miranda rested her chin on the top of Blackie's head and was suddenly certain he knew that her father was gone and would never be coming back. And she had another scary, eerie feeling that the dog knew something about her father's death that she would never know. "Blackie," she said to him, "if you could talk, is there something you could tell me?"

In the green library now there is the sudden scent of Shalimar as Miranda's mother enters the room, a little breathless. "Sorry to be late, darling," she says, "but I couldn't get a cab and ended up walking all the way from Forty-fourth Street." She gives Miranda a peck on the cheek. She has changed into flats, but the two crescents of pale hair that frame her face are still perfectly in place. She steps to a mirror, touches her hair, and flicks an invisible speck of lint from the sleeve of her navy Chanel suit. Then she moves quickly away from the mirror, glides back across the room, and sits in the green leather chair opposite Miranda, under Monet's painting of water lilies, where the museum light shines down on her hair, giving it frosty glints.

It is another of her mother's mysterious talents, Miranda thinks—to be able to position herself perfectly in a room, under a painting where her white skin reflects the tone and texture of the lily blossoms, and where the lamp echoes the reflected sunlight in the lily pond.

Milliken arrives with iced tea in a silver goblet, garnished with a lemon wedge and a sprig of fresh mint.

"Thank you, Milliken." Miranda's mother fishes for a cigarette from the silver box on the coffee table, screws it into a silver cigarette holder, and lights it with a silver table lighter. Everything seems to glimmer in the lighter's blue and orange flash. In her mother's world, Miranda thinks, everything works, including silver table lighters, which never work for anyone else.

Her mother glances at the silver bowl. "Cheese Doodles," she says. "Dear me. Remind me to tell Milliken to throw out all those Cheese Doodles in the larder."

"I happen to like Cheese Doodles, Mother."

Her mother throws her a quick look. "Do you? Dear me. Well, *chacun à son goût*. There's apparently a young man who wants to write your father's biography. What would he say if we told him that your elegant father's favorite snack was junk food?"

"Do we want Daddy's biography written, Mother? He never wanted it done."

"I asked Jake Kohlberg the same question. He feels that if we don't cooperate, this man might decide to write the story anyway, and we'd have no—leverage, as Jake put it, over what he decides to say."

"Control, you mean."

"Exactly. Anyway," she continues, without skipping a beat, "the will's been read, that's over and done with, and we all know where we stand. Too bad about Blazer, because your father really was going to relent and leave Blazer something. Not a lot, I think, but something."

"But still—"

"You know why your father did that to Blazer, don't you? It wasn't just because of the things Blazer said to him that day. It was because he hoped that leaving him out of the will would galvanize Blazer into finding a job. 'Shock therapy,' your father called it. Anyway, there's nothing to be done about that now, is there? And"—she blows out a long thin stream of smoke—"we've got more important things to discuss, you and I. We've got to decide what's going to happen next."

"Yes."

"I had a long talk with Jake Kohlberg after you left," she says. "He feels very strongly, and I agree, that we ought to sell the store."

"Oh, no!" Miranda cries.

"Apparently Continental is planning to make us a nice tender offer, and there are a couple of other bidders, and Jake thinks, and I agree, that we ought to accept the best offer as soon as we can. A bird in the hand, as your father used to say. It's the only sensible thing to do, darling."

"But we can't give up the store, Mother!"

"Why can't we? We'd all be paid a lot of money. And obviously I can't run the place, and neither can you."

"I'd sure as hell try!"

"Darling, I know you've always *said* you'd like to run the store, but do you have any idea what it's really like? Of course you don't. Do you have any idea of how to deal with the market? You don't even know the market. Those are tough guys out there, those market people. Your father was a tough cookie, and he could deal with them. You'd be an innocent abroad, a babe in the woods. You'd be like a minnow swimming in a sea of sharks. They'd gobble you up in no time."

Retailing, Miranda thinks, is perhaps the only business in the world where the term "the market" does not mean the customers. It means the designers, the manufacturers, the suppliers, Seventh Avenue. And it is true that she has had absolutely no experience dealing with the market. "But what about Tommy?" she says.

"If the new owners want to use Tommy's—talents, they can do so. Tommy's a bright boy. He'll always land on his feet. I'm not worried about Tommy."

"And what about me?"

"Your job, you mean? Well, it isn't much of a job, is it, darling? Not that you don't do what you do very well. But I suppose if you still wanted to work for the store, the new owners might be able to find something for you—if you wanted something. But why should you? You'll have plenty of money."

"It's not just money, Mother!"

"Darling, everything is money in the end, isn't it? Of course it is. If I were Miranda Tarkington, age twenty-four, I wouldn't be worried about a job. I'd be thinking about finding an eligible young man to marry. I've never understood how you could have let that nice David Belknap slip through your fingers. They're calling him the new wunderkind of Wall Street."

"I didn't want to marry the wunderkind of Wall Street."

"At your age, I was already married to your father."

"I'm not you, Mother. You Consuelo. Me Miranda."

"Of course, darling. But the point is, under the new management, you surely wouldn't want to work there. It would be Tarkington's in name only. It would be an entirely different store."

"But that's exactly what I don't want to see happen!"

"It's got to happen, darling. You saw what *The Times* called your father—the last of the dinosaurs. This store is the last of the dinosaurs too, struggling in vain against extinction. It's an anachronism, Miranda. The women your father used to call 'my kind of woman' are either dead or dying or their husbands are being carted off to jail. As Jake Kohlberg said to me tonight, and I agree, Tarkington's is an idea whose time has come and gone. Jake reminded me of one of your father's favorite sayings: 'Running a store like mine is like putting on a piece of theater. It's show business.' Well, as Jake says, this piece of theater has had a nice long run, and now it's time to ring down the curtain and post the closing notice."

"Jake Kohlberg, Jake Kohlberg, stop telling me what Jake Kohlberg says!"

Her mother looks at her, then stubs out her cigarette. "I may not always have agreed with Jake Kohlberg," she says, "but I've followed his advice and never regretted it. And I intend to follow it this time. We tender our stock to the best offer that comes down the road."

"Well, I'm *not*."

"Think about it a little bit, Miranda," her mother

says gently. "Think about it, and you'll agree with me. Your father's grand dream—for a specialty store to end all specialty stores—is as dead as he is."

"I can't believe you're talking about this so cold-bloodedly," Miranda says. "This store that he built from nothing, single-handedly, from scratch—"

"Well, he had a little help," her mother says with a small smile.

"Help from whom?"

"From me, among other people. As Jake Kohlberg said to me this very afternoon, I've been the best advertisement your father ever had for his store. Do you think that's been easy? Do you think it's easy to stay on the Best-Dressed List? It takes time and effort and study—working with designers, studying the competition, being seen at the right places with the right people. I've done all that, and I did it for him and for his store. The only thing was, I never got paid for it. Now I'm ready to get paid. And I'm also ready to relax, get out of my girdle, and stop worrying about how I look every time I step outside my front door. I'm thinking of doing some travel, the Mascarene Islands, the Seychelles. I'm ready to let my hair down, Miranda."

"Will you give up your beauty routine? The Dead Sea mud packs?"

"Well," she says, still smiling, "some habits are harder to break than others," and she reaches for another cigarette.

"Will you give up this apartment?"

"Of course, when the store is sold. I've always hated this apartment, you know. Everything in it is fake, including—but never mind."

"Mother, where was Blackie when Daddy died?" Miranda asks suddenly.

"Blackie?"

"Blackamoor. Daddy's dog."

"Why, in his kennel, I suppose. Yes, I'm sure he was in his kennel. Why do you ask?"

"Sometimes he swam with Daddy."

"Well, he didn't on Saturday," her mother says. "But I don't understand what—"

"What became of the TV set?"

Her mother looks briefly at her hands, then up at Miranda. "The TV set?"

"The TV set that President Ford gave him. It was always in the pool house. It wasn't that night."

"Oh, that," her mother says. "It was sent out for repairs several weeks ago, I think."

"Where was it sent?"

"To a repair shop, I suppose! I don't know *which* repair shop your father sent it to, for heaven's sake!"

"Sent out for repairs in its Lucite case?"

"I suppose! I just remember your father mentioning something about repairs. Really, Miranda, I—"

"There was a power outage in the whole pool area of the farm that night. Did you know that?"

"Yes. Yes, I remember one of the maintenance men mentioning that. Something to do with a circuit breaker. It was fixed the next morning."

"Yes, I know."

"What do you mean you know?"

"I went out the next morning, and everything was working fine."

"That's what I just told you! There was a problem. It was fixed. But I really don't understand this line of questioning, Miranda. What has any of this got to do with—?"

"I think you're lying to me, Mother. I think there's something you're not telling me."

"Lying? Why would I lie to you? Don't be ridiculous, Miranda! What have dogs, TV sets, and power failures got to do with what we were talking about? We were talking about our need to sell the store. We were talking about my travel plans and—"

"I think Blazer was right this afternoon," Miranda says evenly. "All you ever cared about was Daddy's money."

"Oh, Miranda!" her mother says with a sob. "What a dreadful, wretched, cruel thing to say to me! You don't understand anything, do you? You understand absolutely nothing at all!"

At that moment Milliken appears at the library door. "Supper is served," he says.

Consuelo Tarkington rises from the green leather chair in one swift, synchronized motion. Miranda also rises and follows her mother out across the marble foyer to the dining room on the opposite side, where the smaller of the two tables is set for two with lighted candles in a seven-branched candelabrum.

As Milliken seats Miranda at her place, she says to him, "Do you know what happened to Daddy's TV set, Milliken, the one he kept in the pool house?"

"Ah, the one the President gave him. It was apparently stolen, ma'am."

"Stolen? Was that it?" Consuelo says brightly. "I thought it was sent out for repairs. Well, I knew something happened to it."

"Very proud of that TV set he was, too, ma'am. He always used to show it to visitors. We apparently had a prowler that day at the farm. I heard the dog barking, and I went out to investigate. The first thing I noticed was that the television set was gone."

"Was anything else missing?" Miranda asks him.

"Yes, ma'am, there was. There was an underwater watch that I believe you gave him for his birthday several years ago. He was very fond of that watch too, though he didn't wear it all that much. He kept it in the pool house, and that was missing too. His clothes were hanging in the dressing room, and I found that his billfold was missing from his right rear pocket, where he always carried it. I doubt there was much money in it. He never liked to carry cash, but the burglar got that too." He turns to Miranda's mother. "I'm sorry, ma'am, but I didn't tell you any of this at the time. I thought you'd had enough that day to upset you. Because, you see, when I found his clothes in the dressing room, that was when I went out to the pool and found him—Mr. Tarkington, your poor father, ma'am—floating there."

"*You* found him, Milliken? I thought you found him,

Mother. That's what the paper said. That's what you told me."

"What difference does it make?" her mother cries. "One of us found him first, and then the other came! I can't even remember it all that clearly!" Miranda looks across at her mother, and tears are streaming down her face, and Miranda realizes that she has never seen her mother weep before. Her mother makes small balls of her fists and pounds them on the polished tabletop, and the china and glassware rattle and the candle flames dance. "What I want to know is why you're doing this to me, Miranda! The most horrible day of my entire life, and you keep harking back to it, harking back to it, trying to make me remember all the horror I've been trying so hard to forget! Let sleeping dogs lie, for God's sake! Leave me alone—just leave me alone!" She dabs at her streaming eyes with her linen napkin. "Now look what you've done! Cook has made this beautiful crabmeat salad, made it with her famous Armagnac mayonnaise—my favorite— and I've lost my appetite completely. With all I had to do today, I skipped lunch. When I came home tonight, I was hungry, but now my appetite's completely gone!" She flings her napkin onto her untouched plate, pushes back her chair, rises from the chair with a simple fluid motion, and runs sobbing from the room.

As quickly and discreetly as he can, Milliken withdraws from this unhappy domestic scene into the pantry, and Miranda sits alone.

Arriving at his small cottage at the far end of Heather Lane, about four miles down from Flying Horse Farm, Thomas E. Bonham III parks his Mercedes, pockets the keys, and walks up the flagstone path to his front door. This cottage was once the gatekeeper's lodge on one of the big estates, long since broken up by a developer into half-acre plots with split-level houses selling in the $450,000 to $750,000 range. Split-level or not, this is still Old Westbury, a fashionable country address.

This cottage is Tommy Bonham's weekend getaway

place. Normally, on a Monday night, which this is,
Tommy would be in Manhattan, in his apartment on Sut-
ton Place. But today, with the store closed in Si's honor,
and with Tommy's only appointment having been drinks
with Miranda at the Pierre, he has decided to spend an
extra night in the country and drive back to New York in
the morning.

In his front entryway, Tommy Bonham tosses his
Mark Cross briefcase in a chair, kicks off his Gucci loafers, and moves, in his stocking feet, into the lighted living
room, loosening his Turnbull & Asser necktie and unbut-
toning the collar button of his shirt. He tosses the necktie
over a lampshade. Then he sheds his jacket, tosses it into
a chair, unbuttons his shirt cuffs, and sinks into the big
Victorian sofa, causing a large pile of retail trade journals
on the sofa to slide precipitously toward him.

Nino, his Filipino houseboy, whose full name is
Saturnino Salas, greets him, making clicking noises with
his tongue. "Could burn your tie like that, Tommy,"
Nino says, but instead of removing the necktie from the
lampshade, Nino merely turns off the lamp.

Tommy Bonham is a notoriously slipshod housekeeper, and Nino doesn't appear to do much to help. A
number of people who have visited Tommy, both in New
York and here, have wondered how such an elegantly
put-together man can live, apparently quite happily, in
such disarray. Though Miranda has never been in the Sut-
ton Place apartment, she has visited her neighbor's weekend cottage a number of times, and what is she apt to see
there? A pair of dirty tennis sneakers on the coffee table,
a half-filled cup of coffee on the windowsill with a dead
fly floating in it. Coming in from the pool, he will drape
his wet trunks over this same lampshade to dry.

His dining room table is always covered with at least
a week's worth of newspapers and journals, along with
paper clips, ballpoint pens, pencils, scissors, and a great
deal else. This, he explains, is his "desk" when he works
at home. His bedroom is even worse. Miranda has never
seen his bed made. Overfilled dresser drawers hang open,
their contents—socks, underwear, handkerchiefs—spill-

ing out. In one corner of the bedroom is a stack of cardboard cartons, the kind you can pick up at a supermarket when you're packing to move, and Lord knows what these contain. When Miranda used his bathroom, his jockstrap was hanging from the doorknob, and one peek at the unlovely contents of his medicine cabinet was enough for her—uncapped, half-empty tubes of toothpaste and shaving cream squeezed from the middle, slivers of soap, rusted razor blades, broken combs, hairbrushes matted with blond hair, ragged toothbrushes caked with dried paste, an open box of condoms, and a brown and gluey substance spilled across the glass shelves in which a rusting nail file, several pills and capsules of dubious origin, and a rolled condom had become more or less permanently embedded.

"Why don't you let me straighten this place up for you?" she asked him once.

"No!" he had cried, almost in panic. "Right now, I know exactly where everything is!"

The kitchen, which is Nino's domain, always seems to be piled with dirty dishes and pots and pans. Nino's only duties seem to be laundering and ironing Tommy's shirts, pressing his suits and dinner jackets, polishing his shoes, and preparing his meals.

Now, at the bar, Nino fixes drinks for them both and then comes and sits beside Tommy on the sofa, pushing the pile of magazines to the floor. They touch glasses. Then, with a sigh, Tommy says, "Well, Nino, phase one is completed."

"You offer her big job?"

"Uh-huh."

"And she say?"

"I didn't expect her to give me an answer right away," he says. "I think she was a little overwhelmed. It's a job she can't possibly handle, of course, but she was definitely flattered when I told her I thought she could."

"Flattered? What is flattered?"

"Happy. Pleased with herself. Pleased that I think she's smarter than she really is. But she'll be putty—you know what putty is?" He makes kneading motions with his hands. "She'll be putty in my hands, Nino, and I'll be completely in charge of things, wait and see. It'll be my store at last."

"And you need her because? Explain again."

"So I can get control of how she votes her stock, before the enemy does."

"Is like war."

"Yeah. That's why they call it a hostile takeover."

"Tell me again, Tommy, what is stock?"

"Shares. Shares of ownership of the store."

"And when you have that, and war is over, we go to Paracale?"

"Yes, Nino, *caro* Nino. Then we'll go to Paracale, and we'll go there rich."

Nino, staring into his whiskey glass, swirls his ice cubes thoughtfully. Then, as though he has seen a vision in the glass, his whiskey-colored face breaks into a smile. "Oh, you must see Paracale, Tommy," he says. "Is not a big place, not like New York. Is a very, very small place, and only one road leads there. But is so beautiful, you will love it, Tommy. The sea—the sea is so blue, bluer than any blue sky you ever see. And in the morning, even before the sun comes up across the sea, the fishermen, in their little boats, are going out. . . . My father, he will be there . . . my mother . . . my sisters. . . ."

Tommy Bonham closes his eyes. He leans back against the sofa and runs the tip of his left index finger slowly up and down the inner curve of Nino's thigh. He has heard the description of Nino's village in the Philippines so often that he knows it by heart. He yawns and pinches Nino's knee. "I've got to get back to the city early in the morning, Nino," he says. "Let's get to bed."

8

Now it is Tuesday morning, and Moses Minskoff is on the telephone again. "Ah, Mr. Martindale," he is saying. "How good of you to call me back, and to call me back so promptly. May I call you Al? Or do you prefer Albert? . . . Please call me Moe, then, Albert—all my good friends do.

"Now what I have in mind for you, Albert—for you and Continental—is a two-tiered tender offer. I'm going to suggest that you make Tarkington's shareholders an offer of sixty dollars a share for their holdings. . . . Whoa! Hold on. Yes, I know that seems a bit on the high side, Albert, but let me finish, please. Once I finish telling you my full proposal, everything will become as clear to you as a summer's day. Let us start with the sixty-dollar figure. You will offer them eighty percent of this figure in cash and the rest in Continental's stock, notes, debentures, what-the-hell—what we on Wall Street call cramdown paper. Who knows what that paper is worth? Nobody. Whatever the market will stand for, right? But everybody appreciates the value of cash, don't you agree? Of course you do.

"Now, Albert, this is going to be a two-tier offer with a kind of special spin on it, which I'll get to momentarily. The first tier of the offer, the cash tier, will have a tight deadline on it. I'm suggesting a deadline of ten business days, Albert. . . . Why so tight? I'll tell you why. For one thing, we don't want to give the enemy any time to organize any kind of poison-pill defense. For another thing, it's important to act fast because right now the company is in a state of shambles. Since the old man died, nobody knows who's running the store. The whole family is at each other's throats. The widow wants to sell the store, the daughter doesn't. The son got zip in the old man's will, and he may decide to sue. If he sues, the whole shmeer gets tied up in litigation, we'll be up to our ass in lawyers, and none of us is gonna get anywhere. . . . How do I know all this? Let's just say I got my sources. So strike while the iron is hot, Albert. Strike while the iron is hot.

"Okay. Now, if the shareholders don't agree to accept the two-tier offer within ten business days, they lose their chance to get any cash at all. All they'll get is cram-down paper, whatever junk your company's got lying around. This will force family members, and any die-hard Tarkington loyalists, to sign agree-to-sell papers fast and will put pressure on other shareholders to do the same. The widow and the daughter are important. They're not a majority, but we need to get them in our pocket. . . . Of course it's legal. Would I propose anything to a man of your caliber that wasn't legal, Albert? All I want to do for you is help you maintain your record as a winner.

"Now here's the beauty part. Once we announce that Continental is about to do a hostile on Tarkington's, I'm counting on our competitive bidders to come in with higher bids and force the price up. Let's say you play the game for a day or so—raise your bid a point or two. Now the ball's in play, right? At this point the press will be having a heyday with the story, and all the shareholders will be rubbing their hands over how much money they'll be getting. This is the point at which you'll announce that you intend to drop out of the bidding, 'cause the price is just too high. . . . Now wait a minute, Albert, please let me finish. You haven't heard the spin yet.

"At precisely this point in the scenario, I leak the store's secret figures to the press—the overvalued inventory, the accounts receivable, the whole shmeer, making Tarkington's look like a two-bit shlock house. Your competition will back out fast, withdraw their offers. That's when you come back into the game with a much lower offer—let's say thirty bucks a share as a ballpark figure. The shareholders kick and scream, but what can they do? You've got their signed agreements to sell. These agreements don't mention any price. They don't sell, we can sue them for breach of contract. They're in a take-it-or-leave-it situation. . . . I tell you it's legal, Albert. I have checked with my attorneys, and it's perfectly legal. It's just that it's never been done quite this way before. Albert, you're going to end up—you and me, that is—with America's top fashion label for thirty, thirty-two bucks a share max. And we'll have reamed them, Albert, baby— we'll have reamed 'em all! That's the spin I've put on this ball for you. . . .

"Ah, you mention my personal shareholding in Tarkington's. I was just coming to that, Albert. I personally own only about twelve percent of the voting shares. But I am willing to sell you those shares at the price I mentioned earlier, sixty dollars a share. . . . Now, wait! Hold on, Albert. I know that's a high figure, it's an arbitrarily high figure, but there is a sound reason for that high figure. There's a method to my madness, heh-heh-heh. You need to pay me that high a figure to establish your *credibility*, Albert. Once it becomes publicly known that you have purchased my shares, got your toe in Tarkington's door at sixty dollars per, this establishes the sincerity of your offer. In real estate parlance, this can be called your earnest money. It establishes the earnestness of your intent. The other shareholders will be led to believe that sixty is your genuine offering price, even though —heh, heh—it really isn't going to be in the end. To establish your credibility at the outset of this deal is very important, Albert. We've got to make the others *think* that's the price they're going to get, too. . . .

"Yes. . . . Yes. . . . But of course. At that price, I'm going to make a very special deal for you, Albert. At that price, I'm willing to accept only *fifty* percent in cash, not eighty. We won't publicize that little aspect of the deal, naturally. That little aspect will be strictly between you and I—*entre vous,* as they say in French. The other fifty percent I'll take in whatever cram-down paper you want to offer me, any junk you want to let me have to make up. . . . Now, Albert, I'm not implying that any of your notes or bonds are junk. I'd be proud to be the owner of any paper you want to pass along to me in the deal, just for the prestige of being associated with your good name. But, you see, throwing in fifty percent in paper reduces your cost per share considerably. And, when you stop to think that you're gonna get the rest of the shares you need for between thirty and thirty-two— eighty percent cash—that drops your cost per share even more. It's a beauty of a deal I've worked out for you, Albert, and as your financial adviser in this takeover, I must recommend that you accept it. . . . Yes, I realize you've got a board of directors to consult. You do that, Albert, and get back to me. I'll be in the office all day long. Just remember, that time is of the essence if we're gonna pull this deal off, and *tempo fugit,* as the fella says, Albert, *tempo fugit.*"

He hangs up the phone and, with a look of distaste on his face, briefly studies a slip of paper on his desk. Then he picks up the phone again and dials an 800 number. "Yes," he says to the young woman who answers the phone. "This is Mr. Harvey B. Knowlton calling, and I'd like to order an item from your current catalogue, please. The item number is fourteen-C. . . . Yes, that is correct, the four-piece matched set of hand-tooled alligator luggage. Forty-six hundred dollars. . . . No, it is not for me. It is to be sent as a gift to a friend. . . . His name? His name is Mr. LeRoy Goldfarb, three-two-three West Ninety-seventh Street, New York City. . . . No, no monogramming. Mr. Goldfarb does not like monograms.

. . . Yes, let me give you my American Express credit card number. The last name is Knowlton, K-N-O-W-L-T-O-N, and the credit card number—"

The details completed, he hangs up and makes another call.

"Goldie? Moe here. Look, Goldie, we got a set of alligator luggage coming from the Smith and Summers catalogue. Forty-six hundred retail. You oughta get at least fifteen hundred for it off your truck, and I'll take my usual percentage. . . . Listen, Goldie, I'm planning to sorta phase myself outa this aspect of my business. Too busy with heavy-duty arbitrage. So maybe you better look around for someone else to scout up credit card numbers for you. . . . Whaddaya mean where do ya find 'em? Dumpsters. Garbage cans. Give ya a tip. I passed a line of dumpsters on Park between Seventieth and Seventy-first on my way to the office this morning. That's where you find the johns with the high credit limits, in the higher rent districts."

Smyrna, his secretary, calls from the outer office. "Tommy Bonham on one, Moe," she says.

"Ah, Tommy," he says, picking up the phone. "You're up bright and early this morning, aren't you? Thank you for calling me back, thank you very much indeed. Look, reason why I called is I need those figures from you right away, buddy. I'm particularly needful of your accounts receivable figure. . . . Why? Now, Tommy, we've been through all this before. I just need it, is all. Just say I need that figure if I'm gonna help you take over the store, never mind why. . . . Tommy, Tommy, I want to be your friend in this, so don't give me a hard time, okay? And I don't need to mention that other little matter we both know about, do I? It would be . . . unfortunate if that got out, wouldn't it? Just give me that figure, and we'll still be buddies. Remember, you owe me one, Tommy. You owe me a big one."

There is a sign on Moe Minskoff's office wall: EVERYTHING IS LEGAL IF YOU DON'T GET CAUGHT.

·   ·   ·

Tommy Bonham has called a meeting of the store's full staff for nine o'clock that morning, but Miranda has arrived a little early, and she taps on the frame of his office door just as he is hanging up the telephone. He smiles and waves to her to come in.

"I found three," she says, and places a pale blue Tarkington's shopping bag on his desk. "I've taken all three out on memorandum."

"Three what?"

"Clutch bags. In silver." She lifts one out of the bag. "This is my favorite. It's seven ninety-five."

"What—?"

"For your rich Texas broad. The Lone Star klepto. Didn't you say she needed a bag for a party tonight?"

He laughs. "You're right. I'd forgotten all about it."

"I'd have messengered these over to her, but I didn't know her name."

"I'll have Linda take care of it." He rises from his chair and takes her hand. "Thanks for remembering," he says. "See why you and I are going to make good partners? Now let's get into our meeting."

Some ninety-two employees of Silas Tarkington's store have gathered in the store's fifth-floor employees' cafeteria this morning, an hour before the store is scheduled to reopen its doors for business. There are the merchandise managers, the buyers, the saleswomen and men. There is Paul, the comptroller; Celestine, the credit manager; Walter, the display director, and his two willowy assistants who dress the store's windows. There are Molly and Odile, the two little dressing-room maids in their starched black-and-white uniforms; Oliver, the night watchman; James, the doorman; Sam, the tailor in charge of the alterations department, and his two seamstress assistants, Becky and Francine. All their faces look solemn, and some look apprehensive. As she and Tommy enter the room together, Miranda notices two conspicuous absentees. Pauline O'Malley is not there, having telephoned to say that she is still too devastated by the loss of her boss to appear in public. Also, Smitty is not there. Miranda whispers this fact to Tommy, who merely shrugs.

Miranda takes a seat, and Tommy moves to the front of the room and takes an informal pose, seating himself on the edge of a cafeteria table with one perfectly pressed dark trouser leg swung over the side.

"Good friends," he begins. "Good friends of mine, good friends of the store's, good friends of Silas Tarkington's: I don't need to tell you that this is a sad occasion for all of us here today. The sudden death of our founder —Mr. Si, as most of us called him—last Saturday was a profound shock to all of us. Not only will he be deeply missed; he can probably never be replaced.

"I would like to say at the outset that I asked you all to come in early this morning not because I see myself as his successor or replacement, and not because I am assuming the title of the new president of Tarkington's. That will be up to the store's board and stockholders to decide. On the other hand, I feel—and I am sure all of you would agree—that Mr. Si would have wanted us to carry on during the next few trying weeks, just as we did when he was off on one of his buying trips, just as though he were still here. Therefore, I would ask that there be no long, sad faces in Mr. Si's store today. I would ask that our clients—who are also our friends and our guests—be treated with the same bright helpfulness, the same attention to service and detail, as always. Some of our clients may express condolences to you. I would suggest responding to this with a simple 'Thank you.'

"Now, since it may be several weeks until a new president is named, I'd like to address myself to some of the problems we may be facing in this period. You've all heard, I'm sure, the rumors that Tarkington's has become the object of a hostile takeover. My friends, these are more than rumors. These are facts, and the company making the most aggressive moves right now appears to be Continental Stores, Incorporated, of Chicago. Two foreign companies have also made overtures. Now that Mr. Si is dead, these overtures will certainly become more aggressive. Naturally, whether such a takeover succeeds will depend on the votes of our stockholders. I can only say this: I have no quarrel with Continental Stores. They have a right to exist, just as we have a right to exist. But I think you'll agree with me that if Tarkington's were to become part of the so-called Continental Family of Stores it would become a very different sort of store from the one Si Tarkington created, the store we have known and loved. I, for one, would be very sorry to see that happen. A number of you in this room are stockholders. I should like to ask you that in the event of a proxy war you vote with me, against a takeover."

There is a polite round of applause.

"I would like to be able to tell you," he continues, "that we are in a strong position to fight any such takeover. Unfortunately, this is not the case. I would also like to be able to tell you that Si Tarkington died leaving the store in a powerful financial position. Unfortunately, this is not the case either. As all of you know, the past eighteen months have been very difficult for all retailers. Retailers' profits nationwide have fallen between thirty-five and forty percent. I wish I could say that Tarkington's has stayed ahead of the pack. But, in fact, in the fiscal year ending last January thirty-first, gross income was down to five-point-five million, from eleven million dollars the year before. That's a drop, ladies and gentlemen, of fifty percent.

"Even so, with a gross like that, you might say our balance sheet ought to look good. It does, but it is also misleading. Retailers such as ourselves list, in our balance sheets, something called Accounts Receivable, and Accounts Receivable are listed in the assets column. Accounts Receivable simply represents merchandise that has been sold but not paid for. Thus, while our Accounts Receivable figure appears as a very large asset on our balance sheet, it represents no cash whatsoever. Mr. Si, of course, believed in a very liberal credit policy. He never pressured clients to pay their bills. I believe, in the future, the store is going to have to take a very long, hard look at that policy. Don't you agree, Celestine?"

"Absolutely!" replies the credit manager tartly. "I have one client—I won't mention her name, but a lot of us know who she is—who's owed the store twenty-seven thousand dollars for the past two years. The other day she was in the store, and I posted an eight-thousand-dollar Geoffrey Beene to her account, and she still hasn't paid a penny! It costs my department ten dollars a month just to send out a bill. I used to say to Mr. Si, 'They're taking advantage of you, these clients.' Not all of them, but some."

"There are other areas in which I think we could be more cost-efficient," he continues. "For instance, Mr. Si never believed in keeping an item of apparel in the store for longer than a season. This is sound policy. But before shipping a garment out to be resold—to Filene's Basement, Value City, Loehmann's, and the rest—Mr. Si insisted on removing the Tarkington's label. Obviously, we could get much better prices for our merchandise if we sold it label-in. It would be a change in policy that most of our regular clients would never be aware of, and it would greatly increase cash flow."

"Hear, hear!" several department heads say.

"Of course, any changes a store like Tarkington's makes should be made very slowly and carefully," he says. "We still like to be known as expensive, and even a bit intimidating. That's part of our glamorous image. For instance, Si never believed in having a sale. I could see his point. Shoppers tend to develop a sale mentality. They never set foot inside a store unless there's some sort of sale going on. As a result, there's hardly anything being sold in New York anymore at the full retail price. I'm not suggesting we go the Saks route, where there's something on sale in the store every day of the year. But I might suggest, with fall and the Christmas season coming on, that we have one storewide post-Christmas sale once a year, the way, for instance, Harrod's does."

"Hear, hear!"

He nods in Miranda's direction. "I'd even be in favor of advertising that sale."

"Hear, hear!"

"You know, and I do too, that other merchants in town call Tarkington's an anachronism. I don't want us to become an anachronism."

"Hear, hear!"

Miss Rubinstein, head of the Bridal Department, raises her hand.

"Yes, Sarah?"

"Tommy, let me ask a question," she says. "You were talking about storewide gross figures a minute ago. If the store's profits are down fifty percent from a year ago, why are my department's figures down *sixty* percent? And why are Diana Smith's jewelry department figures *up* ten percent? We're both selling luxury goods. By the way, where is Smitty?"

"She was notified of this meeting," he says. "You have a good point, Sarah, and it's another problem we face. Demographics show that our clientele is growing older. Every time I see in the paper that a rich society woman has died, I kind of groan and think, There goes another of our customers!"

There is laughter at this.

"And not enough rock stars, women like Madonna, are coming along to take those women's places."

More laughter.

"Rich older women still buy jewelry. But they're out of the market for bridal apparel."

Still more laughter.

"But seriously, Sarah, you have an important point. I've often thought that Tarkington's ought to have a department offering designer apparel for children, and also for teenagers, so that we could start educating women to be Tarkington's shoppers while they're young."

"Hear, hear."

"I'd like to end this meeting on one final, even more serious note," he says. "If we're going to have the capital necessary to fight a takeover attempt, our company is going to have to do some serious belt tightening. I'm going to propose something you won't like, but I hope it will be only temporary—a ten-percent cut in base pay, of those at the executive level only."

There is a collective groan.

"To offset this, I'd like to increase the commission percentage to salespeople who exceed certain goals. And

I'd also like to allow sales staff members to sell merchandise from departments other than their own."

There is silence, as the members of the sales staff do mental arithmetic to try to figure what such a move will do to their take-home pay.

"You mean," says one, "that I could take a customer from Small Leather Goods up to the fur department and sell her a mink?"

"Absolutely."

"That would work fine for *you*, wouldn't it?" says a saleswoman from the fur department. "It wouldn't work so fine for me, the other way around."

"It would work fine for you, Eunice, if you could sell the client the mink first," Tommy says, giving her his best smile. "Well, that's all I have for you this morning. Except to say that I hope you'll all bear with me during this difficult interim period, while we all may literally find ourselves fighting to save Tarkington's. Thank you, and God bless you all." He hops down from his perch on the tabletop.

There is applause. Muted applause, but applause.

"Well, you may not be president of the store yet, Tomcat," Miranda says to him when they are back in his office, "but you were certainly acting like one. That was a good meeting, and they liked nearly everything you said. Except salaries, of course. You wouldn't have expected them to like that. Is the situation really that serious? With Continental?"

He nods. "I'm afraid it is. Albert Martindale has already sent out feelers to me about acquiring my stock. Of course I told him it was not for sale. But I sense a big fight coming."

"And I guess Daddy was a bit of a fuddy-duddy. A bit behind the times. He didn't prepare the store for this at all, did he?"

"Your father was your father. He did things his own way." He picks up a slip of paper from his desk, reads it, and hands it to Miranda. "This explains why Smitty wasn't here today," he says.

Miranda reads the note headed *From the desk of Diana Smith*.

Dear Tommy:

Mr. Jacob Kohlberg, who is the attorney for Si Tarkington's estate, has informed me that I have been named in Si's will as Special Curator of the Tarkington Collection of Art when it is turned over to the Metropolitan Museum. This is an exciting new career opportunity for me in the field of Fine Art, and one I accept eagerly.

Since such a curatorship will be a full-time job for me, I am herewith submitting my resignation, effective immediately.

Smitty

"So that solves that problem," he says. "You should be pleased."

"I just hope she really has that new job," Miranda says grimly. "The representative from the museum didn't exactly do handstands when he learned that Smitty came along as a condition of the gift."

"But it means we have one less salary to pay," he says with a little laugh. "Every little bit helps, I guess. What would you say if I gave Jewelry to Gertie Elson of Small Leather Goods? She seemed happy with my idea of interdepartmental selling, and the two departments are right next to each other on the floor. Gertie could buy for both."

"Good idea. Or what about Sarah Rubinstein of Bridal? They sort of go together: brides, wedding rings. And she complained that her figures weren't as good as Smitty's."

He lowers his voice. "Frankly, I think Sarah's problem is her merchandise. Her figures are weak because her merchandise is lousy. If it were up to me, I'd get rid of Sarah and find someone else with a younger point of view. Sarah's bridal apparel looks like it was designed for weddings in the nineteen-fifties."

"I haven't been in the Bridal Shop recently," she admits. "I'll stop by there and have a look." She sits in a chair opposite his desk. Unlike his house in Old Westbury, his office is meticulously tidy, his desktop clear, the quilted pillows on his sofa plumped invitingly. But perhaps this is his secretary's doing. "Now tell me," she says, "who are these stockholders, besides Mother and myself, who we'll have to deal with if there's a takeover attempt?"

"You and your mother each own about twenty percent of the voting shares," he says. "I own roughly five percent. Moses Minskoff owns about twelve percent."

"Moe Minskoff is a *stockholder*?"

"Unfortunately, yes."

"How in the world did that happen?"

"He advanced your father money over the years. Your father repaid him in Tarkington's stock. Then there's your father's sister, Mrs. Belsky—"

"My father's *sister*? I never knew my father had a sister! You mean I've got an aunt I never knew about?"

"Yes, she's your father's younger sister, Simma Belsky. Mrs. Leopold Belsky. She lives in Florida. She owns another twelve percent."

"Does my mother know about her?"

He hesitates. "I'm sure she does," he says.

"More dumb family secrets!"

"Apparently something occurred in your father's family years ago, and there was a serious falling out between your father, his sister, and his mother. I don't know what it was all about. Money, probably—these things usually are. But there's been absolutely no communication since. Did you know that your father's mother is still living?"

"I have a grandmother *too*?"

"Yes, you do. She's a very old lady now. She lives in a

nursing home near Palm Beach, and I understand she's completely senile. On Mother's Day your father used to send her something now and then—not often—from the store. But they haven't spoken to each other in years."

She looks at him wonderingly. "You're telling me about relatives I never knew I had! Of course I know why nobody ever mentioned those women. They were family skeletons, weren't they? That's quite typical of my parents. Those two didn't match the Tarkington's image. They weren't glossy enough. They weren't Tarkington types. They reminded Daddy of his quote-unquote humble origins, so he swept them under the rug, turned them into non-persons. Right?"

"I really don't know the whole story, Miranda. Your father never discussed it with me. All I know is their names from the company books as stockholders."

"My grandmother is a stockholder too?"

"She doesn't own as much as your father's sister. She only owns about three percent of the company. She always has."

"Wait a minute," she says, as a thought suddenly flashes across her mind. "What does she look like, this grandmother? Is she short and fat with long white hair? Did she used to live on West End Avenue?"

He spreads his hands. "I don't know. I've never met her either."

"Do you remember, years ago, one evening at the farm—" But she breaks off. "Never mind."

"Anyway, those are the six major shareholders. The other shares, the remaining twenty-eight percent, are owned in small blocks by individuals. Some are employees. Your father often rewarded longtime employees with gifts of Tarkington's stock in lieu of raises. He felt it made them feel as though they owned at least a little piece of the company they worked for. And there are other individuals who've bought up shares whenever they appeared for trading, over the counter. I can show you the complete list, if you like."

"What percentage of the twenty-eight percent is owned by our employees, do you know?"

"About half. Actually a little less than half."

"Will they be loyal to us? Will they help us fight a takeover?"

"Who knows? It will depend on what form Continental's tender offer takes. Never underestimate the human capacity for greed. I'd hope they'd be loyal. That's why I made that little spiel to them this morning."

"But," she says, quickly counting on her fingers, "if you and Mother and I and even *half* the employees refused to sell their shares, that would give us a clear majority, wouldn't it? Nobody could take us over!"

"That's right," he says. "But your mother wants to sell."

She bites her lip. "Yes," she says. "At least that's what she's saying now. But let me work on her. I wasn't very nice to her at dinner last night, but let me try being nice to her again. Let me see if I can butter her up. I'll work on her and you work on the employees—take them to lunch, tell them what a great job they're doing, what a great store we're going to make this into, and I'll tackle Mother. How's that for a division of labor?"

He shakes his head. "I wish I thought it would work," he says.

"Why not? Why won't it work? I'll make it work."

"Your mother's a very determined lady," he says. "And I think you underestimate the depth of her bitterness."

"Bitterness?"

"Over your father's relationship with Smitty."

"But Smitty wasn't the first, and she wouldn't have been the last. There were lots of others—others Mother knew about, and others she probably didn't."

"I think she knew about them all," he says. "But Smitty was different. Your father was besotted with Smitty." He fixes her with his deep blue eyes. "I can't lie to you, Miranda," he says. "I've got to tell you the truth. This isn't going to be easy, but you've got to know."

Her dark eyes flash. "What is it?"

"On the day he died, your father was planning to leave your mother and run away with Smitty."

She takes a quick intake of breath. "How do you know?"

"I found a letter. About a week before he died, your father had gone out to lunch, and I needed some figures he had. As I rummaged through the papers on his desk, I found a typewritten note. And—I'm not proud of this—I read it. It was from Smitty. It named the date and time when they planned to meet at the farm, where they planned to confront your mother, and then go off together to Bermuda. That date was the day he died. Strange coincidence, don't you think?"

"Tommy, you don't think—"

"I don't know what happened that day at the farm," he says, "but something did. The whole thing was handled so strangely. First, your mother finds him floating in the pool—"

"No, Milliken found him. Then he called Mother."

"Oh?" he says, raising his eyebrows. "Is that the story now? Well—"

"That's what Milliken told me last night. And Mother doesn't deny that that was the way it happened. She says she doesn't remember."

"Anyway, nobody called the police or an ambulance. Instead, Si's old crony Harry Arnstein is called from twenty-five miles away in Manhattan. He pronounces death from natural causes—no tests, no autopsy—and your father is whisked off to the crematorium. All this before anyone else is notified—not me, not even you."

"Tommy, you don't think that Mother—"

"Hell hath no fury like a woman scorned," he says. "But I honestly don't know what happened that day, Miranda, and now I suppose no one ever will. But I did think you ought to know about the letter, and the fact that on the day he died your father had other plans."

His gaze at her is so burning and intense that she looks away from him. "I think," she says carefully, "that I hate him now."

"Don't say that, Miranda. He was your father. Women were attracted to him, and he was susceptible."

They sit in silence for a moment, and then he says,

"In the meantime, have you given any thought to that proposition I made to you yesterday afternoon?"

"Of course I have," she says. "I've been weighing the pros and cons of that kind of an arrangement. There are a few of both, it seems to me, and I haven't reached any decision yet."

"I want to give you something," he says. "I took something out on memorandum myself this morning." He reaches in his pocket, removes a small blue box, and hands it to her. "Open it," he says.

She lifts the lid. "What a beautiful diamond!" she says. "But Tommy, you can't give this to me!"

"Why not? Diamonds are a symbol of faith and trust. I want you to have this as a symbol of the faith and trust I have in you to run this store in full partnership with me."

"It's beautiful, but—"

"Three point nine carats. Extra River Gem quality. Fifty-eight facets. Thirty-three above the girdle, twenty-five below."

She looks at the ring with some misgivings.

"Put it on," he says. He picks up the ring and slips it on the ring finger of her right hand. "Wear it on your right hand, so nobody will think you've become engaged. Wear it as a symbol of the faith I have in you to become as great a merchandising force as your father was. Wear it to remind you how much I believe in you, Miranda, and of how much I believe in our partnership. Wear it while you make up your mind."

Back in her own small office, Miranda sits down hard in her chair and distractedly sorts through her morning mail, pushing pieces of paper this way and that, to no particular purpose, while the ring glitters on her finger. She should not have let him give it to her, and she starts to remove it and slip it in her purse when she smells the unmistakable scent of Equipage. She looks up and sees Smitty standing at her door.

Smitty's face is pale. "I came by to collect some of my things," she says. "My Rolodex, things from my desk. It took some courage to come up here to see you, Miranda, but I felt I had to. I know you've never liked me, but I wanted to tell you how sorry I am about your father. I loved your father, Miranda, and I thought I could make him happy. That's really all I have to say, that I'm sorry, and to say goodbye, and I hope we can say goodbye like ladies." She extends her hand, and Miranda extends her own.

"Goodbye, Smitty."

Suddenly Smitty screams, "*Where did you get that? That ring is from my department! That's my merchandise! Give it to me!*"

Miranda withdraws her hand. "Since you no longer work here, Smitty," she says, "I don't see how you can talk about *your* department and *your* merchandise."

"Give it to me! It's mine!"

"It should take you about fifteen seconds to get from here to the elevator," Miranda says. "I'll give you ten."

9

On Friday afternoons—at least when he was in town—Miranda's father would pick her up outside the entrance to the Brearley School in his car and they would drive together out to Old Westbury for the weekend. Oh, those were the best times.

Miranda loved those Friday rendezvous. They seemed to her displays of pure theater. The Rolls-Royce Corniche would stop grandly at the curb on East 83rd Street, and the chauffeur, in his snappy uniform—gray doeskin breeches, patent leather knee-high boots, tight jacket with silver buttons, and shiny cap—would hop smartly from the car, cross from the front, tip his cap smartly to Miranda, and hold the rear door open for her as she stepped into the back seat, with its mink lap robe, and took her seat beside her famous father. Then she would wave a gay goodbye to her schoolmates as they waited for their buses, the car door would close, and they would glide away. Other girls her age might have been embarrassed by such shows of raw privilege, but not Miranda Tarkington. In those days, she enjoyed being something of a show-off.

What I was was a little snot, she thinks now.

On that particular Friday—she is not sure of the year, but she must have been about twelve—the little princess in her Brearley uniform had been helped into her royal coach by her royal coachman and had waved a royal farewell to her less fortunate countrywomen, and the car had headed toward the Triborough Bridge. The day was special. The weather was brilliant. The East River sparkled like diamonds in the sunlight. Often, her mother joined them for this drive to the country for the weekend, but this week she had left for Old Westbury the day before, and today Miranda had her father all to herself. But even more important matters accounted for Miranda's buoyant mood. Tonight, Tommy Bonham was coming to the farm for dinner, and Miranda was to be seated with the grown-ups. Since her mother and father sat at opposite ends of the table, this meant Miranda would be seated facing Tommy, where she could feast her eyes on him, and where he could feast his eyes on her. The dress she planned to wear was cut off-the-shoulder.

Meanwhile, a friend at school had introduced her to a paperback romance series called Lovedrenched. All the novels in the Lovedrenched series were about seduction, and Miranda had been wondering whether it would be possible to seduce a man twenty years her senior. Would her mother notice if she padded her bra with Kleenex for a little extra fullness in the bosom? The royal princess's loins throbbed with quite plebian lust.

Her father was deep in the pages of *Women's Wear Daily,* and Miranda was deep in seductive fantasies, when her father had suddenly put down his newspaper and said, "Wait. I've forgotten something." He leaned forward and gave the driver an address on West End Avenue. So the chauffeur turned west and headed across town through Central Park. "Just a quick errand," her father said. "A small package to drop off."

When they arrived at the address on West End Avenue, between 112th and 113th Streets, if Miranda remembers correctly, it turned out to be a drab brownstone sandwiched between two massive apartment buildings.

Perhaps half a dozen doorbells were arrayed beside the front door. "I'll only be a minute," her father said, and got out of the car, his briefcase in his hand, and rang one of the bells.

The woman's apartment must have been on the ground floor, because Miranda saw her come to the door —a little fat old lady with flowing white hair, wearing glasses and a dirty apron. She seemed pleased to see him, let him in, and he was gone for several minutes. Then he came out again, got back in the car, and the driver headed back toward the Triborough Bridge.

Miranda was mystified. "Who was that?" she asked him at last.

"Who?" He seemed preoccupied.

"The fat lady. The woman whose house you just went into."

"She's just one of our clients. You know I sometimes have to make deliveries in person."

Miranda giggled. "She certainly didn't *look* like a Tarkington's client, Daddy," she said. "A fat old lady in a dirty apron."

"The woman you saw was my client's maid," he said.

She giggled again. "She didn't even look like a Tarkington's client's *maid*," she said.

"Well, that's who she was," he said with a tone of finality.

"What was it you were delivering?"

"It was a—a gold bracelet. My client wants to wear it to a party tonight."

Miranda was determined to get to the bottom of this mystery. She was positive he was holding something back from her.

"I didn't know Tarkington's clients lived in places like that," she said. "A crumby old brownstone with dirty windows and torn window shades, a brownstone that's been cut up into at least six itty-bitty apartments."

He looked at her. "My, aren't you the observant one," he said at last. "Don't you know that curiosity killed the cat?"

"Come on, Daddy. Tell me who she really is," she said.

He leaned forward and rolled up the window that divided the passenger seats from the driver's seat. "Well, if you must know," he said quietly, "she's someone I take care of."

"What do you mean, take care of?"

"Ssh! I just realized it's the first of the month. Her rent's due."

"You mean you pay her *rent*?"

He nodded. "Please, Miranda, not so loud."

"But why?" she whispered.

"She's a very poor woman. She's penniless. If it weren't for me, she'd be a homeless person."

"What's her name?"

"I have no idea."

"You mean you pay the rent for some old woman you don't even *know*?"

He nodded again.

"But *why*?"

"I found her begging in the streets, Miranda. Several years ago. There was something about her face. She seemed so pitiful. I gave her some money, and she said, 'God bless you,' and my heart just went out to her. I asked her where she lived, and she said, 'Nowhere,' and I felt terribly sorry for her. It didn't seem right for people like us to have so much, and for decent people like her to have so little. She has no one—no family, nothing. I decided to find an apartment for her. It's just a little place, as you can see, but it's clean, and in a safe neighborhood, and she's able to take care of herself. I pay her rent and give her a little extra."

"Why, Daddy, what a super thing to do!" It was in the days when Miranda and her classmates were always using words like "super."

"At least she's safe and off the streets."

Later, when they were across the bridge and on the Long Island Expressway heading east, she said to him, "Does she know who *you* are, Daddy?"

"Of course not," he said.

"Really?"

"Did you ever hear of Maimonides, Miranda?"

She shook her head.

"Maimonides was a great philosopher in the twelfth century. He wrote about 'the golden ladder of charity.' The highest rung on that golden ladder, he wrote, is when you give to someone whom you do not know, and when that person does not know who the donor is."

"Does Mother know you're doing this?"

He seemed to hesitate. Then he said, "Yes."

She reached out and squeezed his arm. "She must be very proud of you," she said. "I know *I* am. I think this is just the nicest, kindest, most super thing you're doing, Daddy. It really is."

"Well, one tries to do what one can to help the less fortunate in this world," he said, with a little sigh. "Now, are you quite satisfied, Miranda?"

"Oh, yes!"

He leaned forward and rolled down the window that separated them from Billings, the driver. "Think we'll have rain this weekend, Billings?"

"No, sir!"

Now, sitting alone in her office, unable to take her eyes for long from the diamond ring Tommy placed on her finger and thinking of the things he said to her, and of all the events and revelations of the past few days, she wonders: Could the little fat old lady on West End Avenue actually have been his mother, her own paternal grandmother—a grandmother whose very existence she has been denied? A grandmother! Just think of it! There, all along, had been a dear little grandmother whom she could have taken Easter baskets to, who could have joined the family for Sunday dinners and at Christmastime; she had been right there, all through her childhood, just a few city blocks away. She had always been told that her father was an orphan. She had been robbed of a whole segment of her family history.

But did that explain the curious scene that took place

later that same evening, after dinner at the farm? Not only had Miranda been seated at the grown-ups' table but her mother had allowed her to be served wine, and after dinner they had all withdrawn to the sun room for coffee. Miranda's mother had picked up her needlepoint, and the two men were discussing, of all things, zippers. A manufacturer's rep had shown Tommy some new zippers from France that were so skinny and narrow they were almost invisible, and Tommy was proposing that these new French zippers be introduced in the Custom Salon.

There was a lull in the conversation, and Miranda said, "Daddy, tell Uncle Tommy about the little fat lady on West End Avenue."

Her mother dropped her needlepoint. "I think not," she said sharply.

"Oh, but it's a super story, Daddy," she persisted. "Tell it."

"Miranda," her mother said warningly, "I said I think not."

"Tell him about Maimonides and the golden—"

"Miranda, what did I just tell you? Your Uncle Tommy would be bored to tears."

Miranda looked imploringly at her father, who was looking uncomfortable. "Perhaps not," he muttered. "Perhaps not tonight."

"But—"

"Actually, I'd like to hear the story," Tommy said pleasantly.

"No!" her mother said. "Miranda, it's past your bedtime. Run along to bed."

Red-faced, humiliated, Miranda rose to her feet. "But Mother—"

Her mother clapped her hands. "Off to bed! Say good night to our guest and then off to bed with you, young lady."

As she left the room, she heard her mother say brightly, "What has the store decided to do about designer jeans?"

Alone in her bedroom but far from asleep, Miranda had been furious at her mother. She had been seated at the grown-ups' table, she had been served wine, she had tried to keep up her end of the conversation, and then, at half-past nine, which was *not* her bedtime—and in front of Tommy Bonham, the man with whom she had decided she was passionately in love—she had been ordered to bed like a little child. She lay there, fully dressed, on top of her bedspread in the dark room, wanting to cry but comforting herself by plotting some sort of hideous and elaborate revenge against her mother. She would put itching powder in her sleep mask. She would put a whoopee cushion under the seat of her chair the next time she had a dinner party. She would poison the fish in the lake in her mother's Dell Garden. She would . . .

Later, she heard Tommy Bonham's car drive away, and the light from his headlamps arced across her ceiling. Now she heard her mother and father exchanging loud words from the floor below, and she crept out of her bedroom and tiptoed to the head of the stairs to hear what they were saying. Her mother seemed to be pursuing him from room to room, and their angry voices rose and fell as they went.

"Goddammit, Connie, it's the first of the month! You know how she gets when I'm late!"

"Why did you have to take Miranda along? What kind of cock-and-bull story did you tell her anyway?"

"Goddammit, Connie!"

"Why do you have to include my daughter in your dirty little secrets? Isn't it bad enough that I got dragged into it? Isn't that bad enough? 'To protect you,' Tommy said. How can I protect you when you won't even protect yourself? And now you've dragged my daughter into it too!"

"She's my daughter too, goddammit!"

"A lot you care! I've tried to protect her from you. Now you've dragged her into it!"

"She doesn't know a goddamned thing!"

"What if she finds out? What if she starts asking questions? What am I supposed to say? Answer me that one, Si? Or shall I call you Sol?"

"Shut up, Connie!"

"Why couldn't you have had Billings deliver the money? Why did you have to drag Miranda along?"

"And get Billings involved in it too?"

"Billings is *already* involved! He drove you there, didn't he?"

"I told him I was delivering merchandise to a client."

"Why couldn't you have sent a messenger from the store? Why couldn't you have just dropped a check in the mail? I'll never understand—"

"Because those are her terms, goddammit! *Those are her terms!* The money is to be delivered *in cash*. By me. *In person*. No messengers. No banks. I've told you all this a thousand times before. She set the terms. She calls the shots, whether you like it or not."

"But there's nothing in the terms about dragging Miranda along!"

"I didn't drag her along! She waited in the goddamn car!"

"But she saw her! She knows about her! She suspects something, doesn't she?"

"She doesn't suspect a goddamn thing! Now shut up, Connie."

"Don't tell me to shut up! I'm sick to death of trying to protect this family from your sordid, messy little secrets!"

"Who pays the bills for this family?"

"And who's seen to it that this family's name hasn't been dragged through the mud? I'm sick to death of covering up for you. I'm sick to death of covering up your filthy tracks, sweeping up your filthy messes!"

"When have you ever covered up for me?"

"*When?* I'm talking about June nineteen-seventy. *Where?* I'm talking about Boston and the Ritz-Carlton Hotel!"

"Moe Minskoff worked that one out for me, damn it! You had nothing to do with it!"

"But I got dragged into it anyway, didn't I? By you— and Moe—and Tommy! I've been covering up for you for the past nine years! Do you think that's been fun for me?

But I did it—and I did it for you! And this is the kind of thanks I get. If it hadn't been for me and Tommy—"

"And Moe! Don't forget Moe!"

"—you could have gone to jail! If it hadn't been for me, you could still be in jail!"

"Goddammit, Connie! Leave me alone!"

"And why did I do it? I did it for you. . . ."

Their voices faded as they moved into another room, and Miranda crept back into her bedroom.

The next day Miranda asked her mother, "Who is the fat old lady on West End Avenue?"

"I don't know what you're talking about, Miranda."

"You sent me to bed early when I asked Daddy to tell about her."

"You were boring Mr. Bonham, dear."

"I was not! What's more boring than talking about zippers?"

"Please, Miranda," her mother said, passing her hand across her forehead, "I don't want to talk about this anymore. I have a terrible sick headache, and I'm going up to take my nap."

And that was all Miranda ever knew.

In the northwest corner of Flying Horse Farm, Miranda's mother had created what she called her Dell Garden. A natural hollow in the land provided the setting and suggested the name, and Consuelo had a deep artificial lake built at the center of the hollow, where it was fed by a nearby spring. In this lake swam many brightly colored carp and calicoes and koi fish, some of them quite rare and valuable. Along the shallower edges of the lake bloomed aquatic plants, lilies and water irises and water hyacinths, but the center of her lake she wanted at least twenty-five feet deep, so the fish could find plenty of room to survive, in semihibernation, under the winter ice. Also, she had been told that the deeper the lake the purer would be its reflective powers with sunlight and clouds and stars. Over the years, the fish had thrived, multiplied, and grown to considerable size.

Connie Tarkington had designed her garden without any formal training in landscape design. She had arranged her plantings by hunch. Along the banks of the lake she had planted low stands of dogwood, crab apples, oak-leaf hydrangeas, azaleas, willows, and golden bamboo that rustled in the breeze. Along the rim of the hollow she had wanted deeper greens, and so this was planted with ilex, boxwood, and Norway spruce. In early spring, the slopes of the garden exploded with swaths of yellow daffodils and blue grape hyacinths. Later came tulips, iris, tall lupines, and delphiniums. In summer there were bright patches of hollyhocks and daylilies, and in fall the Dell Garden was still bright with asters, chrysanthemums, and the reddening leaves of the dogwoods.

Across the lake ran an arched wooden footbridge, in the Japanese moon-gate style. Along the bridge, spaced at intervals, were redwood benches, where the visitor could sit and look down at the reflection of clouds in the dark water and at the playful herding and leaping of the bright fish. It was on this footbridge that Richard Avedon posed Consuelo Tarkington, in a series of romantic outfits, for that famous fashion shoot in *Harper's Bazaar* in the spring of 1980, the year she climbed to the top of the International Best-Dressed List.

In the summer of that same year, Miranda and her half brother were seated on one of the benches on the garden footbridge. He was seventeen then, and a freshman at Yale, and she was thirteen, in her first year at Ethel Walker. Over the past year, her passion for Tommy Bonham had faded, and now she was in love with Blazer, though he didn't know it. Blazer wore his hair long in those days, in a shaggy ponytail pulled back with a rubber band, a style chosen—she is certain today—only because it was designed to infuriate his father. Their final blowup had not occurred, and Blazer still came down from Connecticut to visit his father at the farm on certain weekends, and this was one of them. Miranda and Blazer were feeding the fish.

One particularly obnoxious blue-and-yellow koi was hogging all the food pellets, and Miranda and Blazer were trying to aim their pellets so the swarms of smaller fish would get their share, but the big koi was too fast for them, and when he opened his huge mouth he could engorge dozens of pellets at a time.

"Tell me about your mother," Miranda asked him. "What's she like?" She had always been curious about Alice Tarkington, whose name was taboo in Miranda's household.

"Like? Well, let's see," he said. "To begin with, she's ten years older than your mother and a little heavier."

She laughed. "You mean she's fat?"

"No, not fat. But she's not as skinny as your mother. Your mother is too damned skinny, if you ask me."

"She has to be a model size to wear the clothes she likes."

"Yeah, I know." With a strong overhand, he pitched a handful of pellets far out into the water. "There!" he said. "There's some that that overweight bastard won't get."

"What else about her?"

"Well, she's nice-looking. At least I think she's nice-looking. She's not a blonde, like your mother. She's got red hair." He grinned. "And a temper to go with it. Hell, I guess she'd have gray hair if she let it go natural. She, you know, dyes it."

"And?"

"And, let's see. She's very athletic, my mother. She plays lots of tennis and golf. I guess you'd call her a very outdoorsy woman. She loves the out-of-doors."

"My mother loves to garden."

"Ha! Your mother doesn't *garden*, Mandy. She just stands out here with her parasol and points out places to gardeners where she wants them to plant her trees."

"My mother thinks the sun can be very damaging to a woman's skin."

"Well, my mother doesn't subscribe to that philosophy. She likes a year-round tan. In the summer she's always out-of-doors. In the winter she goes to a tanning salon. At least she used to."

"In other words, she's just the opposite of my mother."

"Yeah, I guess you could more or less say that."

"I wonder if I'll ever meet her? I'd like to."

"Well, don't take this the wrong way, Mandy, but I don't think you ever will. She doesn't want to meet you. She's very bitter."

She had tried not to feel hurt by this. "Bitter?" she said.

"Yeah, she's bitter, all right. She's about the bitterest woman I've ever known. After all, the old man asked your mother to marry him even before he asked my mother for a divorce. Wouldn't you be bitter? I'll tell you how bitter she is. If I come out here for the weekend, she won't even ask me how it went. She won't ask me what I did or anything, and she won't listen when I try to tell her. I've learned not even to mention Flying Horse Farm to her, or anything about Dad's new family. When *Architectural Digest* published all those pictures of the farm, including this garden, she refused to look at the magazine. Needless to say, she won't set foot inside the store. She won't even walk on that side of Fifth Avenue when she's in that part of town. If she happens to be walking across the street from the store, she won't even look in the store's direction. That's how bitter she is."

"That's sad," Miranda said.

"Yeah, I guess so. But it was a pretty bitter divorce."

"Do you remember any of it?"

"Nah, I was too little. But that's another thing she's bitter about. She felt the old man abandoned her and her two-year-old kid."

She sighed. "What a strange family we are," she said. They had run out of fish-food pellets.

"Yeah. Strange. Sad. And add a couple of more S-words: shallowness, superficiality, and secrets. That's what this family is all about, Mandy. I could add another word beginning with an S, but I couldn't use it in front of a well-brung-up young lady."

"Shallowness, superficiality—?"

"What's Tarkington's all about, anyway? Putting a

lot of shallow, superficial dresses on the backs of a bunch of shallow, superficial women, trying to turn them into something they're not, telling some rich old broad she looks divine in a dress that makes her look like an Eighth Avenue hooker—an *expensive* Eighth Avenue hooker, but an Eighth Avenue hooker just the same."

"Daddy says running a store like ours is like putting on a piece of theater."

"Yeah, right, and what's a piece of theater? Pretense. Make-believe. Lies. Phoniness. You don't think a piece of theater is anything like *life,* do you? And Tarkington's isn't even good theater, if you ask me. It's more like Hollywood, like an old Joan Crawford movie. Its more like television, that tells you if you'll just buy a Cadillac your neighbors will think you're John D. Rockefeller. Or if you'll try our deodorant you can have a date with Robert Redford. I'll tell you what the store is *really* like. It's like Chicago. Ever been to Chicago?"

"Uh-uh."

"Chicago is the phoniest city in the world. All along the lakefront are these big mansions and apartment buildings with doormen in fancy uniforms. But walk two blocks inland from the lake and you're in Scuzbagsville—cheap bars, flophouses, and porno shops. Chicago is all facade. Behind the facade, Tarkington's is just a tarted-up version of the *shmattes* business."

"Shmattes?" She giggled again. "Another S-word. What does shmattes mean?"

"Rags. Junk. Trash. That's what all the family lies and secrets are designed to protect: the fact that the old man's in the rag business. Secrets on top of secrets, lies on top of lies. Nobody even knows the old man's age, for Chrissake. No, we gotta keep the old man's age a secret to protect the image."

"He says age is a boring, unimportant statistic."

"Sure—so nobody will know how old he is. Or where he was born, or who his parents were. That might hurt the old image, right? Image! It's all done for image, for illusion. It's all done with mirrors, so step right up, folks, and see the little lady sawed in half onstage. That's about how real he is. Everything *about* the old man is phony, Miranda. Silas Tarkington isn't even his real name. He was Solomon Tarcher before he changed it. My mom told me that."

She remembered her mother's words: *Or shall I call you Sol?*

"And look at the phonies he surrounds himself with —men like Tommy Bonham."

"Is he a phony?"

"The only thing he likes about Bonham is that he *looks* good. More facade. Bonham looks good, so he's good at buttering up the ladies."

"Blazer," she asked him, "is my mother a phony too?"

He hesitated. "I've got no quarrel with your mom," he said. "I like her, actually. But she's his shill, his beard, his showpiece, his flagship customer. She's *the* Tarkington's woman. But I'll say this for her, she doesn't seem to mind letting herself be used like that, to display the merchandise. That was one reason—one of the main reasons —why the old man divorced my mom and married yours. After I was born, Mom got a little heavy. She didn't look good in designer dresses anymore. So the old man traded in a size twelve for a size eight, and got a ten-years'-newer model in the bargain. I once heard your mom say that when she was pregnant with you she only gained eight ounces. Can you imagine that? Eight ounces! No wonder you were such a shrimpy little thing when you were born."

She laughed. "Shrimpy? Was I?"

"I remember when they first showed you to me in your whatchamacallit—bassinet. You were only *yea big.*" He stretched out his hand. "I could have held you in the palm of one hand. You were even shrimpy-colored. Pink."

She was enjoying this immensely. "Tell me what else you remember," she said.

"I guess you don't remember the old man before he had his face lifted, do you?"

She looked at him, amazed. "I didn't know he'd had his face lifted!" she said.

"Oh, yeah. It must have been around nineteen-seventy. It changed his looks completely. My mom thought it was a big joke. 'Now that he's bought himself a new young wife, he's bought himself a new young face to go with her,' she said. More phoniness."

"You think that? That he *bought* her?"

"That was my mom talking. Remember, she was very bitter."

"It made him look younger, I suppose."

"Not just that. It made him look completely different. He used to have a small mustache. After the facelift, that went. His nose was smaller. His eyes were bigger. He used to have dark hair. After the facelift, he decided that silver hair looked better with the new young face. For contrast, you see. New young face but older hair. But silver with a blond rinse thrown in so the hair didn't look *too* old. Facade again. When I first saw him after the facelift, I didn't even recognize him. That's how much it changed him. The only thing it couldn't change was his voice. It wasn't until he spoke to me that I knew who he was!"

They sat in silence for a moment or two. "Secrets," she said. "There's a little fat old lady who lives on West End Avenue."

"Huh?" he said. "Who dat?"

She told him then of the odd experience the year before, and of its even odder aftermath.

He shrugged. "Probably one of the old man's old girlfriends that he's paying off," he said.

"You mean, blackmail?"

"Just a guess. But you won't get him to tell you who she is." He wagged his finger at her. "That's a secret, Mandy! That's for him to know and you to find out. To hell with it. It's just more lies, more phoniness. Who gives a damn? Let him have his secrets."

There was another little silence, and then she said, "What are you going to do after you graduate from Yale?"

"Do? Probably nothing."

"But you can't just do nothing."

"Why not? That was one thing my mother got out of him. A nice little trust fund that'll be mine when I'm twenty-one."

"But still, you can't just do nothing, Blazer."

"Well, I'm sure as hell not going to work for his phony store," he said. "I'm not going into the shmattes business, that's for sure."

"I think he'd like it if you did."

"Well, I'm not. And what about you? What are you going to do when you grow up?"

"I *am* grown up!" she said. "But I'll tell you what I'm going to do when I'm even *more* grown up! I'm going to be the queen of the circus and marry the man on the flying trapeze. I'm going to be Miranda, the daughter of Prospero, the Grand Duke of Milan! That's who I'm named after, you know—Miranda in *The Tempest*. I'm going to create a tempest of my own, and not in a teapot! I'm going to be a star! 'Here she comes,' they're going to say. 'There she goes!' I don't know how I'm going to do it yet, but I'm going to do it, wait and see. I may go to work at Tarkington's, but if I do I'm going to end up running the store—you wait and see!"

"Just watch out for the phonies," he said.

There was another, longer silence. Then she said, "Blazer, is everything phony for you? Do you think I'm a phony too?"

He grinned. "Of course not. You're not a phony. You're too young to be a phony. You're just a kid. Phoniness happens later."

"I'm not a kid! I'm a young woman, in case you haven't noticed." She hesitated. "But, sometimes—sometimes I feel so strange."

"Strange? How strange?"

"Like right now. I feel strange. Not knowing if I'll ever be able to do all the things I want to do."

"Hey," he said. "Just a minute ago you were the daughter of Prospero, the Duke of Milan! The world at your feet."

"I know," she said, and her tone was wistful.

"Hey," he said again. "I bet I know what you need. You need a neck and shoulder rub. My mom says I give great neck and shoulder rubs, and she always feels better afterward. Want me to give you one of my famous rubs?"

"All right," she said.

"Turn around."

She turned her back to him, and he began to massage her neck and shoulder muscles with his long, strong fingers.

"Let me tell you your future," he said. "You shall have towers. Towers and minarets and spires and palace gates, forests, shores, and islands, gems and pearls and scepters and all the emperor's diamonds, and everything brilliant in King Oberon's bright diadem. For you, I foresee temples and mosques and fountains, fountains and waterfalls and tapestries and flowers and little thornless roses, rings on your fingers and bells on your toes—"

"Blazer," she interrupted him, "have you ever been in love?"

"Oh, yes," he said easily.

"What's it feel like?"

"Not much fun. Kind of like an ache in the pit of your gut."

"I think I'm in love," she said.

"Tell me about this guy," he said, still kneading her shoulders and the back of her neck.

"Well, for one thing, he's older than me."

"Hmm," he said, rubbing her back more slowly. "What else?"

"He's tall. And he's dark. And handsome."

"What else?"

"He's—" But she couldn't bring herself to finish the sentence.

He withdrew his hands. "Back rub's over," he said. "Feel better now?" He stood up and stretched. With his arms above his head, he appeared to be nine feet tall. She thought he had a beautiful body. "Well, I don't much like the sound of this guy," he said. "I think something better will come along. If you ask me, you're just in love with the *idea* of being in love. I think I'll go for a swim. Care to join me?"

"Okay," she said, and she also rose.

He reached for the old duckbill cap he often wore, and put it on his head with the bill in the back, the way he liked to wear it, and she followed him across the foot-bridge.

"Blazer," she began.

"Yeah?"

"I don't know how to say this, but I like you—very much."

"Yeah, you're a good kid, Mandy," he said, and she felt as though her heart were breaking. There were tears in her eyes, but since she was walking behind him he could not see them.

When they got to the pool, their father was swim-ming his laps, up and down, and Blackamoor, his Labra-dor, who was just a big puppy then, was swimming beside him, while the television set, placed on the pool's flagstone coping, broadcast the news.

Now, in her office at the store, Miranda is thinking of Blazer, who in the end did not even get his trust fund and now has been disinherited in his father's will "for reasons he will understand." Poor Blazer. Will he ever forgive his father? On an impulse—not that she has any-thing in particular to say to him except hello and to ask how he's doing—she picks up her phone and dials his number. After several rings, she hears, "You've reached the number of Blazer T. You got my machine, but you ain't got me. I'm either out or I'm fast asleep. So leave your name when you hear the beep. You may want to leave a message too. If you just hang up, well, then, fuck you!"

"Blazer," she says. "It's me, Miranda. I'm at the of-fice. Please give me a call when you get a chance."

Not many blocks away, Moses Minskoff is also on the telephone. "Listen, Albert," he is saying, "this Bonham character seems like he's dragging his heels a little. . . . Sure we need him, so I'm suggesting you sweeten the deal. Offer him an employment contract. Offer him three hundred big ones for the next five years. Hell, with that kind of a deal, he won't even have to come into the office. . . . What's that add up to for you? Just a mil and a half over five years, and that's peanuts, Albert, compared to what you're going to walk off with. Peanuts. Shall I relay that offer to him? . . . No, to hell with the girl. She'll do what her old lady tells her."

In the end, it had not been a ponytail that precipitated the final break with his father. It had been a T-shirt. Or perhaps you could say it was a bikini.

The ponytail disappeared at Yale when Blazer Tarkington took up diving. "A diver looks dumb bouncing on a diving board with a ponytail flopping up and down behind him," his coach had told him. "Also, it can affect your scores. No matter how clean an entry you make into the water, a judge will knock off two points if the entry's attached to a lot of hair." So the ponytail had been sheared off. Begrudgingly.

Several years earlier, Blazer's father had realized that something was happening to the city of New York—and to the world at large—when he had seen a young woman skating down Fifth Avenue, the city's most fashionable thoroughfare, on roller skates, wearing a Walkman shoulder pack, earphones, and a bikini. Silas Tarkington had returned to his office and immediately called a meeting of his staff and announced that, no matter how far the standards of the world might have fallen, the store must never lower its own rigid standards.

He had often lectured on the value of what he called "the intimidation factor" to a store like Tarkington's. Human beings actually enjoyed being a little bit intimidated, a little frightened, a little apprehensive, he argued. Fear was a positive, exciting emotion. Fear stirred the adrenal glands. How else did one account for the popularity of horror novels and horror movies? Some retail establishments had lost their power to intimidate. A prime example of this was Tiffany & Company. Years ago, Tiffany's had been an intimidating store to shop in. But then had come *Breakfast at Tiffany's,* the popular novel and film, and now Tiffany's was nothing more than a Manhattan tourist attraction where crowds came to browse and admire the merchandise but not to buy. Cartier's, by contrast, had maintained its ability to daunt the shopper, and probably the most intimidating Manhattan merchant of all was Harry Winston. No one passed through Winston's grand and fearsomely gilded gates unless he or she had a serious jewelry purchase in mind. The girl in the bikini on roller blades would never have dared to enter Winston's. On the intimidation scale, Silas Tarkington saw his store as somewhere between Cartier and Winston.

Silas often compared his store with the Ritz Hotel in Paris, a hostelry that was always deliciously intimidating. The Ritz was a small hotel, with less than a hundred rooms. Tarkington's was a small specialty store of less than twenty departments. Was there ever a more intimidating stretch of real estate than the Ritz's arcade of display cases that ran from the lobby on the Place Vendôme to the rear entrance on the rue Cambon, where goods from all the most expensive shops in Paris were trapped behind gleaming glass? Silas Tarkington wanted the aisles in his store to have the same awe-inspiring feel as the Ritz arcade. If you're not our type of shopper, he wanted his store to say, you really should not be here. He also admired the way the Ritz staff treated its guests—warm and cordial to the people the hotel knew, but aloof and just a touch condescending to strangers and people who did not look as though they belonged there. He urged his staff to try to emulate that Ritz attitude, a delicate balance between coziness and hauteur.

At that meeting, he had announced that the store would adopt an unwritten dress code for its clientele.

Anyone who did not "look right" or was not "dressed right" would be shown to the door, politely but firmly.

The young man in the reversed duckbill cap, granny glasses, T-shirt, and jeans approached the Fifth Avenue entrance to the store, but James, the doorman blocked his path. "Deliveries through the side door, around the corner," James said. Indeed, the young man did look like a delivery boy and was carrying a fat manila envelope under one arm.

"Wait a minute, fella," Blazer said. "Don't you realize who I am?"

This immediately posed an agonizing dilemma for poor James because he did indeed now recognize the owner's son. But, at the same time, he had been given strict instructions that men in T-shirts were not to be admitted to the store. "We have a rule against T-shirts on the selling floors, Mr. Tarkington," he murmured. "So would you mind—?" He glanced nervously toward the corner and the service entrance.

"What the hell! You mean I gotta go in my old man's store like I'm a goddamned delivery boy?"

"If it's your father you've come to see, Mr. Tarkington," James said, "he's not in the store at the moment. He left about half an hour ago, saying he'd be back around two."

"That's okay. I just want to leave this envelope on his desk."

"Perhaps I could take it up for you, then," James suggested.

"No, I want to take it up myself. I need to write him a note when I get up there. It's important." He patted the manila envelope. "These are important legal papers, damn it!"

"Well, let me see what I can do," James said, and he pressed the button by his station that connected him with Tommy Bonham's office. "Mr. Tarkington, Junior, is downstairs, sir," he said. "I wonder if I could ask you to

come down, sir." Turning to Blazer, he said, "Mr. Bonham will be right down."

And so Blazer waited, fuming, on the sidewalk.

Presently Tommy appeared through the door and immediately grasped the situation. He took Blazer by the
arm and said, "Let me take you down the street, Blazer,
and buy you a cup of coffee."

In the coffee shop, the two of them settled in a booth,
and Tommy said, "Have you had lunch? Would you like a
sandwich? They do a good Reuben here. Good burgers,
too."

"Nah. Just coffee's fine. Black."

"Blazer," Tommy began easily, "lots of places have
dress codes. All the best restaurants in New York require
jackets and ties on men, and some will not even permit
blue jeans."

"I don't go to phony restaurants like that."

"Well, phony or not, don't you think restaurants
have the right to enforce a dress code?"

"We're not talking about a restaurant, damn it."

"Let me put it to you another way. Suppose you were
taking a date to the Yale Prom—"

"I wouldn't be caught dead at the Yale Prom!"

"Then let me put it still another way. Suppose you
were invited to a dinner dance, or a friend's wedding, and
the invitation said 'black tie.' How would you—?"

"I wouldn't go!"

"Suppose this is your best friend's wedding. He has
asked you to be his best man. The wedding is to be black
tie."

"I still wouldn't go. I wouldn't accept."

"If he's your best friend, wouldn't he be hurt if you
turned down the honor of being his best man?"

"A phony who'd have that kind of wedding wouldn't
be my friend!"

"I see," he said. "Your father tells me you're fond of
classical music."

"So? What's that got to do with it?"

"I'm thinking of hypothetical situations, Blazer. Suppose there's to be a Mozart symphony performed, by an

orchestra you've always wanted to hear. Your seats are in the dress circle—"

"I wouldn't sit in the goddamned dress circle."

"What if the *only seats available* are in the dress circle, Blazer?"

"Then I'd stand in the back of the hall!"

Tommy Bonham sighed. "Blazer," he said, "don't you think it's rude—don't you think it's actually insulting to the other people around you—not to dress the way other people consider appropriate for certain occasions? Don't you think that's actually hostile behavior?"

"Nope. People are what they are, not what they wear."

"But don't you think your attitude is maybe a little bit childish? I mean, I could understand this sort of rebelliousness from a fifteen-year-old. But you're a grown man. You're twenty-one, and you'll be graduating from Yale at the end of May. You're going to find a different world out there, a world where you're going to be expected to conform to certain—"

"Don't give me a lecture about the big bad world out there!" Blazer snapped. "I've heard all that shit before."

"Well, let me put it to you one final way," he said. "Your father and I run a business. It's known as a service business, which means that our job is to please and be of service to our clients. We are not in the business of insulting them. And our clients are people accustomed to observing certain standards of dress. And if any of our clients had seen you walking through the store this morning, dressed the way you are right now, our clients would be so upset and insulted—insulted, Blazer, that we'd allow such a thing to happen—that they'd never set foot in our store again. So, as far as we're concerned, our dress code is simply a matter of good business. It's simply a matter of dollars and cents. Would you dress like that to meet the Queen of England?"

"I wasn't going to meet the Queen of England, for Chrissakes!"

"No," Tommy said with a slight smile. "But the Queen of England has shopped in our store."

Blazer said nothing, merely looked down at his empty coffee cup, and Tommy Bonham looked at him evenly. "You have no respect for your father, do you, Blazer. No respect at all."

"I've got no beef with the old man," he said. "It's just this fucking, phony shmattes game he's in."

Tommy Bonham's eyebrows went up. He took a final sip of coffee and folded his paper napkin carefully on the table in front of him. "No wonder your father hates you," he said.

"I hear we had a little problem with Blazer this morning at the store," Si Tarkington said to Tommy Bonham later that afternoon.

Tommy steepled his fingers. "Your son's attitude seems to me—well, a little bit immature," he said.

"James did absolutely the right thing, and I told him so. We may decide to make exceptions to the rule now and then, but certainly not for members of my own family. If anyone in the store had recognized him, it would have looked even worse for us."

"That was the only argument I didn't use with him," Tommy said.

"I mean Miss Garbo may look a little—peculiar when she comes into the store. But she's Miss Garbo, and everyone knows who she is. She's earned the right to dress as she chooses. Blazer hasn't."

"Mrs. Onassis and her sister happened to be in the shoe department at the time."

"And he would have walked right past them on his way to the elevator!"

"He said he had some important legal documents to show you. He didn't say what they were."

Si Tarkington looked grim. "I think I know," he said. "What would you do with him, Tommy? If he were your son, how would you handle him?"

Tommy spread his hands. "It's hard to say, Si. But at times like this, I'm grateful that I've never been a parent. It isn't easy, I know."

"It's his mother's fault, of course. It's his goddamned mother's fault. She encourages this sort of behavior. She *applauds* it! It's all her goddamned fault."

"If I might make one small suggestion, Si," Tommy began.

"What? What is it?"

"Perhaps—perhaps if you tried a little harder to show him that you love him, Si. Perhaps that might help."

He nodded. "I'm going to have a word with him," he said. "Meanwhile, thanks for helping out with James this morning, Tommy. You certainly have better things to do with your time than deal with my family problems."

"That's what I'm here for, Si. To help you in any way I can." He paused. Then he said, "He referred to our business as the shmattes game. He called it 'this fucking, phony shmattes game.'"

And Tommy Bonham watched as Silas Tarkington's face grew white with fury.

That evening, after the store had closed for the day, Blazer Tarkington appeared at his father's office as he had been invited to do. He was dressed as he had been earlier in the day, but now he wore an unzipped leather airman's jacket over the T-shirt. Unknown to him was the fact that, in the closed office next door, Tommy, at Si's request ("So you can tell me how I do with him"), would be eavesdropping on this meeting over the intercom.

"Sit down, son," Si said, and Blazer slumped in the chair across from his father's desk.

"We are a divided family," his father began. "That fact is painful to me, but it is a fact that cannot be avoided. You are the product of a broken home, as they say, and I'm sure you blame me for the breakup of that home. All I can say to you is that in any divorce there are two sides to the issue, and the two people who are involved will probably never agree on who is to blame for the breakup of the marriage. Each partner in a divorce action thinks his side is right and the other side is wrong. I ask you to accept the possibility that, in your mother's and my case, there were rights and wrongs on both sides. I have never tried to paint myself as the hero or your mother as the villainess. The greatest mistake, I suppose, was that your mother and I got married in the first place. But then, Blazer—but then we would not have had you, whom we both love very much.

"I'd also like you to believe, son, that I have done everything in my power to make this divided family as happy and as privileged as I possibly can—to do everything I can for you, Miranda, and your mother. As you know, I've tried to give you and Miranda the finest of possible educations. Your stepmother and I have tried to make you feel welcome in our home. We wouldn't do any of this, son, if we didn't love both you children equally."

"Bullshit," Blazer muttered.

His father pretended not to hear this. "And we wouldn't have been able to do any of this," he went on, "if it hadn't been for my business. Now you may think that this is a phony business; I won't argue with your right to think that. Perhaps any business designed to fulfill human needs is a phony business, but all I can say is that I would not have been successful in the business I'm in if I had not found a way of fulfilling certain needs. In my case, it is women's needs for beautiful clothes, designed to make them look more beautiful. My success is proof of that need, son, and all I ask is that you understand why I am proud of it, very proud. This is a business I built from scratch, from nothing, with no help from anyone. And I didn't build it just for myself, though that was certainly part of it—I won't deny I have an ego—I also built it for my family, my wife, my children, and my children's children, so that future generations of this family would have something to hold on to. That's about all a man has in this life: his business, his family, and the future of his family. It's like a religion. It's like a love affair. For what are religion and love all about if it isn't trying to find some security in the uncertain future? I ask you to try to understand that. Of course I used to think and hope that you—that you and I, as father and son—but never mind that."

"Yeah, what about me?" Blazer said.

His father studied him. "I'm asking you to understand me," he said at last. "Is that too much to ask? Maybe it is."

"Yeah."

"You had your twenty-first birthday two weeks ago," his father said, and Blazer nodded.

"I assume you received your birthday check?"

Blazer nodded again.

"That's wrong. I don't assume. I know you received it because you endorsed it, and the check has cleared the bank. I suppose I was asking too much to expect some sort of thank-you note from you for a check for five thousand dollars."

Blazer sat forward in his chair. "But what about this?" he said, slapping the manila envelope on his lap. "What happened to my fucking trust fund? I took these papers to Jake Kohlberg this morning to collect the money from my so-called trust fund, and he tells me all the money's gone! Where is it?"

"I know about this," his father said. "Jake Kohlberg called me this morning. This is a matter you will have to take up with your mother."

"But this was supposed to be *your* trust fund! For *me*!" He waved the manila envelope in his father's face.

"Please don't do that, Blazer," his father said, holding up his hand. "It's true that I funded the trust. But the two trustees were your mother and the First National Bank of Stamford, Connecticut. Somehow the funds have been expended. Don't ask me how. Ask your mother."

"But what the fuck am I supposed to do, Dad?"

"I suppose you could sue your mother."

"That's what Kohlberg said. He wants me to hire him to sue my own mother!"

"I doubt that Kohlberg, Weiss would be willing to represent you in such an action," his father said, "since they are my legal counsel."

"Sue my own mother! That's typical of you, isn't it? You'd sue your own mother! I know all about you! All this bullshit you've been slinging me about your business

—how you started it from nothing, from scratch, with no help from anybody! You started it by jewing your own mother out of her inheritance! You jewed your sister, too. You jewed your mother and your sister, you jewed them both with your dirty Jew tricks. Mom told me all about it, Dad. I know all about it!"

"Your mother is a highly emotionally unstable woman with a serious drinking problem. And, it would seem, a serious streak of larceny."

Blazer jumped to his feet. "Don't say such things about my mother!"

"Your mother is a lush. You know that as well as I do."

He raised his fist. "I'm warning you!"

His father reached for a button on his desk. "Are you going to strike me?" he said. "All I have to do is push this button, and Oliver from Security, who is a Pinkerton detective, and armed, will be here in a matter of seconds."

"You're not worth hitting," Blazer said, lowering the fist. "You're not worth it, Mr. Solomon Tarcher. Mr. Phony Silas Tarkington!"

His father's eyes drew into narrow slits. "Did you refer to my business as the shmattes game?"

"Who told you that?" Blazer's eyes were round.

"I asked you a direct question, and I want a direct answer. Did you refer to my business as the shmattes game? *Did you ever refer to it as that?*"

"Yeah, sure! Because that's all it is! Fucking, phony shmattes game!"

"Get out of here, you filthy little piece of slime," his father said. "Get out of here in your filthy jeans and filthy T-shirt and filthy shoes and everything else that's covering your filthy body. *You're* shmattes, is what you are. When you were a baby, your mother almost dropped you on your head and killed you in one of her drunken rages. Sometimes I wish she had succeeded. Get out of here. I never want to lay eyes on you again."

Blazer hurled the manila envelope at his father, who caught it deftly in mid-air, ripped the envelope in half, and dropped the two halves into his wastepaper basket.

And Blazer charged out the office door.

"I guess you heard all that," Si Tarkington said when Tommy rejoined him in his office. Si's face was drawn and weary.

"All of it," Tommy said. "Si, you were magnificent. You gave him every opportunity. Some of the things you said—I made some notes. 'What are religion and love all about, if it isn't trying to find some security in an uncertain future?' My God, that's beautiful! It's poetry. It almost brought tears to my eyes. But he didn't hear a word of it. Give up on him, Si. The kid's not worth it. And you're right, it's all his mother's fault. She's completely poisoned his mind against you—against you and against everything you've ever done or tried to do."

Silas Tarkington rose a little slowly from behind his desk. His face was pale and his shoulders sagged, and he suddenly seemed a man of even slighter stature than he actually was. "Worthless," he repeated. "What should I do now?" His voice was soft, imploring, almost childlike.

"For God's sake, just don't give him any more money. He made it perfectly clear that's all he wants from you. Don't send any more good money after bad. Look at all you've given him, Si. The finest education money could buy—Hotchkiss, Yale—and this is the way he rewards you."

"But he's my son," he said. "My own flesh—"

"Take him out of your will, Si. Lord knows you've threatened to do that often enough. Show him it wasn't just a threat. Show him you mean it. Put your money where your mouth is. God knows what would happen if he ever got his hands on any Tarkington's stock. He'd have this place down the tubes in five minutes. The little bastard doesn't deserve a plugged nickel. Cut him off without a penny."

"It's hard, Tom. It's damned hard."

"Of course it's hard. But it's time for you to play hardball now."

"The things he said about my mother . . . my sister."

"Your mother and your sister were well taken care of

—you and I know that. You were dealing with greedy and ungrateful people, and you had to be tough. You're dealing with a greedy and ungrateful person now, and you've got to be tough again. Besides, you'd be doing him a favor. Let him learn that he can't go through life living on handouts from a rich father. Let him learn that if he's going to make a living he's going to have to do it by the sweat of his balls—the way you did. A kid who'd speak to his father the way he just did to you? Cut him out of your will. Show him who's boss."

"You're right . . . you're right."

"Listening to the things he was saying to you, it was all I could do to keep from walking in here and punching him in the face. After all you've done for him. For God's sake, Si, don't let this kid shit on you any longer. Be a man! Let him go. It's called tough love."

"You're right. I'll call Jake Kohlberg in the morning."

"Good man. Now you're talking like Si Tarkington. Now you're talking like the legendary Silas R. Tarkington, the merchant prince."

"And doesn't he . . . doesn't he understand I couldn't have done any of it if I'd kept the old name?"

"Listen, that kid has never even *tried* to understand you!"

"You understand me, don't you, Tommy?"

"Damn right I do."

"But still—where did I go wrong with him, Tommy?"

"You didn't. You're not to blame. You said it yourself—it's his mother's fault, it's Alice's fault. She's taught that kid to hate you since he was old enough to talk."

"You're right . . . you're right." Si Tarkington lowered his head, and his fingers riffled aimlessly through some papers on his desk, staring hard at the day-end sales figures as though they held the answer to some inscrutable riddle. He pressed his palms hard on the top of his desk and appeared to sway.

Tommy Bonham stepped forward. "Are you okay, Si?" he asked.

"Oh, yes. . . . But still . . . but still, I had such high hopes for him," he said. "My only son, and he called me a dirty Jew. I feel . . . I feel like camels just shat on my father's grave. Blazer. . . . He was supposed . . . he was supposed to blaze across the sky like . . . a comet, like a shooting star. I wanted so much for him, Tommy . . . so much. Maybe I wanted too much. And now I have . . . no son."

"Look, Si," Tommy began gently, "you'll always have—"

He had been about to say "me" when he realized that the founder and C.E.O. of Tarkington's was weeping, that teardrops were falling across the page of sales figures, so Tommy Bonham left the rest of that sentence hanging in the air.

"You're doing the right thing," he said instead.

"You're right . . . you're right."

"His mother has poisoned his mind against you, Si. He'll never change."

10

It is Wednesday, and Miranda has arrived to assist Pauline O'Malley clear out her father's desk, bookshelves, cabinets, and files. "Pauline needs help going through the things in your father's office," Tommy Bonham told her. "Someone in the family should be there when she does this. Can you give her a hand?" Materials pertaining to the store's operations will, of course, stay where they are, but personal items—her mother's photograph in its silver frame, his silver calendar and water carafe, his collection of Baccarat *millefleur* paperweights, and so on—will be packed and shipped out to Flying Horse Farm. The shipping department has sent up cardboard cartons for the job, along with bags of Styrofoam peanuts for packing the more fragile things.

This is Pauline's first day back at work since Silas Tarkington's death. She has taken his death very badly. When Miranda first encountered her this morning, she looked terrible. Her eyes were red from weeping, her hair was a mess, her lipstick was smeared, and her desk was awash with piles of wadded-up Kleenex. Seeing Miranda, she rose from her chair and quite literally threw herself into Miranda's arms with a fresh burst of sobbing. "Oh, Miss Miranda," she moaned, while Miranda patted her shoulder, "we've lost him . . . lost him . . . we'll never see him again, will we? Never in this world. Your poor mother. How is she taking it?"

"She's—bearing up," Miranda said.

"Oh, the poor thing! She must be devastated, absolutely devastated. I should have written her a note, but I just couldn't bring myself. I still can't believe it. Our Mr. Si is gone . . . he's gone . . . he's gone!" Tears streamed down her pale cheeks.

"There, there," Miranda said.

"Tell your mother I'm making a very special novena for her. This is my fourth day. I'm asking Our Lady to bring your mother peace."

"She'll be very touched to hear it," Miranda said.

Now Pauline has more or less managed to collect herself, though there are still occasional sighs and sniffles as they pack the boxes. From her father's bathroom, Miranda fetches a fresh box of Kleenex. She supposes that Pauline was secretly in love with her father—how else to justify such an excessive display of grief?—and she even wonders whether Pauline and her father had been lovers once upon a time. Was Pauline O'Malley ever pretty? It is hard to say at this point. Perhaps, but now she has developed the white papery skin and fine worry lines of secretarial spinsterhood. Why does a spinster's skin become like parchment? Miranda doesn't know, but it does.

"When we finish this, I'm going to have to clean my own desk out," Pauline says, gently wrapping a paperweight in tissue paper and nestling it in a box of plastic peanuts.

"Whatever for?" Miranda asks her.

There is a little sob. "I can't stay on here. I can't stay on here now that Mr. Si is gone."

"Oh, but we don't want to lose you, Pauline. Mr. Bonham's going to be running the store, at least for the time being. Couldn't you stay and help him out?"

"I could never work for Mr. Bonham!"

"Why not?"

"Never! There was only Mr. Si. He was the only one I could ever work for, ever. No one can ever take his place." Another sob.

"But what will you live on, Pauline?"

She blows her nose noisily. "There's my pension fund account. Every Tarkington's employee with more than ten years' service has a pension fund account. And there's my Social Security. That will be more than enough."

"If it's any comfort to you, Daddy left you some money in his will."

Her eyes grow wide. "He *did*?" she gasps.

"Ten thousand dollars. I know that's not—"

"Ten thousand dollars!" she cries. "Why, that's more money than I've ever had at one time in my entire life! What in the world will I ever do with that much money?" There is a fresh burst of sobbing. "Oh, what a wonderful man he was, your father, what a wonderful, generous man. . . . I'll have to ask my brother-in-law to help invest it for me. He's a C.P.A."

Miranda is beginning to lose patience with this woman and her teary heartbrokenness. Here, after all, is a woman who always seemed to Miranda so coolly efficient and unemotional that she verged on iciness; her father's death has reduced this virginal automaton to a blubbering mass of woe. Here is a woman who has spent thirty-four years working in a store where women spend ten thousand dollars for a single dress without giving it a thought, and Pauline is treating this sum as though she has been handed the output of King Solomon's mines. "Come, come, Pauline," she says a little crossly. "Please try to pull yourself together." After all, she thinks, I am the one who should feel bereaved. She finds herself wishing her father had left this woman nothing at all, though she knows these thoughts are unworthy.

All her comment produces, however, is another freshet of tears.

"Look here," Miranda says. On impulse, she picks up the signed photograph of President and Mrs. Ford. "I want you to have this too."

"Oh, no, Miss Miranda! Not that! That was his most prized possession! That's a signed photograph of a living United States President! Do you realize how valuable that is? That's *priceless*, Miss Miranda!"

"I hardly think so," she says. "The Fords handed them out to everyone they met. But I'm going to make it even more valuable for you."

She slides the photograph out of its frame and, beneath the inscription (*To Silas Tarkington, with grateful good wishes, from Gerald and Betty Ford*), Miranda writes in her own hand, *Presented to Pauline O'Malley, devoted secretary to Silas Tarkington, with gratitude and affection by his daughter, Miranda.*

"There," she says, handing it to her with a flourish. "That gives the photo a bit of a history, as the art dealers say. Now, no more tears, okay?"

"Oh, Miss Miranda, I shouldn't accept this."

"But you will, right?"

Pauline reads the new inscription. " 'Devoted,' " she says. "Yes, that's right. I was devoted to him. I'd have laid down my life for him."

"And this too," Miranda says, and reaches for a paperweight that is particularly nice. "I want you to have this too, as a little personal remembrance. Look, it's even dated on the bottom: seventeen-eighty. Daddy was told that it once belonged to Catherine the Great of Russia." She presses the paperweight into Pauline's hand.

"But what would I ever do with it?"

"Just place it somewhere where it will catch the light."

Now there is yet another spell of weeping. "Oh, Miss Miranda. You've always been so kind to me. All your family. How can I ever thank you? My cup . . . my cup runneth over." When she has managed to compose herself again, she says, through her Kleenex, "Now, what about these? What shall we do with these?" She points to a line of books bound identically in dark blue leather bindings. "These are his diaries."

"Diaries? I didn't know he kept a diary."

"Well, they're not diaries really. They're date books, where he recorded his personal appointments. There's one for each year. They go way back to when he opened the store."

"Well, if they're personal, I think they should go to the farm."

Miranda starts plucking the books from the shelf and stacking them in an empty carton. Then an idea strikes her. She picks up the most recent volume and turns to the date he died, Saturday, August 12. The page contains only a single notation: *D.S.—11 a.m.*

She feels her heart sink. D.S. Diana Smith. So Tommy was right. He was planning to meet Smitty on the day he died.

She turns the pages backward, and a letter in its envelope falls out. It is addressed to him in what seems amateurish typing, and the envelope is marked *Personal/ Confidential.* Pauline is busy in another part of the room, so Miranda drops the letter quickly in her purse, to read later.

Then she remembers another date: June 1970. She runs her finger back along the books until she finds that year's volume and begins turning the pages for the month of June. There, scrawled across two dates—June 24 and 25—she finds the notation: *Boston, Ritz-Carlton, res. conf. #384–86J.*

She replaces the book in its proper sequence and continues packing the diaries in their carton.

Back in her own office, after she and Pauline have finished, Miranda cancels her luncheon date, pleading urgent family business. Instead of having lunch with an ad salesman from *The Times,* Miranda goes to the public library. She is not sure, exactly, what she is looking for, but she has found out that the library files copies of the *Boston Globe* on microfiche.

She takes her little spool of film to one of the projection machines and begins running through June 1970. When she gets to the twenty-fourth, she slows the film down and begins studying the newspaper page by page as it moves across her screen. She finds what she wants in the issue of June 25. It is not a big item.

MODEL, 19, PLUNGES TO
DEATH AT RITZ-CARLTON

A sometime model and actress, whom Boston police have identified as Christine Wandrous, 19, of South Braintree, either jumped or was pushed from a window of the Ritz-Carlton Hotel yesterday evening. Her body struck the sidewalk on the Arlington Street side of the building, opposite the Public Garden.

Miss Wandrous, a spokesman for the hotel said, was not a registered guest at the time, and elevator operators could not recall transporting the young woman to an upper floor. Although there was no immediate sign of foul play, neither was any suicide note found. A thorough police search of all guest rooms immediately above the site of her fall revealed no guests who had any knowledge of, or acquaintance with, Miss Wandrous, who most recently worked as a part-time model for Filene's.

A sister of Miss Wandrous, Mrs. Helen McCullough of South Braintree, was contacted by police. "Somebody had to have done this to her," Mrs. McCullough asserted. "She would never have committed suicide. She was a happy, healthy, beautiful girl, whose life was full of hope and promise."

Funeral arrangements will be made in South Braintree.

She flips through more editions of the paper, to see if there are any follow-up stories. She finds only one. It appeared two days later, buried in a back section of the paper:

AUTOPSY REVEALS MODEL
WHO PLUNGED TO DEATH AT
THE RITZ WAS PREGNANT

The Suffolk County Coroner's Office revealed that in an autopsy performed on the body of Christine Wandrous, 19, the part-time model and actress who plunged to her death from the Ritz-Carlton Hotel Wednesday evening, it was discovered that the young woman was pregnant. Assistant Coroner James J. Bailey said that Miss Wandrous appeared to be in the second trimester of her pregnancy. The sex of the fetus was undetermined.

A sister of Miss Wandrous, Mrs. Helen McCullough of South Braintree, told the Globe, "I had no idea that Christine was pregnant. But I'd noticed that she'd been terribly nervous and despondent in recent months. I could tell that something was deeply troubling her, and weighing on her mind. She would suddenly burst into tears for no apparent reason. I assumed it had something to do with her inability to find work."

Occupants of the hotel rooms and suites situated directly along Miss Wandrous's line of fall expressed no knowledge of the young woman, leading police to speculate that she may have jumped from the roof. But how she could have reached the hotel's roof is unclear, since access is possible only through the use of a specially magnetized key-card, supplied only to members of the hotel's maintenance staff.

A police investigation continues, with an interrogation of all hotel employees.

Well, a police investigation may have continued, but there is nothing about it in subsequent issues of the newspaper; Miranda runs the film through the next several weeks to be sure. The whole story seems to have been dropped.

Several things strike Miranda as odd about the story.

First is the girl's last name, Wandrous—like Gloria Wandrous in *BUtterfield 8*, whose party-girl career ends with her fall into the paddle wheel of a ferryboat. Was Gloria Wandrous pregnant too? Miranda can't remember. Then she thinks of the phrase "jumped or was pushed." If Christine Wandrous managed to enter an unoccupied hotel room and jump out, she would have left behind her an open window. If she had been pushed by a guest of the hotel, would the murderer have left the window open? No, he would have closed it, to make it appear she had fallen from the roof. Neither of the stories mentioned an open window, which would have been the first thing the police looked for.

But oddest of all is the way Mrs. Helen McCullough's description of her sister changed over the course of two days. First, Christine Wandrous is a happy, healthy, beautiful girl whose life is filled with hope and promise. Two days later, she is despondent, deeply troubled, bursting into unexplained crying jags at the drop of a hat: unemployed, pregnant out of wedlock, suicidal. At least Miranda's father appears to have nothing to do with the tragedy, beyond the coincidence that he happened to be in Boston and staying at the Ritz-Carlton when it occurred.

Deciding that she has been pursuing a red herring, Miranda rewinds the tape and snaps off the machine.

Now, in the back seat of the Rolls with Billings at the wheel, Miranda is being driven out to Old Westbury. Beside her on the seat, as well as on the floor and in the front seat beside Billings, are packed cartons. Still more are in the car's trunk. Each carton is labeled as to its contents. She is still thinking of her mother's words that night: "I'm talking about June nineteen-seventy! . . . I'm talking about Boston and the Ritz-Carlton Hotel!"

And her father's reply: "Moe Minskoff worked that one out for me."

But her afternoon in the library has provided no clues as to what it all means.

Then, suddenly, she remembers the letter that fell out
of her father's date book. She opens her purse, reaches for
the letter, and shakes it out of its envelope.

It is a very short letter, typewritten on a single sheet
of plain white notepaper without a letterhead, and it has
the look of having been typed in great haste. She reads:

My darling—

Our long talk this morning has made this the
happiest day of my life. This is my promise to you:
We'll leave that horrible old, boring, nagging *hag*
behind—forever—and let me become the kind of
new wife you've always deserved, one who loves
you beyond measure, and then all the heartache I
have endured for these past years—loving you un-
bearably, but knowing that I could not have you,
all of you, all to myself, as I have so longed to do,
my dearest—seems worthwhile. I have made our
reservations at the Princess, and Bermuda should be
lovely at this time of year. I am walking on air,
hardly able to wait until Saturday, when I will be
all yours, and you at last will be *all mine.*

The letter is signed, *With all my love, the soon-to-be
new Mrs. Silas Tarkington.*

She is stunned. She feels as though she has been dealt
a blow to the center of her stomach. She reads the letter
once more, her hands shaking. She looks at the postmark.
It was mailed in Manhattan. Then, all at once, she recog-
nizes something else. She presses her nose into the fold of
the letter, and there it is, unmistakably: the scent of Equipage. This is the letter Tommy told her about. Everything
he told her was true.

Her temples are pounding, her breath feels short, and
she feels almost physically nauseated. On the day he died,
her father was planning to leave her mother and the family he professed to care so much about and not only run

off with Smitty to Bermuda—of all the cliché places—but also to marry her. *Oh, Daddy, Daddy,* she thinks, *how could you have wanted to do such a thing to us?* She tears the letter into tiny shreds, rolls down the window, and scatters the pieces into the wind from the speeding car.

Billings, glancing at her in his rearview mirror, senses that something is wrong. "Are you all right, ma'am?" he asks her.

"Yes, I'm fine."

Her next reaction is rage—total, absolute, and unadulterated fury—not so much at Smitty as at her father. What had happened to her gutsy father? How could he have allowed himself to be reduced to such a state of groveling servitude, to have become so *besotted* with this woman, to use Tommy's word? How could he allow this woman—or any woman, for that matter—to get him to promise to give *all of himself* to her? How could he allow this woman—any woman—to speak of her beautiful mother, his wife for almost thirty years, in such a trashily bitchy way? Had Smitty managed to castrate him? Had he become suddenly senile? This was not the father she knew at all! All at once her father the man has become her father the wimp. All at once she has nothing but contempt for him. If this was the way he planned to treat his family, Miranda is almost happy that he is dead.

Her next wave of feelings are of total confusion and disorientation, as Miranda asks herself how she can ever face her mother again, how she can ever look her mother straight in the eye again, without having to tell her mother the truth.

Unless, of course, her mother already knows.

Her mother greets her in the entrance hall with a little kiss. She is looking lovely, as always, relaxed from her massage and rested from her nap, wearing a long hostess gown of pale blue chiffon, belted with three silver chains that tinkle as she moves. Billings is taking the car around to the garage, where the cartons of her father's things are to be stored temporarily. "Darling, come into the drawing room and meet our other dinner guests," her mother says. Miranda was hoping to have a serious discussion with her mother tonight, without anger or recriminations, but apparently this is not to be. Some sort of party is going on.

"Do I need to change?" she whispers.

"Darling, you look perfect," her mother says.

They enter the drawing room together, and two young men, both in black tie, rise from their chairs. One is fair, the other dark. One looks familiar, the other does not. "Darling, you remember Mr. David Hockaday from the Metropolitan Museum," her mother says. "And this is Mr. Peter Turner, who is interested in writing a book about your father. Is it a book? Something, anyway. Mr. Turner, this is my daughter, Miranda."

She shakes hands with the two young men. "Though we've never met, I feel I know you, Miss Tarkington," the darker of the two says. "I saw you once when you came down to visit your brother at Yale. Blazer and I were both in Calhoun."

"Oh, yes . . . I remember now. It was in the fall of Blazer's sophomore year. Mother and I had driven up from New York. You were standing in the quad."

"You really remember that?"

"Certainly. You were wearing a red shirt."

"You know something—I think I *was*!"

"Mr. Hockaday has come to look at your father's art collection," her mother says. "I thought that made sense, since most of it is here, scattered about the house. The only important piece in this room is the Gauguin over the fireplace."

Mr. Hockaday's eyes travel to the Gauguin, and he steps closer to it. "I hadn't noticed it," he says. "Forgive me."

"I understand it's an early piece, before Gauguin went to Tahiti," Connie says.

Milliken appears to take drink orders and then to pass hors d'oeuvres.

"Tell me how your husband assembled his collection,

Mrs. Tarkington," Mr. Hockaday says. "Did he work through any particular dealers?"

"Oh, no," Connie says. "He didn't trust dealers. He read in a book somewhere that people like Duveen often got Bernard Berenson to falsify the authorship and provenance of paintings in order to make sales."

"That's true," he says. "Did he buy from galleries and auction houses, then—Sotheby's, Christie's?"

"Never. He didn't trust the auction houses either. He bought only from private collectors."

"He didn't want there to be any publicity about what he bought," Miranda says. "That was another reason why he never went to auctions."

"But I assume he did turn to one or more art experts before making his purchases," Mr. Hockaday says.

"Well, in recent years he often consulted with Diana Smith—the woman mentioned in his will—before making an acquisition."

"But you say she is not an art historian."

"No, but he admired Smitty's—taste. And before that he used to consult with Tommy Bonham."

"An art historian?"

"No. Tommy was—well, I believe he was a drama major in college."

"I see," he says. "Very interesting."

"And even before Tommy—you see, my husband began his collection long before he and I ever met—he often made purchases through his friend Moses Minskoff. But always from private collectors."

"Ah," David Hockaday says. "Moses Minskoff. The name rings a definite bell. A European, isn't he? Based in Paris? An expert on the Fauvists?"

"No," Miranda's mother says. "I think you must be thinking of someone else. This Moses Minskoff is—" She turns to her daughter. "How would you describe Moe Minskoff, Miranda?" she asks.

"Moe Minskoff is a financial person," Miranda says.

"I see," he says. "Very interesting. I look forward to seeing the full collection."

"You will, after dinner," her mother says.

"I take it that you yourself have very little interest in art, Mrs. Tarkington."

She laughs her tinkly laugh. "None at all, I'm afraid, though I think some of the paintings are awfully pretty. My favorite is the Monet water lilies, which is in the New York apartment. No, my interests are gardening and music. My late husband's art collecting was something he did strictly on his own. It was his principal hobby, and I stayed out of it completely."

Milliken appears at the doorway. "Dinner is served, ma'am," he says.

During dinner, Miranda's mother keeps the conversation bright and lively with her usual skill, shifting her attention back and forth between her two male guests. "We must all try to remember our favorite stories about your father," she says to Miranda. "To help Mr. Turner with the story he's writing. Oh, I remember one: Doris Duke and her dogs. There's a rule about dogs in the store —I think it's a city ordinance, in fact. And one day several years ago my husband happened to see this woman strolling through the store with two borzois on a double leash. My husband was about to speak to her, when suddenly Jimmy, the doorman, came running up behind him and whispered, 'Mr. Si, that's *Doris Duke*!' Isn't that funny? Jimmy the doorman recognized Doris Duke, and my husband didn't. He'd been about to ask Miss Duke to leave the store. He often told that story on himself, so you see he had a sense of humor. . . . What else, Miranda?"

"Well, when I was nine years old, he persuaded American Airlines to let me pilot a seven-twenty-seven between New York and Washington."

"Miranda, Mr. Turner wants to hear stories about how your father ran the *store*—not stories about airplanes!"

"Well, there was one client in Florida who used to keep dresses for months and months and then return them for credit." She eyes her mother. "Is that a suitable story?"

"Mrs. Curtis LeMosney?" Peter Turner says.

"Yes. She's dead now, so you can use her name if you

want to. Once it got into the papers, and my husband was terribly embarrassed. It happened dozens and dozens of times. We always knew the clothes had been worn. She'd return them with wine stains, lipstick—"

"But she always was given credit."

"Yes, and each time she returned a dress for credit, she bought something else. And she always paid her bills on time. So what she had was kind of a revolving credit line."

"Do you remember Mrs. LeMosney's fingernail, Mother?"

"Oh, yes, tell that story, Miranda!"

"Well, Mrs. LeMosney had these very long fingernails. They were sort of her trademark, and she always painted the undersides of her nails too—bright red, as red as the shirt you were wearing that day, Mr. Turner—"

"How can you remember that? It was at least ten years ago!"

"Anyway, she was terribly proud of her fingernails. And one day she was in the store, trying on some things, and Daddy was helping her, and suddenly from the dressing room came this blood-curdling scream. The little dressing room maid came running out, crying, 'Mr. Si! Mr. Si! It's Mrs. LeMosney!' Well, Daddy naturally thought she'd died in there or something—she was well over eighty at the time, and Daddy was always worried that one of his—well, that one of his less youthful ladies would die in the store. So he went rushing into the dressing room, certain that Mrs. LeMosney had literally shopped until she dropped. There stood Mrs. LeMosney in her bra and half slip, in tears, staring at her left hand. 'I've broken a fingernail!' she sobbed. Well, the first thing Daddy did was to call Pauline and have her make an appointment with a manicurist to try to repair the damage—with a false nail or whatever. And after Mrs. LeMosney had gone off to the manicurist's, still in tears, Daddy went back to the dressing room. Crawling around the floor on his hands and knees, he found the broken-off nail in the carpet. He had the nail embedded in the center of a Lucite cube as a paperweight, and he had the cube inscribed *Left Index Fingernail of Audrey LeMosney, Broken at Tarkington's Fifth Avenue, September 23, 1983* and had it gift-wrapped and sent to her."

"For Christmas. He sent it to her for Christmas."

"And speaking of Christmas, do you remember my terrible Christmas, Mother?"

"I do indeed. You were a very naughty girl. Tell that story, Miranda."

"I must have been five or six—"

"Five and a half."

"And it was Christmas Day, and we were spending it in the apartment over the store. That morning, I'd opened all my presents, and by ten o'clock or so I was bored with them all, so I went downstairs to the store, which of course was closed. In the middle of the center aisle on the street floor, the display department had set up this magnificent Christmas tree. It seemed at least twenty feet high—"

"Well, perhaps not quite. The ceiling is only eighteen."

"It seemed that tall to me. Anyway, it was covered with candy canes and tinsel and popcorn balls, and underneath it were all sorts of packages, beautifully wrapped in different colored papers, tied in gorgeous ribbons and bows—big packages, little packages, packages of all shapes and sizes. I suddenly got it in my head that this was a Christmas tree my parents had forgotten about and that all these packages were more Christmas presents for me, so I started tearing open the packages—there were hundreds of them. Of course each one I ripped open turned out to be nothing but an empty box, but I kept at it, thinking that at least some of them had to contain gifts for me. I don't know where the store's security staff was while I was doing this—maybe in the basement, having a cup of Christmas cheer. But when I'd opened every gift box and found them all empty, I started on the candy canes and popcorn balls. They turned out to be made of papier-mâché, but I kept pulling them off the tree, anyway—as high up as I could reach—hoping to find a real one. I was in a gift-getting frenzy!

"Well, when somebody finally came to look for me, I was mad as hell. I was crying, stamping my feet, and saying, 'There's nothing here for me!' When my parents saw what I had done, something told me that they were not pleased."

"It was the most godawful mess," her mother says. "Your father was furious."

"Naturally. That display was supposed to stay on the floor until after New Year's. The store was going to open the next morning. Someone was going to have to rebuild the whole thing. I was miserable. I wasn't just miserable for myself, but I was miserable because I soon realized all the trouble I was causing everybody else. Cyril Marx was still director of display then, and he had to leave his Christmas dinner on Staten Island and come in to supervise. So did two of his assistants. Everybody was in the basement, rewrapping boxes. Even Daddy helped."

"So did I," her mother says.

"I could tell how furious everybody was with me— people muttering, 'Damn little kid, damn little brat.' People worked halfway through the night, trying to find new candy canes and popcorn balls that hadn't had bites taken out of them. I knew that my own Christmas was ruined and that I'd ruined Christmas for a lot of other people as well.

"Well, while all this work and cleanup was going on, I guess my father realized how miserable I was. I'd been sent to my room, but suddenly my father came in and said, 'Come downstairs with me, Miranda.' As I went down in the elevator with him I thought I was going to be in for more punishment. The mess around the tree had been cleaned up, but there was one gift box under it, wrapped in—I remember—gold paper, with a red ribbon. 'There's one package you forgot to open, Miranda,' he said. 'It's for you. Go ahead, open it.' I opened it, and inside was the most beautiful French doll I'd ever seen, wearing white lace. I still have that doll. I don't know where he managed to find it, on Christmas Day, with all the stores closed—"

"Actually, I think it was a display piece," her mother says. "But it was an antique doll. It was a pretty doll."

"And so, it was probably the worst Christmas of my entire life. But it was also one of the best. It was certainly a Christmas I'll never forget." She feels her eyes mist over, remembering it. "God, I was a rotten little kid, wasn't I, Mother?"

"No, just a normally active five-year-old," her mother says. "Angry as your father was, he realized that."

There is a silence around the dinner table now.

"And what about his philanthropies?" Miranda says suddenly. "There was a little old lady on West End Avenue whom he used to take care of—"

Her mother clears her throat and makes a face. "Let's not go into that, Miranda," she says. "She caused us a lot of trouble. She died about five years ago, thank goodness!"

"What sort of trouble, Mother?"

"She became very—demanding. Let's just say that some of your father's charities backfired." And Miranda decides that the little old lady on West End Avenue cannot have been her long-lost grandmother, now living in Florida, after all.

There is another brief silence, and then Peter Turner says, "How did you and Mr. Tarkington meet, Mrs. Tarkington?"

"Meet? Oh, that's an amusing story too. It was my twenty-first birthday, and my father had given me a check for a thousand dollars. That was quite a lot of money in those days, and my father said, 'Bobolink'—he called my two sisters and me his bobolinks—'Bobolink, I'm giving you this only on condition that you buy yourself something pretty at Tarkington's.'" She breaks off, and her face grows pensive. "The day Si died was also my birthday. Funny coincidence, isn't it? Two birthday presents. The day I found him, and the day I lost him. . . .

"Anyway, I came into the store, and who should come up to greet me but the owner himself? I was terribly impressed. 'May I show you some of our things, Miss

Banning?' he said. Goodness, I thought. The great Silas Tarkington himself was waiting on little me."

"Well, you were pretty well-known even then, Mother. Three years earlier, you'd been named Debutante of the Year. Your picture had been in *Life* magazine."

"Yes, but later I found out that Fa had set up the whole thing in advance. Fa—that's what we called my father—had phoned Silas Tarkington and told him I was coming in. It was part of the birthday present, getting the owner himself to greet me at the door and wait on me personally. But I was certainly impressed. And later, when I had decided on a dress—it was a white piqué short summer evening dress, by Dior, with red and yellow tulips appliquéd on it—he said to me, 'May I tell you that you are one of the most beautiful women who have ever set foot inside my store?' And naturally that impressed me too. Later I found out that he said that to every first-time client. But at the time I was most definitely impressed. Oh, yes." She touches the corner of her napkin to the corner of her eye. "Shall we take our coffee in the next room?"

Once the foursome has moved into the sun room for coffee, Miranda's mother says, "Now, Mr. Hockaday, why don't you just wander through the house and look at the collection? You have the complete catalogue from Mr. Kohlberg's office, and you'll find paintings in nearly every room. Just wander through the house and take your time. . . . Miranda, darling, why don't you read Mr. Turner's cards? Find out if he's a suitable biographer for your father."

"Would you like me to, Mr. Turner?" she asks him. "Among my other talents, I'm an excellent tarot reader—or diviner, as we say in the fortune-telling business."

"Please call me Peter. Can you really do that? Tell my fortune?"

"Absolutely. It's one of the more important things I learned at Sarah Lawrence. In Psychics One-oh-one."

"Please do it," he says eagerly.

She fetches the tarot pack from a drawer in the card

table. "Come sit beside me," she says. "Now, first I have
to select your significator card. This will be the card that
represents *you*." She studies his face. "Since you have
dark brown hair and eyes and are a young man, your
significator card will be the Knight of Cups. You see, even
though this method of divination was devised by the ancient Celts, it's very scientific. Remember that it was the
ancient Celts who built Stonehenge, by which they predicted the solstices and the phases of the moon." She
makes a droll face. "This means that everything I say
about you will be absolutely true." She winks at him,
removes the Knight of Cups from the deck, and places it
face upward on the table.

"I'm really amazed that you remember me from
Yale," he says. "Out of five thousand students."

"It was your red shirt," she says. "It was fire-engine
red. And you were—well, sort of staring at me."

"Yes, I guess I was."

"Now, I want you to shuffle the cards three times,
very carefully, and while you're shuffling them, I want
you to think hard, really concentrate, on any question
you want answered or any problem you want solved.
. . . Now cut the cards into three piles, away from your
heart, to your left. . . . Now give me the leftmost pile."
She begins to lay out her tableau. "This first card covers
you. This card represents the general atmosphere surrounding the problem, or the question you want answered. . . . The atmosphere is favorable, as indicated
by the Sun. . . . You will attain your personal goals.
. . . And now the Hanged Man, in this quadrant, is another favorable sign. It suggests that you are introspec-
tive, spiritual, willing to make sacrifices. . . . I believe
the question you have asked concerns a young woman.
Am I correct?"

"You're right!"

Miranda's mother picks up her needlepoint, the cover
she is making for her tennis racket.

"This is unusual," Miranda continues. "All the Major Arcana have fallen in this quadrant. One day you will

be very famous. That is, your name will be known, but not your face. . . ."

Presently, Mr. Hockaday returns. "Mrs. Tarkington, I wonder if I could have a word with you in private?" The expression on his face is grave.

She hesitates, starts to rise, then sits again. "No, I think you can say whatever you have to say to me in front of Miranda and Mr. Turner. After all, Mr. Turner has been promised that we'll hold nothing back about my late husband."

"I don't quite know how to put this to you, Mrs. Tarkington," he begins. "But I'm afraid your late husband was—or whoever advised him on his purchases was —well, it was the Gauguin in the drawing room that first aroused my suspicion."

Her needlework falls briefly into her lap, but she picks it up again and quickly draws another pale blue thread through her canvas, completing a stitch. "Is it a fake?" she asks.

"I'm afraid so, yes."

"The Vuillard?"

"Also."

"The three Cézannes?"

He nods.

"The Van Gogh sunflowers?"

He nods again.

"The Utrillos?"

"Yes."

"The Hoppers and the Bentons?"

"Yes."

"All of it?"

"All."

"I see," she says.

"These are high-quality copies, Mrs. Tarkington. But —copies, I'm sorry to say."

There is a silence, and then Miranda hears her mother say, "Well, that, I suppose, is that. It's rather like Miranda's empty Christmas boxes, isn't it?"

Miranda, who has been staring hard at the tableau of

cards spread out in front of her, reaches out now and squeezes her mother's hand, and their eyes lock briefly.

"You mentioned a Monet water lilies, Mrs. Tarkington."

"Yes. That's in the apartment in the city."

"I'd like to have a look at that too."

"Certainly," she says. And then, quickly, "No! I don't want to know."

"I think I'd better go now, Mrs. Tarkington."

"No. You haven't had your coffee. After she finishes with Mr. Turner, Miranda will want to read your cards. She's very clever. Do you take cream?"

"Now here in the King of Pentacles," Miranda says, touching the cards with her fingertips, moving from one column to the next. "He is a very strong figure in your life. Pentacles and Swords dominate. . . ."

And now Miranda is alone in the sun room. It is almost midnight, and she is not thinking about love, exactly, though love is a part of it. The two male dinner guests have departed, and her mother has said good night and made her way up to her bedroom.

"Will you be spending the night here, dear?" her mother asked her from the doorway.

"Would you like me to, Mother?"

"Whatever you like."

"Well, if it's okay with you, I think I'll borrow the station wagon and drive back to the city. After all, tomorrow is another working day."

"Oh, dear, I hate to hear you say that."

"Why? I do have a job to do."

"The store, the store. It's always the store. It's dominated our lives. But soon we'll be rid of it."

"No!" she said sharply. "The store is part mine now, and I'm going to keep it."

"Miranda, such foolishness—"

"What would you have me do instead, Mother? Sit

on my fanny for the rest of my life, doing nothing—like you?"

Her mother turned on her heel, the silver chains at her waist tinkling as she did so. "Well, if you change your mind and decide to stay, just let Milliken know and Margaret will turn down your bed for you." Then she was gone.

Miranda sat alone for a while, her thoughts racing, sipping what remained of her coffee. The coffee was cold, but she sipped it anyway. Her mother was a riddle that seemed to have no answer. She decided to make one more attempt at making peace, so she tiptoed up the stairs and down the hall to her mother's room.

Her mother's door was partway open, and her mother lay across the bed, propped up by many white lacy pillows, her face masked in a mud pack, her hair in its net. At the foot of the bed sat Margaret, who was massaging a cream called PrettiFeet between her mother's toes. In her mud pack with its tiny slits for her eyes, nostrils, and mouth, Miranda's mother looked both pitiful and comic—mummified and yet alive—and Miranda had to stifle an urge to laugh.

"Is that you, Miranda?" her mother said. "Did you change your mind?" Her mother's voice was hollow, for it was difficult to speak behind the pack. Any movement of her facial muscles tended to crack the drying mud. The mud smelled of cordite. At this point in her evening toilette, Consuelo's bedroom smelled of a mixture of Guerlain and brimstone, Shalimar and sulfur.

"I'm sorry, Mother. I didn't mean to snap at you," she said. "It was just that you took Mr. Hockaday's terrible news so—calmly. But then you always seem to take bad news calmly. I wish I could learn to do that."

"I'm not thinking of the paintings," her mother said in the same hollow voice, trying not to move her lips. "I'm thinking of poor Smitty."

"Poor *Smitty*?"

"Yes. She's been named special curator of an art collection that apparently doesn't exist. Never did exist."

"I think Smitty is getting exactly what she deserves!"

"Oh, no," her mother said. "Not this—not this, on top of everything else."

Miranda felt herself about to lose her temper once more, but she refused to let that happen, so she simply said, "Well, I'm off. Good night, Mother." And she turned and ran down the stairs.

And yet here she still is, in the quiet sun room at Flying Horse Farm. The house is asleep. She should be in the station wagon by now—its keys hang on a little board just inside the kitchen door—driving down the express-way toward Manhattan, speeding toward 11 East 66th Street and her comfortable apartment and her quiet bed. Outside, the garden is dark, for there is no moon. Some-where in the invisible distance is her mother's Dell Gar-den, with its deep lake and the moon-gate footbridge running across it, where she and Blazer fed the swarming fish and he had warned her to beware of the phonies.

"These are high-quality copies, Mrs. Tarkington. But copies, I'm sorry to say."

The house is sleeping, but suddenly it is full of voices.

"Actually, it was a display piece. But it was an an-tique doll. It was a pretty doll."

And so there is another illusion shattered—the pic-ture of her father, bundled up against the winter cold and snow, trudging through empty streets of closed and shut-tered shops in search of a special gift that would in some way salvage, at least in part, a little girl's unhappy Christ-mas. All he had done was go down to the basement Dis-play Department and pick out an item from its carefully boxed, catalogued, and numbered contents. From the shelves of dismembered mannequins, the boxes of orna-ments and trimmings and artificial foliage, he had found a doll with a china head and moving eyes wearing a white lace nightie.

"You have to be very cynical in this business," her father had said to her—yes, it was right in this room—when she was desperately trying to persuade him to give her a job in the store. "You're not cynical enough, Mi-

randa. This is a business for gamblers, high rollers. I don't
see you as a born gambler. Everything about designer apparel is in the roll of the dice. I've often compared retailing to show business, but, believe me, retailing is even
riskier. A true gambler gets as much of a thrill out of
losing as he does out of winning. That's what gamblers
call 'heart,' but a gambler's heart is hard and his blood is
cold. I don't see you as a hard-hearted, cold-blooded person. You're not tough enough for this business. You're
soft, you're feminine, you're easily hurt and easily disappointed. Cynicism is what you lack, knowing that you're
either going to win or lose, and that winning is all a matter of luck, of chance."

"Just give *me* that chance, Daddy," she said.

On the card table, the tarot cards are still spread in a
fan shape, face down. If I'm going to place my faith in
luck and chance, she thinks, I might as well place a little
of my faith in magic too. *Think hard, really concentrate,
on any question you want answered or any problem you
want solved.* She thinks hard, and the question comes.

It is: *Who am I?* She picks a card at random and
turns it face up. It is the High Priestess.

Interesting. The High Priestess is the most powerful
female court figure in the deck. She symbolizes wisdom
and secret influence. She is also a figure of mystery and a
certain ambiguity. She wears a strange headdress—an orb
with antlers, signifying her ability to rule and also to fight
for what she wants. A blue robe cascades from her head
and shoulders and falls across her knees and feet like a
freshet of spring water, denoting fluidity and an ability to
compromise. Behind her grow palm and pomegranate
trees, and in the far distance, on a hill, stands a castle—
riches. The face of the High Priestess stares directly and
serenely at Miranda. Studying that face, Miranda thinks,
I am that loosely draped lady, she is me. See how surely
and squarely she sits, chin tilted upward, resolute, proud,
secure in her world, unafraid of the future. See how she
seems to be spreading her wings, prepared to fly, borne by
the wind. She is me. Oh! She is me.

Who am I? I am not my father's soft and easily hurt

and disappointed daughter. I am not his little china doll. I am tough and I am strong and I am cynical and also flexible, and flexibility was not exactly your strong suit, Daddy dear, and I am going to show them all how strong and tough and cynical yet flexible I can be. Oh, yes.

Of course there is another side to the High Priestess that reveals itself when the card is held upside down. She also symbolizes love, marriage, motherhood, relatedness, sexual passion, and supportiveness of friends and family, and suddenly, Miranda has another revelation. *I will gather up the pieces of this fragmented family and put them together again.* I will find my long-lost grandmother and the Aunt Simma I never knew I had. I will bring back Blazer, too, and even his mother. That is all a part of my destiny, according to this little card. She feels a sudden rush—a rush of adrenaline almost like a burst of sexual excitement—as she contemplates all that she has suddenly been assigned to do.

Everything my father broke, I will mend.

I will even let myself fall in love again, for love is just another of the tools with which one builds a life.

Impulsively, she turns over another card, and there he is, the Magician, who denotes the power to turn mere ideas into action, to turn dreams into reality, to translate promises into deeds. He is Tommy Bonham, who has offered to help her. Of course.

In the distance, the hall clock strikes twelve, and still Miranda stays at the card table, studying the esoteric symbols in her hand.

It is the memory of that little gesture of Miranda's—reaching out from that magic card table to touch her mother's hand—and the look of a deeply shared intimacy that seemed to pass between the two women, that Peter Turner has carried home with him. Earlier, he had sensed a certain tension between them. But in that brief gesture they became a mother and a daughter.

Talk about grace under pressure, he thinks. Both women demonstrated that rare asset tonight. Considering the pressures they both must have been under during these past few days, he is even more impressed. Miranda is beginning to see the whole fabric of her father's life, that he had stitched together as elaborately as a needle-point design, fly apart before her eyes, he thinks. How much more will come?

As he slides his long legs between the cool sheets of his narrow bed at the Dakota, he also thinks, She noticed me standing there that day in the quad outside Calhoun. She remembers my red shirt. I remember her fiery mane of chestnut hair.

He turns out the light and, with a little sigh, realizes that tonight he has managed to fall in love with Miranda Tarkington.

Again.

From *The New York Times*, August 18, 1991:

87 KILLED, HUNDREDS INJURED
AT EAST ST. LOUIS ROCK EVENT

Many Listed as Critical After
Fans Storm Stadium Entrance

EAST ST. LOUIS, ILL., Aug. 17—At least 87 people, most of them teenagers, lay dead last night as thousands of screaming fans stormed a single narrow entrance to the Riverside Stadium in this impoverished and predominantly black city to hear a concert by the Hot Jockers, a popular heavy metal rock group. At least 300 others were admitted to local hospitals with injuries, many of them critical. The basement of the A.M.E. Church here was turned into a temporary morgue, as distraught families stood in long lines to identify their dead.

The concert, scheduled for 8 P.M. yesterday evening, was sold out, according to its promoter, Milton Prokesch, 47, and thousands of young people had gathered outside the stadium waiting to get inside. When, by 8:15, the gates failed to open, the crowd grew noticeably restless, and police officers with nightsticks attempted to restore order. And when, inexplicably, only one of the twelve gates was unlocked at 8:25, the crowd of impatient fans rushed toward this single entrance, less than ten feet wide. In the ensuing stampede, many young people were crushed to death under the feet of others, while still others appeared to have died from suffocation. By the time order was restored, many trampled and mangled bodies had literally to be scraped off the surrounding streets and sidewalks, and at least one mother, Mrs. Lula Barner, 26, was only able to identify her teenage son by the color of the sneakers he was wearing. A full list of the deceased is as yet incomplete.

The seating capacity of the stadium is 70,000, but police estimated the crowd outside was considerably larger than this. It is speculated that many of the rock group's fans intended to hear the concert from outside the open-air arena, though many of the dead still clutched valid tickets in their hands. East St. Louis Fire Commissioner Julio G. Gomez, 56, insisted today that the event could not have been oversold. "This office regulates these matters very carefully," Commissioner Gomez stated. "We were on top of the situation in every sense of the word. What happened here last night certainly should not have happened, but it did. It is too bad, but no one is really to blame. It was more like an act of God."

"Kids' Own Fault"

Commissioner Gomez did suggest, however, that the use of alcohol and drugs might have been a contributing factor to the slaughter. While drugs and alcohol are prohibited within the stadium proper, "There is no way of controlling the use of these substances outside the gates," he said. Arriving quickly at the scene of the carnage, Commissioner Gomez pointed to the numbers of crushed beer cans, broken bottles, and at least one shattered hypodermic syringe that lay among the corpses and the bodies of the injured. "There's your villain," he announced, brandishing the twisted needle for photographers. "The kids like to get high before these concerts. When they get high on a controlled substance, they tend to act in an irrational and antisocial manner. In some ways, this was those kids' own fault. This department expresses sympathy to their nearest and dearest."

The concert's promoter, Mr. Prokesch, conceded that the concert may have been overbooked "by one or two seats." This, he said, is customary procedure, "just as our finest and safest airline companies deliberately overbook seats," to allow for no-shows. He added that seating at the concert was so-called festival style, a common arrangement at such events, whereby the best seats are available on a first-come basis. When the doors open, there is often a sudden surge on the audience's part for the seats closest to the stage and the performers.

As to why only one of twelve gates was unlocked to admit a capacity audience, Mr. Prokesch had no explanation. "You'll have to ask the stadium's management about that one," he said. "All I do is hire the hall. I wasn't even at the stadium when it happened. I was having dinner in my hotel suite across the river. I first learned about it on television."

The stadium is owned by the City of East St. Louis but is managed by a concessionaire, Halcyon Entertainments, Inc. Calls to Halcyon Entertainments were referred to the office of East St. Louis Mayor Clarence M. Thomas, who is no relation to the Supreme Court nominee, and calls to Mayor Thomas's office were referred to Fire Commissioner Gomez.

Meanwhile, Sonny Lemontina, 21, the Hot Jockers' lead guitarist, said he and his group, still backstage when the mob first surged toward the stadium entrance, were unaware that anything unusual was taking place. The sounds of police and ambulance sirens rushing to the scene and the screams of the injured and dying were apparently drowned out by the group's own amplifiers, and the group itself did not learn of the tragedy until after their performance ended. "I thought we just had your normal, happy audience," Mr. Lemontina said. "They gave us three encores. We're all real, real sorry that there were people got killed."

11

Mrs. Consuelo Tarkington (interview taped 8/17/91)

I can't really say I'm surprised that the art collection turned out to be fakes. I'm disappointed, of course—for my late husband's sake, and poor Smitty's. But the people who advised him, and the people he bought from—they were simply not experts. They knew nothing about art, and neither did he, but then neither did I, which was why I stayed out of it. Whenever Si bought a painting, I'd say how pretty it was and help him hang it, but that was it. Collecting was his hobby, not mine.

Thank God Mr. Hockaday didn't come back to us the other night and say some of the paintings were stolen! I don't know why, but that was my greatest fear, that some of the pieces might have been stolen from other collections and fenced to my husband. You see, when I learned that someone like Moses Minskoff had acted as his agent—but never mind. It doesn't matter now. At least Mr. Hockaday didn't say anything about stolen paintings, and now we're done with him, thank God. I must say I didn't care for Mr. Hockaday.

When I married my husband, I made only one promise to myself: No matter what happened, I was going to be Silas Tarkington's final wife. Not just his second wife but his final one. I knew there had been other women in his life, and there probably always would be. People don't change. A wife can't change her husband; she's foolish if she tries. My father taught me that. My father was a rather old-fashioned mid-Victorian man. He said it was in a man's nature to have a roving eye, and if that happened, as it probably would, I was not to mind. "Remember, Bobolink, there has never been a divorce in this family," he said to me, "and there must never be. And so, if you marry this man, you are marrying him for life, for better or for worse, from this day forward, as long as you both shall live." I promised him that, and I kept my promise.

No, I won't say that Si's and mine was a happy marriage. What does the phrase mean, anyway? Are there any happy marriages? Perhaps, but I don't know of any. My sisters certainly don't have happy marriages. They have successful marriages, which is not the same as happy. In many ways, I consider myself the luckiest of the three, because I loved my husband, though love isn't a happy state. Love is a matter of constant compromise and sacrifice, and in any sacrifice there's bound to be anger, bitterness, and resentment. Love is a matter of adapting your needs to the needs of the person you love, and this is never easy, but it must be done. Miranda gets very angry with me when I talk like this, but I've lived longer than she has, and I know it's true. Let the feminists say what they want. It's still a man's world.

How did I adapt my needs to his? In many ways. He was in the designer apparel business, running a fashionable women's store. Therefore, I had to be fashionable. That was where his first wife had let him down. By refusing to be fashionable, she was hurting his business, and his business meant everything to him. He told me once that he liked me because I had class, so it was up to me to maintain that class, to fit the image of his classy store.

It wasn't easy. It's not easy to get on the Best-Dressed List, and it's even harder to stay on once you're there. It's all politics; it's like running for President of the United States every year, and almost as expensive. There's a committee and all sorts of other people you have to be nice to and pay court to—designers, fashion writers, photographers—people you otherwise wouldn't notice. But my husband wanted me to be on the list, for the store's sake, and so I went to work on it. It's all about publicity, so in the beginning I hired a P.R. man. But it can't be just any P.R. person. Ideally, it should be someone who also represents at least one major designer, a couple of other ambitious women, and a fashionable restaurant. Then the P.R. person arranges for his lady clients to meet for lunch at his restaurant, wearing his designer's clothes. Then he arranges for someone from *Women's Wear* to photograph everyone going in or out of the restaurant. The designer then publicizes the women, the women publicize the designer, and the designer and the women publicize the restaurant. Everybody publicizes everybody else.

After I learned the ropes, I was able to dispense with the publicist, but in the beginning he was indispensible—and, I was told, tax-deductible—even though I didn't always enjoy the things he had me do.

As I think I told you, my main interests are music and gardening. The Westbury Garden Club has been after me for years to join, and the town of Manhasset has been struggling to start its own symphony orchestra and has begged me to be on the board. But I couldn't afford to do either of those things. Not visible enough. Not high-profile enough. I was told to go on the board of New York Children's Hospital because it has the biggest, splashiest, highest-profile fund-raiser of the year.

I hate hospitals. People die in hospitals. I've visited enough people in hospitals to know I never want to be in one. But what did I do? I agreed to chair the committee for the hospital benefit. I've done that now for nine years. For months ahead, I traipse around Manhattan, hat in hand, begging for underwriters. Any successful charity event should be completely underwritten. I call on retailers and corporate executives, begging them to advertise in the program. I go begging to Seagram's to get them to donate the liquor and wines. I beg Mobil to donate the flowers, someone else to pay for the music, someone else to pay the cost of the room. I hit up designers for gifts for the raffle, and people like Estée Lauder to give the items for the goody bags that have to be at each place setting. Oh, those goody bags! People will kill for them! I once had the idea that, at each table, there would be a little X symbol under one of the chairs, and the person who had the X-marked chair would get to take home the table's floral centerpiece. Two Social Register women got into a hair-pulling fight because one of them claimed that the X had been under her original chair, but she'd changed places during dinner. A fight over a centerpiece! I'd tell you who these women were, but they're too well known.

Sometimes I envy Margaret, my maid. She gets to sit home with a tuna sandwich and watch her afternoon soaps. She has a favorite, called *Another World,* that goes on at two. But every weekday I'm busy at that hour being visible with my lunch ladies—either Tarkington's clients, or potential Tarkington's clients, or what I call my committee ladies. So I'm never home at two o'clock, and I've never seen a single episode of *Another World.* Margaret tells me the plots. Will Felicia find her long-lost daughter? Will Olivia give Marley the baby? Who put the chain around the baby's neck before it was given up for adoption? Will Marley let Iris raise the baby? It all sounds so much more interesting than what I get to talk about at Le Cirque or Grenouille.

You see, I no sooner finish putting on one year's hospital ball than it's time to start planning next year's. There's much more to it than just selling ad space in the program, finding sponsors and underwriters, and getting freebie bottles of perfume for the goody bags. After that's all done, you have the problem of what the French call *le placement.* Everybody who's had anything to do with the evening wants to be *bien placé.* Even the hairdressers nowadays expect to be seated at the best tables, and if they're not they have their ways of getting revenge, believe me. Planning the seating for a party like that can take months, working with big charts laid out on the floor and pushing around little slips of paper. Mrs. A won't sit at a table with Mrs. B and wants to sit at Mrs. C's table and so on. You try to keep everybody happy, but you just can't keep everybody happy. A lot of people are going to be unhappy, no matter what you do. And who are they angriest at? Me, the chairwoman! I spend my life making enemies. I chair the hospital ball in order to make people hate me. And those who don't hate me are jealous of me. The other day on the street a woman recognized me, and I heard her say, "That's Consuelo Tarkington. I wish I had her money!" How does that make me feel? Wounded. Unappreciated. And through it all, I always have to be perfectly dressed, perfectly groomed, every hair in place, because I've got my place on the Best-Dressed List to keep, and the competition out there is unrelenting. Voracious! Waiting for me to make a mistake, hoping to make me slip a notch on that damned list! Does this sound like a happy life to you, Mr. Turner? It's a miserable life. Sometimes at night, after a particularly awful day, I go home and cry myself to sleep.

But I've done it, and I never complained to my husband. And why did I do it? Because it was what he needed and what he wanted. I did it because I loved him and was determined that no other woman would ever take him away from me, because I was determined to do what I did better than any other woman could. And so I did what I had to do—for the man I married.

A happy marriage? No, but a *successful* one, because it lasted.

Miranda doesn't understand any of this, that marriage is *work,* hard work, not fun.

Miranda takes after her father. Si was essentially a simple man, an uncomplicated man, by which I mean there were no deep, hidden facets to his personality and psyche. Oh, he had secrets, of course. His age. His background. His family. Things he never liked to talk about. His mother, for instance, is still living. She's a very old lady now, living in a nursing home in Florida. His sister, Simma, also lives in Florida. These were secret relatives, and I've never met either of them, but now that he's dead

I see no reason to keep those secrets any longer, do you? If you like, I can tell you how to get in touch with them. They might have something to say about his background, his early days, and why—before I met Si—his mother and sister became . . . estranged. I imagine it had something to do with money. It usually does, in families. I never asked, because he didn't want me to know.

That was another thing he trusted me to do—not to ask too many questions about matters he found unpleasant. You see, he had a very trusting nature, my husband. Sometimes, he was too trusting; I guess the art collection is an example of that. When people betrayed him, or disappointed him, or let him down, he couldn't understand it. When this happened, he usually just dropped those people, but some people were hard to drop, and that made his life difficult.

I tried not to complain about how hard I worked for him and for his store—at work I hated—because that would have been letting him down. Oh, I'm not saying I never got angry with him, never nagged. I'd be lying if I said that. I did my share of ranting at him, but mostly it was when I felt he was being too trustful and other people were taking advantage of him. I hated to see people taking advantage of him, and of course he hated it when I pointed out that this was happening. I tried to protect him from those people, but, as my own father warned me, most men don't like to feel smothered by a protective woman, and they hate it even more when they know they need to be protected. That's when we'd have our blowups.

Thank God for the farm! If it weren't for the farm, I don't know what I would have done. On weekends at the farm, I could relax, let down my hair, shake all the cobwebs out of my mind, be by myself with my own thoughts, and stop worrying for a little while about how good a job I was doing at being Mrs. Silas Tarkington. At the farm, I could wear jeans and sneakers and a big floppy hat. I could walk in the woods, or supervise the planting of a crab-apple tree, or just sit on the bridge in my Dell Garden and feed my fish. Fish have no problems, except being fed. They're even more relaxing to watch than the daytime soaps. They have babies too, but they don't worry about putting them up for adoption.

But still, at the farm, I couldn't do that all the time. Si didn't like seeing me in jeans and sneakers and a big floppy hat all that much. At the farm, there were still house guests to entertain, parties to give, parties to go to. For those, I would still have to be *on,* still have to be Mrs. Silas Tarkington, the perfect wife, the perfect hostess. Sometimes I wonder what I would have done with my life if I hadn't married Si. Not very much, I suppose. He was my life.

That's why I think I've been so lucky. He gave me something to do, something to really work at. And look —I won! I was his final wife. Nobody was able to take him away from me . . . until God did.

Not even Smitty, bless her poor heart.

12

Over the years, a great deal has been written about Consuelo Tarkington's beauty. "The Beauteous Bannings," as they were called in their debutante years were also described as "heiresses to an Old Guard Philadelphia Main Line fortune." This has always struck Consuelo as amusing.

True, she and her sisters grew up on the Main Line and attended proper Main Line day and boarding schools. And, true, their father, George F. Banning, was a prosperous Philadelphia lawyer, with some Old Guard Main Line clients, at least one of whom George Banning had saved from going to the federal penitentiary for tax evasion. But George Banning was born in San Francisco, where his father ran a hardware store. And Consuelo's mother, née Nielsen, was from Minneapolis, where the Nielsens were regarded as part of that city's Dumb Swede population. Did that make the Bannings Old Guard Philadelphia Main Line? Connie herself thought not. "Where does the press get this stuff?" she used to ask her husband.

"Never correct the press," he used to say to her, "if

you want to keep the press your friend. Besides, the fewer hard facts the media know about you, the better off you are. Always."

And he didn't mind reading that he was married to an Old Guard Main Line heiress. How grand that sounded!

The press elevated all three Banning sisters into the firmament of Philadelphia's aristocracy. George Banning managed—with help from that blue-blooded client who really should have gone to jail—to get his three daughters presented at the Philadelphia Assembly, very definitely an Old Guard Main Line affair. And all three had gone on to make "brilliant" marriages, which was to say marriages to very rich men, which was precisely what their father wanted for them.

From the time they were very little girls, George Banning taught his daughters how to make their way, as women, in the world. They were taught how to perform a deep curtsy, of course, but they were also taught how to enter rooms. They were taught how to smile and how to accept a compliment. ("Thank you.") They were taught how to cross their legs, ankle on ankle, when seated. ("Knee on knee causes the calf to bulge ungracefully.") They were taught to speak in richly soft, cultivated voices. He taught them to dance, and he taught them to flirt. All three became expert flirts, which probably persuaded men to think them prettier than they actually were. Flirtation is not an art taught to young women of today's generation, perhaps, but it was taught to the Banning sisters by George Banning himself.

They called him Fa and he called them his bobolinks, and long before they were old enough to have any interest in boys, he would gather the little girls on his lap in his big study chair and give them lessons on how to deal with the opposite sex.

"Bobolinks," he would say, "always remember that when a young man calls to pick you up for a dance or a dinner date, you should make him wait for you a little bit. That's very important—the little wait. When he rings your doorbell, never come running down the stairs, ready to go, even if you are. Make him wait for a few minutes. That makes it much more exciting for him when you finally appear. Now remember, Bobolinks, most young gentlemen are not good conversation-starters, so it becomes the young lady's duty to start the conversation. That's why it's important to find out, ahead of time, what the young gentleman's interests are. If he happens to be interested in baseball, you can start the conversation by saying, 'Wasn't that an exciting White Sox game on Saturday?' After the conversation's started, though, you should let him do most of the talking. There's nothing that impresses a gentleman more than a lady who's a good listener. That's why it's important to ask him questions about what interests him. For instance, with this baseball chap you might say, 'I love baseball, but I've never understood what constitutes an inning.' Then let him explain to you what an inning is, even if you already know. Gentlemen enjoy explaining things to ladies. They do *not* enjoy ladies who seem to know all the answers. They do not enjoy that *at all*. Then, while he's explaining whatever it is to you, you should look him straight in the eye, as though what he's telling you is the most interesting thing in the world to you, even if it isn't."

"Is it important to be pretty, Fa?"

"No, Bobolinks," he said firmly, "it is not. But it *is* important to be attractive. If a gentleman finds you attractive, he will also find you pretty. What do I mean by attractive? Do you remember what I told you about attractiveness?"

"A gentleman is attracted to a lady if she makes him feel witty, worldly, wonderful, and wise."

"Correct. The four W's. Very important. That's why, when a gentleman says something to a lady that he thinks is witty, she should always laugh politely, even if she doesn't find what he said particularly funny. Not a loud laugh, of course. Just a soft, polite laugh. Remember Mr. Shakespeare: 'Her voice was ever soft, gentle, and low, an excellent thing in woman.' Now, unfortunately, some young men are mashers. Do you remember what I told you about mashers?"

"A masher is a man who likes cheap women, Fa."

"That is correct. Since well-brought-up young ladies are not cheap women, you must treat the masher very carefully. Here are some of the things a masher may try to do. In the theater, on a streetcar, or in an automobile, a masher may try to put his arm around your shoulders. Simply reach up and remove his arm. On the dance floor, the masher may let his hand drop below your waist. Simply reach behind you and move his hand up where it belongs. In the theater, he may rest his knee against yours. Simply withdraw your knee. If he persists, just reach out and tap his knee sharply with your fingertip, like this." He demonstrated the tap on each of his daughters' kneecaps, and the girls giggled. "A masher may try to tickle you," he said. "Do not let him."

The little girls squealed. "Tickle us, Fa!"

And so he tickled them, tickling the backs of their legs, under their chins, between their shoulder blades, until the three girls were shrieking with wild laughter.

"Now that's enough," he said at last. "But just remember that only your Fa has tickling privileges with his Bobolinks.

"Now here's another important thing to remember. A time may come when you will find yourself at a party with a young man who has had too much to drink. If you should happen to sense this has happened—if you see his eyes begin to roll, or if he seems unsteady on his feet—you must simply leave the party. Do not say good night to your escort. Do not even tell him you are leaving. Just find someone else to take you home or telephone for a taxicab. When the young man discovers you have left, he will be so ashamed of himself that he will telephone you in the morning, and apologize, and beg you for another date. Do not give that to him right away. Make him call you a second time, or even a third.

"Remember, Bobolinks, what I told you about accepting a date from a young gentleman you have not dated before. The first time he asks you out, tell him you're sorry but you're busy, even if you're not. The second time he asks you, tell him you'll think about it. The third time he asks you, it will be proper to accept, if you wish to do so. The point is, you want a young man to keep coming back . . . coming back . . . again and again. A gentleman finds a lady *particularly* attractive if she is hard to get, so never let him think you are easy to get. If a young lady is too easy to get, a gentleman finds her unattractive in the end and will lose interest in her.

"Of course, this is all while you are waiting to decide which man you intend to marry. Once you are married, you will become your husband's property and you must do what he tells you to—love, honor, and obey. Is that clear, Bobolinks?"

"Yes, Fa."

And, quaint though these lectures sound today—and there was a great deal more in this vein—the three Banning sisters learned their lessons well. They adored their father. They thought him the wisest man in the world, as well as the handsomest and the kindest and of course the best.

Consuelo Banning Tarkington used to try to pass on some of her father's wisdom to her own daughter, Miranda, but it fell on deaf ears. She wouldn't listen then, and she'll certainly never listen now.

What is the secret of raising children in today's world? Dressing for dinner, Consuelo Tarkington consults her mirror for the answer.

13

Miranda Tarkington (interview taped 8/19/91)

My mother jumped on me when I tried to tell you this story the other night at the farm. I don't know why. Maybe she thinks it's too childish a story. But I think it illustrates the special feeling I had about my father when I was growing up. Why I loved him so.

In 1976, when I was nine years old, my father and I flew down to Washington, D.C., together. This was to be a very important mission. A few days earlier, a secretary from the White House had phoned the store to say that Mrs. Betty Ford, the First Lady, would like to look at clothes for a state visit that she and the President would be making to France, and in the belly of the jet was a whole wardrobe carton filled with designer dresses, shoes, bags, and accessories for the First Lady's consideration.

Jackie Kennedy had been dressed exclusively by Oleg Cassini when she was in the White House. She didn't become a Tarkington's client till after. Incidentally, that reminds me of a little selling trick my father used to use. He'd have an important client in his office, and he'd have

Pauline telephone him from the outer office. He'd say, "Yes, Mrs. Onassis. . . . Yes, we have a new shipment of those little tops you like so much. . . . We have it in moss green, in shell pink, in pumpkin, in tobacco, and in navy. . . . You'd like one in each color? Certainly, Mrs. Onassis." By the time he hung up on this phony order, the customer's eyes would be popping out of her head. She'd say, *"Let me see those little tops!"*

My mother probably wouldn't like me telling that story, either, because it was—well, I suppose a little bit deceptive. But it used to make me laugh.

Anyway, back to Mrs. Ford. Daddy used to complain that there hadn't been a stylish woman in the White House since Jackie. But then Mrs. Ford went on a diet and slimmed down to a size six, and Daddy had been dropping hints that she might consider shopping at his store. And so, when that call came, he was thrilled, and naturally he decided to accompany his merchandise and show it to her personally.

The airline had been notified of the significance of this trip, because the cargo handlers needed to be alerted to the special nature of this big packing box. God forbid that any of the garments should arrive damaged by grappling hooks or even the slightest bit out of press. A Secret Service man had even helped supervise the packing, in case someone tried to slip a bomb into the yards and yards of pink tissue paper.

Why my father took me on this sales trip, I had no idea at the time. Later, I learned he had said, "I understand the Fords are a very family-oriented couple. So I think bringing Miranda along would be a nice touch—to show them I'm a family man." Even then, my mother and I were being used as window dressing for Daddy's store—not that I minded in the slightest.

Daddy was terribly excited, particularly since these were clothes that were to be worn in Paris. "We'll show those French fashion snobs what American designers are all about!" he said.

I was excited too. All my classmates at Brearley were green with envy that I was going to the White House. So were my teachers. I was going to write a special report on my visit and deliver it in front of the entire school when I got back. Oh, I was Little Miss Important, believe me! I was even going to get to wear a little light lipstick, which was taboo in the fourth grade. My mother says being envied makes her feel sad. It didn't make *me* sad. I loved it!

Beforehand, my mother tutored me carefully on how to greet the First Lady. "No curtsy, just a handshake and a nice smile. Remember, a smile is in the eyes, not the mouth. Just say, 'How do you do, Mrs. Ford. How very nice of you to let me come.' Then, while she looks at the garments, you just sit there, with your hands folded in your lap and your legs crossed at the ankle. Don't speak to her unless she speaks to you, and if she should speak to you, answer as politely as possible. First impressions are most important, Miranda."

Then my mother and I had a dress rehearsal for the visit, with Mother standing in for Betty Ford. "How do you do, Miranda," Mother said.

"How do you do, Mrs. Ford. How very nice of you to let me come."

My mother held an imaginary garment at her shoulders in front of an imaginary mirror, turning this way and that. "What do *you* think of this dress, Miranda?" she asked.

"I think you would look lovely in it, Mrs. Ford," I said.

My mother clapped her hands. "Perfect!" she said.

And of course my mother selected my clothes with great care, rejecting outfit after outfit. "You must look like a Tarkington's woman," she said, though the store didn't have a children's department. Finally, she settled on a white cotton blouse with a yellow ribbon at the throat, a yellow pleated skirt with a matching bolero top, blue low-heeled shoes, and a yellow straw hat with a blue ribbon down the back. "A lady visiting the White House during the daytime should always be hatted," she explained. "In the evening, never." Where did she come up with these rules? I wondered. I'd never worn a hat before, and it was my first pair of pantyhose.

I modeled my White House clothes for her. "Oh, you look just like a little yellow tulip," she said, clapping her hands again. "You're really an awfully pretty little girl, you know."

She'd never told me that before, and it impressed me. Come to think of it, she never told me again.

So my father and I sat beside each other in the first class section of the big plane. He didn't seem to be nervous, but I knew he was, and I certainly was, at least a little. I concentrated on keeping my hands folded in my lap.

We'd been in the air for about ten minutes, and the seat belt sign had been turned off, when my father summoned the stewardess. I remember she was a young black woman with hair so shiny and pulled back so tightly across her head that it looked as though it had been painted on. It looked like trompe l'oeil hair. "I'd like to visit the captain in the cockpit," my father said.

"I'm sorry, sir, but F.A.A. regulations do not permit passengers to visit the flight deck while the aircraft is in air operations," she said.

My father reached in his pocket. "Please give the captain my card," he said, and handed it to her.

"Certainly, sir."

My father winked at me. "We'll have some fun with her," he whispered.

Well, she was back in a flash, all smiles, saying, "Mr. Tarkington, Captain Brown has invited you to join him for a few minutes on the flight deck. Is this your little girl? Perhaps she'd enjoy visiting the flight deck, too. Please follow me, sir."

And so we went forward to the flight deck, where we met the captain, the first officer, and the flight engineer, who explained what the hundreds of little dials and knobs and buttons and switches on the control panel meant and how they worked. "We're delighted to have you on board, Mr. Tarkington," the captain said. "I've been assured that your cargo went on board intact and will receive priority care when we get to Washington National."

"Now that my daughter has had her first flying lesson," my father said, "perhaps she'd like to take over the controls of the aircraft for a few minutes. Would you like that, Miranda?"

Well, the captain looked a little nervous at this suggestion, but the next thing I knew he was unbuckling his seat belt and strapping me into the pilot's seat.

Now, I'm quite sure I was not really *flying the plane*. But my hands were on the stick, or whatever it's called, and it certainly *felt* as though I were flying it. I'm sure the first officer was fully in control of things, and the captain was right over my shoulder, in case I pushed a button that would send the plane into a nose dive or something. But there I was—in the captain's seat!

Later, back in first class, my father said, "Well, what do you think of that, young lady? You were flying this seven-twenty-seven. That'll be something to tell your friends at school, won't it?"

"Yes!" I gasped. I'd already decided that this was going to be the highlight of the essay I was going to write for school. To heck with meeting the wife of the President of the United States!

At the airport gate, we were met by reporters and photographers. This was what Daddy called "trickle-down" publicity, and it was the kind he liked best. The store hadn't needed to publicize this special White House visit. American Airlines had done it for them. The next morning, there would be stories with headlines like: FIFTH AVE. FASHION STORE COMES TO WHITE HOUSE VIA AMERICAN AIRLINES.

"No photographs of me, please," my father said, holding up his hand and stepping to one side. "But you may photograph my daughter, Miranda."

And so Little Miss Important posed at the door of the plane and, later, with the big carton of dresses as it was being carried out by four uniformed baggage handlers.

"Open up the carton!" one of the photographers said. "Let's see the dresses!"

"Not until Mrs. Ford has made her choices," I said, somehow knowing this was the right thing to say.

Everything that happened later on that trip seemed like an anticlimax to me, after flying the plane. My father and I were driven to the White House in a limousine, with another one following us with the dresses. We were ushered into the executive mansion and upstairs to the family's private living quarters. I watched as Mrs. Ford examined seams and necklines. She'd had a mastectomy, I found out later, so nothing could be too low-cut or too short-sleeved, and my father had borne that in mind. She tried on a number of the dresses and ended up with four for evening and five for daytime, and she asked to keep one or two other pieces to decide on later.

"What do you think of this one, Miranda?" the First Lady asked me.

"I think you look lovely in it, Mrs. Ford," I said, just as my mother had taught me.

After she'd made her selections, Mrs. Ford took us both on a short guided tour of the White House, including Lincoln's bedroom. And at one point the President himself stepped into the room and introduced himself, and I shook his hand. As we left, my father and I were each given envelopes embossed with the White House crest, and in each was a signed photograph of the President and Mrs. Ford. Mine, which I still have, was inscribed *To Miranda—fondly, Betty Ford.*

Finally, before heading back to the airport, my father, who was just in the greatest mood, asked our driver to give me a quick tour of some of Washington's most famous sights—the Washington Monument, the Lincoln and Jefferson memorials, the Capitol building, the Supreme Court building, the Smithsonian, and so on.

But nothing in Washington quite matched the thrill when I'd had the actual controls of an American Airlines jet right in my hands. Sometimes I wonder, What would the other passengers have thought if they'd known that their plane—for a few seconds—was in the hands of a fourth-grader from the Brearley School? To this day, the thought makes me smile. And what nine-year-old girl could fail to adore a magic father who, with the flip of a calling card, could manage to bring about miracles like that?

My mother, on the other hand, was not amused. "You are not to use that airplane story in your essay," she said. "I will not allow it. That was a very foolish, childish thing your father did. The pilot could lose his license."

Well, maybe that was part of it. But mostly I think my mother doesn't like that story because it is about how my father liked to show off his power. She was always uncomfortable about the show-offy things he did, like Billings in his knee breeches and patent leather boots, and the mink lap robe in the back seat of the Rolls. Those show-offy things embarrassed her.

But the show-offy things she disliked were the things I loved most about him. To me, his store was a magic place, and he was the magician. Whenever the Magician comes up in the tarot pack I think of my father, the symbol of the power to translate ideas into action. To me, my father was the Wizard of Oz. Oh, I know the Wizard of Oz turns out to be a sham in the end, and maybe my father was a bit of a sham too. But even the sham wizard had his heart in the right place, and so did my father—most of the time, at least.

I don't think I'll ever really understand my mother. She always seems just a little bit too—well, too self-absorbed. She's the only person I know who refuses to talk on the telephone in the morning until after she's brushed and flossed her teeth—as though the person on the other end of the line might detect her morning breath. I'm sure she's told you how hard she works for the annual hospital ball, and she does work hard, and it's always a big fundraiser and a beautiful party. But it always seems to me that she works much harder on herself, maintaining her famous beauty.

Over the years, I've studied my mother's face, both in photographs and in the flesh, and tried to pinpoint what her secret is. The flaws and imperfections of her face seem pretty obvious. Her lips are a little too thin, her nose a little too sharply aquiline, her jawline is a little too wide, and her chin is a little too pointy. But then there are those big blue eyes, those high cheekbones, that luminous skin, the pale hair, and that long Modigliani neck—and somehow all the disparate elements of her features come together as a kind of work of art.

Then there's her posture; I think that has something to do with it. She's tall—five-eight, taller than my father was—but there's none of the awkwardness that's often associated with tall women. She stands and sits perfectly, and there's an almost catlike grace about the way she moves. The act of rising from a chair, for instance, which is perhaps the most difficult movement for a woman to perform gracefully, she seems to do like an act of levitation. She just seems to float upward. She can accomplish the same trick from a seated position on the floor, rising in a single, fast, fluid motion. "It's all a question of balance—balance from the shoulders downward," she once explained to me. "You have to think of your shoulders as being attached to your belly button." Well *I* can't think of my shoulders as being attached to my belly button! Watching her rise from a chair or come down a staircase, I sometimes think my mother could balance a lighted candle on the top of her head without spilling a drop of wax or causing the flame to flicker.

At fifty, she naturally pays a lot of attention to what she calls "my war paint." But she's so skillful at applying makeup that she seems to be wearing none at all, except lipstick to add fullness to her lips and, if you look closely, just the faintest trace of pale brown eyeshadow on her upper lids. This isn't an easy look to achieve, believe me. It takes time and skill in front of that lighted four-way mirror on her dressing table. But there's more to it than that. My mother works on her beauty even while she sleeps.

Here's the way her daily routine goes, at least on weekdays when she's in the city. Her day begins at eight in the morning when Margaret, her maid, taps on her bedroom door and comes in to open the curtains and place her breakfast tray beside her on the bed. The contents of this tray are always the same: a cup of plain yogurt, half a grapefruit, a coffee cup and a pot of black coffee, and the morning's mail and newspapers. While Margaret arranges all the little lacy pillows behind Mother's back and shoulders, Mother removes her sleep mask and unties the gauzy hair net that has kept her hair, in big rollers, in place for the night. A box of Kleenex and a bowl of cotton puffs are always placed beside her bed, and, while Margaret draws the bath in the room next door Mother removes the night creams from her face and throat, using many tissues. I once suggested to her that she should buy stock in Kimberly-Clark because she must be their biggest Kleenex customer.

Then, while Mother eats her grapefruit and sips her coffee—into which she spoons a dollop of yogurt—she and Margaret go over the menus for the day, if any meals are to be taken at home. If not, they'll discuss the latest plot developments on *Another World,* a soap that Margaret watches every afternoon and that Mother enjoys hearing about vicariously.

Now the tub will be filled and bubbling with Guerlain salts and bath gel. Margaret disappears with the breakfast tray, and Mother slips out of her nightie, ties a towel, turban-style, about her hair in its rollers, and steps into the tub. She likes a long bath, and there are all sorts of little scrubs and sponges on the bath tray with special uses—for between her toes, behind her ears, for her face and breasts and underarms. At last she rises from the tub, wraps herself in an oversize bath towel, and steps to the washstand, where Margaret will have placed a bucket of ice cubes. Mother presses ice cubes all over her face and throat, then pats herself dry with more tissues. Then, using a French toothpaste that's supposed to add pinkness to the gumline, she scrubs and flosses her teeth for exactly five minutes.

Then, changing to a dressing gown, she goes to her dressing table in the bedroom and sits down to apply her makeup, beginning with moisturizers for her face, arms, and hands. No one can do this for her. She must do it herself—outlining and filling in the lip gloss just so, patting her face with many tiny sponges and badger brushes. This takes another forty-five minutes or so.

By now, it is nine-thirty. The store won't have opened yet, so this is the best time for a hairdresser to arrive from the salon downstairs to remove the rollers from Mother's hair and give her a comb-out. When he finishes this, it will be ten o'clock.

Now, still in her dressing gown, she will go to her desk. Here she will glance briefly through the newspapers and open her mail.

At least another hour must be allowed for the next process, since Mother believes in answering every letter on the day that it's received—in an almost illegible handwriting, I might add. Tommy Bonham, who's an amateur graphologist, once joked that he couldn't possibly analyze Mother's handwriting—which is full of wild hooks and crazy downstrokes and little wedges for punctuation— because he couldn't read what she had written. Mother says it doesn't matter whether her letters are legible or not. It's the thought that counts. This hour is also spent making and receiving her morning telephone calls. Everyone who knows my mother knows she's never available on the phone before 10 A.M.

By eleven o'clock, it's time for her to go into her closets and select what she'll wear for lunch. This also is a lengthy and complicated process. Every padded hanger in her closet is tagged and numbered and color-coded so that every garment there can be coordinated and accessorized with shoes, scarves, bags, jewelry. Also, there are elaborate charts showing which outfits she wore with which friends, at which occasions, and at which restaurants, so she will never be seen to duplicate herself. By twelve-fifteen, she's ready to go downstairs, looking radiant and smelling of Shalimar, where Milliken will offer her a glass of chilled *champagne de pêche,* her only alcoholic beverage of the day. On the tray with the wine will be her vitamin, calcium, and iron pills. Mother insists that vitamins are much more effective when washed down with a bit of the bubbly. Milliken will receive his instructions for the balance of the day, and Billings will be outside with the car to drive her to lunch.

Okay, now cut to the chase. Lunch! This is the most important part of my mother's day. This is when she does her so-called work. You've heard of the Ladies Who Lunch. My mother invented them, long before there was such a phrase. Her lunches are either with her various committee heads or with designers she's trying to wangle out of goodies for party favors or door prizes or raffle prizes or silent-auction items or whatever. This latter part can't be very hard to do, because all the designers want to be on Tarkington's good side.

In any case, these lunches are always at least two-hour affairs. God knows what they talk about. Eating, incidentally, has nothing to do with it. My mother doesn't really *eat lunch*—oh, maybe a couple of asparagus spears or a bit of grilled fish. And did I tell you that my mother always times her lunch dates so she arrives exactly five minutes late? That's so she can make her *entrance,* which is so *important*!

Have you heard enough details of my mother's arduous day? Well, there's more. On Tuesday and Thursday afternoons, at three o'clock, her masseur arrives at the apartment to give her a full body and facial massage. This is a two-hour ordeal. On Mondays, Wednesdays, and Fridays, these hours are spent with her personal trainer, who supervises her exercises on the rowing machine, the stairclimbing machine, the stationary bicycle, and the other pieces of Nautilus equipment in the exercise room. The masseur is for skin and muscle tone. The personal trainer is to avoid measurement problems at all costs. After these sessions, Mother likes to take a half-hour nap. After the nap, there's a second, shorter bath, and after the bath the whole moisturizing-makeup process begins again. If she's dining out, as she often is, the hairdresser from downstairs arrives at six to shampoo and set her hair. While her hair is drying under the big professional hair dryer that she keeps in her dressing room, Margaret will lay out the clothes Mother has selected for the evening. From shampoo to comb-out takes about an hour and a half.

When the evening's over—and Mother likes to be home no later than eleven fifteen—an even more elaborate routine begins. First, if she's been entertained at someone else's house, she'll sit down at her desk, before doing anything else, and write her hostess an illegible thank-you note. These notes, she insists, should be no less than a page and a half of notepaper in length and should include glowing comments on the food, the décor, the hostess's appearance, and the brilliance of the other company. Some people even claim to be able to read these notes. Billings will then take the thank-you note directly to the post office so that, with luck, it will be delivered to the hostess in the next day's mail. Or, if the hostess is a neighbor, Milliken will hand-deliver the note the following morning, accompanying it with a long-stemmed rose.

Now, with her bread-and-butter duty done, Mother will begin to prepare herself for bed. I've often sat with her in her bedroom while she undressed, as she moved about, taking those light, quick steps, between her closets, dressing room, bedroom, and bath, chatting away about the details of the evening, reappearing in a succession of garments as she went. Wasn't it Mary Poppins who astonished the children with the way she could put on her nightgown first and then remove her street clothes from underneath the nightgown? Mother's changing-for-bed act is something like that. She'll vanish into a closet in a ball gown. Then she'll reappear in a slip or teddy. She'll disappear again and return in a long dressing gown. She'll disappear *again* and reemerge in a nightie and fluffy peignoir. Then the peignoir gets replaced with a bed jacket. These changes are so quick that they seem to be done with mirrors, and the result of this sleight of hand is that I've never in my life seen my mother naked or in anything more revealing than a swimsuit.

Now it's time for her to put her hair up on the big rollers and to tie the rollers in place with netting. Then she removes her makeup with creams and more tissues. Soap, Georgette Klinger tells her, must never touch a woman's face. Every night, on her dressing table, Margaret places two halves of a lemon in saucers and, while

Mother works on her face, she rests her elbows in the lemon halves to bleach them. With the makeup off, more groceries appear: cucumber slices. She pats the cucumber slices all over her face and throat. Next come the various night-working creams, some for the forehead, some for the earlobes, some for the lips. There are also special night creams for the elbows, the knees, the arms, and the legs, creams for the backs of the hands, creams for the palms, creams for the toes and the soles of the feet. Applying these creams takes at least half an hour, while the whole bedroom begins to smell of lemons and cucumbers and aloe and beeswax.

But once a week, usually Friday night, the room smells of brimstone. This is when she's applying her mud pack. This is no ordinary mud, mind you. Her masseur introduced her to this mud several years ago. It's imported from Israel, where it's scooped up from the bottom of the Dead Sea. It's the color of caviar, costs twice as much, and smells like rotten eggs. But the dried mud from the Dead Sea caves helped preserve the scrolls at Qumran for over two thousand years, didn't it? Just think of what it ought to do for a woman's face to help erase the tiny little lines of aging!

She spreads this mud in a thin layer all over her face and throat. Then must come a full facial mask of stretchy Ace bandage material to keep the mud in place while it dries for an hour. This mask has holes for the eyes, nose, and mouth, so my mother looks like an extraterrestrial, or a bandit in a ski mask about to hold up a bank. With the mask on, it's hard for her to talk because she can't move her lips without cracking the mud. When the mud is dry, the mask comes off, and the mud gets chipped away. Then come more night creams.

Then comes a glass of hot skim milk sipped through a bent hospital straw, and finally the sleep mask and the cold-cream-lined night gloves, and the long slender gloved hand reaching out, half blindly, to switch off the final lamp.

On weekends at the farm, the routine is a little less stringent, but there's still a routine. At the farm, she'll wash and set her own hair and do her own comb-outs. Instead of the trainer and the masseur, she'll play tennis, or walk in the woods, or work out on the machines in the gym in the pool house. Instead of a nap, she'll meditate on the bridge in her Dell Garden before bathing and dressing for dinner. After all, in Old Westbury there are still lunches and dinners to go to, and house guests to entertain.

All this she does in the name of Beauty. Beauty is in the eye of the beholder, they say, but what is in the eye that the beholder beholds? To me, my mother is a riddle.

There's another question I've often asked myself. Did my mother and father ever fuck? I guess they must have, at least once, as I guess I'm the living proof. But how did they accomplish that through all the masks, the creams, the nets and rollers, and the smelly Jewish mud? Was it any wonder that he took a mistress?

My mother often complains that I don't tell her enough about what's going on in my life. It's true, I don't. Because if I told her some of the things I'm doing she simply wouldn't understand. It's like she comes from a different planet. She doesn't understand why I want to run the store. I haven't told her about the marketing and business courses I'm taking at night at N.Y.U., because she wouldn't understand that either.

She couldn't understand why I didn't want to marry David Belknap, who was my last beau, if that's the word for it. What if I told her that David Belknap hit me? Would she have understood that?

David's an account executive with Merrill, Lynch. He makes a quarter of a million dollars a year, comes from a quote-unquote good family, and is good-looking in a Brooks Brotherish sort of way. To my mother, David seemed like Mr. Ideal for me.

David and I were pretty serious there for a while. At least we were living together, which I guess makes it serious. But things began to get unserious after about six months. You see, David wanted to marry me, move me to

Scarsdale, and start me having his babies. I wasn't at all sure I was ready for that, and I told him so, and we argued about it. But our final argument started over, of all things, the woman sommelier in a restaurant where we'd just had dinner.

"That was the only thing that spoiled the dinner for me," he said. "The lady wine steward."

"I thought the wine she suggested was excellent."

"Yeah, but women shouldn't be wine stewards," he said. "Wearing a black bow tie, a man's mess jacket, and a skirt—she looked ridiculous."

"Are you saying that women can't know as much about wines as men do, David?"

"There're just some things women shouldn't *do*," he said. "Wine stewarding is one of them. Being professional jockeys is another. Last week, on my flight to Atlanta, a woman's voice came over the loudspeaker and said, 'This is your captain speaking.' Everybody on the plane was scared shitless."

"You mean the men on the plane were scared shitless. The women on the plane would have felt very reassured."

"Person sitting next to me was a woman. She looked scared shitless."

"Hmm," I said. "I flew a Boeing seven-twenty-seven when I was nine years old."

"Aw, come *on*," he said. "I've heard that story. You didn't really fly that plane. But there's one thing a woman like you should do."

"What's that?"

"You should marry a guy like me and have a nice little baby."

"We've been through all this before," I said. "I haven't changed my mind."

"Even your mother thinks you should. Just the other day she said to me, 'When are you and Miranda—' "

I turned away from him. "I don't care what my mother thinks," I said.

"Don't you think I'm good enough husband material? And father material?"

"That has nothing to do with it, and you know it," I said. "It's because of my job, my career."

"Career? What kind of a career is that? Placing the same little ad in the same newspapers day after day. Some career you've got!"

That made me mad. "There's a lot more to it than that!" I said. "I'm working my way up in my father's business. Someday I'm going to run the store." It was the first time I'd told him that.

"Not if you marry me, you won't," he said. "You're going to have to choose between your so-called career— and me."

"Well, aren't *we* the Mr. Macho Man?" I said. "Aren't we Mr. Sexist Old World Husband? No women wine stewards! No women pilots! Join the twentieth century, David. This is nineteen ninety-one."

"Sorry, but that's the way I am, sweetheart," he said. "The girl I marry is going to be a *wife,* not some sort of career type. In *my* household, there's only going to be one breadwinner—me. The girl I marry is—"

"So now we're *girls,* are we? Really, David, you're beginning to sound like Stanley Kowalski."

"Well, what you see is what you get," he said, and a hard edge had crept into his voice. "And what you see is a guy who's ready to get married and start a family, because the girl I marry is going to start having babies *bing-bing-bing,* just like that."

"Babies!" I cried. "Well, you're looking at the wrong woman for that assignment. Maybe I'll have a baby someday, but I'm certainly not going to start having babies *bing-bing-bing,* just like that—not for you or for anybody else!"

"Take it or leave it," he said flatly. "You say you love me. If a woman loves a man, she has his babies."

"Well, I'll certainly leave it, if that's my choice. If all you want me for is to be a machine—a machine that turns out babies like so much sausage—go find yourself another sausage machine. Babies! First it was just *a baby,* singular. Now it's a whole nursery full! I happen to be advertising director of Tarkington's, with a brilliant career ahead of me, which doesn't include flopping around your house barefoot and pregnant all the time. Why do you want all these babies? So you can prove how much juice there is in that pathetic little sausage you seem to think is God's gift to women? So you can prove how masculine you are? So you can brag to the boys in the club locker room about how high your sperm count is?"

That was when he hit me, hard, across the face, with the back of his hand—a hand that had a heavy gold signet ring on it.

The blow sent me reeling into the sofa, and I sat there with my hand across my mouth. I remember that I just whispered, "You hit me!" just like that—more in wonder than in anger, because I'd never had a man hit me before. I looked at my hand, and it was covered with blood. The signet ring had split my bottom lip.

"You're damn right I did," he said, "and I'll do it again if you can't button that foul little mouth of yours, sweetheart!"

"You don't want a wife," I said, "you want a beautiful ornament to show off to your friends and customers. You want a whore. You want someone like—someone like my mother, who'll let a man walk all over her like a doormat and kick her when she disobeys. Well, I'm not like my mother!"

"Damn right. Your mother is a lady!"

"And if you're looking for something to kick around the house, buy a dog!"

"That," he said carefully, "is not such a bad idea, sweetheart," and he turned on his heel and started toward the door.

I stood up then. "David," I said in the sweetest voice I could muster, "please come back."

He hesitated, and then he turned and stepped toward me. He held out his arms and took me by the shoulders. Then he dipped one hand inside my blouse, and started to fondle my breast, and bent his face toward me to kiss my bloodied lip. "Now that's more like it," he said. "Now you're acting like my good little girl."

That was when I brought my knee up, hard, into his

groin. I'd never done that before to a man, but I'd read enough in romance novels as a kid to know it was something a woman could do to make a certain point, and it worked.

He howled and doubled over in pain, clutching at himself. "You fucking bitch!" he moaned.

"That," I said calmly, "is one of the sweetest things you've said to me in a long time, David. Now get out of here before I call security. Get out of here and don't come back."

That night, half waking from a crazy dream, I reached out across the big bed, half expecting to touch his shoulder with my hand. Then, fully awake, I realized he wasn't there, and wasn't ever going to be there again, and I opened my eyes wide in the darkness to find myself—triumphantly alone! I sat up in bed, then stood up and threw a robe across my shoulders. It happened to be his robe, but that fact only added to my sudden sense of triumph. Tying the robe's sash around my waist, I made my way through the darkened rooms of my apartment.

My apartment is on the twelfth floor, and it has a small terrace, and I stepped out onto the terrace and gripped the iron railing with both hands. I'd never had what I suppose you'd call an epiphany, but I knew I was having one now. The night was chilly, but the cold air felt good on my swollen lower lip, and the light breeze swirled the skirts of the long robe. I felt like Athena Nike in the Louvre. From my terrace there's a skinny view of Central Park and, across the park, a better view of the lights of the West Side. Everything—the wind, the park, the lights—seemed to be supporting me as I stood, with my wings spread, at the top of the Louvre's grand staircase, looking out and down. Through the trees, the lights of the West Side—the Dakota, the Majestic, the San Remo, all those grand old solid buildings in this city I love and know so well—they were twinkling for *me*. And I thought, *Oh, my city!* It was as though the lights bowed and returned my salute.

I made a solemn promise to the city, then, and to the lights. Never again, I told myself, never again will I let myself be pushed around by a man. Never again will I let myself be used like that, never, ever, as long as I live, as long as I have air to breathe, never will I let what happened to me with David Belknap happen again, ever, so help me God.

It was as though the lights of the city had witnessed my vow and were winking back their approval. And I knew, more surely than ever before, that someday I was going to run my father's store. The winking lights agreed. They signaled their assent. They would conspire to help me.

Of course David didn't come back. The next day, he sent a sheepish-looking friend of his around to collect his things. I made no attempt to hide my swollen lip, and I'm sure the friend knew what must have happened.

Of course, looking back, I wonder if I wasn't to blame for that particular quarrel. I certainly helped start it. I certainly could have helped stop it. Maybe the things I said were needlessly harsh and cruel. Unnecessary roughness, they call it in sports, and players get penalized for it. Maybe he was genuinely sorry for what he did. It doesn't really matter. A month later, I read that he'd become engaged to a pretty blonde from East Orange.

The only thing I know for sure is that I'd done something my famously beautiful, ladylike mother would never have done, and I'm proud of that.

Maybe I'm just not cut out to be partners with anyone. Maybe anything I do I'll have to do on my own. Maybe I'm just not designed to be . . . a partner.

But listen to me! Whatever you're writing is supposed to be about my father, and all I've been doing is talking about myself. It's not me you're interested in, is it? Is it?

I'll tell you one story about my parents that may interest you, because it shows the differences in their attitudes toward things. Neither one of them really approved of the fact that David Belknap and I were living together, though neither of them actually said anything about it. Not long after we broke up, my mother said to me, "When are you and that nice David going to get married, darling?" She was on her way out to one of her lunches, and she was checking in her purse for her keys and gloves.

"He hit me, Mother," I said.

"That's nice," she said. "It shows how much he cares about you, darling." Then she was out the door.

With my father, I tried a different approach. "David and I have broken up," I told him.

"Good," he said.

"He hit me."

"I may be old-fashioned," he said. "And I know that many young unmarried couples live together nowadays. But in your case, it just wasn't good for the store's image."

It was like—and I still remember this—when I brought home my first report card from Brearley. It was all A's, except for one B—in Citizenship, if I recall.

My father said, "You're going to have to work to bring that B up to an A, Miranda."

My mother said, "Remember, darling, that boys aren't attracted to girls who seem to be too smart."

So I'd pleased neither of them.

I remember thinking to myself, Doesn't anyone care about me but me?

Part Two

ROSE'S CHILDREN

14

Mrs. Rose Tarcher (interview taped 8/27/91)

Well, you're finally coming around to me, the one who finally knows something. If it hadn't been for me, there wouldn't have been any Silas Tarkington, because how can there be any son if you don't have a mother in the first place? Answer me that. It was I who started everything. Well, here it all is.

My husband, Abraham Tarcher, was born in 1888 in Bialystok, which was then in Russian Poland. If he was alive today, my Abe would be a hundred and three. Think of that. He was named after his grandfather, whose name was Avram Tarniskovsky, but Tarniskovsky was I guess too much for the immigration people and so it came out Tarcher on the official papers, and my Abe told me his parents were too scared of the authorities to try to change it back again to what it should have been, so they settled for Tarcher, the way it was on the papers.

My Abe had two sisters, one older and one younger. The older one was murdered. When he was only nine years old, my husband was forced to watch as his older sister was raped by a gang of Russian soldiers. After that, they cut her stomach open, and he was forced to watch that too. Think of it. He used to have nightmares about that, even years later, after he and I were married and our own children were growing up. His younger sister died earlier, from some childhood disease I think it was, so when the family came to America there were just the three of them, Abe and his parents. That was in 1902, when Abe was fourteen.

It was decided that he was too old to go to school—to start all over again in an American school, which would have meant going to first grade—so he started the way everybody else did in those days, with a pushcart on Hester Street. There were other streets on the Lower East Side, of course, but Hester Street was the main one. It was where everybody shopped. It was where all the pushcarts were. Sometimes you could hardly walk down Hester Street because of all the pushcarts. What you did was, you built your own. My Abe built his pushcart out of an old wooden crate and a set of old baby-buggy wheels he found in an alley. He started out selling borscht, which is a soup made with beets and sour milk that his mother made on her own stove. His mother was famous for her borscht. The secret was cow parsnips. She told me that after he and I were married. She boiled cow parsnips and added that to the beets. It was delicious, if I do say so. Anyway, he started with the borscht, and later he added fresh bagels, which his mother also baked in her own oven. Still later, he branched out into undershirts and buttons, and when I met him he was selling watches, ladies' and gentlemen's watches. Nice watches, too. Anyway, that was Hester Street.

I have a good title for your book, if you want one: "From Hester Street to Heather Lane." What do you think of that?

My own family was of a cut above. We were considered to be of a better class. My parents came from Hungary, which is considered to be a better place to come from than Poland, and I was born in the United States, which made a big difference in those days. My family had a better name, too: Roth. My father used to say that we were probably related to the Rothschilds. He said Rothschild means Child of the Roths. He was full of baloney. It means Red Shield, but I didn't know the difference. Anyway, we considered ourselves superior types. My mother nearly died when I said I was going to marry a Polack, and my father sat shivah for me when I married him—think of that! He tore his shirt in ribbons and sat shivah for seven days, as though I was a dead person, all because I was a native-born American and my husband was a greenhorn with an accent.

Of course, when my father saw how successful my husband would turn out to be, what a good provider he was for me, he changed his tune—but fast! Times are different now, but back then it was a very bad thing for a girl to marry against her father's wishes. But I was always a very independent type. I said to my father, "This is America! The land of the free! I'll marry whatever man I want to!" And I did.

So. Where was I? Oh, yes, my family background. We were considered a cut above. My father was a scholar of the Talmud; my husband's father worked in a shoe-repair shop. All this background is important, you'll see, when you try to understand my son Solly—or Silas Tarkington, as he called himself, after all that other business happened.

Oh, I'm not saying my family was rich. We weren't rich at all. I suppose we were as poor as everybody else, but I never thought of myself as coming from a poor family. I was very strictly brought up, and we always seemed to have enough to eat. We lived on the Lower East Side too, at number fourteen Henry Street, in a little apartment—they called it a railroad flat—one room in front and one in back; the toilet, it wasn't even a bathroom, was on the floor below, and we shared that with four other families. Baths were in the kitchen sink. It was a sixth-floor walk-up, but I didn't mind the stairs. I thought we lived in the lap of luxury. Living here now, in an elevator building, *really* in the lap of luxury on what they call the Gold Coast of Florida, remembering that two-room apartment on Henry Street, I think, Oh, my!

It's funny. They talk about what a bad place the Lower East Side was to live in, but I didn't think it was all that bad. It was the smells of Hester Street that I liked best, wonderful smells. There was always the smell of food cooking, delicious smells of onions, cabbages, carrots, fresh-baked bread. There was also the smell of the sea, like there is here, because the Atlantic Ocean wasn't very far away. The smell of the sea would be mixed with the smell of a brisket boiling—salt and cloves—and then there was the smell of people, because Hester Street was always filled with people. But even though nobody took baths that often, I don't remember any bad people smells. The people smelled as sweet as newborn babies. I remember my mother's skirts always smelled of starch, and my father always smelled of cigars and mustache wax—my father had this great, black, bushy mustache that used to tickle me when he kissed my cheek. But I'm getting away from my story. Back to my mother, who is really a very important part of the story of Solly Tarcher. You'll see how she fits in. Without her and without me, Solly Tarcher would have been nothing but a schlepper, or maybe even worse.

My mother was a seamstress, a beautiful seamstress. She taught me to sew when I was just a little girl, and after a while she began letting me help her with her sewing. There wasn't anything my mother couldn't do with a needle, but her specialty was hats—beautiful hats that she designed and made herself, hats with embroidery and sequins and silk flowers and feathers, lacy veils and ribbons and all sorts of trimmings—and I used to help her, and by the time I was in my teens Leah Roth's hats were quite famous. So while my father studied his holy books, my mother had a nice career of her own.

A lot of uptown society women heard about my mother's work and started ordering hats from her. No two were alike, of course, and I remember when I was eighteen I started delivering hats to the great Mrs. John Jacob Astor, who lived in a great big house on Fifth Avenue and whose husband went down on the *Titanic*. Mrs. Astor only wanted black hats, because she was in mourning for her husband, you see, but even her black hats were awfully pretty. I used to just hand the hats in their boxes to the butler at the front door, but one day I met the great Mrs. Astor herself. She was just a little thing, just a girl, really, and she didn't seem much older than myself. That surprised me, somehow. I had thought Mrs. John Jacob Astor would be an enormous woman, but here was this tiny little creature, with a whispery little voice. "Oh, how lovely," she whispered—like that—as she lifted the hat out of its box and tissue paper.

All this is important; you'll see, when I get to that point in my story. Because I used to tell Solly about how I'd met the great Mrs. John Jacob Astor, and it stuck in his mind. It influenced him.

Anyway, about that time I met my future husband. I was walking home from school one afternoon with my books, and some older boys started to tease me. There were six or seven of them, and they gathered in a circle around me and wouldn't let me through. I was pretty in those days, believe it or not, and I was a little frightened. The boys kept pushing closer, asking me to give them a kiss. Well, my future husband saw what was happening, and he pushed right into that crowd of boys with his pushcart, and the boys went flying. Then he got a friend to mind his pushcart, and he walked me home to Henry Street.

It was love at first sight, or so it seemed at the time. He wasn't tall, and he wasn't very handsome, but he had nice dark eyes, and every afternoon he'd wait for me outside school and walk me home. Sometimes we'd stop at Mr. Levy's drugstore where they made good egg creams, and I think we both knew we were in love, though we didn't talk about getting married. I knew my father would not like the idea of me marrying a man who was seven years older and sold watches from a pushcart. Abe only mentioned marriage once. He said, "In America, when you're twenty-one years old, you can do as you please. You don't have to ask your parents' permission for anything." I knew what he meant. That was proposal enough for me.

On my twenty-first birthday, Abe Tarcher and I went down to City Hall and got married, just like that. That was when my father screamed and raged and carried on, tore his shirt into shreds, and said "My daughter is dead!" He said he was going to sit shivah for me and told me never to darken his door again. I didn't care. I was that independent. I had my new husband now, with his own place to live. I just stuck out my tongue at my father, marched out the door, and slammed it in his face, expecting never to set foot in fourteen Henry Street again. My Abe was waiting for me on the street downstairs. "We're free!" we kept saying. "We're free!" And we held hands and skipped down the street like children. That was in 1916.

My Abe had rooms in Norfolk Street, number thirty-five, which was really not that many blocks away, and I was very happy keeping house for my new husband. Oh, we were very happy, and I loved tidying the rooms while he was off on the street at work. In the corner of the front room, he kept a pile of old magazines. Sometimes I would pick up one of those magazines to read, which made him very nervous, and I wondered why. The magazines—*Collier's, Saturday Evening Post,* and so on—were all very old, and there wasn't very much of interest in them, and one day I said, "Abe, why don't we throw all these old magazines out? They're just taking up room." "No!" he cried. "Don't ever touch those magazines!" Then he showed me why.

At the bottom of the pile, the magazines were stuffed with lots of dollar bills: ten-dollar bills, twenties, even fifties. That was where he kept his money. He didn't trust banks, and he figured no burglar would be interested in running off with a lot of old copies of the *Saturday Evening Post,* you see. It made a certain amount of sense. We counted out the money that he had saved there. It was more than a thousand dollars! It seemed like a fortune at the time, but that was what he had saved from his push-cart business over the years.

Well, it made me a little nervous having all that money lying around the house, you'd better believe it. But I also made sure the news got back to number fourteen Henry Street that my new husband had savings of over a thousand dollars, though I naturally didn't say where he kept it.

Oh, my. You've never seen such a change come over a man as came over my father when he heard that! Suddenly he forgot all about sitting shivah for me. Suddenly it was shalom, shalom! Come for dinner! Come for the lighting of the shabbat candles! Suddenly my new husband was like his long-lost son. He was always full of baloney, my father, but I did love him, and I loved my mother, and it was nice that we were all one big happy family again. That thousand dollars was all it took to do it.

It was during these family gatherings that both my mother and my father got interested in my new husband's business methods, and my new husband got interested in my mother's millinery business and the good customers like Mrs. Astor. It was my father who suggested that my husband might take some of his savings and open a little shop where my mother could sell her hats. Abe liked the idea, and that was how he got rid of his pushcart and we all got into the millinery business. You see how it all hangs together now, don't you? Because it was in the millinery business that my husband made his real money.

At first, our shop was also on Norfolk Street—just a little place. But it was so successful that we soon needed more room, and so in 1920 we rented space on 14th Street, just off Union Square, which was still the fancy shopping area, where all the rich women bought their clothes. By then, my mother mostly just designed the hats. I helped too. But we had four girls in the back room who did the cutting and the sewing and the trimming. My husband ran the store and kept the books. My father pretty much kept out of our hair—too busy scribbling questions in the margins of his Talmudic texts, arguing with God.

Nineteen-twenty was also the year that Abe's and my first child was born. We named him Solomon Tarcher, in

honor of my husband's father, Samuel, the shoe repair-
man, who had died the year before. People often did that.
The first initial of the baby's name was in honor of a
relative who had recently died. So that was the birth of
the man who became Silas Tarkington. "Born in abject
poverty," the obituary said. Ha! When my baby was
born, I had both a nursemaid and a wet nurse for him.
My milk was short. With both my children, my milk was
short. All the women in my family have had that trouble,
I don't know why.

Oh, he was a beautiful baby! Once when I was
wheeling him in his carriage, a strange woman stopped us
and said, "That is the most beautiful baby in the Bronx!
That is the most beautiful baby in the Bronx!" She said it
twice. I forgot to tell you that we'd moved to the Bronx
by then, to a beautiful apartment in a new building right
on the Grand Concourse. My husband was certainly a
good provider. And Solly was such a well-behaved baby.
He hardly ever cried. And when he was old enough for
school, he did so well. He brought home such wonderful
report cards, always with wonderful comments from his
teachers. It was only after his sister Simma was born that
he began to change.

I'm not saying it was Simma's fault. Perhaps it was
because I waited nine years to have another baby. I've
often thought that. But he was terribly jealous of the new
baby. Perhaps that was natural, because he'd been the
kingpin so long—like the only child—that he couldn't
stand having to share any of my attention with a baby
sister. But a new baby just does take more time and care
and attention than a nine-year-old boy. There was just no
way I could pay as much attention to Solly as I had before. It used to frighten me. He'd be with her, and I'd hear
her screaming, and I'd rush into the room. "I was only
playing with her, Mama," he'd say to me, but I worried
that he wasn't playing with her, that he was hurting her,
and after a while I decided I couldn't leave the two of
them alone in a room together. I was terrified that he'd
try to harm her in some way. And she was a sickly, colicky baby, too.

Right about that time, his grades in school began getting worse. His teachers would write me notes, saying, *Solomon needs to apply himself more.* "What does that mean?" he'd ask me. "What does it mean, *apply* myself more?" "It means you've got to work harder, study harder. Have you done all your homework for tomorrow?" "Of course I have," he'd say. But still the notes came home. *Solomon's homework assignments were incomplete again. Again!* He'd been lying to me, but what could I do? By then it was the Depression, times were hard, and my husband and I were working harder than ever in the shop, trying to make ends meet. And times kept getting worse. Women weren't willing to spend fifty dollars on a hat. They weren't even willing to spend five dollars. Mrs. Astor had died, and there didn't seem to be any more women like her left in the country, let alone New York City.

Yes, I think it was waiting those nine years that did it. If his sister had been more of a contemporary, less of a rival, it might have been different. But during those nine years I was so busy helping my husband build his business I couldn't even think about having another baby. Those nine years . . . and then the Depression hit us. Oh, my.

Solly began hanging around with a different crowd of boys, an older crowd, a tough crowd from the East Bronx, a crowd I didn't like and I told him so. It went in one ear and out the other. The Bronx was changing. It was not so nice anymore. Even the Grand Concourse was not so nice. In our building, apartments were getting robbed. The *shvartzers* were moving in. "Should we move?" I asked my husband. But moving is just about the most expensive thing you can do. Our nice new building was getting to smell bad. There was rubbish in the streets. It was getting worse than the Lower East Side ever was.

Then I discovered that Solly had been playing hooky. The truant officer came to our door. "Your son has not attended school for the last three weeks," he said. He'd been going off each morning with his books, supposedly to school, but he'd never gotten there. God knows what he'd been doing, running around with that fast new crowd of his. Some of those boys had cars—stolen cars would be my guess. I spoke with him. His father spoke with him. We pleaded with him. It all fell on deaf ears.

At thirteen he was supposed to be bar mitzvah. He refused. He had refused even to go to *shul*. And at sixteen he announced that he was going to quit school altogether. His father and I begged him not to do this. "What are you going to do?" his father asked him. "I'm going to work," he said. "I'm going to make a million dollars." "You can't work for me," his father said. "I can't afford to hire any extra help in the store." This was 1936, the Depression was at its worst, three of the four girls in the back of the store we'd had to get rid of, and we were down to just one. My mother had developed Parkinson's, and just the three of us were doing everything—the one girl, my husband, and me. "Yes, where are you going to work?" I asked him. "Nobody's hiring anybody."

"What about your famous friend, Mr. John Jacob Astor?" he asked me, kind of freshlike. "How did he make his money?" "In furs," I told him. "Then I'll go into the fur business," he said. "Just see if you can find *any* job, Mr. Know-It-All," I said to him.

Well, I must say, he made good on that promise. He did find a job, schlepping furs on a rack for a manufacturer on Seventh Avenue, and for the next few years we didn't see too much of him. He'd found a place to live, he told us, somewhere on the West Side near his job. And I must say he seemed to be making good money. I didn't know there was that much money to be made schlepping furs on a rack, but whenever he showed up he always seemed to have plenty of money in his pockets, plenty of nice new clothes. "I'm on my way to making my first million," he used to say, showing off the fat bankroll in his billfold. Well, his father and I thought, times were beginning to get a little better. Once, on my birthday, he turned up at our place and gave me a solid silver tea set: teapot, hot water pot, sugar, and creamer on a solid silver tray. Once, for his father's birthday, it was a solid gold Bulova watch. "Well," my husband said, "maybe he's becoming a success after all."

Pearl Harbor came, and we didn't hear from him for a long time. Maybe he's been drafted into the army, we thought, because he was that age, and naturally we worried. But then, in December of 1943, he showed up again with Hanukkah presents for all of us: a gold necklace for me, silver hairbrushes for his father, and even a silver ring with a diamond in it for his sister, Simma, though it was too big for any of her fingers and she had to wear it with a piece of adhesive tape around it. Simma was fourteen then. "Do you suppose he stole these things, Mama?" she asked me later. It was an omen.

"It's been so long since we've heard from you," I said to him. "We thought maybe you'd been drafted into the army."

"Flat feet," he said with a wink.

I don't know for sure, but I never believed that. I think he just never bothered to register for the draft. A mother should know that, shouldn't she? If there was anything the matter with her son's feet?

Anyway, the worst moment came a few years later, in 1949. A policeman came to our door. He had a warrant for Solly's arrest. Grand larceny, they called it. Grand theft. Of course he didn't live with us, and we didn't know how to find him. But somehow they found him. And they arrested him. Oh, my . . . oh, my. . . . Do you need to keep that machine running? Yes . . . turn it off.

Fine. I'm better now. It was just remembering all that. They arrested him for selling fur coats off the racks he'd been schlepping in the streets. His boss had been missing certain garments for some time. He suspected it was one of his employees, and he sent out a company spy to try to catch whoever it was. Solly was schlepping a rack of mink coats down 34th Street, and this spy approached him and said he was interested in buying a mink coat for his wife. Solly offered to sell him one for five hundred dollars, and that's how they knew who it was.

Oh, my. I'm not saying it's all right to sell garments

that belong to the boss, but was it right for the boss to catch him that way? With a spy he sent out? Somehow, it just doesn't seem right to me.

Naturally, we were devastated, his father and I. Abe met with the boss and offered to pay full retail for all the missing garments. He went down on bended knee, begging. But the boss had a heart of stone. He wouldn't let Solly off. He refused to drop the charges. And so there was a trial, and Solly was convicted, and the judge sentenced him to ten years in the state penitentiary, upstate in Hillsdale. Ten years!

Of course his father and I were heartbroken. Abe wanted to sit shivah for him, but I wouldn't let him. I remembered how I'd felt when my own father did that to me, and I reminded him of that. What does sitting shivah mean? I asked him. It means meaningless.

But it broke poor Abe's heart. He was never the same after. I know it shortened his life. It had to. After that, he suddenly looked old. He died just a few years later, in 1954. His only son in prison. It was too much for him. He died of a broken heart. So young, only sixty-six.

Solly could have come to the funeral. They would have let him. But he would have had to come to the synagogue in handcuffs and shackles, and he didn't want anybody to see him like that, and I can't say as how I blame him. I could understand that.

But the good thing that came of it—there's a good side for every bad side, my mother used to say—was that when we went through my husband's things we kept finding all these little bankbooks, hidden under his underwear and in places like that. He still didn't really trust banks, and so, instead of putting all his money in one bank, he put it in a lot of different ones—a thousand dollars here, five thousand dollars there. "Don't put all your eggs in one basket," he used to say. And when we added up all the money in the different banks, it came to over a million dollars! Just think of that!

My late husband, may God rest his soul, hadn't made any will, so the court ordered that the money be divided three ways, between Solly, in prison in Hillsdale, and Simma and me.

I must say that Solly must have behaved himself at Hillsdale, because, instead of making him serve the full ten years, they let him out in a little over six. Time out for good behavior, they call it. They let him out in 1956.

The first I heard of it was in a telephone call from his parole officer. I remember the man's words exactly. "Your son is now completely rehabilitated, Mrs. Tarcher," he said. "To be honest with you, we in the New York State correctional system have never seen such a complete rehabilitation of a prisoner in our lives." In fact, he said, in the whole history of New York prisons, as far as he knew, there had never been a case that had turned out as well as Solly. He'd made a complete turnaround, he said, and it really did the prison people's hearts good to see it. A former felon was turned into a model citizen, just like that, and the parole officer agreed that my early training of him had a lot to do with it. He told me how I was certainly an admirable mother, and how much the prison people, and Solly too, appreciated it, everything I'd done. "Your son Solomon has seen the error of his ways," he told me. "He is like a whole new man, and he is ready to embark upon a whole new and productive life." Solly would be sticking to the straight and narrow from now on, he told me. And he told me that now everybody in the New York State prison system was just hoping for a little more assistance from me. "I am confident we can count on you for that, Mrs. Tarcher, can't we?" he said.

I thought that was the best news I'd had in years. I'll never forget that nice parole officer's name. It was Moses Minskoff.

"Just tell me what I can do for you, Mr. Minskoff," I said to him.

"Your son is already a prince among men," he said to me. "You're going to help us make him a king!"

15

They were standing at the southwest corner of 59th Street and Fifth Avenue gazing at the stolidly Renaissance seven-story building on the corner diagonally opposite them.

"What you see here is the prelude to a great metropolitan tragedy," Moe Minskoff was saying. "This is the last of the great private residences on this section of Fifth Avenue, an architectural gem of historical significance. It was commissioned by the late Truxton Van Degan before the turn of the century and was designed by the great Stanford White before his untimely demise a few years later. No expense was spared in the mansion's construction, and it is as solidly built as the Rock of Gibraltar.

"And yet it is slated for the wrecker's ball. The Van Degan heirs, unable to find a purchaser for the building and unwilling to pay for its upkeep, have allowed this magnificent structure to be sold for taxes, and the purchaser, a demolition company, plans to raze the building and sell the property for the construction of an office tower. What a waste! But the president of the demolition company happens to be a very, very good friend of mine, and this magnificent building can be yours, Solly, for a mere three hundred thousand dollars."

"But what would I do with it, Moe?"

"I might even be able to get him down to two-fifty."

"But—again—what would I do with it?"

"Solly, I've known you for nearly seven years. Those years we spent at Hillsdale, sharing the same cell—I feel I know you inside and out. I feel you're my best friend, which is why I'm making this offer to you and you alone, but I also see you as a young man with great promise. You're young, you're smart, and now with all that other business behind you, I see you cut out for great things.

"What you are, Solly, is a retailer. That little business that got you in trouble was nothing more than a retailing transaction. What is retailing, after all? It's just buying something for less and selling it for more. That's the origin of the word retail. Re . . . tail. You buy at the tail end of the market and resell at the top. Maybe what you were doing before wasn't quite within the letter of the law, but it was essentially the same thing, and it's something for which you have a natural talent. Retailing's in your blood. After all, your father was a retailer. Your mother is still a retailer. I see this building"—and he gestured toward the Van Degan mansion with his palm upward—"as becoming a great retailing establishment, on the most fashionable shopping street in the city if not the world, selling merchandise of the highest quality and the highest price—the same kind of merchandise you used to deal in, Solly."

"But three hundred thousand—"

"I said I think I can get it for two-fifty."

"Even that would wipe out most of my inheritance. I'd have nothing left to set up my inventory, to—"

"That's why it's important that we get your mother to back you in this enterprise."

"I don't know, Moe. My mother's pretty tight with her money."

"Ah, but I have a plan, Solly."

"Care to tell me what it is?"

"From what you tell me, your mother is a woman

who is impressed with officialdom. My name means nothing to her. What if I were to present myself to her as your parole officer and indicate that this enterprise is part of the state's overall long-term plan to bring about your rehabilitation? I think the old lady might go for it, Sol."

"She'd need more than just your word for it, Moe."

"Ah, of course, my friend. There are at least two things we can offer your dear mother. One is stock in our new enterprise. In return for her financial contribution, she would receive shares of stock. Shares of stock are simply a matter of going to a printer and ordering them. With shares of stock, your mother would become part owner of our store. We can offer her more than that. I visualize this store of ours as a series of small shops, or boutiques as they're now called, each featuring a different type of merchandise. The layout of the rooms in the house suggests this plan. Leah Roth's millinery styles are already quite well known and well respected. Suppose we offered your mother a Leah Roth's boutique in our store? The Leah Roth's label on Fifth Avenue would have more prestige than it does on Union Square. And she'd be getting her space rent free."

"Well, I don't know, Moe," he said. "I don't think that even with my mother's money in it I'd have enough —not enough to run the kind of store I'd like to run, the kind we used to talk about up at Hillsdale. I'd like it to be a really super-specialty store, really fancy, really exclusive. For a really exclusive clientele. But that was just prison talk. I think what I'll do, now that I have a little cash, is put it in some safe stocks and see if I can live off the dividends until—"

"The dividends from three hundred and thirty-five thousand would be peanuts," he said. "Peanuts, Solly! I'm talking about big bucks. I'm talking about your golden opportunity!"

"Yeah, well, I don't think so," he said, and started to turn away.

"Wait," Moe said. "There are other sources of capital."

"Where?"

"What about your redheaded sister? She got the other third of the old man's estate."

"Simma? That's out of the question. She hates me. She always has."

"I have a plan for her as well."

"Oh? What's that?"

"That red hair of hers. Where'd she get it? Suppose we tell her what you told me—that her father wasn't who she thought it was? That it was Dr. What'sisname?"

"Weiss. Sidney Weiss, the dentist. But I don't *know* that, Moe. It was just something the kids at school used to tease me about. They used to say my mother was having an affair with Sidney Weiss because he had bright red hair, and after Simma was born she had the same red hair, and nobody else in our family had red hair."

"But would your sister like that rumor spread around? After all, your mother and Dr. Weiss are still living, and Dr. Weiss also has a wife."

"That sounds like blackmail," he said.

"Nah, it's called persuasion. It's called influence. It's called salesmanship, which is something you and I are pretty good at, Solly."

"It still seems like a shitty thing to do to Simma."

"Do you give a damn? You never liked the bitch, you told me."

"She made my life miserable from the moment she was born. Kids at school calling my mother a whore—"

"See? So why don't you let me try both these little tactics, my boy? What can it hurt? Just let me try it, and see what happens. Faint heart never won fair lady, as I read somewheres."

"I don't like her, but that doesn't mean I want to screw her out of her money."

"You won't *be* screwing her out of her money, Sol. We'll be getting her to make an investment. An investment in your future, your glorious future. Once your store is opened, both your old lady and the bitch sister will start getting dividends."

He shook his head. "No," he said. "It won't work, Moe. Even with my mother's money and Simma's money, there *still* wouldn't be enough. Look, that store was just a pipe dream, Moe. It was just something you and I used to talk about to pass the time. That's all it was—just talk."

Moe Minskoff stared at him. "You know what I think when I hear you talk like that, Solly?" he said. "I think, What a waste. What a waste of talent. You know what your talent is, Solly? Well, first of all there's your looks. Hell, I know what I look like. I look like a fat schmuck. That's why I'm always a behind-the-scenes type person. I don't look like a front-and-center type. The first thing you judge a guy by is how he looks. Now maybe you ain't as handsome as a Rock Hudson, but you have the looks of a high-class type. You look sincere, and that's a number-one point in business. Number two, you're well liked. I was never well liked at the joint, strictly because of how I looked. But everybody in the joint liked you. All the guards liked you, even Shitface. Remember Shitface? Shitface used to give you smokes—I seen him, and it wasn't because you gave him blow jobs, either. A lotta new grubs think they can get favors from a guard by giving him a blow job, but they're just wasting their spit. You never did that, but even Shitface passed you smokes."

"Maybe it was because I never called him Shitface," he said. "Not to his face, anyway."

"That's right. You called him sir. And that brings me to talent number three. You got high-class manners, Solly. You got them manners in the joint."

"I used good manners because I wanted to get out of the joint as fast as possible."

"Right! But it takes talent to use good manners like that. Me, I ain't got that talent, either, which was why they kept me in longer than they kept you. You actually improved yourself in the joint, Solly. Most grubs, it's the other way around. They come out worse than they went in, but not you. You took those courses. You took a bookkeeping course and got an A. You even took a course in French and learned to speak it like a real Frenchman—I heard you. And some of the books you read up there, like that one by Andrew Carnegie."

"Dale Carnegie," he said.

"Right, and that brings me to talent number four."

"What's that, Moe?"

"Your smile, Solly. You may not be as handsome as Rock Hudson, but you've got a great smile. With the right smile, a man can sell anything. Me, I never learned how to smile right, which is why I'm a good behind-the-scenes man. I can talk good, but I don't smile good. But you, when you smile at a guy you look him straight in the eye, and that's the real key to success. You know something? When we was roommates in the place, I used to catch you looking in the mirror, practicing that smile. Am I right? That smile of yours didn't come natural. You worked on it, and you learned to do it right."

He was smiling now, but he was not looking at Moe. His eyes had traveled to the empty Van Degan mansion across the street. "Dale Carnegie says a man's smile is more important than his handshake," he said.

"And Andrew Carnegie was right." Moe had caught the direction of his friend's look. "Well, that's the end of Moses Minskoff's Sermon on the Mount," he said. "But when I hear you talk like this, turning down this golden opportunity to buy that magnificent historical structure there, it makes me sad. Sad to see all those wonderful talents of yours go to waste."

His friend said nothing.

"There's other sources of financing, of course," Moe said.

"Such as?"

"I have certain friends, Solly. Friends with influence. Bankers. Private bankers. Venture capitalists, you might call 'em. They're often interested in investing in high-class-type businesses. They might be persuaded to back us, if I approach them the right way. And then there are always your regular commercial banks."

"Aw, the commercial banks would never lend me money, Moe. I'm Solly Tarcher, remember? I'm an ex-con who's served time for grand larceny."

"Ah, but you don't understand, my friend," he said. "You are not going to *be* Solly Tarcher anymore. You are not going to *have* any record. You are just going to be a bright young fellow who's recently come into a little money, and have a plan to make some more, who isn't going to be just a merchant prince but a merchant king!"

The way it worked, Moe explained, was like this. You went out to a cemetery, any cemetery—Woodlawn would do, since it was big and close to town—and looked for the grave of a man who had been born in approximately the same year as yourself. Then you went to the Bureau of Vital Statistics, which was open to the public, and looked up that man's death record, which listed his place of birth. Then you wrote to the Bureau of Vital Statistics in that city and, for a four- or five-dollar money order, you obtained a copy of the birth certificate.

After you had the birth certificate, everything else was a piece of cake. With a birth certificate, you could obtain a Social Security number. With a birth certificate, you could obtain a driver's license. With a birth certificate, you could obtain a passport. Before you knew it, you had a whole new identity.

Moe Minskoff knew how easy it was. He had done it himself. Twice. It was even easier for a man who'd had only one arrest. He would have only been fingerprinted once. And, naturally, it behooved that person to stay out of further trouble. But Moe would handle everything.

"Think about all this very carefully," Moe said, as the two men turned and headed down the avenue. Moe tucked his hand into the crook of the younger man's elbow. "This could be your golden opportunity," he said.

He had been interested in this young man ever since they had been assigned the same cell at Hillsdale and became friends. There was something about this young man, maybe it was those good manners, maybe it was the way he practiced his smile before the mirror, that smelled of promise and success. Moe had been released from Hillsdale about a month after Sol and had quickly gone to New York to look his friend up.

He was even more interested in Sol Tarcher after learning that Sol had inherited $335,000—or, more specifically, $335,953.77.

. . .

Two weeks later, Moe Minskoff appeared with his younger friend's new credentials in his hand. "You are now Silas Tarkington," he said triumphantly. "You're in luck, because I even got you the same initials. Anything you got that's monogrammed, you don't need to change it, ha-ha-ha. Like your prison fatigues. Ha-ha-ha." Then he reached into his jacket pocket. "I also got something else for you," he said, and handed him a cashier's check for $200,000.

"Where did you get this?"

"One of my friends I told you about. One of my venture-capitalist friends. He's highly interested in our project and asked to come on board. In the real estate game, you'd call this earnest money."

"What's your role going to be in all of this, Moe?" the younger man asked carefully, staring at the check in disbelief.

"Why, your partner, of course! Your silent partner. I'm a behind-the-scenes type person."

"But I'm to be in charge. That's clear."

"Oh, absolutely. You're going to be the president of Tarkington's Store, or whatever the hell you decide to call it. Me, I won't even set my foot inside the door. You wouldn't want a Moe Minskoff type inside this fancy store of yours."

"Will this really work, Moe?" His look was suddenly anxious.

"Hell, yes," he said. "I make just three rules for you, Solly—I mean Silas. Rule one, never go back to your old neighborhood, not even to see your old lady. Rule two, grow a mustache. It will change the way you look, but it won't spoil your smile. Rule three, always remember: the richer a man is, the more he's loved."

16

"In the parlance of penology, your son has been transferred from New York State's list of correctionally correctables to that of the correctionally corrected," Moe Minskoff said. "Congratulations, Mrs. Tarcher!"

"Hmm," she said.

"I must say what a great honor it is to meet you, Mrs. Tarcher," he said with a bow. "It is a great honor to meet the mother who has produced and raised such a wonderful son, Mrs. Tarcher. You must be proud, very proud indeed. It isn't often that we officials with the New York State penal system have the honor to meet a mother of your caliber. Some of the mothers we have to deal with, Mrs. Tarcher—well, you just wouldn't believe some of those other mothers. Believe it or not, there are mothers out there who have no interest in their sons' rehabilitations or their sons' futures. But you, I can see, are a special case, just as your son is a very special case on our docket of prisoner rehabilitation cases. And may I compliment you, too, on this attractive shop? I can see from the items of millinery displayed here that you do beautiful work."

"Thank you, Mr. Minskoff," Rose said. "It was my own mother who started this business. My mother is Leah Roth. She still does some of the designing, but she hasn't been all that well lately."

"Ah, I'm sorry to hear that, Mrs. Tarcher, truly sorry."

"Thank you. But now tell me what I can do to help Solly."

"Well, let me begin by explaining what we of the penal system have been able to accomplish thus far," he said. "As you know, our job is to see to it that your son, recently released from his incarceration, takes his place as a useful and productive member of our society. That's the American way, and I'm sure your own wishes for your son's future are the same. As you can imagine, one of the greatest problems facing a recently released convict is the stigma of his incarceration. The stigma of incarceration can affect a man's ability to find work and his ability to establish credit, as I'm sure you can understand. But, fortunately, the people of this great state of ours have empowered officials such as myself to help the former prisoner overcome this stigma, particularly a former prisoner of such sterling promise as your son. To help someone such as your son overcome any such stigma, we are empowered to provide him with a new legal identity, including a new name."

"A new name?"

"Yes. In order that your son's past record will not come back to haunt him, the State of New York has supplied your son with a new legal appellation. We want to help him make a clean break with his criminal past and make a fresh start in civilian life with a clean slate. Maybe you've heard of our criminal protective program, which is similar to our witness protection program. Your son will henceforth be known as Silas Tarkington. We felt this was close enough to his former name to be acceptable. His full name, incidentally, is now Silas Rogers Tarkington."

She looked suspicious. "Tarkington?" she said. "That's a goy name, isn't it?"

"Possibly," he said. "But it has a certain distinction,

don't you think? There's a certain drumroll quality to it: Silas Rogers Tarkington."

"Silas Rogers Tarkington," she repeated. "So my son is now Silas Rogers Tarkington."

"Correct," he said. "Naturally, it will be to your son's advantage, and to the advantage of our overall rehabilitation program, if you no longer refer to your son as Solomon Tarcher. In fact, if I may make a suggestion, you may wish to think of Solomon Tarcher as a dead person, or at least as a person who is no longer a part of your life. Your friends, I think, would understand and sympathize with this attitude, considering the disgrace and humiliation he put you and your late husband through at the time of his arrest, trial, and conviction."

"Oh, yes," she said sadly, shaking her head. "It was awful, Mr. Minskoff. It shortened my Abe's life, I know it did. He was never the same afterward."

"But in your heart, Mrs. Tarcher, you will always know that you have not lost a son. Instead, your son has been reborn, as a new man. He was a young man who had started down a dangerous and wayward path, but now, reborn, he is headed along the path of righteousness. That must be a very comforting thought for you to hold, Mrs. Tarcher."

"Yes." She nodded. "It is—I suppose."

"Of course it is! What mother wouldn't be bursting with pride at such a development? What a pity your late husband couldn't have lived to see it!"

"Yes," she said.

"Now," he said, "in addition to helping erase any traces of your son's, shall we say, untidy past, the State of New York is willing to go even further in his behalf. Isn't this a wonderful state we live in, Mrs. Tarcher? Over in Jersey, they don't do nothing—excuse me, anything, like we do here. What I am also empowered by New York State to do for him is in the important area of employment. We must help this young man establish himself in a career. Now, it occurred to my office that an ideal career for him would be in retailing. Retailing, after all, is in the blood that courses through his veins. You, your late husband, and your mother have all been successful and highly respected retailers. Prior to his arrest, your son gained some experience in the fur business, and even fencing furs—though we don't like to use that expression—is a form of retailing, is it not? Up in Hillsdale, your son took courses; this is one of the services our great state's penal system offers. He took courses in business management and accounting and excelled in both of them. He also studied manners and diplomacy under the great Andrew Carnegie himself. He acquired all the aspects of a successful manager of a retail operation.

"Now, my office has located an excellent site for a retailing operation such as your son is so ideally suited for. It is an old abandoned mansion on Fifth Avenue, right in the heart of the city's most prestigious midtown shopping district. It is slated to be torn down but can be saved from the wrecker's ball for a price. The building itself is in excellent condition, though the interior will require some work to convert it into retail space, and this will also cost some money. The State of New York is willing to provide some funding for this enterprise but unfortunately, as in any bureaucracy, there are certain budgetary limitations and restrictions. Your son himself has, as you know, come into an inheritance from his father, and he is eager to put most or all of that sum into the start-up costs of his new business, which the State of New York, I might add, has carefully examined and found to be highly feasible and potentially highly profitable, with someone of your son's caliber running it. The State of New York has unilaterally approved every aspect of the plan. Unfortunately, the State of New York, with its budgetary limitations, cannot completely underwrite the project. It can only help. The project—of which we officially approve, of course—is a highly ambitious one. Your son wants to create a retail establishment of the highest caliber, which I'm sure is what you'd want for him yourself. He wants a class act, in other words, and who can blame him? He comes from a family that's always been a class act. And so, to help defray the start-up costs of the enterprise, it occurred to me and others in my office up in Albany that you yourself might be willing to be an investor in the project."

She looked at him narrowly. "If Solly needs money, why doesn't he come and ask me for it himself? Why did he send you?"

"Silas."

"Silas—that used to be Solly. Why?"

"My dear Mrs. Tarcher, there are really two answers to your question," he said. "One is that I am simply doing my job. It is my job in the Rehabilitation Office to do whatever I can to help ex-convicts get back on their feet, to explore every possible avenue to achieve that objective. It's a heartwarming job, I must say, trying to help men who have strayed from the paths of righteousness, and help give new direction to their lives, to help them recover from the trauma of incarceration, but you're not really interested in hearing about my job. The second answer to your question is that your son asked me to come and state his case to you today because he is still too ashamed of what he did six years ago to face you. He is afraid you might not wish to see him. He is still too filled with shame over the disgrace he brought down upon his family and his family's good name. I'm sure you can understand these feelings, Mrs. Tarcher. He is, after all, a man. He is afraid that if he saw you at this point, he might break down. This is how deeply ashamed he is of the deep hurt he inflicted on you, his own mother, the only mother he'll ever have, and the mother he worships more than any woman in the world." Moe Minskoff wiped a tear from his eye. "Forgive me, Mrs. Tarcher. In my line of social work, it's hard not to get emotionally involved in certain aspects of my case load."

She hesitated. "Do you always do this?" she said. "When you're trying to get an ex-convict back on his feet, do you always come to the mother and ask for money?"

"Certainly not, Mrs. Tarcher."

"Here. Use my hankie. It's clean."

"Thank you." He blew his nose noisily into the proffered handkerchief. "Certainly not," he said again. "Most of the mothers of ex-convicts don't have a pot to piss in.

Excuse my French. In my business you get used to a lot of rough language. What I'm saying is that most ex-convicts are not of your son's caliber, and most mothers of ex-convicts are not women of your caliber and social position. You'd be surprised how many mothers don't give a rat's ass what happens to their sons—pardon my French again."

"That's okay. You can use rat's ass with me."

"That's the only word for it," he said. "But it's true. You are a special case. You are a very caring woman, I can tell. You've raised two fine children—"

"Huh! One of those fine children just got out of prison."

"Oh, you won't recognize him now, Mrs. Tarcher. That's how much he's changed. But the real point I want to make to you, Mrs. Tarcher, is that I did not come here to ask you for money, as you put it. Remember that this is all a part of a carefully organized rehabilitation plan that has been worked out in Albany. What we are offering you is an opportunity to invest in a new business that we in Albany have studied thoroughly and feel will be very lucrative and profitable. Other investors have already approached us and are highly eager to get on board. But we felt—I felt, my superiors in Albany felt, and your son also felt—that you, of all people, deserved to be let in on the ground floor of an operation that is going to make you a lot of money. Who deserves to get rich from this more than you, who brought the retailing genius of Silas Tarkington into the world?"

"Hmm," she said. "What would I get for this investment?"

"You would get shares of stock in Tarkington's, Incorporated, class A stock. It is expected that, once your son's store's operations are under way, quarterly dividends will be paid at the rate of nine percent per annum, which I think you'll agree is a nice return on your money. I could send you a prospectus, but there's not much time. Too many other investors want to get on board."

"Don't bother. I could never read those things. My late husband could, but not me."

"Your son plans his store as a series of small, select boutiques, each specializing in a different category of choice merchandise. It occurred to your son, and we in Albany agree, that in view of the fine reputation of Leah Roth millinery, a Leah Roth boutique might be placed somewhere prominently on one of the selling floors. Your son thought you might like having an outlet right on Fifth Avenue, the city's principal shopping thoroughfare, rather than down here, which is a bit out of the way nowadays."

"Hmm," she said thoughtfully. "The millinery business isn't what it used to be, I'll say that much. It used to be that every woman worth her salt had to have a hat for every occasion—for morning, noon, and night. Mrs. John Jacob Astor certainly did. She was a client of ours, you know. But women just don't seem to wear hats anymore, except to special things like weddings and funerals. Now everything's hair, hair, hair. Women spend more on their hair than they do on hats. When did hair take over from hats? Don't ask me how that happened."

"And of course, as an initial investor and as a family member, you'd have your space on the floor rent free."

"Rent free?"

"Absolutely."

She hesitated. "Well, let me think about this," she said. "Let me talk it over with my lawyer."

"By all means, Mrs. Tarcher," he said. "But of course while you wait for a legal opinion, the shares the State of New York wants you to have first crack at will most likely have been snapped up by other investors, and you'll have missed the chance of a lifetime. All you'll be left with is a big legal bill. But do talk it over with your attorney, and let's just hope there are a few shares left for you. I hope there will be. But I can't promise anything."

"Let me talk it over with my son-in-law, my daughter Simma's husband. He's an accountant, and he's very smart when it comes to money."

He began rummaging in his big briefcase, which seemed to be filled with many important-looking documents. "Well, I'm afraid I've been barking up the wrong tree, Mrs. Tarcher," he said at last, with a little sigh, "when you start talking about son-in-laws and shyster lawyers. The State of New York does not wish to involve itself with persons of that order. It does not wish to, and it does not need to. The State of New York does not need your investment or your participation in this project in any way. I'm afraid I misjudged you. Your son was merely hoping to be able to do something for you that would partly compensate you for all the suffering he's put you through, but I can see you're not interested in any gestures of generosity from him. I can see you're not interested either in your son's future or in a highly lucrative financial investment that would make you a very rich woman. I'm sorry to have taken up so much of your valuable time." He started to pull himself out of his chair.

"Now wait a minute," she said, holding up her hand. "Sit down. My time's not so valuable. I'm not so busy. You haven't seen so many customers trying to bust down my doors for the last hour or so, have you? And I haven't said I'm not interested, have I?"

"I shouldn't have listened to what your friend Dr. Sidney Weiss said about you."

Her eyes widened. "Sidney Weiss? What did he say about me?"

"That you were a real human being."

"I am a human being."

"That you were a warm and wonderful woman."

"I am a warm and wonderful woman!"

"He said you were very smart."

"I am smart!"

"He also said that when he first met you he thought you were the most beautiful woman he'd ever seen."

She smiled and lowered her eyelids. "So Sidney said that?" she said softly. "Well, I did use to be pretty, believe it or not, if I do say so myself. I haven't seen Sidney in years. He was our family dentist," she added quickly.

"Yes, I know," he said. "The State of New York has investigated your background very thoroughly." He glanced at his watch. "Well, I must be on my way."

"Now hold your horses," she said. "What's your hurry? Sit down."

"Well, I have several appoint—"

"Just sit where you are for a minute, Mr. Minskoff. So you're talking Fifth Avenue? Rent free?"

"Yes, of course, but—"

"So let's talk dollars and cents for a minute, Mr. Minskoff. Just exactly what kind of an investment are you talking about having me make?"

"For three hundred thousand dollars, I can offer you a six percent interest in Tarkington's, Incorporated."

"Too much," she said. "I can't afford that. Let's make it half of that. A hundred and fifty."

"Let's split the difference and make it two twenty-five."

"I said a hundred and fifty."

"Very well," he said. "For an investment of a hundred and fifty thousand dollars, you would receive three percent of the outstanding shares of the company's stock. Do we have a deal?"

"I'm going to think about it."

He looked at his watch again. "I'm afraid there won't be time for that," he said. "As I mentioned to you, there are investors all over town scrambling to get onto this bandwagon. If we wait as much as twenty-four hours, there won't be any more shares of stock available for purchase."

"Street floor," she said.

"What?"

"My Leah Roth boutique. I want it on the street floor."

"In most specialty stores, I believe the millinery department is located on one of the upper floors."

"I'm afraid of heights," she said with a wink. "I want street floor, near the main entrance."

He hesitated briefly. Then he said, "Very well. I'll see to it that that's arranged."

"Then we have a deal," she said, and extended her right hand.

"Good," he said, taking her hand and pumping it. "This is a very wise and wonderful decision you are making, Mrs. Tarcher. I can assure you that you will not regret it. And may I add that everything Dr. Weiss said about you is true."

"Thank you," she said. "And if you see Sidney, give him my—regards."

"I'll surely do that," he said.

"So—now when do I get to see Solly?"

"Silas. Remember?"

"So, Silas. When do I get to see him?"

"As soon as we get this little bit of paperwork out of the way, I'll arrange a meeting for the two of you," he said. He gathered up his big floppy brown briefcase, which had THE STATE OF NEW YORK emblazoned in large gold letters on the flap. "Of course that meeting should not be here, or at your apartment in the Bronx. We must try to keep him away from his old influences, to avoid any temptations."

"It was that bad crowd he ran around with. He ran around with a bad crowd."

"Exactly. Now, if you'll just have a cashier's check ready tomorrow, payable to Tarkington's, Inc., I'll bring around all the necessary papers for you to sign. How's tomorrow afternoon at three o'clock?"

She nodded. "It should be interesting to see him. Now that he's so changed and all."

"I think you'll find the change in him absolutely astonishing," he said. He smiled at her. "The thing Dr. Weiss told me he remembered most about you was your beautiful green eyes, Mrs. Tarcher. I see what he meant."

She returned his smile. "Tell me something, Mr. Minskoff," she said. "Do you have a wife?"

"I do indeed. A beautiful wife, if I do say so."

"What's her coloring?"

"She is a blonde. A beautiful blonde."

"Good. I have a gift for her." She moved to a cupboard at the back of her shop, opened the door, and removed a pink straw sailor hat from its stand. "This was designed and made for a rich society girl from Long Island, also a blonde," she said. "It was to have been part of her wedding trousseau. But at the last minute she broke the engagement and called off the wedding. You know how young people are these days. I could have charged her for it, of course, but I don't like to do business that way. I'd like your wife to have this, Mr. Minskoff."

"What a beautiful hat, Mrs. Tarcher!"

"Each of those little silk roses was individually made by hand. It takes a girl almost two hours to make a single rose."

"My wife Honeychile will love it, Mrs. Tarcher."

"Let me put it in a box for you."

"Thank you, Mrs. Tarcher! We state social workers don't make much money, you know. It will be a real thrill for Honeychile to own a Leah Roth hat."

"May she wear it in good health," Rose said.

Outside, in the street, he knew he should spend the rest of the afternoon trying to round up more investors. But there were a couple of fillies running in the fifth at Aqueduct that he was interested in. The IRT station was right across the street, and if he caught an uptown train, then switched to the F train, he could be in Ozone Park by post time. He ran down the subway steps, the hatbox swinging by its cord in one hand, the big briefcase in the other. For a large man, Moe Minskoff moved fast.

"We got a hundred and fifty big ones from your old lady," he said that evening. "We're on our way, Silas baby, we're on our way!"

"Si," he said. "I think I'd rather be called Si."

"Whatever you say, pal. But we got a hundred and fifty big ones from the old lady. A hundred and fifty big ones—and a hat." He tossed the pink-and-white hatbox onto Silas Tarkington's sofa.

"Watch it, Moe!" Si snapped. "My mother puts a lot of work into those hats of hers!"

"Aw, come off it, Si. Shit. It's just a hat the old lady couldn't sell."

"And stop calling my mother the old lady!"

Moe Minskoff stared hard at his friend. "What's

with you, pal?" he said. "You got a wild hair up your ass or something?"

"I don't like the way you're talking about my mother."

"Shit. You never gave a shit about your old lady, and she never gave a shit about you."

"She just gave you a hundred and fifty thousand bucks, didn't she?"

"Shit. That was because I promised her a nine percent return on her money and some rent-free space in our store."

"She's still my mother, and that's still her money—and she gave you that for *my* store, not *our* store."

"Your store, our store, what's the diff? I still got the dough out of the old lady."

"I said stop calling her that, Moe!"

"Jeez," Moe said. "What's all this *mother* shit all of a sudden? She never once came to see you in the joint."

"That was because she was too busy—working to make a living for her family."

"So all of a sudden she's the Virgin Mary? She was too busy gettin' it off with Weiss, the tooth doctor, is what it was. He was drillin' her in more ways than one, that's for sure."

"Shut up, Moe!"

"You shoulda seen how her eyes lit up when I mentioned that fucker's name."

"I said shut up!"

"Jeez," he said. "I get you a hundred and fifty big ones from your old lady, and I get this shit. Some gratitude I get. Some thanks."

"You can take your hundred and fifty big ones and blow them out of that big fat ass of yours, one by one!"

Moe Minskoff's eyes narrowed to tiny slits. "Come off it, pal," he said. "Don't give me no shit. I know what you're pissed off about. I know you like a book. It's not me calling your old lady your old lady, is it? Shit, no. It's because you wouldn't have shit if it weren't for your old lady and your old man. Here's you, Mr. Big Shot, quittin' school and sayin' you're gonna make a million bucks, like

Mr. John Jacob Astor. What happens to you? You wind up with zip to ten in the slammer. What happens to the old man and the old lady? *They* end up makin' the million makin' and sellin' ladies' hats! They amounted to somethin', and you didn't amount to a shit sandwich. That hurts, doesn't it, pal? That's a tough booger to swallow, ain't it? Knowing you wouldn't have a pot to piss in if it weren't for the honest dough your old man and your old lady were making with the honest sweat off their honest balls, while you were making license plates in the joint!"

Si lunged toward the other man, seized his necktie by the knot, jerked his head backward, and punched him with a hard right to the jaw, a blow that sent Moe crashing on his backside to the floor. "Take that, you fat shmuck!" he said.

For a moment, Moe lay there, looking dazed. Then he leapt to his feet and charged at Si. With his left elbow, he pinned Si's neck against the wall and, with his right fist, began slamming punches at Si's face, while Si concentrated his returning punches on Moe's gut, trying to deliver a certain little liver punch he'd read about. He needed that little liver punch to free himself from Moe's weight.

Now pause, reader, for a moment, and consider the physical disparities between the two combatants.

Si Tarkington was eight years younger than Moses Minskoff, and he was also in better shape. At Hillsdale, Si had exercised regularly and developed a wiry, muscular physique. Moe's principal athletic activities in prison had been sleeping, eating, and watching television. On the other hand, Si had never been in a fist fight before. He had steered clear of the fights that occasionally broke out, had learned to walk away from a fight even when challenged, concentrating on earning points for good behavior. By contrast Moe Minskoff, who by his own admission was not well liked at Hillsdale, often found himself at the center of some prison brawl. Moe's great advantage was his weight. At two hundred and eighty pounds, he weighed nearly twice Si's hundred and forty-five. He was also three inches taller than Si, who was 5 feet 7 inches in his stocking feet.

Moe, who had Si pinned against the wall with one massive elbow, only had one fist with which to deliver blows—his right—and he concentrated on punches to the face. Si, meanwhile, had two free fists to fight with, and he concentrated on Moe's midsection, continuing to try to find Moe's liver. This, he knew, was located somewhere just below the rib cage, but with Moe's bulk the rib cage was not easy to find. He continued with rapid blows aimed at Moe's belly and above. A picture fell from the wall with a shattering of glass, then a mirror, then another heavier picture. A lamp fell over.

"Call me a shmuck, you little mama's boy?" Moe was saying. "You think I liked it, going out and begging for more of your old man's money for you? Doing a snow job on your old lady that you were too chicken to do yourself?"

Then Si found his target and delivered a series of hard, mean, fast punches with both fists to his opponent's solar plexus. Moe bellowed and fell back again heavily into the sofa, crashing on the hatbox. The sofa's frame cracked and Moe fell thunderously to the floor while Si danced around him, fists in the air, shouting, "Shmuck! Shmuck! Stand up, shmuck! I'm not finished with you yet!"

But it was over. Si's nose was bleeding, and his left eye was almost swollen shut and turning purple. Saliva dribbled from Moe's mouth, and he was clutching at his belly. The living room of Si's small apartment was a shambles. The wallpaper was spattered with blood, and an upstairs neighbor was banging loudly on the radiator pipes for peace.

Moe wiped his mouth with his sleeve. "Why are we doing this?" he asked numbly. "This is no way for partners to be. We shouldn't be fighting, babe. We should be celebrating, 'cause I even got more good news for you. My friend who owns the demolition company? He'll let us have the place for two and a quarter. How's that for good news? I got him down to two and a quarter, but he wants cash. Cash money, in hundreds. No checks. But that's no problem. We can get two and a quarter in hundreds. For two and a quarter in hundreds, the place is ours, Si, baby!"

Si spit some blood. "You okay, Moe?"

"Yeah, I'm okay. You?"

"I'm okay."

Moe heaved himself up from the collapsed sofa and the floor. "Shake?" he said and offered his hand.

"Shake. Want a beer, Moe?"

"Beer! We should be drinking to this deal with champagne," Moe said.

Even by flashlight—for the windows of the Van Degan mansion were boarded shut and the electricity had not been turned on—Silas Tarkington could see the potential of the building, and for the first time since Moe had pointed it out to him he began to feel a sense of excitement about the possibilities of his new purchase. The six matched Baccarat chandeliers (though he had not yet learned they were by Baccarat) that hung from the ceiling of the long entrance corridor were thick with dust, but they could be cleaned, and they would stay. The wide double staircase with its carved rosewood railings would have to go, but perhaps the railings and the marble steps could be used elsewhere. In place of the staircase would go a bank of elevators, for the single wire-cage Otis lift that had served the family would hardly suffice.

He flashed his torch up at the high carved-plaster and coffered ceilings and along the linenfold walnut-paneled walls. Most if not all of these interior details could be retained.

What impressed Si most about the mansion was the way, on each of its floors, the large rooms extended out from a central corridor, suggesting, as Moe had said, a series of intimate boutiques, each devoted to a different variety of merchandise. The house had been designed, it suddenly seemed to him, as though the Van Degans and Stanford White had actually had his store in mind.

It was then that he had his most important merchandising idea. Suppose some of these elegant rooms could be leased out to other merchants—quality merchants, of course. The income from these leased spaces could provide Si with working capital as he developed his store. If his own areas of the store turned out to be successful, he could little by little take over the leased spaces for his own merchandise. He had seen pictures of the Ponte Vecchio in Florence, with its row of little shops on either side. Each floor of his store would become a separate Ponte Vecchio. Leasing space would give him income and elbow room—room to grow. He decided, on a hunch, not to share this idea with Moe Minskoff.

But all at once, standing in the empty mansion with his flashlight, Si Tarkington could almost see his dream—that pipe dream he had dreamed aloud in their prison cell at Hillsdale—beginning to come true.

"Well," she said, when he joined her at a back table of the little restaurant on West 47th Street they had chosen.

"Well," he said.

"You're looking well, Solly," she said. "I like the mustache."

"I'm feeling pretty good, Mama," he said. "But I'm not Solly anymore."

"I know that," she said, "but you'll always be Solly to me. Oh, I know I'm not supposed to call you Solly in front of other people. I'm to call you Mr. Tarkington. It seems wrong, somehow, to have to change your name. But perhaps it's for the best."

"Yes. And how are you feeling, Mama? Are you feeling well?"

"Oh, I'm feeling pretty well. Except my eyes. The doctor says I'm not to do close work anymore."

"It's been a long time."

"Yes."

"I'm sorry, Mama."

"Well, it was hard, Solly. I won't say it wasn't hard.

It was even harder on your poor papa. He died of a broken heart."

He nodded, not looking at her. "You never came to see me, Mama," he said.

"No. Your papa didn't want me to."

"Yes."

"Even after he died, I thought I should respect his wishes."

"Yes. I understand."

"No, that's not true. I didn't want to go. I didn't think I could bear it, seeing my only son in a place like that."

He nodded again. "But thank you for helping me, Mama. With the money, I mean."

"Oh, well," she said, and let her voice trail off.

They sat in silence for a while, not looking at each other, and Rose Tarcher's fingers toyed with the paper napkin in her lap.

"Mr. Minskoff says you're going to be a big man. He says you're going to be a big success," she said at last.

"I hope so, Mama. I think so. I'm going to work real hard."

"Good. It's good you're going to work hard. It's good you're going to be a success. Your papa would have liked that. I wish he could have lived to see that."

"Yes. So do I."

"I'd like to live to see it too," she said. "I'm not getting any younger. I'll be sixty-two my next birthday. I'd like to go to my quiet grave knowing my only son was a success."

"You will, Mama."

Another silence.

"How is Grandma Roth?"

"Not too well. Getting older, bless her heart."

"Give her my love."

"I will."

A waiter approached them. "Oh, my goodness," Rose said. "We haven't even looked at the menu. Can you come back in a few more minutes?"

"The soup of the day is cream of lentil."

"Thank you. . . . Simma sends her love. I told her I was meeting you today. I hope that's all right. She said to give you her love."

"Give her my love too, Mama."

"I will. Oh, my. This is difficult for us, isn't it? It's difficult because there's so much to say. I don't know where to begin."

"Yes."

"Well, you know Simma's married now, of course. She has a nice husband. He's an accountant. He makes good money. Oh, and guess what? Simma told me this morning she thinks she's pregnant again. Doesn't know. Just thinks."

"That's nice."

"That will make my third grandchild!"

"Yes."

"That will be something to look forward to."

"Yes."

"Well, I'm glad you're going to be a big man," she said. "That will be something to look forward to, too. I'm glad you're going to be a success. That would have pleased your papa. I talk to your papa every day, you know. I know he doesn't hear me, but I talk to him just the same. I'm going to tell him that tonight, when I get home, that his son is going to be a big man. A big shot, as he would have said."

"Oh, Mama." He reached out and seized her hand. "Oh, Mama, I promise never to hurt you again. I promise you, I promise you, never to hurt you again."

17

He had been giving a lot of thought to the way his mother and father—and Grandma Roth before them—had run their small millinery business and why they had been successful.

The women who bought hats with the Leah Roth label certainly didn't need them. Mrs. Astor hadn't needed all the hats she bought. She bought Leah Roth hats because they were pretty, because they were one-of-a-kind. She bought them, in other words, because of the way they were presented to her, *because of the way they were sold to her.*

The kind of women customers Si Tarkington wanted to attract to his store were women who really didn't need anything at all. They already had more of everything than they would ever really need, and except for certain essentials such as soap and toothpaste they never shopped for necessities. Yet they shopped. Why? Because they enjoyed having attractive merchandise presented to them. They enjoyed being *sold.*

He began making the rounds of the city's smart specialty shops and department stores to see how well other merchants sold their merchandise. At the Small Leather Goods Department in Saks, he stood for twenty minutes waiting for someone to offer to help him. Meanwhile, not a dozen feet away, two saleswomen appeared to be chatting about a movie they had recently seen. He finally walked away. That sort of thing would never happen in *his* store, he decided. In the Better Dresses department at Lord & Taylor, he told the saleswoman that he was interested in buying a sweater set for his wife, only to be curtly told that he was in the wrong department. The woman neglected to mention the table stacked with sweaters right around the corner. That sort of thing would not happen in his store either.

At Bergdorf-Goodman, he was told it was the wrong season for sweater sets. The salesperson failed to suggest an alternative gift for his wife. He telephoned the Gift Department at Bloomingdale's and counted while the phone rang thirty-two times before anyone came to answer it. At Altman's, he asked whether the sweaters he was looking at were cashmere or not. "I don't know," the saleswoman replied. "Look at the label. If it is, it'll say so." He began making notes of all these shortcomings of salesmanship.

He decided to pretend to be interested in buying a new car and stopped at a Park Avenue showroom that sold expensive Jaguar automobiles. The salesman appeared indifferent to his interest; when he asked to test-drive a model with a $12,000 price tag, he was told, "That's the showroom model, that ain't no demo." Si thanked the salesman for his trouble and left, and the salesman didn't even say goodbye.

On his shopping excursions, he was quickly struck by the similarity of the merchandise offered by the different stores. He found the same red-and-white print Clare McCardell shirtwaist dress at Saks, Bloomingdale's, De Pinna, Lord & Taylor, Altman's, Best's, Bonwit's, and Macy's. All were identically on sale, at $59.95, marked down from $79.95. How many red-and-white print Clare McCardell shirtwaist dresses would a woman want to own? Only one, and she would buy it from the store that presented it most attractively and sold it most effectively.

He began making lists.

SALESPEOPLE

1. Salespeople should be attractive-looking, well-dressed, with good taste in clothes. They should appear to be well-educated, which means well-spoken. Certain foreign accents (esp. French) may be acceptable. No obvious physical deformities. No Negroes.

2. Salespeople should be polite, attentive, help-ful, cheerful, but not kowtowish. The sales-person who does not have the item a customer is looking for in his or her department should escort the customer to department where item is located.

3. If item the customer seeks is not sold in the store, salesperson should suggest an alterna-tive purchase, e.g., "I'm afraid the store doesn't carry that, but before you go let me show you something pretty that just came in."

4. Once customer gives his or her name for charge purchase, salesperson should address customer by name afterward. "Let me have this wrapped for you, Mrs. Jones. . . . Here is your package, Mrs. Jones."

5. Salespeople should record customers' sizes, tastes, and color preferences, etc., etc. *Never* look a customer up and down and say, "You look like about a size 14, Mrs. Jones."

6. If a customer has made a purchase in excess of $200, salesperson should write customer a note (handwritten) on store stationery the next day, thanking customer for purchase.

7. Good customers (in excess of $1,000 in purchases per year) should receive Christmas cards from salesperson. Also, if ascertainable, birthday and anniversary cards, etc.

8. Salespeople should keep track of customers' lives through society pages, etc. "I read about the lovely coming-out party you had for your daughter, Mrs. Jones."

9. Salespeople (without being pestish) should telephone customers periodically with store news or special events. "Some beautiful new coats just came in from Paris, Mrs. Jones, and I immediately thought of you."

10. Salespeople should *never* gossip behind counters, stick pens or pencils in hair or behind ears, wear pants suits, wear ankle-strap shoes, chew gum. . . .

The list continued at some length. Si had already decided that his store would specialize in female designer apparel, so he began to draw up another list.

MERCHANDISE

1. Manufacturers tend to produce too many pieces of one design. Result: Same dress appears all over town at the same time.

2. Tarkington's apparel must be available *only at Tarkington's.* This means manufacturers (in NYC and Europe) must be persuaded to create a special line just for us. This may be hard to do at first, but make this our long-range goal.

3. No garment shall remain in store longer than one season. *No garment shall go on sale.* Each unsold garment will be disposed of elsewhere after its season—label out. No woman will find Tarkington's label in Filene's Basement.

4. For custom couture, Tarkington's should find its own in-house designer. Advertise for him . . .

Not long after this item appeared on Si Tarkington's list, the following advertisement ran in the male Help Wanted columns:

Designer Wanted

Small select Manhattan specialty shop looking for
young, talented, unknown designer of haute couture. No experience necessary, only distinctive designing flair. Chance for rapid advancement. Bring
portfolio. For appointment, call 555-3400.

A stream of applicants followed, and Si set aside several hours of each business day to interview these
hopefuls and scrutinize their work. He didn't know what
he was looking for, exactly, but was certain he would
recognize it when he saw it. He divided the portfolios into
two stacks, marked POSSIBLE and NO.

One day he felt he had found what he wanted in a
twenty-two-year-old Pratt graduate named Antonio
Delfino. There was something about the young man's
fluid, floating designs that seemed to say he understood
the female figure.

"I would hate to have to design anything for a
woman over a size ten," the young man said. "I don't
design for porkers."

Si liked this young man's cocky confidence and spirit.
He also liked his name. He could envision the sign DESIGNS
BY DELFINO above the entrance to the couture salon. He
negotiated a contract with Mr. Delfino to design an exclusive collection for the future store, giving him two
years to come up with "the most exciting couture collection in the world." It was a tall order, but Antonio
seemed delighted with the challenge.

Si also added a new item to his lengthening list of
merchandise rules:

47. No item of female apparel will be offered
    larger than a Size 10. Let Lane Bryant have
    the porkers.

He might not have realized it at the time, but Si was
developing a merchandising philosophy.

Si had formulated a two-year plan to prepare his

store for its grand opening, which he was planning for the early autumn of 1958. Nothing was to be rushed. No corners were to be cut. Everything must be perfectly in place by that date, which was naturally calculated to take advantage of the Christmas shopping season. In addition to his many lists, he devised an elaborate work and production schedule, which included a two-week "dress rehearsal," during which no customers would be admitted, but he and his staff would go through every phase of the selling operation in each department in an effort to iron out any possible wrinkles. Si often found himself waking in the middle of the night to jot down ideas on a pad he kept beside his bed.

> *Telephone switchboard operators: No New York accents! Try for British accents if possible. Have them say, "Good morning, this is Tarkington's." Or, "Tarkington's, at your service." Which? Decide!*

> *Couture salon: Have soft, classical music piped in. Have full bar there. Bartender in white mess jacket, gold trim. Like pic in* Life *magazine of grand saloon on* S.S. Mauretania. *Grand piano in one corner.*

The next morning, he was able to find a magnificent Bösendorfer in rosewood and walnut, with its four extra keys in the treble and the bass. The sounding board was cracked, which was why it had found its way to a second-hand furniture store. Artur Rubinstein would have scorned it, but then Artur Rubinstein was not going to play it. It was appropriate to the room he had chosen for the couture salon because, Si had discovered, that room had originally been Mrs. Van Degan's music room.

The Van Degan mansion, meanwhile, was proving to be even more compatible with Si's plans than he had first imagined. With the windows unboarded and the lights turned on, Si and his crew of workmen had discovered wonderful things. The floors, stripped of years of grime, turned out to be Carrara marble, which polished to a high gleam. Several of the stained-glass windows, when layers of city soot had been removed, turned out to be signed creations of Louis Comfort Tiffany. Nearly all the major rooms had working fireplaces, each with a distinctive carved wood or marble mantelpiece, and all these architectural details would be kept. The groin-vaulted windowless room that had been the Van Degans' library was lined, floor to ceiling, with bookshelves behind glass doors, and the room even came with its own set of rolling library steps. These shelves could be used to handsomely display the sweaters, scarves, and so on, from the store's collection of designer sportswear.

The innards of the house, on the other hand, were another matter. The original copper plumbing was, for the most part, in good shape. But the electrical system was not, and as Si's remodeling crew worked with their power tools they were continually blowing fuses and seeing noisy sparks crackling out of outlets. Moe Minskoff insisted he had a friend who had a friend in the city's Department of Buildings who, for a small consideration, would see to it that the building passed the department's inspection. But Si, who had seen the frayed and sputtering wiring himself, decided that such a course was far too risky. The entire building would have to be rewired and a costly circuit-breaker system installed.

In the Van Degans' day, the house had been heated by a huge coal furnace, and one vast area of the basement had been the coal bin. This would be converted into workrooms and storage rooms, and the coal furnace would be replaced with a smaller and more efficient gas heating and air-conditioning unit. As each of these costly jobs was completed, Si ticked off another item on his lists.

In a way, it was a good thing that he and Moe had had their fight. It cleared the air. It also established a chain of authority, and there was no longer any question as to who was in charge of this project. Moe was useful when it came to rounding up investors. He seemed to have dozens of money sources. Most of these were for relatively small amounts—one or two thousand dollars each—but it all helped, and Moe had come up with one other $150,000 investor, whom he wouldn't yet name.

But, though Moe raised money, the handling and spending of it was done by Si alone. Only Si was empowered to sign the checks to the contractors and subcontractors working for him; after his courses at Hillsdale, he had become an excellent bookkeeper. For each of Moe's contributions, Moe was given a receipt or promissory note, nothing more. Si knew that Moe was a gambler, and no gambler can ever be entrusted with cash.

One night on the scratch pad by his bed, Si Tarkington found himself writing:

> As soon as start-up costs are recovered and we begin to see some black ink, think of ways to start easing Moe out of this.

Moe had been right, of course. Si did feel little pangs of guilt, knowing that much of what he was spending represented his father's lifetime savings, the father whom he had disgraced, and that he had also dipped into nearly half of his hardworking mother's inheritance. But he kept promising himself that once his store was making money he would start to pay her back. And, he could rationalize, his own inheritance from his father was not his fault. If anything, it was his father's fault, for being so imprudent as to leave no will. Perhaps his father had not really *wanted* him to have this money. But if he hadn't wanted it, the old man should have been smart enough to see that he didn't get it.

Besides, unbeknownst to Moe—or to anyone else, in fact, except his lawyer, Jake Kohlberg—Si had another source of money. It was not a huge sum, but it could always be tapped if need be. From his days in the fur business, he had saved close to twenty thousand dollars. He had placed this money in the Dime Savings Bank of New York because he had been impressed with the bank's claim that one could start an account there for as little as ten cents. During his years at Hillsdale, this sum had been gathering interest and had mounted up. He had not swept these funds into the store's general operating account yet, but if it became necessary he would. By now, creating the kind of special store he had in mind had become an obsession with him.

He was also having some success with his idea of leasing sections of the mansion to other merchants. He had discovered a jewelry store on West 47th Street called Bosky & Gompertz whose lease would soon be up and whose landlord was demanding a twenty-percent rent hike to renew. He approached Irving Bosky and Mel Gompertz and offered them what had been the Van Degans' billiard room on the street floor. The partners were definitely interested. Si had only one request. He explained to them the kind of store he planned to open and the kind of clientele he hoped to attract. Somehow, he said as politely as he could, a jewelry shop in Tarkington's called Bosky & Gompertz did not sound quite right. He explained that his own name was an Anglicized version of the original one. In return for a favorable lease, would the partners consider renaming their store? Flipping through the Manhattan telephone directory in search of stylish-sounding names, he even came up with a new name for them. What about Delafield & Du Bois? The partners agreed.

Si was now working on a similar arrangement with a retailer who sold fine women's footwear on the Upper East Side and was interested in the street-floor space that had once been the Van Degans' morning room. All these extra sources of income would help.

Still, he was troubled by the fact that Moe Minskoff seemed to be becoming more of a liability than an asset, as his plans for his store drew slowly toward completion. Moe, for instance, seemed to have become unduly concerned about Si's sex life, or lack of it, and during those busy months Si's sex life was indeed nonexistent. As the end of each week approached, Moe would drop by and say, "Let's go out and get ourselves a coupla broads for the night. Whaddaya say?"

"No, no. I've got to work on the books."

"All work and no play makes Jack a dull boy!"

"No, no."

"C'mon. Gotta get your rocks off sometime. I got a friend who knows this redhead that gives terrific head. Only twenty bucks, and she's got a girlfriend."

"No, no thanks, Moe."

Though Moe claimed to be devoted to his wife, Honeychile, he also said, "A man's gotta get a little strange pussy every now and then. It's good for him, and it helps save the marriage."

"Not tonight, Moe."

"Whaddaya do for kicks, pal? Mrs. Fist and her five daughters? Jackin' off ain't good for you. It drains the vital fluids."

"Honest, Moe, I've got work to do tonight."

"Well, you're missin' out on a great piece of strange pussy, pal."

"Maybe some other time."

Now, on the pad on the table beside his bed, he found himself writing, and underlining, and following with a string of exclamation points: *Think of a way to get rid of Moe!!!!!*

Actually, there was one woman who, when he permitted himself to think about women at all, he thought of often. Her name was Alice Markham and she too was a redhead, though not from the same walk of life as the one Moe Minskoff had in mind.

Assembling the kind of bright, attractive, and attentive sales force he wanted was turning out to be harder than he'd thought. In fact, of all the problems involved in preparing his store for its opening, this was easily the most difficult to solve. He'd decided that advertising for salespeople would not work. Most people who were looking for jobs wanted to go to work right away and were not interested in waiting several months for jobs to become available. And it was not economically feasible to put promising people on the payroll and give them nothing to do. He had decided on a word-of-mouth approach. As he made his rounds of Seventh Avenue designers, trying to persuade them to produce lines of clothing that would be sold exclusively at Tarkington's, he let it be known that he was looking for salespeople who would look just right, talk just right, handle a customer just right. A few possibilities had turned up, but one particularly attractive young woman, who had been the directrice at Anne Klein, had said to him, "Well, if nothing better turns up between now and when you're ready to start your training program, I'll give you a call." Si decided that this was not the sort of attitude he wanted at Tarkington's.

But Alice Markham was different. She was more than merely attractive. She had lovely red hair that she wore in a short, fluffy style, and she did not have the sort of pale, freckled skin that usually accompanies red hair. Her skin was smooth and lightly tanned, and she looked like a California girl, which, as it turned out, she was. She was a slim size six, and from the casual way she had tied a bright Hermès scarf across one shoulder it was obvious to Si that she had a sense of style. She needed, and wore, very little makeup other than brown lipstick. It was that quirky, distinctive touch that he admired most—the brown lipstick. She had passed the Van Degan mansion a number of times, had noticed the renovations going on, and, when a designer friend had told her that an expensive specialty store was soon to open there and was looking for salespeople, she had come to apply for a job.

As Si took her on a tour of his still-unfinished store and she exclaimed over some of the architectural details that Si had preserved and at the quality of the new work that was being done, she told him a bit more about herself. She was twenty-eight years old, a graduate of Stanford, where she had majored in Art History, and was a recent widow. Her husband had been an Air Force captain who was killed on a training mission. "We'd been married less than a year," she told him. "And we were stationed at Mather Air Force Base in Sacramento. His plane simply blew up in the sky over Arizona. The cause of the accident was never determined, or, if it was, it was never officially explained to me. All three men aboard the plane were lost. The Air Force shipped a coffin home to me, and when I asked that it be opened they did so with some reluctance. There was nothing inside but one of his uniforms, carefully pressed and folded, so that was what I buried. After that, I decided I didn't want to live in California anymore, so I came here." She told this sad story without bitterness, only with a certain sense of bewilderment and resignation.

He escorted her into the room that would be the couture salon. "Oh, what a beautiful fireplace!" she exclaimed. "And look—a Bösendorfer! That must have cost you a fortune!"

So she knew good merchandise when she saw it.

"Promise not to tell anyone, but it has a cracked sounding board," he said.

She laughed. "I promise not to tell a living soul," she said, and Si found himself also admiring her soft, lilting speaking voice and rich, throaty laugh. "Cracked sounding board or not, that piano is the perfect touch. This is going to be the most elegant store in New York, Mr. Tarkington."

"That's what I'm aiming for, Mrs. Markham," he said, looking around him. "But there's still an awful lot of work to be done."

"Don't worry. I can visualize it perfectly. I can see what it's going to be like in my mind's eye. I'd love to work in a store like this, Mr. Tarkington."

"Please call me Si."

"Then you must call me Alice," she said. "If I worked here, I'd be Alice in Wonderland."

"There's only one problem," he said. "Even if everything goes completely according to schedule, we can't possibly be ready to open before early October. And I can't put anyone on the payroll until then."

"That's all right," she said. "I'll gladly wait. To be honest with you, I really don't *need* to work. My husband left me a very nice life insurance policy, and I have his Air Force pension. But I *want* to work. And I can't think of any place I'd rather work than in this beautiful store, selling beautiful things to beautiful women."

Alice Markham, he decided, was going to be nothing short of the perfect Tarkington's saleswoman.

That night on the note pad by his bed he wrote, *Find more Alice Markhams!!!!* But that, it turned out, would not be an easy task.

He began telephoning her every week or so, to give her reports on the store's progress. A strike of the electricians' union had been threatened and had been called off, but there were other, almost daily problems. Labor disputes in France were delaying shipments from the Paris couturiers. Seventh Avenue designers were bickering over display space. Mollie Parnis would not have her garments displayed in any part of the store where they would be visible from Pauline Trigère's collection. Cyril Marx, who had been hired to head the Display Department, was sick with the flu. The *faux*-porcelain mannequins that had been special-ordered from Goldfinch & Brewer in Chicago arrived, mysteriously, with only one leg apiece. "No arms, we could fake!" Cyril Marx screamed from his sickbed on Staten Island. "But we can't have all our mannequins standing on just their left legs!" Then Cyril's lover got on the phone and screamed some more. "Do you realize he has a temperature of a hundred and *two*, Mr. Tarkington?" he said. "What are you trying to *do* to him, Mr. Tarkington? Are you trying to *kill* him? What *are* you, some kind of *fiend*?"

All these problems came to Si Tarkington for him to try to settle and solve, and Alice Markham listened to them, and sometimes she even had useful suggestions. "What if you put Parnis at one end of the elevator bank and Trigère at the other?" she suggested. "The spaces are equal, the amount of traffic through them would be the same, and nobody could see one collection while looking at the other one."

"Damn, why didn't I think of that?" he said.

Mostly, he telephoned her because he didn't want to lose her. He had begun to see her as irreplaceable. But also, he realized, he telephoned her because he liked listening to her soft, cultivated voice and hearing her ripply, throaty laugh.

"Tell me," he said to her one day, "am I ever going to find any more people like you?"

There was the laugh again. "Well," she said. "You just might. There's my friend Beverly Hollister, a girl I play tennis with. Bev is green with envy that I'm going to have this job. She's got great chic."

"More chic than you?"

Once more, the laugh. "Want to see for yourself? Shall I have Bev call you?"

"Please do," he said.

But when he put down the phone, he was certain that, whatever Beverly Hollister turned out to be like, there would never be another Alice Markham.

Do we dream in color, or do we dream in black and white? That question is often argued. That night Si Tarkington dreamed in color: red hair—and brown lipstick.

18

Silas Tarkington would never really know at what point, exactly, he became certain that his new store was going to be a hit. The certainty came gradually, and only seemed to increase the fury of his pace.

In the final weeks of preparation, he seemed to be everywhere at once, at all hours of the day and night, and those working under him began to believe that he never slept. They would encounter him on one of the selling floors adjusting a mannequin's pose (the missing limbs had finally been delivered) or running a vacuum cleaner over a stretch of carpet. They would see him with Windex and a dust cloth, polishing a display case, or on a ladder in the sportswear department, arranging sweaters according to size and color. In the middle of the night he might be found in one of the Fifth Avenue windows—still curtained, with muslin, from public view—helping Cyril Marx mount a window display or pinning up the hem on a gown from Antonio Delfino's couture collection. He seemed tireless in his quest for absolute perfection.

"Why has that door been left standing open?" he

would suddenly bark. "That door should remain closed at all times!

"Where are the Porthault towels for the ladies' rest room?

"Why is there no toilet paper in this stall?

"That 'T' in our letterhead looks more like a 'P,' and the word 'Tarkington's' should have an apostrophe, for God's sake.

"I want the lid on the piano down, not up, to show off the wood.

"The ficus tree is blocking the view from the entrance. Move it three feet back.

"What about self-covered buttons, Antonio? What do you think?

"Where is the rest of my shipment from Chanel? They've only sent us three pieces. We ordered twenty."

There was some grumbling, naturally, about Si's constant nitpicking among the members of his staff. But since he pitched right into the exhausting work along with them, they for the most part accepted it—though once, when an electrician angrily threw down his tools and threatened to walk off the job, Si had to chase the man out into the street to cajole him to come back. And as the number of weeks until opening day grew shorter, the tempo of everyone's work grew faster to the point of frenzy.

"I ordered gold elevator buttons, not bronze!

"That sofa has a spot on it!

"That mirror is chipped!

"Where is the rest of my shipment from Chanel?"

Now Si hardly ever left the store.

He did, however, sleep. The top two floors of the mansion, which had contained the Van Degans' servants' rooms, were still unfinished, and in one of these cubicles Si had tossed an old mattress. Here, between bouts of work, he retreated for ten- or fifteen-minute catnaps. One workman, finding his boss sprawled face downward and fully clothed on his mattress, thought for an awful moment that the king had died. That was what his staff had begun to call him, "the king," though some people had already started to call him Mr. Si.

It had been Alice Markham's suggestion that the store have two gala preview parties. The first would be for the fashion press. The second, also by invitation only, would be for people in New York society who might be expected to become Tarkington's customers. The parties would take place on two succeeding Thursday nights. "Thursday's the most fashionable night for entertaining in New York," she said. "Don't ask me why. If we get good press from the first party, people will turn out in droves for the second one. The press will make this *the* place to be on the night of the second party. We might get some society press for that party as well, if the right names show up."

"How do we make sure they do?"

"New Yorkers will turn out for anything, if the food and liquor are free," she said, "but here's a start," and she handed him a small black-and-red volume called *The New York Social Register*. In it she had checked off certain names, and as he leafed through the little book he was surprised to see her listed in it:

Markham, Mrs. Erickson B. (Alice L. Boynton) Jl.

"What does that mean, Jl?" he asked her.

She laughed her throaty laugh. "Junior League," she said.

Si was impressed.

"It's just a glorified telephone book," she said. "But it might be useful for the sort of party you have in mind."

Now, in addition to other things, Si worked on the guest list and invitations, which would read:

Tarkington's
cordially invites you
to a special gala preview
of our new store
Thursday, October 9
Fifth Avenue & 59th Street
Six to nine p.m.
Cocktails and dancing   *R.s.v.p.*

"Who should we get to do the printing," he asked her, "Tiffany or Cartier?"

"Not printing, please," she said, with that lovely laugh of hers, "engraving. By Cartier. It's much more chic."

He realized he was relying upon her more and more for advice, and yet somehow he didn't mind. Everything about this girl impressed him.

In addition to attending to dozens of small problems that kept arising, Si spent the final two weeks before the first preview party putting his sales staff through the training program he had devised for them. His object was to impress upon them the kind of service-oriented establishment he intended Tarkington's to be. He had finally assembled twenty-four sales men and women who seemed more or less satisfactory to him, and now he went from department to department, acting as though he were a customer and presenting them with as many selling problems as he could think of.

"I'd like to buy this for my wife," he said to Beverly Hollister, Alice's tennis-playing friend. He fingered the hem of a lime-green chiffon peignoir, its sleeves and neckline trimmed with white maribou, that she was holding up for him. "But I don't know her size."

"Is she about my size, sir?"

"No. Taller."

"Then she's probably an eight. But don't forget Tarkington's pickup and delivery service. If it's the wrong size, we can send a messenger to pick it up and deliver another in her correct size at the same time. It's pretty, isn't it? I just wish I could afford it for myself."

"But I live in California."

"That's perfectly all right, sir. We use a nationwide delivery service."

"Well, I think maybe I'll wait till I get home," he said.

"Certainly, sir," she said, carefully refolding the garment. "I'm sure you could find something similar out there. You won't find the same garment, though. Tarkington's has this design exclusively."

"Hmm," he said, scratching his chin. "It *is* pretty."

"Tell me," she said. "Is this a gift for a special occasion? Her birthday? An anniversary?"

"Our wedding anniversary, yes."

"An important one?"

"Yes, our seventy-fifth."

"Oh, how nice," she said without batting an eyelash. "That will be your platinum anniversary, did you know that? Had you thought about a piece of jewelry? You might want to look in our Delafield and Du Bois boutique. They have some lovely things."

"No, I wanted it to be lingerie."

"Then let me show you just one more thing," she said, and pulled open a drawer. "It's a silver lamé bed jacket, which is the closest thing to platinum. And it just slips over the shoulders, like this, so it fits all sizes."

"Very good, Beverly," he said. "I liked what you said about wishing you could afford to buy it. The customer is flattered when you assume he's rich. You're going to make a good saleswoman."

"I just hope I'm still around for your seventy-fifth wedding anniversary, Mr. Si."

He patted her shoulder. "You'd also make a damned good actress," he said.

But now, just days before the first of the two preview parties, an even more pressing problem arose. The full consignment of dresses he had ordered from Chanel in Paris had still not arrived, and Si was frantic. The Chanel boutique was finished, with its distinctive double-C logo over the door in gold, and he had no stock for it. "How can I open a Chanel boutique with only three pieces?" he moaned. Every morning—starting at 5 A.M. to take advantage of the six-hour time difference and catch them at the beginning of their business day—he was on the telephone to 31 rue Cambon, using his best French. All they could tell him was that the shipment had left Orly. "*Ils sont parti d'Orly, monsieur,"* he was told repeatedly *"C'est tout que je sais."*

"What am I going to do?" he wailed.

"Let me see what I can do," Moe Minskoff said.

At four o'clock on the afternoon of the party, an unmarked panel truck pulled up to Tarkington's shipping dock and three large crates were unloaded. As Si and Cyril Marx worked furiously to arrange the display in the boutique before the first guests started to arrive, Si saw immediately that these were not the dresses he had ordered. But they were by Chanel, and they would have to do.

"How did you get these, Moe?" Si asked him.

"Don't ask questions," Moe said. "You got your dresses, didn't you?"

"How did you get them?"

"Just say I may not be well liked, but I got friends."

"Moe, tell me where you got these dresses!"

"Let's just say they fell off a conveyor belt at Idlewild," Moe said.

It was five minutes of six, and there was no time for any further discussion of the matter.

Of course Si Tarkington did not realize it at the time, but just across the street, at Bergdorf-Goodman, a buyer was screaming into the telephone, *"What do you mean my shipment from Chanel got lost?"*

Alice Markham had suggested that, instead of standing at the Fifth Avenue entrance and greeting his guests as they arrived, Si should wait upstairs in his fifth-floor office until most of the guests were there and were enjoying the cocktails, the music, and the hors d'oeuvres that were being passed by waiters in pink-and-white mess jackets, the store's colors. "Let them wander around and get the feel of the store," she said. "As they say in the fashion business, let them get their 'eye in.' Then, when I see that all the important writers and editors are here and everybody's having a good time, I'll phone you and you can come down."

And so, while the members of the fashion press milled around downstairs, asking, "Where is he? Where is this Mr. Tarkington?" Si sat alone upstairs, nervously chain-smoking mentholated cigarettes. Finally the telephone rang. He stubbed out his last cigarette in the overflowing ashtray, stood up, straightened his necktie, put on his jacket, shot his shirt cuffs, ran a comb through his hair, brushed away any dandruff that might have settled on his shoulders, and headed for the elevator.

As he made his entrance, emerging from the elevator on the street floor, someone—could it have been the savvy Alice Markham?—cried, "Here he is!" And Silas Tarkington's entrance was greeted with a burst of enthusiastic applause, while he beamed at his guests.

Now flashbulbs started to pop, and instinctively Si reached up and covered his face with his hands. "Please," he begged, "don't photograph me. Photograph the store . . . the store . . . the store. . . ."

Much later that night, Alice Boynton Markham raised herself on one elbow in her dark bedroom, and said, "I think I had too much to drink at the party tonight. I shouldn't have let you seduce me."

"I've wanted to do this for a long time," he whispered. "I've wanted to do this for a long, long time."

From *The New York Times,* October 10, 1958:

NEW TARKINGTON'S STORE
APPEARS TO BE A HIT

Tarkington's, a new name on the fashion horizon, made its first bow to New York last night when fashion editors and writers were treated to a special preview of the new store's resplendent delights. The store will officially open its doors to shoppers next Friday.

For months, Fifth Avenue merchants and other retailers have been gossiping and speculating about what was going on behind the McKim, Mead & White facade of the former Truxton Van Degan mansion at Fifth Avenue and 59th Street, and eagerly awaiting a chance for a glimpse inside. The result seems to have been worth the wait. The mansion, which was slated for the wrecker's ball two years ago, was saved in the nick of time by the young merchant Silas Tarkington and has been transformed into handsome retailing space that is in many ways unique.

Architectural Details Preserved

By dividing his selling space into a series of intimate boutiques, Mr. Tarkington was able to preserve much of the mansion's original floor plan. Other architectural details that have been preserved are marble floors and fireplaces, Tiffany stained-glass windows, Baccarat chandeliers, and wall panelings of exotic woods.

The merchandise, all of it decidedly on the pricey side, lends itself perfectly to this arrangement. On the street floor, near the Fifth Avenue entrance, is the Leah Roth boutique, a well-known name in designer millinery. For the press opening, Leah Roth offered a display of hats designed for the late Mrs. John Jacob Astor. The hats, borrowed from the Astor estate for the occasion, are all in black, since Mrs. Astor wore only black after her husband went down on the S.S. *Titanic* in 1912. Also on the street floor is the glittering boutique of Delafield & Du Bois, a new name in jewelry.

On an upper floor, in a room graced by an antique grand piano, is the salon of Antonio Delfino, a young designer never before shown in New York, whose airy, witty creations suggest that he is slated to become a name of considerable importance in the fashion world. Thus has Mr. Tarkington, a shy man who dislikes being photographed, cleverly combined the old and the new. Displays and windows, designed by Cyril Marx, manage to be both elegant and amusing at the same time.

In the gala party atmosphere of last night's press preview, it was impossible to tell whether the level of the store's service will match its magnificent array of fashion merchandise and its stunning decor, but if the enthusiastic response of last night's invited guests is any indication, Tarkington's seems well on its way to joining the pantheon of New York's fine specialty stores.

"What's a pantheon?" he asked her. The newspaper was spread out on the bed between them.

"It's a roster of the gods," she said. "You're about to become one of the gods, my darling."

He swung his feet over the side of the bed. "I've got to get to the store," he said.

"So do I," she said.

The clean-up squad was already at work when they arrived, by separate taxis. Someone had dropped a lighted cigarette on an Oriental rug, leaving an ugly burn, and a weaver had to be found who could repair it quickly. Cocktail glasses had left rings on many of the display counters, and even on the lid of the Bösendorfer. Bottles of Windex and furniture polish were being brandished everywhere. Merchandise had been pulled out for inspection, and display shelves and counters had to be put back in their original perfect order. Vacuum cleaners droned throughout the store. Si and Alice pitched in with the work, careful not to let their eyes travel toward each other. No one must suspect that they had become lovers the night before.

"Party favors," Alice said at one point during the day. "It would be great if we could have favors for next week's party—something for the women and something for the men."

"What could we give them?"

Alice snapped her fingers. "Antonio," she said. "He's designed a fragrance. Did you know that?"

"I did not know that."

"He gave me a little sample of it, and I thought it was quite nice. Oil of vetiver, clove, a bit of lemon—it's a spicy, woodsy scent. We could give perfume to the ladies, cologne to the gentlemen."

"We've invited five hundred people. Could he have that much by next Thursday?"

"I think so. Right now, his collection's finished. He's the least busy person in the store."

"But bottles! We'd need to bottle it and package it, all by next Thursday. That's impossible."

"I happen to have a friend—" Moe Minskoff offered.

"No, this is Alice's idea," Si said, a little sharply. "Alice will handle it."

"We'd need different bottles for the men's and women's fragrances, of course," she said. "Let me see what I can find in the way of bottles, and if necessary I'll do the packaging myself. If the scent turns out to be popular, we can sell it in the store and pay Antonio a royalty."

"Do you really think you can pull all this off by Thursday?"

"Of course," she said. "This is New York, remember? The great thing about New York is that there's always a little hole-in-the-wall store somewhere that sells whatever you're looking for."

By Monday, she had found her one-ounce spray bottles. "I'd hoped for something a little more stylish," she said. "These are from an Elizabeth Arden line that's been discontinued, but they'll have to do. If the scent's a success, Antonio will design his own bottles." Antonio had concocted his perfume in the kitchen of his apartment, and by Monday afternoon he had put together three full gallons of his essence. Perfume became men's cologne, he explained, simply by diluting the essence base with alcohol. On Tuesday, Alice and Antonio spent the day filling five hundred bottles with medicine droppers. It was a tedious job, and by the end of the day both of them had headaches from the heavy scent.

On Wednesday, the labels arrived from the printer,

pink labels for the perfume and blue for the cologne. The labels read:

Parfum de Antonio
BY
DELFINO OF TARKINGTON'S

The rest of that day was spent affixing the labels to the bottles, and Alice spent most of Wednesday night wrapping the party favors—blue tissue paper with pink ribbon bows for the men, pink paper with blue ribbons for the women. By Thursday morning, the job was done.

They had decided to employ the same tactic: Si Tarkington would not make his entrance until the party was well under way. Tonight, when Si stepped off the elevator, there was also applause. But since tonight's guests were from the worlds of society and the arts, where each celebrity guest was interested in his or her personal appearance more than in anyone else's, the applause was more polite and muted. Si immediately recognized some reasonably well-known faces.

There, in black, was Maria Callas. There was Audrey Hepburn, chatting with Joan Fontaine. There were Arlene Francis and her husband, Martin Gabel. There were Maureen O'Hara, David Niven, Moira Shearer, Nina Foch, Rhonda Fleming, Joan Bennett and Clare and Harry Luce, Charlton and Lydia Heston, Kirk and Anne Douglas. Alice had also managed to snare some European titles—"New Yorkers love titles," she said—and, taking Si by the arm, she introduced him to the Princess de Crouy, the Countess D'Arcangues, and the Princess Colonna. Through it all swirled Antonio—youthful, handsome, and dashing in his dinner jacket—taking compliments on his fragrance and on his designs, in his true element at last. A poor boy from Brooklyn, born to Italian immigrant parents, he had confessed to Alice, as they worked in his kitchen with the little bottles, that he had got his idea for mixing a fragrance while helping his

father make wine in the family's basement in Crown
Heights.

"There's someone you must meet," Alice whispered
to Si. "Monique Van Degan is here. Her husband's grandfather built this house. She's upstairs in Sportswear with
the Begum Aga Khan."

From *The New York Times,* October 17, 1958:

SECOND GALA
TOASTS THE ARRIVAL
OF TARKINGTON'S

The worlds of international celebrity and high society
collided with the tinkle of champagne glasses last night in
the second of two glittering galas to toast the arrival of
Tarkington's, the elegant new emporium on Fifth Avenue
at 59th Street. The store opens officially to the public this
morning at 10 A.M., but last night's entertainment was
by invitation only. Invitations were carefully scrutinized
at the door, and potential crashers were challenged.

Among the invited guests was Adam Gimbel, president of Saks Fifth Avenue and a vice president of the Fifth
Avenue Association. Asked whether Tarkington's might
not provide stiff competition for his own luxury-goods
store, Mr. Gimbel merely smiled and said, "Whatever is
good for Fifth Avenue is good for us."

Another guest was Mrs. Truxton Van Degan III,
whose husband's grandfather, the late railroad magnate,
commissioned the stately seven-story graystone McKim,
Mead & White mansion now occupied by Tarkington's.
"It was a wonderful house," Mrs. Van Degan said, looking around the new store, "but it had become such a
white elephant for the family. No one can afford to live

on this grand a scale anymore. It's wonderful that Mr. Tarkington had the taste and imagination to redo the place. Who would have thought it possible? We thought we were lucky to get $150,000 from a demolition company to tear it down, and *they* thought they were lucky to find a buyer for $25,000 more. The really lucky one is Mr. Tarkington. He's such a charming man."

Mrs. Van Degan looked wistfully up at the ceiling of the street floor lobby, where six matching Baccarat chandeliers are suspended. "I wish I'd had the sense to take just one of those for myself before the sale," she said. "I'd frankly forgotten about them. The last time I was here, they were in bags."

Silas Tarkington noticed the discrepancy in the purchasing price, but he did not mention it to Alice. After all, Mrs. Van Degan might have been mistaken, though she seemed very definite about her figures.

On Friday morning, long before the doors opened at ten o'clock, crowds began to collect on the sidewalk outside the store and lines started to form outside the entrance. Presently, the police arrived, and yellow barricades were set up to control the crowds and get the curious to form a single manageable waiting line. Two mounted policemen trotted back and forth, up and down the block.

Looking out at this scene from his fifth-floor office window, Si could tell that the vast majority of these people were not Tarkington's shoppers. At least from the looks of this crowd, he hoped that they were not. These people would not be coming into the store to buy anything. They just wanted to look around. Still, the word-of-mouth that this kind of excitement would create could only help.

A mounted policeman was bellowing through his bullhorn, "No more than forty persons admitted at a time. . . . Fire regulations. . . . No more than forty at a time. . . ."

Looking down, it amused him, in a grim way, to think that eight years ago he had made his way to Hillsdale in a grimy, unventilated police van, manacled to seven other men, four of them black and all of them older than he. One of them had shit in his pants during the three-hour journey. On that occasion, the assignment for the police had been to protect the public from his unruly ways. Today, the police were lined up outside his store to protect him from the unruly public. "It could only happen in America," as his father used to say.

"Moe, we need to talk," he said.

"Sure," said Moe. "What about?"

"Several things," he said.

"Shoot, pal."

"To begin with, that shipment from Chanel. Where did you get it?"

"I told you. I got friends. I got connections."

"Andrew Goodman was at the party the other night. He commented that our Chanel collection looked a lot like some garments Bergdorf had ordered, but the order got lost. I had to do some fast talking about coincidences and that sort of thing."

"Yeah, that's it. Just a coincidence."

"I'm not sure I convinced him."

"Well, when your own order comes in, you can offer to make a swap. Simple."

"We've already sold several of those garments. How do we account for that?"

"Aw, we'll think of somethin'."

Si looked at him steadily. "I hope so," he said. "Now there's another matter I'm unhappy about, Moe. I think you saw Mrs. Van Degan quoted in last Friday's *Times*. She said we paid the demolition company a hundred and seventy-five thousand dollars for this building. She sounded very definite about it. But you told me the price was two hundred and twenty-five. You handled that transaction. Who's right?"

"I'm right, of course! Would I lie to you?"

"I hope not," Si said carefully. "But I wonder why Mrs. Van Degan came up with a smaller figure."

"That broad's nutty as a fruitcake," Moe said. "I've done deals with her husband, and he's told me she's as nutty as a fruitcake. She spends six months a year at the Hartford Retreat, whenever she starts thinking she's Marie Antoinette and the peasants are trying to murder her. That's how nutty she is."

Si waved his hand to dismiss the subject. "There's a third matter I've been meaning to ask you about. You remember when we were all working so hard to get the renovations finished and the electricians were threatening to strike? That day, a bunch of goons appeared outside the building. Where did those guys come from?"

Moe chuckled. "Electricians went back to work, didn't they? Isn't that what you wanted?"

"But where did the goons come from? I've never seen such a rough-looking bunch."

"I told you, I got connections. People with influence."

"Who are these people?"

"Just friends. Friends of mine. People who owe me."

"And the elevator inspection certificates. They were all put up awfully quickly. But even though I was here the whole time, I never saw an elevator inspector come around."

"There's shortcuts. Shortcuts you can take down at City Hall. Everybody does it. If you went through all the red tape they got for you down there, it would take six months to get an elevator inspected."

"You mean our elevators were never inspected?"

"Look, what are you bitchin' about?" Moe said. "You got your work done when you wanted it done, didn't you? You got everything done on time, with all the necessary permits, strictly legit. So what's your problem?"

"I guess what it all boils down to," Si said, steepling

his fingers, "is that I've started wondering about some of
the investors you've been bringing in. That initial two-
hundred-thousand-dollar check, for instance. That was a
large sum of money. Where did it come from?"

"I told you! Friends, connections, people who owe
me. People who for one reason or another don't want
their names known. In that particular case, it was from a
guy who wanted to invest some money he didn't want his
wife to know he had. So what's the big deal?"

"I don't want any dirty money in my operation,
Moe."

"Dirty money, clean money, what's the diff? It's all
money, ain't it? Money is money."

Si paused for a moment. "Moe, I'm really grateful for
everything you've done," he said at last. "I couldn't have
gotten this place off the ground if it hadn't been for you."

"Now that's more like it," Moe said. "Now you're
talkin' more like I'd expect to hear—a little gratitude for
all I done."

"I *am* grateful, Moe. But this morning I had a meeting with an officer from the Morgan Guaranty Trust. He
came to offer me some financing. Funny, isn't it? A year
ago the big banks wouldn't talk to me. But now that the
store looks like it's going to be successful, the banks send
vice presidents around, begging me to let them loan me
money. Anyway, I'd like to accept this particular offer.
And I'd like to use some of that capital to buy you and
your friends out."

Moe's eyes narrowed. "Oh, yeah?" he said.

"Quote me a price, Moe."

"You ain't gonna buy me out, pal."

"Come on, Moe. Be reasonable. Quote me a price.
Some of that money I've had for two years. Let me pay it
back, with full interest."

"I told you you ain't gonna buy me out! You ain't
never gonna buy me out! This is my store too, ya know!
This is the first respectable high-class business I've ever
had an interest in, and who made it respectable? Me! And
I ain't gonna lose that interest in it—never!"

"Moe, I'm asking you as a friend. With the money I'd pay you, you could go out and buy something else—"

"I don't want nothing else! I worked too damn hard to get what I got right now, and I ain't gonna give it up!"

"Then I'm afraid I'll have to—"

"Afraid you'll have to do *what*? Now, wait a minute, buddy! You better hold the phone! Are you threatening *me*, pal? There ain't a fucking thing you can do to me, and you fucking well know it! How'd you like it if I told your fancy banker friends who this blowgut who calls himself Silas Tarkington really is? How'd you like it if I took a coupla reporters from *The New York Times*, that seems to think you're the hottest thing since sliced bread, out to Woodlawn Cemetery and showed 'em where the *real* Silas Tarkington is planted, deader'n a mackerel? You got a bad case of a swollen head if you think you're gonna get rid of me, Mr. Big Shot! I'll yank that tombstone outa Woodlawn Cemetery and plant that fucker right beside your front door on Fifth Avenue, and you'll be dead! Try any fast ones with me, pal, and they'll be writing your obituary!"

He began jabbing his pudgy forefinger into Si's chest.

"You're stuck with me, pal," he said. "Get that through that swollen head of yours. I made you what you are, and I ain't lettin' you go!"

"You could ruin us both, of course. But I suppose you know that."

"Right! If we sink, we go down together. But we ain't gonna sink, and you know why? 'Cause I been ruined before, and I ain't gonna be ruined again, and you been ruined before and you ain't gonna be ruined again, neither. You gonna let that little shiksa you're screwin' see you turned into a ruined man? Fuck, no! She's only screwin' you because she's screwin' Mr. Big Shot. Well, I made you into that big shot, so you're *my* Mr. Big Shot now, and you're gonna stick with me."

"Just tell me one thing, Moe," he said. "When is my mother going to start getting her dividends? She's started pestering me."

"We got other more important investors to pay off

first, that's when. It's like these're bondholders and preferred stockholders. Bondholders and preferred stockholders always get paid off first. Your old lady is only a
common stockholder, who gets paid off after."

"Who are these preferred stockholders, Moe?"

"I told you! Friends of mine who are venture capitalists, who prefer to remain unanimous, who put up a big
piece of our start-up cash, remember?"

"Are they getting nine percent?"

"In actual fact, they're getting slightly more, which is
what preferred stockholders always get. Anyway, that
was the deal I got you. And don't mess with these guys,
pal. Mess with these guys, these venture capitalist friends
of mine, and you'll find out what trouble really is! These
are big guys, pal!"

"That's another thing I don't like, Moe," he said.
"These friends of yours. I don't like the sound of them at
all."

"Well, you're gonna have to like 'em because you're
stuck with 'em, just like you're stuck with me." He continued jabbing his finger into Si's chest. "You're stuck
with me, and you're stuck with me for *life*! You're not
gettin' rid of me until the *day you die*. And maybe not
even then, pal. Maybe not even then!"

From *The New York Times*, November 12, 1958:

ELEVATOR PLUNGES AT
TARKINGTON'S 5TH AVE.

No Serious Injuries Reported

A passenger elevator plunged from the fourth floor to
the basement yesterday afternoon at Tarkington's, the
fashionable new specialty store at Fifth Avenue and 59th

Street, apparently as the result of a faulty cable. However, no serious injuries were reported, thanks to the quick thinking of one of the elevator's seven passengers.

The passenger, Howard J. Kilgour, 47, of Phoenix, Ariz., told *The Times*, "When I felt the elevator begin to fall, I remembered reading somewhere that most elevator shafts are constructed with a heavy rubber cushioning device at the bottom. So I ordered everybody to sit down quickly on the floor of the car. When the car hit bottom, there was quite a jolt, but at least nobody fell, and nobody was more than a little bit shaken up. There was no panic, no screaming. We were released from the car very quickly into the basement."

Silas Tarkington, president of the glamorous new store, expressed shock at the accident, gratitude that there were no injuries, and had nothing but praise for Mr. Kilgour for his quick thinking and quicker action. "He's a real hero," Mr. Tarkington said. "Our elevators were all recently inspected and safety-certified," he added. "Needless to say, all elevators will be thoroughly reinspected before they are put back into service." The store closed early shortly after the incident to allow for inspection and repairs.

One of the seven passengers in the elevator at the time was Myrna Loy, the motion picture actress, who was in New York from Los Angeles on a Christmas shopping trip. Miss Loy made light of the incident. "I'd come to New York expecting to take a big plunge on some new outfits from Tarkington's. But I hadn't planned on literally taking this kind of a plunge," Miss Loy said.

19

Mrs. Rose Tarcher (interview taped 8/28/91)

Sure, the store was a success. At least they made it sound like a success from all the things they wrote about it in the papers. My hats sold well there. I did a good business. Maybe you remember the big Henry Ford wedding that was in 1959? No? Well, I did all the bridesmaids' hats for that, and there were twelve bridesmaids. Those hats retailed for five hundred dollars apiece. That was a nice order. And a lot of the guests at that wedding wore my hats too.

I never worked at the store. Solly—I guess it's all right to call him Solly now, isn't it, now that he's dead?— he didn't want me to. He said he wanted a younger woman for the saleslady. I think it was because he didn't like my New York accent. But why shouldn't I have a New York accent? I was born and raised in New York. He got some lady with a phony English accent. Millicent, she was. I used to talk to her on the phone. I never met her.

But that arrangement was okay with me. I didn't

mind working out of my apartment. I filled all the orders there, and then, when they were ready, they sent a messenger up from the store to pick them up.

And, as I say, business was good, a lot better on Fifth Avenue than it was on Union Square, and my rent was free, so I had no complaint about that aspect of it. But what I began to wonder about was, where were the dividends on that stock I'd bought? Sure, maybe I didn't expect dividends the very first year, and maybe not even the second. But I'd bought that stock as an investment, and they'd promised me a return of nine percent a year. Now, I may not be the bookkeeper that my late husband was, but you don't have to be Albert Einstein to figure out that for an investment of a hundred and fifty thousand dollars, at nine percent, I should have been receiving an income of thirteen thousand five hundred a year, right? A year went by, then two, and there was no income. Where was it?

I spoke to my son about it. "Where is this so-called income I'm supposed to get?" I asked him.

"Don't worry, Mama," he told me. "There's still some start-up costs we have to cover. As soon as they're paid off, we'll start sending you your dividends. That'll be any day now."

Well, "any day now" was turning into a longer and longer time.

I called that nice Mr. Minskoff, who'd set the whole thing up for me, and asked him about it. He told me that New York State's case with Solly was now completely closed. Solly was now completely on his own, and Mr. Minskoff was off that case entirely. Solly was now in charge of everything, and I should take the matter up with him.

"I've tried taking the matter up with him," I told him, "but I get nowhere."

"There's absolutely nothing further that this office is empowered to do for you, Mrs. Tarcher," he told me. I began to think I was getting the run-around.

In 1960, I had to put my mother, God bless her, into a nursing home, and that was a big drain on my finances. I kept calling Solly, and when I could get him on the phone I'd ask him where my income was, when my dividends were going to start. He gave me more about start-up costs that needed to be recovered and more "any day now." When I could get him on the phone, that is. A lot of times I'd call him, and I'd get a secretary who'd say he was tied up with a customer or something and couldn't come to the phone right now. Remember, I wasn't supposed to let anyone know that it was his mother calling. I was Miss Rose from Leah Roth Millinery.

"I'll have him get back to you, Miss Rose," the secretary would say. But then he started not returning my calls.

I knew I was getting the run-around when I read in the papers that he was fixing up the top two floors of his building and turning them into a fancy apartment for himself. A "twenty-two-room luxury duplex," the papers called it. Well, I thought to myself, if he can afford to fix up a twenty-two-room luxury duplex for himself, why can't he afford to pay me my dividends?

Oh, every now and then he'd send me presents. He'd send me a cashmere sweater from the store, or half a dozen scarves, or nylons, or a nightie, or a couple of nice pairs of gloves. It was as though he thought these presents would keep me off his back. Once he sent me a mink coat. But you can't use a mink coat to put food on your table. You can't use a mink coat to pay the milkman and the butcher. Since I couldn't get him on the phone anymore, and he wouldn't return my calls, I started writing letters to him. "Thanks for the mink," I wrote him, "but where's my dividends?"

No answer to these letters.

That was when I decided to speak to my daughter Simma, whose husband's an accountant, thinking maybe Simma and Leo would have some suggestion about how I should deal with this run-around.

Well, you could have knocked me over with a feather when I found out that Simma and Leo were being given the same run-around as I was! Simma had bought stock in his store too, and this was the first I'd heard about it! Mr. Minskoff had been to see her too, not long after he'd come to see me, and she'd put in a hundred and fifty thousand of her money too, the same as me. But somehow, thanks to Leo, Simma had been smarter. She'd got them to issue her a lot more shares of stock than I got. But her story was the same—no dividends. Why she never told me about making this investment I'll never know.

"Let's face it, Ma," Leo said to me. "Your son's a crook. He always was a crook, and he'll always be a crook. I've shown those shares of stock to my brother the lawyer, and shown him that agreement you both signed, and he says it's got more loopholes in it than a screen door. In effect that agreement says he doesn't have to pay you any dividends until he feels like it, and he obviously hasn't felt like it, and it doesn't look like he's ever going to feel like it. That agreement means meaningless."

"Write him off, Mama," Simma said. "He's no good, so just write him off. We both have. Just don't go sending any more good money after bad."

"How could you have let Simma get involved in this whole thing in the first place, Leo?" I asked my son-in-law. "Me, I can excuse. I'm his mother. But you—you're supposed to be this big-shot accountant. Shouldn't you have taken care of Simma's money better?"

They just looked at each other, guilty-like, like there was some sort of secret between them that they didn't want yours truly to know about. I still don't know what it was. Ashamed, probably, because they hadn't invested the money better.

"Could we sue him, Leo?" I asked him. All this was transpiring around Simma and Leo's kitchen table at their house in Kew Gardens, where they used to live. It was a nice house, too, with a nice kitchen.

"What would we sue him *for,* Ma?" he asked me. "We gave him the money. We bought his stock. You can't sue a company for not paying you dividends." I had to admit he had a point.

"What if we were to tell him that if he doesn't pay us our dividends we'll tell the newspapers who Silas Tarkington really is?" I asked him. Once more there was this funny look between them.

"The trouble with a threat like that, Ma, is that you've got to be prepared to carry through on it," he said. "And what would we get if we did that? We'd get him a lot of bad publicity. Bad publicity for your business too, Ma. Maybe the publicity would be bad enough to put him out of business, and then what have we got? We've got no dividends now, but with him out of business we'd *never* get any dividends."

"You've got a point, Leo," I admitted. "You've got a point." And I didn't really want to put my only son out of business.

"And with him out of business, where would your business go? Your business is in his store."

"You've got another point," I admitted.

"I say write him off, Ma," he said. "Just write him off."

Well, it isn't easy for a mother to just write off her only son as a crook, I can tell you that. It was very, very hard, believe me. I still kept hoping I could get through to him somehow, with the phone calls and the letters. But no such luck.

I kept thinking about moving Leah Roth Millinery out of his store, just to show him I didn't appreciate how he was treating me, and setting up shop somewhere else. There could have been advantages to that. I had certain special customers I called my personals, and they'd have followed me wherever I went. I'd also have been able to put the store's markup into my own pocket, and the store's markup was forty-five percent. I mean those hats for the Henry Ford wedding, for instance, that retailed for five hundred each, I only got a little over two-fifty for. The rest was markup. But a Henry Ford wedding doesn't walk in the door every day, and now we're talking 1959 and 1960, and the millinery business wasn't what it used to be. Even in the old days, how many expensive hats did a rich woman buy a year? Two, maybe three. Now it was more like one hat every five or six years!

Every designer needs a showroom, and the store gave me that, the best showroom I could ask for, right on Fifth Avenue, just inside the front door. So I decided to forget

my aggravation and stay put—until they gave me the
heave-ho, which they eventually did, and which I'll get to.

Go ahead. Change your tape. . . .

Anyway, all this I've been telling you about tran-
spired between 1958 and 1962—four years of aggravation. Then, in the fall of 1962, who should show up out
of the blue at my front door but my son, with this shiksa
he says he's going to marry. "I want you to meet the girl
I'm going to marry, Mama," he says to me. "Alice, this is
my mother."

"I've heard so much about you, Mrs. Tarcher," she
says to me.

"I'll bet you have," I said. Then I said to him, "Well,
it's nice to meet the girl you're going to marry, but when
am I going to shake hands with some of the dividends you
owe me? That's what I'm waiting to say howdy-do to."

"Now, Mama," he says to me. "This is the happiest
day of my life. Let's not start off this meeting talking
about money."

"I'll talk about whatever I like," I said to him. "This
is my house, and in my house we talk about whatever I
decide to talk about."

"Now, Mama," he says.

"I don't so much mind you stiffing *me*," I said to
him. "Maybe I deserve it for being a mother. Maybe
that's what a mother deserves for having a son. But
Simma doesn't deserve it. How could you stiff your very
own sister, a mother herself, with two little children?
That's what has me flummoxed."

He started acting very strange, like he didn't know
what I was talking about. "Simma?" he said. "What's
Simma got to do with it?"

"You know!"

"Honest, I don't, Mama," he said.

"Simma put up the same amount of money as me, is
what I'm talking about," I told him. "She bought stock
too, through Mr. Minskoff."

"Oh," he said, looking kind of funny. "I guess I forgot about that."

"Forgot?" I said. "Forgot about a hundred and fifty thousand dollars from your very own sister? Your poor sister, who's trying to raise and feed two little children, one of which is gifted?"

"Mr. Minskoff didn't give me all the full details," he said, or something like that.

"You can forget about me," I said. "After all, I'm only your mother. What do I deserve for bringing you into the world? But your sister. Your own flesh and blood. That's what I can't understand."

"You always cared more about Simma than you did about me, didn't you, Mama," he said to me.

"Simma was a sickly baby when she was born," I reminded him. "She was always colicky. Chicken pox, mumps, measles, whooping cough, the whole megillah. She took a lot of my attention. You were a healthy boy of nine and already able to take care of yourself." I almost added, And already getting into trouble, but I didn't, because of the girlfriend being there and all.

At this point, the girlfriend started getting into the act. I didn't think much of her. She called me "Mother Rose." She said, "I want us all to be one big happy family for our wedding, Mother Rose."

"We can all be one big happy family when he comes around with some dividend checks for me and my daughter," I told her. "Now that he's found out that his mother and his sister are still in the land of the living, maybe that will happen. I'm not holding my breath, but until that happens, toodle-oo to both of you."

She was crying at that point. But I meant what I said, and I was glad I got a chance to say it. He knew I meant it, because he never came around again, and that was the last I ever saw or heard from any of them.

And of course there were never any dividends. Not to this very day.

The only times I ever heard from the store were when that Millicent, with her la-di-da English voice, would phone me with an order for a hat.

Anyway, he married his shiksa. I read about it in the

papers, a big, fancy wedding. Needless to say, she didn't have the nerve to order her bridesmaids' hats from me, even if they wore any hats, which I don't even know if they did or not.

Then, in 1972, I had a letter from the store, from a Mr. Bonham. I'll read it to you. "Dear Mrs. Tarcher: I regret to inform you that we have reluctantly decided to close the Leah Roth boutique at Tarkington's. The market for custom millinery has declined so sharply over the past decade that it is simply no longer profitable for us to maintain such a department, and we have decided to put the space to other use. I am sure you will understand the necessity of this move when I point out to you that over the past twelve months we have had only three orders for a Leah Roth hat. We regret this decision but wish to thank you for your many years of loyal service to the store. Sincerely, Thomas E. Bonham, Vice President and General Manager."

Well, he was right, of course. I'd seen it coming. I'd seen the handwriting on the wall. All through the sixties, I'd seen my business tapering off, fewer and fewer calls from Miss Millicent. I don't know why, but all through the sixties women seemed to stop wearing hats altogether, much less the expensive custom headgear that I used to design and make. Hats like mine were becoming like the dinosaurs, extinct. Some of them are even in museums now. There's one in Hartford, one in Portland, Oregon, and I forget some of the other places. My hats are a part of history, I guess you'd say. Ancient history. My mother, God rest her soul, would be proud of me.

But that was all right with me. I was seventy-seven then and ready to retire. I had my savings, my Social Security, and the rest of my inheritance from Abe, enough to live on. I'd heard about this retirement community down here, so I came down. I'm not rich, but I have everything I need. We have activities here: bingo, shuffleboard, my bridge club once a week. We have a Happy Hour every Saturday afternoon. Simma and Leo live in Lauderdale—he took early retirement from his firm—and

Simma and her children come to see me all the time. I even have two great-grandchildren now, just think of that. They come to see me too. I guess you could say I'm lucky, Mr. Turner. There are lots of women my age who don't have as much as me.

And now comes this letter from a Mr. Albert Martindale, head of Continental Stores, asking me if I'd be interested in selling my Tarkington's stock. Simma got a letter too. So who knows? Maybe I'll be rich after all. Maybe I'll get back what I should have gotten back from all those years when I got nothing. But at my age a lot of money doesn't mean much. There's nothing more I need, nothing more I want. It's a funny feeling, at my age, to think that you might get a lot of money but have nothing to spend it on. Life's funny, isn't it?

But at least it would give me something to leave in my will to Simma and her children and my two little greats. Unlike my late husband, may God rest his soul, I've made a very careful will.

As for Solly, I've tried to forget about him the way he seemed to forget about me. Forget about him, I told myself. Let him keep his shiksa in the lap of luxury and forget about me. I didn't even know it when he divorced the first one and married another one. I didn't even know it when I had two more grandchildren, one by the first and another by the second. Forget about all of them, I told myself. Why give yourself the aggravation from remembering?

But of course I can't forget about him. And of course I love him. I'll always love him, even though he's dead. A mother can't forget about her firstborn, her only son. A mother can't stop loving her firstborn, her only son. It's just not possible. Because that was what he was, my firstborn, my only son. Oh, my. . . .

Sure, you can talk to Simma. I'll give you her number, but I don't think she can tell you any more about my son than I've already told you. Simma lives in Lauderdale, like I told you, but she's in Las Vegas till the middle of September. I had a card from her today. Since Leo has retired, they do a lot of traveling—Las Vegas, Disneyland, they go to all those places. That means you'll have to make another trip down here if you want to talk to her in person. She and Solly weren't that close. Is it worth it? It's up to you. It's your nickel.

20

Mrs. Alice Markham Tarkington (interview taped 9/11/91)

Si Tarkington? Oh, dear. *De mortuis nil nisi bonum,* I guess I should remind myself. Where to begin? Let's see. . . .

I taught him how to dress. I can take credit for that. He had intuitive good taste and a flair for women's fashions, but that may have been in his genes. After all, both his mother and his grandmother were talented millinery designers, and some of his fashion decisions, such as hiring Antonio Delfino as in-house designer, were strokes of absolute genius, but he had no idea how he himself should dress or what the president of a store like Tarkington's should look like.

He thought he should dress like a banker, in dark three-piece suits, white shirts, sober neckties, and black wingtip shoes. I told him that wasn't quite the look for him, and he seemed to think the only alternative was to dress like a Hollywood producer. I tried to explain that for a successful fashion retailer there was a happy balance in between.

I started out by taking him to Paul Stuart's custom shop. Si wasn't tall but he had a good figure, trim and flat-bellied, with a nice set to his shoulders. They made him a beautiful cashmere double-breasted blazer in navy blue, side-vented of course, and several lovely pairs of slacks in gray and doeskin. Then I picked out some Turnbull & Asser shirts with three-button cuffs and coordinated ties. We traded in the wingtips for brown Gucci loafers, and we bought gray and navy cashmere socks at Dunhill. "There," I said, when we'd finished with my makeover. "Now you look like the president of Tarkington's."

In retailing, how you present yourself to the customer is as important as how you present your merchandise. For the next three or four years, he never bought an article of clothing without consulting me. If he got a reputation as a snappy dresser—"impeccably tailored," I think *The Times* called him in their obituary—it was thanks to me. There's not much else about Si's life or career that I can claim responsibility for. Remember, I wasn't married to him for very long. Only three years.

I really hadn't planned on getting married again. I'd been terribly, passionately in love with Erick, my first husband. Erick's death was a terrible blow. I sometimes think that a love like mine for Erick only happens once in a woman's lifetime. That certainly was the case for me. No one, before or since, ever lighted up my life the way Erick did, and when that light went out I knew he would be irreplaceable. Si understood that. He never objected to the fact that, even after he and I were married, I kept a photograph of Erick in his uniform in a frame on my dressing table. I still do. I didn't keep any photographs of Si, I'm afraid, because there was really only Erick.

But there are different kinds of love, and different reasons for a woman to marry a man. When I first met Si I got caught up in the excitement and adventure of the store he was creating, so caught up I began to feel I was somehow part of that creation. He really didn't know what he was doing in the beginning, you know. He was flying by the seat of his pants and had no idea where he was going beyond some vague goal of opening a super-elegant shop for women's designer apparel that everyone in New York would drop dead over. He was leaving everything to luck, just hoping that somehow luck would carry the day. His plans changed day by day, minute by minute, while he kept his fingers crossed and tossed the spilt salt over his left shoulder. It was, "Shall we have a Small Leather Goods Department? Yes! No, we won't! Yes, we will. Shall we get into lingerie? Never! But why not? Umbrellas—no! But what about designer umbrellas? Cosmetics? The cosmetics business is full of crooks. . . . But what if we put the cosmetics counters here?" It was like that, every day. And it was exciting, because you never knew what would happen next.

It was like the old days of making movies in California. Neither the director nor the writer nor the actors had any idea of what the story was going to be about or how it was going to end, but they started shooting anyway, hoping for the best.

I felt I was a part of whatever it was that was going to be born in this wonderful old building, and I was helping him with the birth. And he was helping me, helping me to stop grieving for Erick, because grief is such a self-defeating emotion. Grief can be a terminal illness, at least it could have been for me.

Sex is grief's opposite. It's so mindless. It's like cooking because, though you enjoy it while you're doing it, you're always glad when it's done, and you can never exactly remember all the ingredients that went into it. At least that's the way I do it, and I'm told I'm an excellent cook!

And Si was a very sexy man. "But he's so *short*," my friend Bev used to say. Well, to me a man doesn't have to be tall, dark, and handsome to be sexy. A man can be short, dark, and handsome—and sexy. Si had a wonderful body, always tanned and well-exercised. He always seemed to radiate good health and—well, I guess you'd have to say virility—from every pore. That's why when I heard he'd had a heart attack—well, it just didn't seem to me the right kind of death for a man of Si's enormous vitality. Now if I'd read he died in Yellowstone wrestling a grizzly, I wouldn't have been the least surprised.

So when Si Tarkington and I became lovers, it all seemed quite harmless and fun. Neither of us was married, and so neither of us was hurting or betraying anyone. We tried to be discreet about it. All love affairs should be discreet, but they should be particularly discreet between two people in the same workplace. Nothing makes a fellow worker more uncomfortable than suspecting that two other people in the office are having a love affair. It doesn't just make other people feel uncomfortable. It makes them mad! "Look at those two damn fools!" they say. Neither Si nor I wanted to be thought of as two damn fools.

So, the way I thought of it at least, we were just having a nice, discreet love affair, nothing more. I didn't ask myself, or him, whether I was the only woman in his life. In fact, I was pretty sure I wasn't. There were the usual hints: Another woman's perfume on his hand, another woman's lipstick on the handkerchief. A matchbook from the Copacabana. A gentleman doesn't go to the Copacabana by himself. I thought, So what? I refused to let myself be upset. After all, I had no special claim on him, and there's nothing worse than a jealous, possessive woman—nothing.

We always met at my place, never his. That was fine with me. He said he was ashamed to let me see his apartment because it was small, in not such a great neighborhood, and, I gathered, sort of messy. He lived very frugally in those days, in order to put as much money as possible into the store. Of course it occurred to me that his own little apartment was perhaps where he took some of his other women, that he didn't want me to see evidence of other women that might be lying around. Well, that's very considerate of him, I thought. No woman likes to see another woman's pantyhose drying on a man's towel bar, no matter what the man is to her—even if the other woman is his wife.

So that's the way it was. He'd come to my apartment. We'd have a drink. We'd talk about the day's business at the store. We'd make love. I'd fix him something for dinner, and then we'd talk about the store some more. We never went out, because we didn't think it would help anything if we were seen together. It was all quite simple between us. It was nice. It was exciting. It was friendly. It was fun. Given hindsight, I can see that it should have stayed that way.

Around 1960, I think it was, he started fixing up the top two floors of the building as an apartment for himself. It was hard to figure out what else to do up there. Those two floors had been the Van Degans' servants' quarters; if you can believe it, the Van Degans once kept forty-three servants in that house. Most of those two floors consisted of tiny little cubicles, just cells, really, and it was difficult to see how they could be turned into retail selling space. We found out that we couldn't tear down too many partitions up there without structurally weakening the building. If too many partitions were removed, the roof could fall in, but he removed as many as it was safe to do. There were two or three larger rooms. The servants' dining room was up there, and that was good-sized. Can you imagine it? The servants used to have to carry their meals up seven narrow flights of back stairs from the kitchen in the basement! I used to wonder whether they really ever bothered. Also, the Van Degan children's nursery was up there, another big room, and that became Si's library. A third big room had been intended as a ballroom but was never finished. That became the living room of the apartment. When *The Times* called it a "twenty-two-room luxury duplex," they must have been counting the walk-in closets—which were former servants' rooms, naturally. Twelve rooms was more like it.

The apartment was pretty, if I do say so, because I helped decorate it. Still, Si cut a lot of corners. For instance, he wanted his library filled with books with expensive-looking bindings. But when he found out how much books like that would cost, he used fake books instead.

After the apartment was finished, he tried to lease it for a while. But nobody wanted to live on top of a busy retail store and share the elevators with the customers. It was not in a residential section of Fifth Avenue. No one liked the idea of being listed as the building's "janitor." And so, rather than let the apartment become a white elephant, Si finally decided to live in the place himself.

"This apartment is too big for one person," he said to me. That was when he asked me to marry him.

It took me completely by surprise. He'd never mentioned marriage to me before, and I certainly never had. But I immediately thought, Why not? It suddenly just seemed to make good sense.

No, I was not in love with him—not, at least, in the wild, irrational sense of the love I'd had for Erick. I was fond of him, yes. I respected him. I admired many things about him. I admired his ambition. I admired his energy, which was boundless. I admired his enthusiasm, and I was touched by his naïve, almost childlike faith in his own infallibility. Having made a success of his store, he was convinced that the course of his life would be a continuous upward curve. He could do no wrong, because he was Silas Tarkington!

But I do think he was in love with me. When I first went to work for him, for instance, I wore brown lipstick. I don't know why. Sometimes a woman likes to have a little trademark, and brown lipstick became mine. But one day I decided I was tired of it, and I came to work wearing red lipstick. That night, when we were alone together, the first thing he said to me was, "Where's your brown lipstick?"

"Sick of it," I said.

"Oh, please," he begged, "please don't give up the brown lipstick! I love you in brown lipstick, darling!"

So I went back to brown lipstick. Yes, I think he loved me.

·   ·   ·

Naturally, when a woman says she's going to marry a man, one of the first things she wants to do is meet his family. At that time, there was only his mother, and I could tell he was reluctant to take me to see her.

I knew about the name change. He told me he'd changed the name for business reasons, because Tarkington sounded snappier than Tarcher, and I must say I agreed with him. Tarkington, with all those clicking consonants, just had a better ring to it, and Silas sounded more distinguished than Solomon. I often wondered whether the store would have had as much success if it had been called Tarcher's instead of Tarkington's. So much in retailing involves this sort of cosmetic doodling and juggling.

I knew he didn't like to talk about his past, so I never asked him about it, though I gathered his childhood had been unhappy, with a much-younger sister whom his mother doted on, while ignoring him, and a father who was all business and never had much time to spend with either of his children. At school, he told me, because he was smaller than other boys his age, the bigger kids picked on him. It didn't seem all that unusual a story.

But what I didn't know was that his mother was the legendary Miss Rose of Leah Roth Millinery. "But then I *must* meet her," I begged him. "I love her work. Those hats she designed for the Ford wedding were so delicious —each one different, and yet they all worked together as a single perfect ensemble of colors." This was true. They did.

So he took me up to see her. Reluctantly, as I told you.

The visit did not go well. She was a tiny woman, but what a tartar! She immediately lit into him about some old family money dispute. She was not the least bit nice to me. For a woman who designed such beautiful things, she certainly had an unpleasant personality and a sharp tongue. I saw immediately why Si preferred to keep his mother at arm's length.

Afterward, Si was very upset. "Now you see," he said. "Now you see why I didn't want you to meet her."

I felt badly, but there was nothing I could do about it.

Si and I were married in his apartment. I'd sent invitations to his mother and to his sister and her husband. There was no response to either of these invitations. I found this all rather sad. But then, there's nothing that can divide a family like disagreements over money.

We'd both decided, beforehand, that after we were married I would no longer work for the store. Employees just don't like working for husband-and-wife teams, and when the husband makes an unpopular decision, the wife gets the blame. Still, living there over the store, I could keep an eye on things, and without ever being bossy with the staff I could make private suggestions to my husband. It seemed to me like an ideal arrangement.

What I hadn't counted on was Si's infidelities. Somehow, when we were just casual lovers, I hadn't minded being just one of several women in his life. And somehow I had the old-fashioned notion that once a man and woman marry they are pledged to all eternity to remain faithful to each other. But in Si's case, at least, I was wrong.

It wasn't long before the little clues started to appear. The strange lipstick, not brown, on the handkerchiefs. The matchbooks from nightclubs and restaurants. The long evenings out, which, he explained, were spent meeting with clients, with wholesalers and suppliers from the market, with designers and their reps. Did these meetings always have to take place at Copacabana and El Morocco? Then there were the telephone calls to the apartment from callers who hung up when I answered. What had never bothered me before bothered me terribly now, because now he was my husband! Looking back, I think Si was a man who was constitutionally unable to be faithful to a single woman. It just wasn't in his makeup. Women were like an addiction for him. He was powerless to resist a pretty woman when she presented herself, and now that he was the president of New York's most fashionable store, a lot of women presented themselves. Women were a kind of drug for him; he got his fix from all different sizes and shapes. I'm sure it wasn't long before his second wife discovered this. I sometimes think women were his tragic flaw. Women were his undoing.

But I don't want you to think that Si's womanizing was the whole cause of the failure of our marriage. I take a lot of the blame too. I was not exactly a rose to live with.

I'm an alcoholic. I'm what's called a *recovering* alcoholic. We alcoholics are never cured of our illness, you see. We are always recovering. I've been sober now for six years—six years, three months, and fourteen days, to be exact, because we count each new day as it dawns—thanks to a wonderful program and three months spent at the Betty Ford Center in California.

Here's an amusing little story. While I was out there, Mrs. Ford came to visit the center, as she often does, and to talk to us. When she was introduced to me, she said, "Oh, Mrs. Tarkington. I'm delighted to meet you because I met your charming husband once, when he brought some clothes from the store to the White House, and he brought your delightful little daughter with him. How *is* darling Miranda?"

I said, "Well, Mrs. Ford, Silas Tarkington is my *ex*-husband, and the daughter you met is his daughter by his present wife. The fact is, I've never met Miranda."

She was very sweet. She just reached out and touched my hand and said, "Just keep up the good work you're doing here, my dear."

How did I become an alcoholic? Well, I suppose it started when I first went to work for Tarkington's, but I don't want to imply that my work at the store, or Si himself, was really to blame, though I did at the time. The alcoholic will find dozens of excuses for drinking. There are really only two culprits, though—the alcoholic and alcohol. I'm no exception. Si and the store had nothing to do with it, though it took the program at the Betty Ford Center to teach me that.

Before going to work at the store, I considered myself a moderate social drinker. But working with Si, helping him start up the store, was stressful. Retailing itself is stressful. People in the theater complain about the horrible hours they have to work, giving performances eight times a week. But no actor is on stage for much more than two hours per performance, and that adds up to working only sixteen hours a week. But in retailing you work from eight-thirty to six-thirty, six days a week, and that adds up to *sixty* hours a week. I'd come home from work and have a few drinks to unwind, to relax, to relieve the day's stress. I'd take my bucket of ice cubes, my glass, and a bottle of vodka, and pour down vodka until that feeling of relaxation came over me. Some nights it took longer than others. Some nights I drank until I passed out on the sofa, and I'd wake up in the morning, still in my clothes, with a half-empty glass of vodka on the coffee table beside me. Staring at me.

I only drank at home and at night. I never drank at work. At least I was smart enough not to do that.

I told myself I drank because of the stress of my work. I told myself that I drank because I was lonely, and because I missed Erick, and because I was not dating anyone. I told myself I drank because my evenings alone were boring, and because I didn't like going out to bars, and because there didn't seem to be anything else to do. I told myself I drank because that was the only way I could get a good night's sleep. Oh, I could give myself dozens of reasons why I drank.

I had too much to drink at one of those opening promotional parties for the store, and that was how I ended up in bed with Si.

When Si and I began our affair, he didn't like it when I drank, so I had to plan my drinking times around him—before he got to my house, after he left, after he fell asleep, and so on. I was very clever. Alcoholics often are. He might never *see* me have more than one or two drinks, but I was still managing to put down my full share.

After we were married, it was the same thing. I was a secret drinker. At least I thought I was keeping it a secret from him, but I'm not sure. Vodka isn't supposed to leave any odor on your breath. And when I found he was still seeing other women, that gave me another excuse to get drunk—anger and humiliation because my new husband was unfaithful. We had terrible quarrels. I don't remember what started most of them, because I was drunk. We'd quarrel, and he'd stalk out of the apartment into the night, and bingo! Another excuse. I'd get drunk because my husband had walked out on me, and left me alone, and was probably out with another woman. Sometimes he'd scream at me. "You've been drinking, haven't you?" And of course that just gave me another excuse. I'd get drunk because my husband had called me a drunk.

No, it was my drinking that destroyed my marriage to Si as much as anything else. I know that now.

I decided that if we had a baby, perhaps that would keep our marriage from becoming unglued. Perhaps a baby would make him give up the other women. It was a foolish notion, but in 1963 I went off the pill and became pregnant with Blazer.

All through my pregnancy, I found myself thinking that the baby I was carrying was actually Erick's baby. Erick and I had planned to have children as soon as his term of enlistment was up, but he never made it, and I found myself telling myself, This is really Erick's baby, my gift to him; this is Erick's legacy, the legacy of our love, of everything we had together and were to each other. I even had the crazy notion of naming the baby Erick, if it was a boy. That would be my revenge on Si for everything he had put me through.

And this just gave me another excuse to drink—guilt that I could think such disloyal thoughts, guilt that whenever Si and I made love I'd pretend I was still making love to Erick, that all through Si's and my affair I'd really been sleeping with Erick's ghost. Once, when Si and I were making love, I even cried out Erick's name. He pulled away from me and said, "I'm Si, not Erick, remember?"

It was all because of my drinking. But I didn't mean to give you a lecture on alcoholism, though they do encourage us to talk about it.

One other thing I noticed about Si after we were married. He had a wonderful eye for fine merchandise. And he was a marvelous salesman. I used to say that Si Tarkington could have sold rainwear in the Gobi Desert, bikinis to the Eskimos, condoms to the Pope. But he was not a businessman. He had no real sense of business strategy. He understood the bottom line, but that was about it. All the details that *got* you to the bottom line just didn't interest him. At the end of each selling day, he'd go over the store's figures, department by department, comparing each department's figures with those of the week before, and so on. In retailing, we have an expression called "making the day." A department has made its day if its figures are at least equal to—or preferably better than—those of the same date the year before. Si would check to see whether a department had made its day. But a lot of other things have to be factored into making the day—national holidays that fall on different dates, world events, the Dow-Jones average, even the weather. A good retailer keeps files on all these factors. Si couldn't be bothered with those little details. And if you'd shown him the company's balance sheet, he wouldn't have been able to make head or tail of it. Si had studied bookkeeping, not accounting.

Business strategy was left to a man named Moses Minskoff, who was sort of a silent business partner. Mr. Minskoff almost never came into the store, never had an office there. But he and Si were often on the phone together.

Mr. Minskoff always struck me as a very shady character. Si called him a diamond in the rough, but to me he was more rough than diamond—a grossly fat man who chewed cigars, smelled of garlic, and had a New York Jewish accent strong enough to start a pogrom. I disliked Moses Minskoff very much, and, even though Si insisted that he was important to the business, I began to suspect that Si didn't really like him either. Whenever Moses Minskoff's name came up, a cloud passed across Si's face —a worried look. I began to think that Si was somehow afraid of Moses Minskoff, even though Minskoff didn't seem all that bright to me. I began to wonder whether Minskoff was blackmailing Si in some way, and I got the distinct impression that Si would have liked to get rid of him but couldn't figure out a way to do it.

Still, Minskoff definitely had his uses. Sometimes a designer's or a manufacturer's shipment would come in short, or we'd suddenly need a certain garment for a certain special client who wanted that item right away and would settle for nothing else. The buyer or the salesperson would bring the problem to Si, and Si would heave a deep sigh and say, "Well, maybe we better bring in Mr. Fixit," as he called him. And he'd call Minskoff and explain the problem, and somehow or other whatever merchandise the store needed would come through right away. Mr. Fixit had fixed it. It was uncanny, because he had no retailing experience whatsoever.

"Moe is a real operator," Si used to say, and I'd have to agree.

Anyway, our son was born in October of 1963. I didn't suggest that we name him Erick. We named him Silas Rogers Tarkington, Jr. Si was thrilled that he had a son, and he was crazy about that baby. "He's going to blaze a trail across the skies, this son of mine," he used to say. That was how we started calling him Blazer—for the trail he was to blaze. "They call me a merchant prince," he'd say, "but this son of mine is going to be a *real* merchant prince," and he'd bounce the baby on his knee.

I really thought the birth of our son was going to mean that Si's and my marriage would get back on the right track, and for a while it seemed to. I was nursing the baby, so I stopped drinking, and that helped things right away. And because it was so easy for me to stop drinking, I told myself I couldn't possibly be that awful thing, an alcoholic. But I was. I was the kind of drinker for whom one drink is too many and ten aren't enough.

Si was a wonderful father. He did more than just bounce the baby on his knee. He bathed him. He changed his diapers and dressed him. He made formula for the supplementary bottle that my doctor had prescribed and sterilized the bottles and the nipples. He fed the baby and loved to watch him feeding at my breast. He loved all those things that husbands are supposed to hate. He didn't want me to hire a nursemaid because he said he could do everything a nursemaid could do, and do them better. And of course he showered the baby with toys—too many toys, I thought, but I didn't say anything. To Si, the sun rose and set on that little boy. He even sang Yiddish lullabies to him that his own mother used to sing: *"Roshenkis mit mandlen, Shluf sie Yidele, shluf. Shlufsie, kind meins shluf. . . ."*

I'd gained weight during my pregnancy, and it wasn't coming off. I was plump now, but I didn't seem to care. I was comfortable in my plumpness, and it seemed such a natural and easy way to be. When I'd worked for the store, appearances were everything, and I'd been a slave to my tape measure. But now none of that seemed to matter. Of course an alcoholic who stops drinking tends to eat a lot of sweets—something about blood sugar—and without even thinking about it, there was usually a box of chocolates within my reach.

And when a woman is nursing a baby, she can't really worry about her clothes. I'd find myself flopping around the apartment in old slippers and a milk-stained robe, and this all seemed wonderfully natural. It didn't occur to me that I might be turning into a slob because—I suddenly realized this—I was *happy!*

And then the strangest thing began to happen. I found myself falling in love with Si. It dawned on me gradually that I was in love again, but the realization came with all of love's force and anguish and terror. It was as though I'd entered a whole new world, and in the center of that universe were my husband and my baby. My memories of Erick were fading. I had to look at his photograph in its silver frame to remember what he looked like. I was finally in love with Si.

"Oh, my darling," I whispered to him as he bathed our little son, "I love you so." He passed the baby into my arms where I waited with a warm towel, and it was as though I'd never lived or loved before, or ever would again, just in that single moment.

And then Consuelo Banning came into our lives.

21

Mrs. Alice Markham Tarkington (interview taped 9/12/91)

I'd been nursing the baby, and when the telephone interrupted my nursing reverie I almost didn't answer it. To this day, I wonder what would have happened if I hadn't. It was an unlisted number, only given to special friends. There'd been fewer of those callers who uttered a little gasp and then hung up, but it still happened, and this call might be from one of them. Anyway, I removed the baby gently from my breast, placed him in his crib, and answered the phone on the sixth ring.

"Mrs. Tarkington?" a cultivated woman's voice said. "This is Consuelo Banning. I'm here in the store, and I wondered if I might come up and see you."

"I just stepped out of my bath," I lied. "Can you give me about twenty minutes to slip into some clothes? Then I'd love to meet you, Miss Banning."

"Oh, certainly, Mrs. Tarkington. I've some more shopping to do. Would half an hour be better?"

"Twenty minutes will be fine. Take the elevator closest to Fifty-ninth Street. I'll unlock it for you, so just press six, and it will take you up express."

I knew Consuelo Banning was one of the store's more glamorous new clients. Her picture had been in *Life* magazine, and more recently she'd been on the cover of *Vogue*, photographed by Irving Penn. Getting her to shop at Tarkington's was quite a feather in Si's cap.

I had no idea why Miss Banning wanted to see me, but I certainly wasn't going to meet her in my spotted housecoat and bedroom slippers. I rummaged through my closet for something to wear and settled on a simple navy wool skirt and matching sweater, a single strand of pearls, and flats. The skirt was too tight and I couldn't get the zipper all the way up, but I pulled the sweater down over the top of the skirt, and the gap at the back didn't show. I ran a brush quickly through my hair, applied the brown lipstick Si liked to see me wear, and pinned a pair of small pearl clips on my ears. Looking at myself in the mirror, I decided I didn't look bad for a woman of thirty-four. The doorbell sounded, and I went out to greet Consuelo Banning in the elevator lobby.

My first impression of her was that she was even more beautiful in the flesh than she was in photographs—the pale blond hair, the light blue eyes with dark lashes, and that extraordinary white skin. She looked incredibly chic, in a simple black suit with hand-feathered fringe on the jacket and skirt and beautifully hand-stitched button-holes—it had to be by Chanel. She was also wearing a small black pillbox hat of the type that had recently been made fashionable by Jackie Kennedy. On any other woman so young—she couldn't have been more than twenty-two or twenty-three—that hat might have seemed a false touch. But on her it looked perfect. Everything about her looked perfect.

"Please come in," I said. "Did you find everything you wanted in the store?"

"Oh, yes," she said. "But that's not really why I'm here. I didn't come to shop."

This response struck me as a little odd, but I led her into the living room.

"Oh, what a pretty room," she said. "But then I knew it would be, with Si's beautiful taste."

"Thank you," I said. "Do sit down. May I get you a cup of tea?"

"Oh, no, thank you. I'll only be a minute. I don't want to take up too much of your time, Mrs. Tarkington." She seated herself in a chair and crossed her beautiful slender ankles, tucking them just slightly under the chair, just so, her shoulders forward, her chin tilted upward. "I do love the *Régence* style," she said.

"Well," I said, taking a seat opposite her. "What a pleasure to meet you. I've read so much about you. My husband and I are delighted that you've become a Tarkington's client."

"Mrs. Tarkington, your husband has asked me to marry him," she said.

Of all the opening gambits in a conversation between two women who've never met before, what could be more startling, more stunning, more shocking than that one? *Mrs. Tarkington, your husband has asked me to marry him.*

I stared at her, feeling the breath go out of me, unable to believe what I'd just heard. Her expression was apologetic, almost imploring, as though, as the bearer of ill tidings, she was saying that she was no more than a dutiful if unwilling messenger. "He never mentioned this to me," I said at last.

"I realize that," she said. "But we thought that you and I, as two intelligent and mature women, should meet and discuss this situation and work out a solution that would be both adult and—graceful."

"In other words, he sent you to do his dirty work," I said. "He didn't have the courage to do it on his own."

"No, that's not it," she said. "He thought that if you and I met first, woman to woman, and discussed the situation calmly and sanely, we could come to an intelligent conclusion on how we are all to proceed from here."

"Calmly! Sanely!" I stood up. "Would you like a drink?" I asked her.

"Oh, no, thank you."

"Then you won't mind if I do." I went to the bar, dropped ice cubes into a glass, and splashed vodka over the ice. I took a few quick sips and then splashed in more vodka, right up to the rim. "Calmly! Sanely!" I said again. "In other words, you're asking me to take this like a perfect lady."

Her face wore an expression now that was almost pitying. "Si and I are very much in love," she said. "We want to marry. We only ask of you that you give him a divorce—a quiet, dignified, civilized, and amicable divorce."

"Quiet! Dignified! Civilized! Amicable!" I was clutching my glass in my hand, and my hand had begun to tremble. "Don't give him a fight that would create publicity that would be bad for business, is that what you're saying?"

"I'd like to say that I'm also prepared to take on the responsibilities of motherhood for your little boy," she said.

"Well, that's one responsibility you're not going to have!" I said. "My son is mine. He's never going to be yours!"

"We want to adopt him."

"Never!"

"Let me say I'll be a good stepmother, then. Si is devoted to that child."

"Not even that!"

"I just meant that, once Si and I are married, we intend to see to it that your little boy is given a wonderful home."

"My son is never going to have anything to do with you, you bitch!"

Her eyebrows went up. "I'm sorry," she said. "I can see I've upset you—"

"Upset? What do you expect me to be? First you come into my house to tell me you're taking my husband! Then you say you want to take my baby!"

"I was just hoping that, woman to woman—"

"*Woman to woman!*" I leaned against the bar to steady myself. I hadn't had a drink in six months, and this one was affecting me as though I'd had several. "I'll tell you what I'll do woman to woman! If you don't get out of here this minute, I'm going to scratch your eyes out! Woman to woman! I'll scratch your eyes out, and then I'll pull your hair out by the roots!" I started toward her with my drink in my hand.

She reached for her purse and rose quickly from her chair. "My dear, drinking doesn't help," she said. "It never really does, you know."

"The hell it doesn't!" I said. "Let's just see if it does. Get out of here, you bitch." And I threw my drink in her face. I was screaming now. *"Bitch! Bitch! Bitch!"*

She turned on her heel and was gone.

I poured myself another drink. The back of the bar was mirrored, and I studied my reflection in the glass. I was not pleased with what I saw. The drink I was holding had smeared my brown lipstick, and I looked like an angry, sneering clown. In the mirror I looked haggard and old and I could see why my husband wanted a younger and more beautiful wife.

I hadn't finished feeding the baby, and from the next room I could hear him beginning to whimper, cross little cries. "I'm coming! I'm coming!" I called. Then I saw that milk from my full breasts had seeped through my bra and had left two dark, wet spots on the front of my navy sweater. Then I burst into tears.

When Si came home, I screamed at him. "Woman to woman!" I said. "You sent your whore here to tell me you wanted a divorce because you didn't have the guts to tell me yourself!"

"I simply thought the two of you could have a rational conversation about the future. But I see that in your case a rational conversation is not possible."

"She's the same as all your other whores," I said. "I know about them too, Si. You've been cheating on me ever since we got married. I thought maybe having a baby would change things, but it hasn't. Does this new whore know about all the others, Si? Shall I tell her about all the others?"

"You're drunk," he said.

I denied it.

"Connie told me you threw your drink in her face."

"That doesn't mean I'm drunk!" I said.

"Whenever you drink, you get drunk. You're always drunk."

"So I threw a drink in the whore's face! That's all she is—a whore," I told him.

"This discussion is getting us nowhere," he said.

"Oh, I know why you want her, this new whore of yours," I said. "You want her because she's younger and prettier than I am, and because she's a so-called famous socialite! You want her because you think she'll be good for business. You want to use her as a shill, a decoy, a come-on for your customers! All you want her for is decoration! You don't want her for a *wife*!"

"Well, you're not very decorative at this point, are you, Alice?" he said. "As a wife or as anything else."

"What do you mean by that crack?" I said.

"Look at yourself," he said. "You've lost your looks, and you've lost your figure. You can't even get your skirt buttoned in the back."

My eyes were streaming now. "I lost my figure bearing your child," I sobbed.

"You lost your figure drinking," he said.

"It was bearing your child," I repeated. "Bearing your child!"

"Look," he said, "you can stay in this apartment for as long as you like, at least until everything's settled between our lawyers. I'll move to a hotel."

"No!" I cried. "I'm not staying here another night! I'm leaving, and I'm taking Blazer with me!"

"No. Blazer stays with me," he said.

"You can't take him away from me! I'm nursing him!" I said.

"I don't want my son drinking the milk of a drunken mother," he said. "He's ready to go on full formula now. I checked with the pediatrician."

"No!" I cried again, and I ran out of the room and down the hall to the baby's nursery, which I'd decorated all in blue and white, where Blazer lay sleeping on his stomach, one side of his face against a blue satin pillow, his thumb in his mouth.

Si followed me. "Don't wake him!" he commanded.

I reached into the crib and lifted Blazer from the pillow, cuddling him against my chest. "I'm taking him," I said.

"Alice, you are not running out into the night with the baby," he said. "It's below freezing outside. Put him back in his crib." He stepped toward me. "Do as I say!" he said.

"No!" I said, moving back toward the wall. "Stay away from me! Don't touch me!"

"Put the baby back in his crib, Alice," he said evenly, stepping toward me again. "Give the baby to me, Alice. Give him to me, Alice—now."

"No! Never!" As I spoke, I suddenly felt the baby begin to slide out of my arms. He was just slipping through my arms. I tried to catch him by the armpits, and then by the neck, and then I slipped to my knees on the floor, still trying to clutch at my baby, at his pajama bottoms, at anything, and when I fell to the floor the baby landed, face forward, on my lap. My lap cushioned his fall.

My husband stood over me in a rage. "Do you see what you almost did?" he said. "You almost dropped him. You could have killed him. Do you see why you can't be trusted when you're in these drunken states? Do you see why I don't love you anymore?"

But I still clutched the child, moaning, "No, no!"

"Don't hold him like that, Alice! You're choking him!"

"Oh, Erick," I sobbed. "Oh, Erick, why did you have to die? Why did you have to die, Erick? Why did you have to die?"

And now Blazer was wailing and screaming—high, shrill screams—and struggling in my arms, kicking his feet and waving his arms, and from the odor I realized his diaper was full, and the destruction of my day was complete.

22

Mrs. Alice Markham Tarkington (interview taped 9/15/91)

Yes, the divorce was pretty awful, though there weren't any more scenes between Si and me as bad as that one. The awfulness was all handled through lawyers after that, and of course I blamed Si and was very bitter about what he was putting me through. But I shouldn't have blamed Si, should I? I should have blamed myself and my mortal enemy, alcohol. I know that now.

The next day, I found a small apartment on the East Side, and my lawyer got a temporary restraining order allowing me to keep Blazer with me. But Si had this shyster lawyer, Jacob Kohlberg, and they were determined to take Blazer away from me. Si wanted absolute full custody of his son and said he'd accept nothing less. I was to have only very limited visiting privileges. They were saying I was an unfit mother, a hopeless alcoholic who had almost killed her baby once.

"It's very rare for a court to take a child this young away from its mother, Alice," my lawyer told me. But he looked dubious. "Still, they're sure to have put detectives on you. I want you to be sure you keep your nose clean."

"You mean my sex life?" I said with a laugh. "It's not me who has affairs."

"I'm not talking about that," he said, and he made a little jiggling gesture with his hand, as though he were holding a glass in it. "I'm talking about the booze."

"That's nonsense," I said.

"They're saying you drink a bit more than is good for you, Alice. You do drink a bit, don't you?"

"Hardly ever," I said. "Sometimes I'll have a glass of wine with dinner, but that's the extent of it." Of course I was lying.

"Do you ever drink in bars?"

"Never!"

"Good. Meanwhile, you do keep liquor in your house, don't you?"

"Of course. In case friends drop by."

"Where do you buy it?"

"Sherry-Lehmann delivers it."

"Watch those deliveries, Alice. Detectives will be keeping track of those deliveries."

How was I going to get vodka into my apartment if detectives were watching my deliveries? I wondered.

"What do you do with your empties?" he asked me.

"Throw them out with the garbage."

"Does your building have an incinerator?"

"Yes, but we're not supposed to throw glass or tin cans into it. Only flammable things."

"Figure out some way of disposing of your empties without putting them in the garbage," he said. "Detectives like to go through garbage."

"Really, you're making much too much of this," I said. "All these things they're saying about me are nothing but lies."

"Hmm," he said. "Well, just as long as you're aware of what they'll be looking for. Think twice about *any*-thing you put out with your garbage—bills, receipts, letters. Your husband's lawyers will be very interested in seeing things like that."

My immediate problem, of course, was how to get liquor into my apartment and empty bottles out. My friend Beverly helped me out. Every few weeks, Beverly would come to spend the night, and in her suitcase would be my vodka. When she left, she'd leave with the empties in the suitcase. See how clever we alcoholics are?

One day Beverly arrived at my place practically squealing with excitement. "You really do have someone watching your building," she said. "When I got out of the taxi today, this man said to me, 'That's a pretty heavy suitcase you've got there, little lady. Can I give you a hand with it?' I said, 'No, thank you.' I was sure he'd try to jiggle it to see if he heard bottles in it." She set the suitcase down on the floor, and we heard a *clank*. "Anyway, here's your stash," she said.

We thought all this was terribly funny. But it really wasn't funny, was it?

I'd told my lawyer I didn't want any alimony. What I wanted was some sort of trust fund set up for Blazer's education. College tuition costs were escalating in the 1960's, and who knew how much it would cost to send a boy to Yale by 1980, when Blazer would be starting college? My lawyer thought we should ask for a fund that would yield an annual income of fifty thousand dollars. That meant about a million dollars. I told him I wasn't sure Si had that much to set aside, but my lawyer said, "We'll start with a demand that's on the high side and let them bargain us down."

Well, naturally that demand infuriated Si, and Mr. Kohlberg came back to us saying that there would be no trust fund at all unless Si was given custody. I was damned if I was going to give Si custody, because he'd begun saying that when he and Connie were married they planned to adopt Blazer, and I couldn't let that happen.

So the battle lines were drawn. For a year and a half I hardly ever left my apartment unless it was to go to a court hearing or a meeting with my lawyer. I was followed everywhere. I was sure my telephone was tapped, so my friends and I talked in code. For instance, when I'd invite my friend Bev for the weekend, I'd say, "Are you bringing your boyfriend?" That meant, *Are you bringing me some vodka?* She'd say, "No, he's going to be out of town." That meant, *Yes, I've got you half a case.*

Finally, after what I gather was a particularly heart-rending performance by my lawyer, the court-appointed referee granted custody of my son to me, and we all heaved a great sigh of relief. I'd won that round.

With that victory, I had a considerable bargaining chip on my side of the table. If Si wanted to see his son *at all,* he was told, he was going to have to come up with some sort of trust fund for him. Dickering over that took several more months.

I'd wanted the income from the fund to be available at age eighteen, which would have been in 1981, when Blazer would presumably be starting college. Si's side wanted the income to start three years later, when Blazer was twenty-one. In the end, Si agreed to pay all Blazer's college costs and to set up a trust that would start paying Blazer an income when he reached his twenty-first birthday. An elaborate schedule of yearly contributions to the fund was worked out, so much each year, until the fund reached a ceiling worth of half a million dollars. It was only half what we'd originally asked for, but my lawyer thought it was a good compromise. In return, I agreed to allow Blazer to spend two weekends a month with his father until he was eighteen, when he'd be on his own.

My divorce from Sol was final in September of 1965, and my lawyer and my friend Beverly Hollister and I all celebrated in my apartment that night, and I'm sorry to say that all three of us got very, very drunk.

Sam, my lawyer, gave us a souped-up rendition of the heartrending performance he'd given before the court referee that got me custody. "Your Honor," he said, standing on a chair, "I ask you to consider the heartache and emotional torment my client has been put through. The young widow of a United States Air Force hero, she came to this cruel city to find employment that would put bread on her table. Here she was taken up by the suave, polished, sophisticated and ten-years-older millionaire Silas Tarkington, the possessor of a twenty-two-room duplex luxury apartment on Fifth Avenue, New York's most prestigious address. Seduced by this older man's blandishments and promises of riches, she agreed to be his wife. But no sooner had the couple entered into the bond of matrimony than the young wife discovered evidence of her faithless husband's philanderings—late nights in expensive nightclubs with ladies of the evening, other women's lipstick smeared on his pocket handkerchiefs, and, yes, Your Honor, in one instance on her husband's underclothing. And yet, despite the humiliation and the heartache caused by these discoveries, the young wife determined to keep up her end of the solemn marriage vows."

His voice broke. He pretended to shed a tear.

"A year later, a child, a son, was born to this marital pair. Added to the travails inflicted upon her by her husband's blatant infidelities were now the duties of sweet young motherhood. Ignored by her faithless husband, she made her infant the center of her life. Today, Your Honor, that infant is barely a toddler. Surely you would not deprive a child of such tender years of its mother, nor a young mother of her only child. Since the outset of this divorce action, Your Honor, my client has devoted herself full-time to the care of her little one, forsaking all social life. In the meantime, she has been forced to hear herself vilified by opposing counsel as a woman of loose morals, an unfit mother, an uncaring parent, and a woman addicted to alcohol, to the demon rum, to the devil's brew. . . . By the way, Your Honor, I'm ready for another drink!"

He had Bev and me rolling on the floor with laughter.

Sam and Bev later got married, by the way. I've lost track of Bev, and it's too bad, because she was my best friend. But she was a friend from my drinking days. That often happens to us alcoholics. When we get sober, the friends from the drinking days just sort of disappear. Today, most of my friends are members of my support group.

Of course my victory over Blazer's trust fund turned out to be a Pyrrhic one, didn't it? By the time Blazer's twenty-first birthday rolled around, there wasn't any trust fund. Si told Blazer I must have raided it, but I swear to you I did not. I never touched any of that money. I never even saw it. Maybe I should have paid closer attention, but I was drinking during all those years, and I let other people handle details like that. In that sense I am to blame for the missing funds—me and my old friend alcohol. Remember, I've only been sober now for six years—six years, three months, and eighteen days, to be exact. And that's a very short time, compared to all those drinking years.

Around 1970, a young man named Thomas Bonham joined the store, and Si placed him in charge of the trust fund, of the annual contributions that Si was making to it. Once a year, Mr. Bonham would come to see me, to go over the trust figures with me and give me pieces of paper to sign. I assumed that everything was going well. Mr. Bonham is a charming man, very intelligent and well-spoken. I have a theory that Si brought him in to be the eventual replacement for Moses Minskoff as his financial detail man. Mr. Bonham was certainly a cut above Mr. Minskoff.

When Blazer found out that his trust fund had somehow evaporated, he was furious. His father had accused me of stealing it, and Blazer actually asked me if I had. "Did you, Mom?" he asked me.

"I swear to you I didn't!" I told him. "I had no access to it. How could I have done it? All I ever did was go over the figures with Mr. Bonham once a year."

"Are you sure? Are you sure, Mom, that maybe sometimes when you were a little drunk you didn't write out some checks, or whatever you do to get at money like that, and then forgot about it?"

"*Why* would I have done that?" I said to him. "I fought hard to get that trust fund for you, all during the divorce. I wouldn't have fought so hard to get that for you, and then have taken it away."

The issue of the vanished trust fund very nearly drove a permanent wedge between my son and me.

There was no way I could get through to Si, so I

called Mr. Bonham to find out what had happened. "I thought everything was in perfect order," I said to him.

"It was," he told me. "Everything was in perfect order until a couple of years ago, when Si made some bad investments in it. I warned him at the time, but he insisted. Then this last recession hit us hard, and there were debts to be paid, and calls for more collateral. I'm sorry, Alice."

I told Blazer about this.

"Then the old man stole it," he said. "He must have."

Blazer and his father had had many disagreements and quarrels in the past, but the missing trust fund drove the final wedge between them. "I hate him," Blazer said at the time. "I really hate him now. I'd like to kill him! I'd really like to *kill him*!"

Well, even though it was awful to hear Blazer talk like that, one good did come out of that trust fund episode—my sobriety.

When Blazer said that to me, about my maybe having done something when I was "a little drunk," I realized that my son had never before used the word "drunk" about me. It woke me up. *My son thinks of me as a drunk!* I thought. It opened my eyes. And I took a good, hard look at myself for the first time.

I realized a number of things all at once. I realized how dependent I'd become on alcohol. I realized how it had come to control my life. My job, for instance. I'd begun editing a weekly fashion newsletter, to give me extra income, to supplement Erick's pension and his $200,000 life insurance policy. It permitted me to work out of my apartment. I didn't have to worry about how I looked or what I wore. I could sleep late on mornings when I had hangovers. In other words, it was a job designed to accommodate itself to my drinking hours.

Other than my job, every minute of my waking day was spent planning on when it would be sundown and time for the cocktail hour. "The sun is over the yard arm, Bev!" I'd say to my friend, and we'd bring out the bottle and the ice and glasses. During the day, I'd check my liquor supply, counting the bottles. Today is Saturday, I'd think. Do I have enough for Sunday, when every liquor store in town will be closed? If I went to a party, I'd stick a flask in my purse, in case the hostess's drinks weren't being poured fast enough. I'd even dream about drinking. I began to have dreams in which a certain seven-digit number kept appearing. I was certain that I was dreaming a winning lottery-ticket number, and one night I forced myself awake and wrote the number down. It was Sherry-Lehmann's telephone number.

I used to say I drank because it helped me get a good night's sleep. I realized it was taking more and more liquor to put me to sleep, and instead of sleeping I was becoming an insomniac. I felt suddenly that my whole life was being washed away in alcohol.

Worst of all, I realized that alcohol and I were cheating my son. There were events in Blazer's life when I was either missing or only half there. In school, he played basketball and, because he was taller than other boys his age, he played center. He'd remind me of the dates of his games, but I'd argue that I didn't care for basketball so I never saw him play. Those games interfered with my drinking time. He had the male lead in the school play, *Onions in the Stew*. I went to see it, but all through the performance I was thinking about getting home and having a drink. "How'd I do?" he asked me afterward. "Just fine," I said, outside in the street, desperately trying to flag down a cab that would get me home to the bottle.

I realized—and this was the most horrible realization of all—that Si had been right: I *was* an unfit mother.

Blazer enjoyed his weekends in Old Westbury with Connie and his father, at the farm they'd bought. He'd try to tell me about the things he'd done there, but I didn't want to hear about any of it. One day—he was only five years old—he mentioned swimming. "You can't swim," I told him. "Yes, I can," he said. "Aunt Connie taught me in their pool." She also taught him how to ride, on the horses they kept at the farm, and she began entering him in horse shows out on Long Island, and he started winning blue ribbons. But he never told me about the blue

ribbons because he knew I didn't want to talk about anything that happened out there. I only found out about
them when I happened to open one of his dresser drawers
and saw them lying there. Neatly, in rows.

I realized that Connie was doing exactly as she promised and giving him a wonderful home—at least, while he
was with them. And where was I? Drinking, thinking,
Hell, I have no pool, I have no horses.

When Blazer was at Yale, Connie and Miranda often
visited him there. Somehow, I never had the time. I realized Blazer had become genuinely fond of Connie, and he
adored his little half sister. That only made me feel bitter,
jealous, and resentful. I knew that Blazer and his father
often quarreled, particularly when Blazer reached his
teens, because Blazer had no interest in retailing or in
following his father's footsteps into the store. At the time,
Blazer talked about becoming a musician, but his father
told him there was no money in it. When I heard about
Blazer's quarrels with his father, it made me feel good. It
made me feel justified as a mother. Can you imagine that?
All because I was drinking.

If I hadn't been drinking, I might have kept a closer
eye on what was happening to Blazer's trust fund and
also what was happening to Blazer.

But mostly it was the shock of hearing my son say,
*Are you sure, Mom, that maybe sometimes when you
were a little drunk . . . ?*

All sorts of things came rushing back to me. One day
when he was sixteen, he sat down at the piano, and I
realized he was playing a Chopin étude. "When did you
learn to play?" I asked him.

He looked at me a little guiltily. "Aunt Connie taught
me," he said. "She's been giving me lessons since I was
six."

All those years, I realized, I'd hardly been noticing
him. But he'd been noticing me. Often in the mornings,
before he'd go off to school, or in the evenings, when I'd
have trouble getting to sleep, he'd come into my room
and give me back rubs, and shoulder rubs, and neck rubs.
"Are you feeling better, Mom?" he'd ask me. All that

time, he knew intuitively that I was sick, with an illness I couldn't control. All those years, when I'd been doing so little for him, he'd been trying to do whatever he could for me.

Sometimes when you were a little drunk . . .

That was when I decided to do something to bring my life under control. I screwed up my courage and went to my first A.A. meeting. It was a very unpleasant experience, but I forced myself to go back. And I began to realize that there were other people in the same plight, who were taking everything out of the bottle and giving nothing back.

When Blazer learned he'd been left out of his father's will, I don't think he was really surprised. I think he expected it, after the trust fund debacle and the bad scene with his father afterward. But who knows? Maybe in the long run it will be good for him that he didn't get a lot of money from his father. Maybe it will force him to go out and do something on his own, the way his father did. He and a friend are trying to open a restaurant in the Village right now. Sometimes I think, looking back, that my insistence on a trust fund from Si was just another example of my own laziness at the time.

My laziness and my vindictiveness. I really wanted that trust fund agreement because I wanted to punish Si. I wanted to extract my pound of flesh. Perhaps God—for I believe in a Higher Power now—didn't want that trust fund to materialize because it was wanted for base and lowly reasons.

And even though Blazer said he wanted to kill his father, I knew he didn't mean it. That was just his hurt talking. He really loved his father; it was love-hate. Lord knows there were times, during the divorce, when I thought of killing his father for what he was doing to me. But now, with the help of this wonderful program I'm in, I've been able to forgive Si. It wasn't me—Alice—whom he wanted to divorce. It was the alcohol that had taken control of me. Blazer and I had a long talk about this very thing the other night. About forgiveness, and the importance of it. "Forgive us our trespasses, and those who trespass against us."

"Have you forgiven your father for the loss of the trust fund?" I asked him.

"Perhaps. Almost."

"Have you forgiven him for leaving you out of his will?"

"Not quite. Not yet," he said.

"You will," I said. "You didn't really mean it when you said you wanted to kill him, did you?"

He shook his head. "No," he said, "but maybe somebody else did."

When he said that, I couldn't help thinking of the odd circumstances of Si's death. . . .

What was odd about it? It was where the obituary referred to Dr. Harry Arnstein, who pronounced the cause of death, as "the family physician." Harry Arnstein was *not* the family physician, certainly not when I was married to Si. When I read that, I immediately suspected some sort of cover-up. What Harry Arnstein *was* was a gin-rummy-playing crony of Si's. Sometimes Moe Minskoff would join them and they'd play poker, and sometimes other men would join them. Why did Connie call Harry Arnstein, of all people? He's not a cardiologist. His specialty is internal medicine.

Also, Si used to joke about what a terrible doctor Harry Arnstein was, even though he was a hell of a gin rummy player. Si used to say if anybody in his family got sick he wouldn't let them get near Harry Arnstein. So— why him?

Blazer had thought of this too.

But if there *was* foul play, and there *was* a cover-up —then who? I immediately thought of Moses Minskoff. Si had been trying to shake himself loose from Moe for years, and I'm sure Moe knew it. Perhaps, in the end, Moe decided it would be easier to get rid of Si. I never thought Moe was very smart, but sometimes stupid people can be more dangerous than smart ones. I'm not suggesting that Moe killed Si himself, but he had contacts with the sort of people who could do it for him. That was why Si distrusted Moe.

And then—Tommy Bonham. Tommy expected to run the store someday, and perhaps he got impatient. I must say Tommy never struck me as a killer type, but perhaps Tommy and Moe, acting in collusion. . . . Both stood to profit from Si's death.

And then, of course, there's Connie. Perhaps she finally got tired of Si's philandering. Hell hath no fury like a woman scorned, as I can personally attest to. She's a very cold woman. I always thought, after that first and only meeting with her, that Consuelo Banning was capable of anything.

Of course I didn't mention any of this to Blazer. He's fond of Connie. She did things for him, while he was growing up, that I didn't do.

And I've forgiven Connie for taking my husband away from me. I've forgiven them both. If there'd been a funeral, I'd have gone to it—inconspicuously, seated in the back. I wrote Connie a short condolence note, and she responded with a formal thank-you card, but with a slash drawn through her printed name and signed *Fondly, Connie,* underneath. I thought that was a bit of hypocrisy, that *Fondly.* Connie certainly isn't fond of me.

And I really shouldn't be speculating with you this way about Si's death, though Blazer thinks something very peculiar happened that morning at the farm.

All I can say is—Harry Arnstein? The family physician? No way!

In his office on West 23rd Street, Moses Minskoff is on the telephone. "Now, Miltie," he is saying, "it's too bad about what happened, and those kids got killed. But that's life, ya know? You took a gamble, and you lost, so what can I say? You got my deepest sympathy. . . . So you got a buncha lawsuits on your hands. I figured you would. A bunch of *shvartzers* get run over in a crowd, and the first thing their folks do is call a lawyer. Think they see a chance to make a buck off whitey. That's just show business, Miltie. That doesn't give you any beef with me. . . .

"Chief Gomez? What about him? He got paid off. . . . Whaddaya mean he didn't get paid off enough? He got twenty-five big ones, just like you and I agreed. . . . Whaddaya mean he only got ten? He's lying to you, Miltie, he's trying to put the squeeze on you. He got his twenty-five big ones, less my commission. . . . Whaddaya mean you got proof? What kind of proof you got? . . . He opened my Fed Ex envelope *in front of you,* and only ten big ones fell out? What is this fire chief, some kind of nut? I knew that fire chief was dumb, but I didn't think he was that dumb. . . . Whaddaya mean he's changed his mind? . . . He's going to the cops and say you tried to pay him off, but he isn't going to accept the payoff? This is nuts, Miltie! This makes no sense! Chief Gomez is trying to act like he's some sort of a saint. I've arranged payoffs for this guy before. Mother Teresa, he ain't. . . .

"Now all this is very strange, what you're saying, Miltie, but I don't see what it's got to do with me. I smell a rat. This Chief Gomez is trying to pull a fast one on you, Miltie. Cocksucker's just trying to hit you up for more. Don't fall for it, Miltie, is all I can advise you, and keep me outa this. . . .

"Now, Miltie, whaddaya mean I owe you fifteen big ones? I don't see it that way at all. . . . I tell ya he's lying. He got his full payment, just like what you sent me, less commission. This could be the ending of a beautiful friendship, Miltie, you talking about me owing you. . . . Now don't talk like that, Miltie. . . . I'm warning you, Miltie. . . .

"Well, I ain't sending you no fifteen big ones, because, A, I don't owe you nothing, and because, B, I ain't got it. I had a bad week at the track. . . .

"I dropped forty grand this week, Miltie, so have a little sympathy. . . . I'm your friend, Miltie. We're gonna be doing a lot more business together, you and me. . . .

"Whaddaya mean you're gonna get Herbie the Heeb

on me? Herbie's my friend from way back. He'll never touch me. . . . Now, wait a minute, Miltie—don't hang up on me!"

He replaces the receiver in its cradle.

Before placing his next call, he rises from his desk and closes his office door. He does this whenever he doesn't want Smyrna to overhear a conversation.

He picks up the telephone again. "Credit card call. . . . Herbie? Is that you? Moe here, Moe Minskoff. You remember me. Minskoff . . . that's right. You remember me, don'tcha, Herbie? You remember all the favors I done you in the past, don'tcha? The Liebman case? The brewery? Sure you remember that, Herbie, I'm sure you do. . . . Listen, Herbie, you wouldn't get involved in this East St. Louis *mishegoss*, wouldja? A man of your caliber. Not to an old pal like me, Herbie. . . .

"Listen, Herbie, let me do some more favors for you. Think up a favor you want me to do. Herbie—*don't hang up!*"

When he replaces the phone in its cradle now, his palms are sweating.

He makes a mental note to call the Mosler people and have the combination on the wall safe changed.

23

Mrs. Simma Tarcher Belsky (interview taped 9/18/91)

I really never understood why my brother resented me the way he did. My mother always claimed it was because I was a sickly baby and he was jealous of all the extra attention she had to give to me. Apparently, I had all those childhood illnesses that kids don't seem to get anymore. I only remember having to spend a long time in a darkened room, and that must have been the measles. When you had the measles, light was supposed to be bad for your eyes. My mother says the QUARANTINED sign was posted on our front door so often that Solly couldn't invite any of his friends to the apartment, and that's why he took to the streets and started running around with a bad crowd. My mother is pretty good at laying a guilt trip on a person. I grew up thinking that if Solly had turned out bad it was probably my fault.

But now it seems to me there must have been some other reason why my brother disliked me so. A nine-year-old boy is usually too far along toward becoming an adult to be jealous of a baby sister. A certain amount of sibling rivalry between my own children was understandable, because they were closer in age—but a nine-year-old versus an infant? It doesn't make sense. Even my psychiatrist says there had to be some deeper explanation.

Of course, in my earliest memories of him, he was already a young teenager. He seemed more like a young uncle than a brother, and I really idolized him. I'd have loved it if we could have been close. But when we were together in a room or sitting around the family dinner table, Sol simply ignored me. I felt like a non-person. My psychiatrist feels this made me mistrustful of the male sex, and I know she's right. One of my early problems in my marriage was that I kept demanding proofs of Leo's love. But you didn't come down here to hear about my therapy.

When Sol got in trouble with the law, that was a terribly traumatic time for me. I was twenty-one and engaged to Leo, and my engagement very nearly broke up because of it. Leo's family didn't want him marrying a girl whose brother was in the state prison, and they came to my parents and told them so. "Disgrace! Disgrace!" That was the only word I heard around my house for months. My father took it worst of all. Subconsciously, because I thought my sickly childhood was responsible for Solly's turning bad, I blamed myself for this disgrace, this shameful thing that had happened to my family. It was my fault we had produced this felon. And my father —he just seemed to withdraw from life. He used to sit in the dark, wide awake, in his chair. I'd come into the room. "Don't you want a light on, Papa?" I'd ask him. "No, I like to sit in the dark, Hadassah," he'd say. He'd started calling me by my Hebrew name. But otherwise there was no communication with him, and not long afterward he died. So there was the blame for another death laid at my doorstep. Is it any wonder my feelings about men were complicated, and it's taken years of therapy to work them out? Thank God for Leo. Leo stuck by me. He seemed to be the only man who would.

When Solly was let out of prison, his parole officer, Mr. Minskoff, came to see me. He explained the rehabili-

tation program that the state was working out for my
brother. They wanted to help him make a fresh start, and
this involved giving him a whole new identity and a new
name. I'd never heard of such a program before, but Mr.
Minskoff explained that it was experimental, and I gathered that Sol was one of the very first ex-prisoners they
were trying it out on, because he had been such an exem-
plary prisoner at Hillsdale. I've no idea whether the program was an overall success or not, though it certainly
was in Sol's case. I don't even know whether the state still
offers such programs to former prisoners—but then how
would I know? The point of the program is to expunge
the criminal's past from the record. And if the program
were publicized, that would defeat the whole point. It
struck me as a wonderfully humane approach to prisoner
rehabilitation, and I've often wondered whether other
states have tried it, though it obviously wouldn't work in
a hundred percent of the cases.

Anyway, Mr. Minskoff explained that the state was
helping to set Sol up in business—a retail store specializing in female apparel. This was because Sol came from a
retailing family and had worked in the garment industry
before he got into trouble. Some state funds were being
made available for this project, but the state was also
asking close family members to contribute to the new
business by purchasing shares of stock in it. "We're only
asking close, caring family members," he said. "We're
only asking people who'd like to demonstrate their faith
in the prisoner's prospects for rehabilitation."

Well, I liked to think that I was caring and that I had
faith in Solly's future, even though he'd never liked me.
And I also thought that by contributing something I could
perhaps atone for some of the grief I'd indirectly brought
upon him and on my parents. But when Mr. Minskoff
mentioned the figure he had in mind, three hundred thousand dollars, that just seemed too much of a Yom Kippur.
I could have afforded it, I suppose. Leo made good
money, and I'd had an inheritance from my father that
was a complete surprise; no one had any idea that he'd
been able to save so much money. But three hundred

thousand dollars would have taken up most of my inheritance. I didn't think I should put all my eggs in one basket. My two children were still little, and I was pregnant with my third, and I thought most of that money should be set aside for their college education.

Mr. Minskoff said the state would gladly accept as little as half that figure, which sounded more like it. But naturally I told him I would have to discuss all this with my husband.

This next part is a little difficult to talk about, because it's been a source of disagreement between my husband and myself over the years. But I might as well tell you. My children are all grown, now, and are mature enough to handle it.

When I mentioned discussing this matter with Leo, Mr. Minskoff asked me a strange question, which really upset me. "Is there any blot on your escutcheon, Mrs. Belsky?" I'll never forget his strange choice of words.

"What do you mean by that?" I said.

"We want to present the new Mr. Silas Tarkington as a man of sterling character," he said. "And that sterling character should also apply to the members of his immediate family. Is there possibly any scandal in your family's background that could come back to haunt you and your family later on?"

"I don't think so," I said.

"Think hard," he said. "The State of New York wants to present Silas Tarkington as a man whose background is simon-pure. Is your own background also simon-pure? This is highly important, Mrs. Belsky."

"Well, I suppose no one's background is *simon*-pure," I told him, "but I've always tried to be a decent person." He was making me very nervous.

"No hint of a family scandal?"

"No—unless you count Sol."

"Silas," he said. "Sol is Silas now, remember. But this particular scandal involves *you*, not your brother, Mrs. Belsky."

"What is it?" I cried. He was really frightening me now.

"The State of New York," he said, "in implementing this prisoner rehabilitation program, does a very thorough background check on each candidate. Not only on the candidate's background but on the background of each member of his immediate family. In your case—well, let me put it to you this way. Does the name of Dr. Sidney Weiss mean anything to you?"

"Certainly. The Weisses are old friends of my parents. Dr. Weiss is our dentist."

"You have bright red hair, Mrs. Belsky," he said. "Dr. Weiss also has bright red hair. Has there ever been any question of your real paternity? Has it ever occurred to you that you may be Dr. Weiss's illegitimate daughter, the product of an illicit union between him and your mother? There have been rumors to this effect."

I knew immediately what he was talking about. In school, my nickname was Carrot Top. I really did have bright red hair in those days. There's a type of redhead whose hair is dark and lustrous, almost the color of mahogany. But I wasn't so lucky. My hair was orange, really a carrot color, and I hated that nickname. Dr. Weiss's hair *was* the same color as mine, and the other kids used to tease me about it. Kids can be so cruel. They'd say, "Are you *sure* that when Dr. Weiss told your mother to lie back and relax in his dentist's chair, all he opened was her mouth?" They'd tease me until I'd cry. If I'm giving you the impression that I had a miserable childhood, it's true; I did. Naturally, I never told my mother about any of this. And I never told my husband.

"Where did you hear these rumors?" I asked him.

"From former neighbors, people in the neighborhood." He patted his briefcase. "It's all in your brother's file."

"You keep these sorts of things in his file? Personal things—about me and my mother?" I couldn't believe what I was hearing.

"Absolutely," he said, and he patted his briefcase again. "It's all a matter of public record, as we say up in Albany. We run a very efficient state, Mrs. Belsky."

I didn't know what to think. It wasn't just my own

reputation I was worried about. What about my mother's? My father at least, thank God, was dead at that point. But what about Dr. and Mrs. Weiss—and their children? What would this sort of thing do to them? And there were my own children. How would they feel if they learned that there was even a possibility that their mother was illegitimate? What would this do to *their* lives? Then there was Leo, and his parents, and his brother and sisters. Those people thought little enough of me as it was! If this suspicion came out, Leo's entire family could turn against me, and what would this do to our marriage? All of a sudden there were at least a dozen other people whose lives could be torn apart by this story. I thought to myself, Haven't I caused enough grief and misery in this family already?

I decided to present this to my husband as my decision, not as if I was asking his opinion of it. This took some doing in itself. Needless to say, he was vehemently opposed to the whole idea. "Why are you doing this for that no-good brother of yours?" Leo wanted to know. "He's never done a damn thing for you!"

"I have my reasons," I said. "Besides, I feel it's my duty and obligation to the family to help him out."

"You'd sacrifice your own children's future for this bum?" he said.

"I don't look at it that way, Leo," I said. "This money came to me from Papa. I feel this is what Papa would have wanted me to do."

"That's nonsense," he said. "Your father had no use for Sol at the end."

"But if he'd lived to see Sol rehabilitated, he would have," I said.

"Huh! What makes you think so?"

"I just know Papa would have believed in giving Sol a second chance."

"Rehabilitated! That'll be the day!" he said.

"It's my money, Leo," I reminded him.

"It's *our* money," he said. "And you're talking about throwing it out the window!"

"No," I said. "That money was left to me, free and clear. And Mr. Minskoff said—"

"Who is this guy Minskoff? I want to meet this guy Minskoff. I don't trust him."

"That won't be necessary," I said. "Mr. Minskoff has promised me nine percent interest on my investment."

"Nine percent? That's crazy, Simma! Nothing is paying nine percent interest these days!"

"This is guaranteed by the State of New York. It's a brand-new program. There's never been anything like it before."

"The State of New York? What kind of guarantee is that? If we get a new governor in the next election, and a new legislature comes into Albany, they could throw the whole program out. And then where will you be, Simma? Then what're you going to do, sue the State of New York? Well you can't do that. You can't sue the government of a sovereign state!"

"I'm not talking suing," I told him. "I'm talking about getting three percent of the shares of stock in the new company."

"Just do me one favor," he said to me. "Just show me you've still got a head on your shoulders. Ask him for a bigger percentage. Ask him for twelve percent of the shares. Hold out for that. At least hold out for more shares."

So I reported this part of the conversation to Mr. Minskoff the next day, and he agreed. For my hundred-and-fifty-thousand-dollar investment, he agreed to give me twelve percent of the shares.

"Are you happy now, Leo?" I asked him.

"Happy? I still think it's craziness," he said. "And mark my words, Simma. You're never going to get a penny back on this so-called investment of yours. You're just throwing that money out the window."

Well, after a few years it began to look as though Leo was right. The store opened, it was supposed to be a big success, but none of us were getting any dividends from the stock we'd bought. We had a little family meeting about the situation around my kitchen table in Kew Gardens—my mother, Leo, and me. My mother turned on Leo. "You're supposed to be this big-shot accountant. Shouldn't you have taken care of Simma's money better?"

I looked at him. "Leo," I said, "would you mind leaving Mama and me alone for a minute? There's something private I have to ask her."

Well, Leo looked as though he did mind, but he got up and went out of the kitchen, and a minute or so later I heard him start up the power lawn mower, so I knew he wouldn't be hearing the conversation between my mother and me.

"What's up?" my mother asked.

There was no point in beating around the bush. I said, "Mama, is Sidney Weiss my real father?"

Her face went white, and I thought she was going to faint and fall off the chair. And right away I knew the answer.

"What did you say?" she gasped.

"I think you heard me, Mama," I said.

"Who told you that?" she said.

"Mr. Minskoff. It was in Solly's file."

"Oh, my God," she said, and she kept repeating it. "Oh, my God . . . oh, my God. . . ."

It was the strangest feeling, having the rumor confirmed like that. I felt as though a whole half of my life had been stripped away. The father I'd loved wasn't my father after all. I started to cry. It had been so much better, not knowing.

"Does Leo know?" she asked me.

"No. . . ."

"Your children—oh, my God, your children! Do they know?"

"No. No one knows, Mama, but you and me."

"And Mr. Minskoff! If it's in Solly's file, the whole State of New York could know by now!"

"All he knows are the rumors," I sobbed. "That's why I gave him the money, if he'd promise to take those rumors out of Solly's file."

"Rumors." Now she was crying too.

"Mama," I said to her, *"how could you?"*

"Simma," she said, "I swear to you it only happened once! I know it was wrong. But your father—my Abe—was so busy with the business, and I was so lonely, and one night I just got carried away! I shouldn't have, but I did. I just got carried away, that was all. I swear to you, Simma, that was the only time—the only time I was ever unfaithful to my husband!"

I stuck my fingers in my ears. "I don't want to hear any more!" I cried. I could feel one of my allergic migraines coming on.

"Will you ever forgive me, Simma?" she said.

Any emotional stress like that tends to bring on an allergic reaction in me. I'd like to read you a report my psychiatrist sent to my allergist the other day. It will give you some insights into the kind of narrow line I've always had to walk in this family.

"Mrs. Belsky's allergies certainly present a problem in terms of her being able to deal with problems in her family. However, she is not physiologically suffering from allergies *per se*. Instead, her problem is emotional, the result of a truncated psychosocial development. Being the child of parents who were emotionally preoccupied, if not absent, she saw her mother as involved with bringing profits to the family business and her father as a man who was at best marginally suited to provide emotional support. She was to bypass critical sexual developmental stages, e.g., anal development was relegated to obsessive cleanliness. Patient's earliest memories involve scenes of her mother boiling her diapers on the kitchen stove. And as for oral gratification, there was never any suckling at breast, unusual at that point in time. Genital stage development was a particularly difficult issue, in that patient's parents weren't engaged in any display of affection. From what patient remembers, parents usually related through issues of money, whether Mother was earning sufficient to provide for family, or how well Father was.

"Money matters became the focus of her life. When excessive anxiety about lack of money surfaced, namely arguments between parents, patient's only recourse was to somatize, since the joys of masturbation, bowel movements, and eating were beyond her grasp. A refuge in physical symptomology was her only outlet.

"Might I add, her marriage is only a further continuation of the repetition compulsion: husband represents the withholding parent who induces guilt readily by declaring a problem in terms of dollars and cents. Wife either capitulates to his whims or suffers an asthma attack. Which is preferable? As you know, 'getting sick' is no panacea, but until she is able developmentally to acquiesce to the transference and work through the debilitating effects of parental influences which have bound her to guilt and shame, she has no chance of ridding herself of the physical symptoms.

"The above is the present focus of psychotherapy."

Isn't that insightful? I think that tells you more about me than I could ever tell you about myself.

Anyway, for a long time I didn't think I could ever really forgive my mother for keeping a secret like that from me. But now I don't see what else she could have done. I was born in 1929. There were no such things as legal abortions then, and the illegal ones were expensive and dangerous. I've never asked whether she considered aborting me. I guess I don't want to know. Anyway, I wasn't, so what else could she have done? She was married; Sidney Weiss was married. If she'd told the truth, she would certainly have wrecked two homes. And thanks to Rita Fiori, my psychiatrist, I've been able to work it out in my own mind, and I can live with it now, though Rita feels that my conflicted feelings on the whole subject are also responsible for my allergies.

So now you're the fourth person to know the whole truth—Mama, me, Rita, and now you. Sidney and Sylvia Weiss are both dead now, and, as I say, my children are all grown, old enough to live with it if they were told. And Leo? Yes, I think Leo could live with it too; I don't think it would matter all that much if I were to tell him the whole story. I just never have. Leo wanted to move down here for the fishing and the golf, and those are really the only two things that interest him now, God bless him, not me and my problems.

Perhaps you're wondering why I'm telling you about the skeleton in my family's closet for this book you want to write. I'll tell you why. It's because I want Leo's brother and two sisters to know the truth. They've never forgiven Leo for marrying me. They talk about my criminal brother. They call me peculiar. They've stayed very distant from Leo over the years, and though he never talks about it I know that's hurt him deeply. They say there had to be something wrong with Leo for marrying me. But there's nothing wrong with Leo. Leo is a saint. He has a beautiful character, and he's stuck with me through thick and thin. But there was something wrong with my mother, for all her talk of coming from a better family and a better background. She was unfaithful to her husband, and with a man who was his best friend, and if you think I believe I'm the result of one time when she just got "carried away," you must think I believe in the tooth fairy. She's the blot on the escutcheon, not my brother, and I want Leo's family to know this once and for all. I want them to stop blaming Leo and put the blame where it belongs, on her, for what she did to my father and my brother and the whole family. As Rita says, once you get the blame placed right, the guilt and pain can begin to go away.

But just do me one favor. If you put all this in your story, don't publish until after Mama dies. She's an old lady now, and I don't want her to suffer any more than she has already. She may deserve the blame, but nobody deserves to suffer. But after you're dead? After you're dead, you don't suffer. So will you promise me that? And me? Well, I think I've learned to live with who I am. Almost. At least I keep trying. Forgive me. . . . Do you mind stopping your tape for a minute until I—?

Yes, I'm all right now. Rita says it's good for me to let out my feelings now and then, not keep everything bottled up inside, the way I tend to do. Sometimes it's healthy to have a good cry. And you can't undo the past, can you? You just have to live with it, like a curse.

And now, out of the blue, just the other day comes an offer to buy my Tarkington's stock—from a man named Albert Martindale of Continental Stores, and guess who's acting as his agent? None other than Mr. Moses Minskoff! Isn't that a coincidence? Mr. Minskoff no longer works for New York State. He couldn't stand the bureaucracy, he says, and—just like Leo predicted, I give Leo full credit—the state's rehabilitation program that was helping Solly was phased out a couple of years afterward. Anyway, Mr. Minskoff now has his own company, specializing in mergers and acquisitions, and he's brokering Continental's buyout of Tarkington's. Mr. Minskoff says this is going to be the deal of a lifetime for me, and I'll get all my original investment back plus a good deal more. Leo says I should hold out and see if we can get a better offer than sixty dollars a share. But I haven't decided what to do. I'm conflicted about that too. I have these feelings of guilt about taking money for shares in my brother's store now that he's dead. Rita and I have been trying to work on that in our last couple of sessions. Sometimes, when I feel conflicted like this, I can't seem to move in any direction, and then I'll get an asthma attack, or a migraine, or break out in one of these terrible rashes. Why do I feel that, if he didn't want to give me any money while he was living, I shouldn't accept any money now that he's dead?

Yes, I was sad when I heard my brother had died. It was kind of an abstract sadness, of course, because it was so long since I'd seen him. And there was guilt, too, thinking that perhaps I should have made more of an effort. I no longer had any mental picture of what he looked like, and that was a terrible feeling.

I knew he'd had two children that I'd never met. I never hear much about the son. But the daughter, Miranda—I see her picture from time to time, in magazines like *Vanity Fair* and *Town & Country*. She's an awfully pretty girl, isn't she? From her pictures, she seems really movie-star pretty.

Any looks in the family come from my mother's side. When my mother was young, she was really beautiful.

And that's another thing I'll never understand. If Mama was going to cheat on her husband, why did she do it with a man like Sidney Weiss, who was just about the ugliest-looking man you've ever seen? If she was going to make me a bastard, why did she have to make me an ugly one, with horrible orange hair?

"And so," Peter Turner says to Miranda, turning off the recorder, "that's your Aunt Simma. That's your father's sister." They are sitting in her apartment at 11 East 66th Street, and she is curled in a chair, looking pensive, her chin in her hand.

"Goodness," she says at last, "what an unhappy woman!" Then she jumps to her feet. "I'm going down there to see her!" she says.

24

"Miranda Tarkington!" Simma is saying. "Solly's little girl! I can't believe you're sitting here in this room with me. When you called from New York, saying you wanted to come to Florida to see me, I couldn't believe my ears."

"I just felt it was high time you and I met, Aunt Simma," Miranda says.

"Aunt Simma! That sounds so strange to me. Nobody's ever called me that before. I'm just Ma to my children and Grandma to my grandchildren. How old are you now, dear?"

"I'm twenty-four, Aunt Simma."

"Twenty-four. Just think of that. It's been many more years than that since I last saw your father. That was more like forty years ago. Well, I must say you're just as pretty as you are in photographs—prettier, even."

"Thank you. You have a lovely apartment, Aunt Simma."

"Yes, we like it. It's right on the golf course, which my husband likes. And the Intracoastal is just two blocks away, where he likes to fish off the bridge."

There is a little silence, and then Miranda says, "Peter Turner let me listen to the tape of the interview he did with you. I hope you don't mind."

"Oh," she says. "That means you know my shameful secret, that I'm illegitimate. Well, I guess that's all right. You're family, after all."

"I don't think illegitimacy is all that shameful," Miranda says. "I think it's rather romantic. In England you'd be called a love-child. Your mother's love-child."

"Love-child? Well, perhaps. But I only wish my mother had picked someone more attractive to have this love-child with."

"Looks are only skin deep, remember. He may have had other qualities—"

"What they were, I can't imagine! After I found out what I did, I couldn't bear the sight of him. I had to switch to another dentist. It was that hard for me to accept."

"Actually, your tapes told me something much more important than Grandmother's involvement with Dr. Weiss. That's one reason I decided I needed to talk to you."

"Oh?" Simma Belsky says.

"You see, since my father died, there are a number of aspects of my father's life and business that I've been looking into, and Peter Turner has been very helpful. I've learned all sorts of things I didn't know before, family secrets that had been kept hidden from me. For instance, I didn't know my father's original name was Tarcher. And I never knew he'd been to prison."

"Did that come as a terrible shock?"

"A bit of a one, yes. But I had to admire the way he'd been able to bury his past."

"The State of New York helped him to do that," Simma says.

"I don't think so, Aunt Simma," she says. "Peter and I have done some checking, and there never was any prisoner rehabilitation program in New York State in the late nineteen-fifties such as Mr. Minskoff described to you and your mother. That was all a lie."

"Really?"

"Moses Minskoff never worked for the State of New York in any capacity. He was not my father's parole officer. Moses Minskoff was a small-time crook who knew my father when they were both inmates at Hillsdale. In fact, when Moses Minskoff first came to see you and your mother, he was on parole himself. I brought along a copy of Moses Minskoff's criminal record at the time he was sentenced to Hillsdale. I thought you might like to take a look at it." She reaches in her purse, withdraws a sheaf of papers, and hands them to Simma.

"My God," Simma says, reading through them. "Fraud . . . petty larceny . . . extortion! I should have listened to my husband. He said we shouldn't trust him."

"I'm afraid he was right. Moses Minskoff is a con artist. He came to you and your mother, posing as a parole officer, in order to extort money to help my father start his store. With your mother, he preyed on her maternal feelings. With you, he resorted to a rather primitive form of blackmail."

"My God!"

"Moses Minskoff has been a fixture in my father's business life for as long as I can remember. He was always on the periphery of things, but he was always there. Daddy used to call him Mr. Fixit. When things needed fixing, Mr. Fixit fixed them. If money was needed, Mr. Fixit found it—somewhere. It begins to look as though, in the early days at least, Moses Minskoff was using Tarkington's to launder money that may well have come from criminal sources. How long that went on, we still don't know. But certainly, in the beginning, Daddy needed money, and Moses Minskoff provided it, and Daddy didn't ask any questions. You see, it's important to remember that, where Tarkington's was concerned, my father was the idea man. He was also a super salesman; it was he who created the store's reputation for fine merchandise and superb service. Moses Minskoff hardly ever came into the store, but he was always there in the background, making deals. When Daddy began to suspect that some of the deals weren't on the up and up, and started asking questions, it was too late. Moses Minskoff had his claws too deeply into him for Daddy to escape."

"It begins to sound as though this man should be thrown back into jail, Miranda!"

"Peter and I certainly think so. But we don't have enough hard evidence yet. Once we do, I'm going to have to decide whether or not to take what I know to the Attorney General's office. There's a danger; that kind of publicity could permanently damage the store's reputation, and we don't want that."

"Of course not."

"I think Daddy was genuinely frightened of what his silent business partner could do to the store. Minskoff had the power to expose Daddy's past. He could blackmail Daddy, just the way he blackmailed you. Or maybe Daddy discovered that, without even being aware of it, he himself had become so deeply involved in Minskoff's shady deals that there was no way he could extricate himself. Minskoff clung to him like a leech. Right up until the day he died, my father was trying to pry himself loose, and at the end he may have thought he'd found a way."

That way, she thinks, may have been a plan to run off to Bermuda with Smitty and leave the whole mess behind him. He had changed his identity once before. Perhaps he was planning to do it again. But she doesn't tell Simma Belsky this. "But then—" she begins. "But then he was found floating dead in his swimming pool."

Simma stares at her. "Miranda, do you mean to say you think your father was murdered?"

"We don't know. It begins to look more and more like that, Aunt Simma, and Moe Minskoff certainly had a motive. But until we find out more, all we can do is speculate. One big reason I came down here is to warn you about him."

"If Minskoff is as dangerous as you say he is, Miranda, isn't what you're doing a little dangerous too? Aren't you a little frightened that something could happen to you?"

She laughs. "Not yet," she says. "But if we're able to

get the goods on him—that's when I'll decide whether to be frightened or not."

"What you're doing worries me, Miranda."

"Well, I also came down here to ask your help," she says. "As you know, Continental Stores is making a take-over bid for Tarkington's, and Moe Minskoff, of all people, is acting as their agent. Various stockholders have already been approached with a two-tiered offer for their shares. It's a very tempting offer, but I'm here to ask that you not accept it, Aunt Simma. To begin with, Tommy Bonham—who was Daddy's vice president and general manager—and I don't want to lose the store. We want to run it ourselves, so we're fighting this takeover. Continental is offering a ridiculously high price per share, so we're certain that if they succeed in this they'll simply sell off our real estate and inventory and close the store. Or they'll turn it into something very different from what it is, and either way that will be the end of my father's dream. My mother and I each own about twenty percent of the shares, but that doesn't give us a majority, and even my mother may decide to jump ship. If she doesn't, yours could be the swing vote, Aunt Simma. And in any case we need every vote we can get to stop Continental."

"I see," Simma says. "Of course I'll have to discuss all this with Leo."

"Of course. I want you to. I want you to discuss it with him very carefully. But remember—any deal that involves Moe Minskoff is a deal that stinks. How he got involved with a chain the size of Continental is a mystery, but believe me, Moe Minskoff means nothing but trouble, and that makes us doubly determined to save the store. And it's such a beautiful store, Aunt Simma. Have you ever been there?"

"Never. I was sure my brother never wanted to lay eyes on me again."

"I don't think that's true, Aunt Simma," she says. "I think he loved you and your mother very much. But I think he was so embarrassed by—so ashamed of—the tactics Moe Minskoff used to get the two of you to invest that he couldn't bear to face either of you after he found out. Posing as his parole officer, for God's sake! I honestly don't think Daddy had any idea of the kind of dirty tricks Moe was using to get you to invest until it was all over."

"Well, perhaps," Simma says, but she does not look convinced.

"I'm sure that's how he felt. Simma, I knew my father longer than you did. There were lots of things about him that I didn't exactly approve of, but I don't think he'd knowingly betray his own mother and his sister."

"If he felt so guilty about the way he'd treated Mama and me, why didn't he leave us the money he owed us in his will? He knew we were still in the land of the living. Why couldn't he have at least done that?"

Miranda bites her lip. "It was a very bitter will," she says. "He was in a very bitter frame of mind when he wrote that will. But I do know that when he died he was in the process of preparing a new will. He was planning to add some additional bequests. I don't know what they were, because he died before the new will could be executed. I wish I could say that you and your mother were going to be remembered in it, but I can't."

Now it is Simma's tone that is bitter. "Mama and I each turned over nearly half of our inheritance to him," she says. "Nearly half! A hundred and fifty thousand dollars was a lot of money in nineteen fifty-six. To me, it still is. Mama kept calling him and writing him about why there were never any dividends. We'd been promised nine percent. But he never answered her letters or returned her calls."

"Again, out of shame. Nine percent was Moe Minskoff's promise, and of course it was an impossible one—another reason why my father couldn't bear to face either of you. He'd already let his family down once. Now, thanks to Moe, he was being forced to do it again. I don't think my father was essentially a dishonest man. But his hands were always tied—by Moe."

Simma shakes her head. "No," she says. "I know a little about psychology. I've been in analysis for thirty years. I know a little about how the human mind works. I think that once he got our money, and got us to sign those papers, it was just easier to forget all about us. He knew we couldn't sue him. So he said to himself, Forget about those two. To hell with them. I got what I needed from them. What more do I need those two for?"

Miranda sighs. "You may be right," she says. "Perhaps he let half of his mind forget you. But I'm sure with the other half he was always remembering what had been done to you—with guilt. Perhaps that's why he was so bitter. But neither of us knows his innermost thoughts for sure, do we? And now he's dead. But I'm not. I'm alive, and I want to make it up to you. That's why, the minute I found out about you, I wanted to see you."

"How are you going to make it up to us, Miranda?"

"Look. Let me tell you the truth. I don't know. If I had the money, I'd pay it all back to you with interest. But I don't. You and I are in the same boat, Aunt Simma. All we have is stock in the company and a ridiculously high offer to purchase it. For me, the stakes are higher since I own more shares. Nobody knows yet what else my father may have left in tangible assets besides his stock. He was supposed to have a valuable art collection, but his paintings turned out to be fakes.

"All I have right now is a belief in Tarkington's. It was my father's dream, and it's become my dream. I'm fighting to save that dream. If Continental buys us, that will be the end of everything, because Continental isn't much more than a glorified J C Penney.

"How do you put a price on a dream? There just isn't any way. You mentioned dividends. Tarkington's has never paid a dividend. Not even my father ever received a dividend on the shares he owned. All he ever received was salary. I wish I could promise you that, if Tommy Bonham and I succeed in fighting off this takeover Moe is engineering, we're immediately going to start paying dividends. But I can't. All I can promise you is that we intend to put the store on a sounder fiscal basis, so that, with any success at all, all of us can start receiving dividends in future. But that's not a promise, Aunt Simma. All it is is asking you to have faith in me, a woman you've just met."

"But this offer from Continental is for sixty dollars a share—eighty percent of it in cash!"

Miranda leans forward in her chair. "That offer is much too high," she says. "It makes no sense. It has to be phony. If Moe Minskoff is behind it, it's a trick. Once we agree to sell, that offer is going to change, and all any of us will end up with is a lot of Continental's junk bonds. The only person who will profit from this will be Moses Minskoff. It's also a very cruel offer. A number of our employees own stock. This offer is intended to divide their loyalties. On the one hand, they'd like to see Tarkington's kept the way it is. On the other hand, the idea of selling out for a lot of money is very tempting. Right now, they're feeling torn. But that's one of the strategies of a hostile takeover—to divide and conquer. One final plea to you, Aunt Simma. It was Moses Minskoff who divided this family. Please don't go along with another scheme of his that will divide us even more. We're more than a store, we're a family."

She considers this. "Well, let me talk to my husband," she says at last.

"Yes. It was thanks to your husband that you got a twelve percent position. Your mother, for the same investment, got only three percent—another Minskoff trick. By the way, I suppose you have your mother's power of attorney and can vote her shares for her?"

"Power of attorney? She'd never give me that. And don't be so sure she'll vote her shares the way I tell her to."

"But I'd heard she was senile," Miranda says.

"*Senile!* I wish she were. It would be a lot easier on me if she were. She's quite alert, thank you very much. She tries to run that nursing home she's in. She goes around to all the residents' rooms at night, seeing to it that they're all properly tucked into bed. She pesters the kitchen staff, either complaining about the food or offering new recipes for them to try. She tries to plan the menus. And her bridge club! She plays bridge for ten cents a point, which none of the other residents can afford, so she has this big stack of IOU's. Once a month, she goes from door to door, trying to collect. Oh, she's a caution, Miranda. Would you like to meet her? After all, she's your grandmother."

Miranda jumps to her feet. "I'd love that!" she cries.

"Well, let's go right now," Simma says. "It's not a long drive up to West Palm. We can take my car. It's right outside." And she also rises.

"Tell me something," Miranda says. "What do her other grandchildren call her?"

"They all call her Granny Rose." They move together toward the front door.

"And tell me something else," Miranda says as they descend the front steps of the condominium toward the parking lot. "Did Granny Rose or any other Tarchers ever live on West End Avenue?"

"In Manhattan? No. Leo and I lived in Kew Gardens. That's really Queens, of course, but Kew Gardens sounds a little better. And Mama lived in the Bronx. We couldn't budge her off the Grand Concourse, even when the neighborhood became completely black, until we moved her down here. And that's all of us there were, for Tarchers."

The old woman runs her fingers gently across Miranda's face. "So you're Solly's daughter," she says. "Yes, I can see Solly in your face. It's in the eyes. But I forget—are you the child of the first one, or the second?"

"The second, Granny Rose."

"Both shiksas, weren't they?"

"Yes."

"Well, I guess I can't complain," she says, "though I didn't think much of the first one. She seemed kind of la-di-da to me. The second one I never met. Well, what do you want? Solly's daughter wouldn't come all this way to see me if she didn't want something. What is it? Money, I suppose. How much this time?"

Miranda squeezes her grandmother's hand, which seems to her surprisingly firm and strong. "I'd like it very much if you'd like me, Granny Rose," she says. "I'd like it even **more if you** could love me."

"Sixty dollars a share!" Leo is saying. "And eighty percent of that in cash, and the rest in Continental bonds! Why didn't you show me this letter before, Simma?"

"Si's daughter was here. Miranda. She's an executive with the store. She doesn't like the sound of this deal. She says don't sell."

"You've got only ten business days to act on this. And you've already let five of those days go by! My God, Simma, you've got to get an answer off right away!"

"I don't think I'm going to sell, Leo," she says.

"Are you out of your *mind*?" he cries. "In cash alone, they're offering you almost a million dollars for the shares you own!"

"I think Miranda's right. The deal doesn't sound right. We smell a rat. Moses Minskoff is his name."

"Are you crazy? Continental stores is offering you almost a million dollars in cash, and you're turning it down? I'm not going to let you do this, Simma. Give me that letter."

"No," she says evenly. "This is a letter to me. This is my stock they're offering to buy, not yours."

"Well, I'm the head of this household, and I'm taking charge, since you're obviously not capable of thinking rationally!"

"You may be head of this household, but you're not telling me what I can or can't do with something that's mine," she says.

"You're crazy, Simma! I *am* telling you what to do!"

"And I'm telling you I won't do it. Rita says I should be more assertive. She says I shouldn't let you boss me around the way I do."

"Who got you to hold out for twelve percent of the shares—*me*!"

"And who didn't want me to buy any stock to begin with—*you*."

"That's my stock as much as it is yours!"

"No, it isn't, Leo. I bought it with part of Papa's inheritance. If it had been your inheritance, from your papa, it would be yours. But I didn't see any inheritance coming from your father, did I?"

"My father left me nothing because I'd married you!"

"Oh. So now that's my fault too, is it? Funny, but I remember things a little differently. As I recall, your father died leaving nothing but debts."

"Give me that letter, Simma—right now!"

"Here. Take the letter. What are you going to do with it? You can't sell my stock for me. Only I can do that. And I'm going to do what Miranda wants me to."

"You're listening to that niece of yours? A niece you've only met for half an hour? A niece who's your crooked brother's daughter?"

"I liked her. I trust her. Rita says I should trust my feelings."

"Simma, how can you do this to your children and your little grandchildren. Simma, think of them. How can you do this to me, who's provided for you for all these years, paid all your bills?"

"The rest of what Papa left me helped to do that, didn't it? As I recall, I turned all the rest of that money over to you."

"I'm not going to let you do this to your family, Simma."

"Well, it's what I'm going to do. Rita says—"

"Rita says! Rita says this, Rita says that! Why do you need all these psychiatrists, Simma? Because you're crazy, that's why. You are completely out of your mind. You are stark, raving mad, Simma. You're a raving lunatic, and I am going to have you placed in a lunatic asylum! I am going to have you declared mentally incompetent and have myself made the legal custodian of your financial affairs, which you are no longer competent to handle!"

"Well, you'd better get working on that, Leo," she says. "You'd better get working on that right now. These things take time, and you've only got five business days left. Today is Thursday. That gives you until five o'clock next Wednesday to have me declared insane. Hurry, Leo! Get out and get cracking on it! You've got to get me declared insane by five o'clock next Wednesday."

"Craziness! Insanity! The more you see these psychiatrists, the crazier they make you!"

"Not really," she says. "Actually, Rita and I seem to be making progress. With all the stress you're putting me through right now, I should be getting an asthma attack, or one of my migraine headaches. But look—no asthma, no migraine. What do you make of that?"

Back in her office at the store, Miranda is going through her telephone message slips and finds a message to call Pauline O'Malley, her father's former secretary.

"Well, Pauline," she says when she reaches her at home, "how are you enjoying your retirement?"

"Oh, Miss Miranda," Pauline says, "I hate to trouble you with this, but something very strange has happened."

"What's that?"

"After I left the store, I applied for my retirement benefits from the pension fund. But this morning I had a letter saying that the pension fund has been temporarily suspended."

"Suspended?"

" 'Suspended until further notice,' the letter says. But Miss Miranda, we all contributed to that, and the store was supposed to be matching our contributions. How can they just suspend the fund?"

"Let me see what I can find out, Pauline," she says. "I'll call you back."

She steps into Tommy Bonham's office. "Tommy, is there some sort of problem with the pension fund?" she asks him.

His face looks grim. "You've been talking to Pauline, I guess," he says.

"Yes. She says—"

"Early in August the store was having a cash flow problem. We needed cash to pay our suppliers. We'd already asked for, and been given, a fifteen-day extension, and our suppliers were threatening not to ship us any more merchandise until they were paid. The pension fund seemed an obvious place to find cash, so your father had those funds transferred to the store's general operating account."

"But Tommy, is that even legal?"

"I begged him not to do it, Miranda."

"But you're the chief financial officer. You let him do this?"

With the tip of his index finger, he wipes a thin band of perspiration that has formed along his upper lip. She notices a small facial tic she never noticed before. The right corner of his mouth is twitching, as though he were about to smile, but he is not smiling. Perhaps because he sees she has noticed this, he covers his lips with his left hand. She sits with her legs together, and his eyes shift away from hers. "Your father was not exactly the kind of man one *let* do anything," he says almost crossly. "If he wanted something done, he did it. He said it was just a question of shifting money from one pocket to the other. It was intended to be temporary. Obviously, he didn't expect anyone to be applying for retirement benefits for a while. And he obviously didn't expect to die."

"Then we've got to get that money back into the pension fund as quickly as possible."

"I agree," he says. "But that's easier said than done at this point. Where are we going to get the money? It's gone."

"Gone," she repeats numbly. She stares at him. "Are things that bad, Tommy?"

The corner of his mouth continues to twitch. "Yes, at this point, I'm afraid they are," he says.

"But what if Pauline should decide to hire a lawyer? What if—?"

"Can you get her to hold off, Miranda? She's always been very fond of you, but she never cared for me. See if you can get her to hold off."

"How much time shall I tell her we'll need?"

He frowns. "Two months?" he says, putting it as a question. "Tell her we're revamping our accounting system, and if she'll just be patient she'll start getting her full retirement benefits in about two months."

"About two months," she says carefully.

"Two months, more or less. Ask her to be patient. Just see if you can get her off our backs."

"Tommy," she says quickly, leaning toward him, "I'd like to see the company's books."

"The books? You mean the daily and weekly sales figures?"

"Those too. But I'd also like to go over the balance sheets, the P and L, bank statements, receivables, inventory—in fact I'd like to see the General Ledger."

"I'm afraid those figures wouldn't mean a thing to you, Miranda." His mouth is twitching more rapidly now.

"Why not? I've been taking some business courses at N.Y.U.'s Stern School. I know how to read a set of books."

"Well, actually those figures aren't kept here."

"Oh? Where are they?"

"I keep those figures at my house."

"Isn't that a little unusual, Tommy?"

"It just makes it easier for me," he says. "I can work on them on weekends without interruptions. I've always done it that way. Your father preferred it. He didn't like to be bothered with accounting problems."

"Could I look at them anyway?"

"They'd make a pretty bulky package for me to lug into the store. But look," he says easily, "why don't you come out to my house for dinner tomorrow night? We'll go over everything." He smiles at her. "We've also got other things to discuss, you know," he says.

"And meanwhile—the daily and weekly sales figures?"

"Oh, those I can give you right now," he says, and reaches for a manila folder on his desk. He balances the folder carefully between the forefingers of both hands. "Funny, but you were never interested in things like this about the store before. How come this sudden interest?"

"If you and I are going to run this store as partners, these are some of the things I'm going to need to know."

He hands her the folder. He is smiling at her now, but the corner of his mouth is still twitching, twitching.

Back in her office again, she opens the manila folder and begins to go through the computerized printout sheets. All the store's transactions are listed daily, by department, by inventory control number, by description of the article sold or returned, by the customer's name and address, by the retail price, and by the manner of sale— "C" stands for cash and "CHG" stands for charge. Then, at the end of each selling week, all this information is summarized, department by department, for comparative review.

Suddenly she comes to the following entry:

DEPT. 101 JWLRY (BYR. D. SMITH) INV #7642 LADIES SQ CT 3.9 C DIAMOND RING PLAT STTNG SRA. A. LOPEZ-FIGUEROA C/O BANCO DE VENEZUELA SA 17 CALLE GUARICO CARACAS VENEZUELA $37,500 CHG SEND

It could be a coincidence, of course. Smitty could have been carrying two such rings in her inventory—Miranda would have no way of knowing—though it seems unlikely.

Then her stomach slowly turns, she experiences a wave of nausea, and her vision blurs. The date of this sale is August 13, the same day that Tommy Bonham gave this ring to her.

Oh, please, let this not be happening, Miranda thinks.

From *The New York Times,* September 20, 1991:

CONTINENTAL IN BID
FOR TARKINGTON'S

Continental Stores, Inc., the Chicago-based retailing giant, announced today that it has acquired a 12 percent interest in Tarkington's, the fashionable Fifth Avenue specialty store. Continental's initial takeover move did not surprise retailing analysts, who have long expected Tarkington's to be targeted by one or another of the larger chains. The smaller store is said to have been experiencing difficulties since the sudden death of its founding chief executive, Silas R. Tarkington, on August 10.

Continental has extended a two-tiered purchase offer to Tarkington's shareholders, according to Albert J. Martindale, Continental's president and C.E.O. Initially, shareholders are being offered $60 per share for their Tarkington stock, with 80 percent of this offer in cash and the balance in Continental bonds and commercial paper.

Besides Continental's own flagship department stores in 12 U.S. cities, Continental owns Milady Fair fashion stores in Texas, Sally's Bridal Wear in Chicago, and the Ritzy Kids chain of juvenile apparel stores in California, Arizona, Washington and Oregon.

Mr. Martindale declined to identify from which Tarkington's stockholder or stockholders he had acquired his initial position. At the famous Fifth Avenue store, where business appeared to be continuing as usual today, with the usual contingent of carriage-trade shoppers, Thomas E. Bonham III, who has assumed the position of acting president since the founder's death, could not be reached for comment.

"By acquiring a prestige label like Tarkington's, Continental will gain prestige," said one retailing analyst. "Continental always has been a solid journeyman retailing group. But they never had class. That's what Continental is in the market for now—a touch of class."

"Was it you, Aunt Simma?" Miranda asks when she reaches her.

"Absolutely not," she says. "I keep my promises. I'm not selling my stock until you tell me to."

"Then I know who it was."

"Who?"

"Moses Minskoff," Miranda says.

"Aha. You know, Miranda, I've actually begun to enjoy this fight. It seems to be curing my allergies!"

"What about Granny Rose?"

"I'm working on her," Simma says. "I keep reminding her of how much Tarkington's did for her millinery business, while it lasted."

"Thank you, Aunt Simma. We need every vote we can get."

This is true. Miranda has been scribbling figures and percentages of share votes on the backs of envelopes. Her own twenty percent interest, plus Simma's twelve, plus Granny Rose's three, will assure them of a thirty-five percent vote against the takeover. Tommy's five percent would make forty percent against, but Tommy, in Miranda's mind at least, has suddenly become a question mark. And even Tommy's vote will not give her a clear majority.

And the employee shareholders? Who knows what they will do? For the past few days, coming into the store before the doors were opened for business, she couldn't help but notice little knots of employees in urgent conversation on the selling floors. The little groups break apart rather too quickly when they see her approaching them, and their good-morning greetings have been a bit too bright. She knows they are discussing the Continental offer, and why shouldn't they? The tension in the air at Tarkington's is now so thick you could cut it with a knife.

What to do? Call another employees' meeting? But that is really not up to Miranda, as director of advertising, to do. That is up to Tommy. This is one of several matters she intends to take up with Tommy when she has dinner at his house tonight.

And Tommy certainly seems to be eager for this dinner to take place. He has poked his head into her office just this afternoon to remind her of their date.

But the person she really needs to work on is her mother. With her mother on her side, she will have a clear, unbeatable majority. She won't need Tommy.

But the trouble is . . . the trouble is she still hasn't come up with an argument that will convince her mother not to sell.

Then, all at once, it comes to her—clear as day, brilliant as a vision—how to do it. It was something her mother said about Smitty. Of course. It is all so simple. She is astonished that she hasn't thought of this before.

She glances quickly at her watch. Her mother should right now be rising from her afternoon nap. She picks up the phone and dials the farm.

"Darling," she hears her mother's lovely voice purr.

"I'm coming out to Old Westbury tonight to have dinner with Tommy," she says. "I was wondering whether I could stay overnight at the farm."

"Of course, darling," her mother says. "That would be lovely."

"And perhaps spend the weekend," Miranda says.

"That would be even lovelier," her mother says. "I have to go to a small dinner dance tonight at the Couderts. If you come in after me, Margaret will have your bed turned down. Or if my light's still on, pop in and say good night."

Tommy is standing at her office door. "You won't forget tonight?" he says.

"No, no. Looking forward to it."

"Want me to drive you out?"

"Thanks, but I'll take my own car. I'm going to spend the weekend at Flying Horse."

"Then my house at seven-thirty," he says, and blows her a quick kiss.

25

Now it is Saturday morning, and Miranda is lying in her bed at Flying Horse Farm, trying to make some sense of the events of the night before. He asked me to marry him, she thinks. New York's most eligible bachelor asked me to marry him.

And all the rest of it.

She had arrived at his cottage on Heather Lane promptly at seven-thirty, and Tommy met her at the front door wearing a brown velvet smoking jacket and matching velvet slippers. "I've got a surprise for you," he said, as he led her into the living room.

"My God," she cried, as she surveyed the scene. "What happened?"

He grinned sheepishly, displaying his three dimples. "I had Nino straighten up the place in honor of your visit," he said.

The furniture in the room had actually been rearranged in a logical way, the big Victorian sofa against the wall, the club chairs facing it, a cocktail table between the sofa and the chairs. Pictures on the wall no longer hung askew, and the curtains at the windows were neatly drawn. "No sneakers on the sofa," she said. "No moldy apple cores between the cushions. Tommy, this room is actually *pretty*! Have you tidied up the entire house?"

"Take a look for yourself," he said.

It was true, she saw, as she moved wonderingly from room to room. The dining room table was no longer strewn with newspapers and trade journals. Instead, it was set for two, with linen place mats, china, silverware, tulip-shaped wineglasses, linen napkins in polished silver rings, and a silver candelabrum sprouting from a center-piece of bright autumn leaves, the candles lighted. In the kitchen, the sink and countertops were clean and empty, cupboard doors and drawers were closed, and the kitchen was filled with the most delicious smell.

"Nino has fixed us his famous chicken adobo and pineapple rice," he said. "It's a recipe from the Philip-pines."

"This place should be photographed for *House Beau-tiful* right away," she said.

He held open the bedroom door. His bed was care-fully made, and his closet doors and dresser drawers were closed, with no underwear spilling out and no sign of laundry anywhere. "I'm witnessing a miracle," she said. "Tommy Bonham, perfect housekeeper."

"I did it all for you," he said, "because I knew you disapproved of my living like a grub. I did it in honor of what I hope is going to be our partnership."

"Oh-oh," she said, pointing to the stack of card-board cartons in the corner of the bedroom. "You're go-ing to have to find some place for those, Tomcat. Maybe in your garage."

"But that's what you came to see," he said.

"What do you mean?"

"Those are the company's books," he said.

"These," she said, staring in disbelief at the stack of cartons, "are Tarkington's *books*?"

She stepped toward the boxes and lifted the lid of the topmost one. Inside was what appeared to be a jumble of loose papers: receipts, invoices, checkbook stubs and canceled checks and statements from various banks, canceled savings bank passbooks, copies of deposit and withdrawal slips, copies of bills and order blanks, credit card receipts, credit and debit memos, sales slips, adding machine tapes, handwritten lists marked EXPENSES and OPERATING CASH, petty cash vouchers, many sheets of variously colored and sized slips of paper with scribbled figures written on them, and even some loose business cards.

"It was the system your father was using before I joined the company," he said, "and I didn't feel I should change it."

"This?" she said, lifting a handful of yellow, pink, green, and blue slips from the carton and then letting them cascade back into the box again. "You call this a *system*?"

"It's easy once you have the key," he said. "For instance, each of the vendors we buy from has a color code and is on a three-by-five card. Pink, for instance is Bill Blass. And every bank we deal with has a color code on a five-by-eight card. Green is Bankers Trust. It's really very simple. I'll explain it all to you. Everything important is in that one large box."

She reached into the box again, and pulled out a dark blue card. "This one has *Shaving gel, $5.95* written on it," she said.

"Dark blue three-by-fives were Si's personal tax-deductible expenses. He figured he had to look his best in the store, so he could deduct the cost of shaving gel. Simple."

"You mean personal expenses are all mixed in with company expenses?"

"Well, it was his company," he said easily. "Come on back into the living room, and I'll fix you a drink."

She followed him, a little numbly, into the next room.

"After all his work, I gave Nino the night off," he said. "So I'm the bartender. What'll you have, Lillet?"

"Thank you," she said.

"You had Lillet when we met that day at the Pierre,"

he said, and filled her glass. "I see you're wearing my
ring," he said, and touched his glass to hers.

"Yes, and I have a question to ask you about that,
Tommy."

"Hmm? What's that?"

"In those weekly sales figures you let me see this
morning—"

"Yes?" The right corner of his mouth had begun to
twitch again, but he touched it quickly with his fingertip
and the twitch disappeared. Perhaps she only imagined
she had seen it.

"On August thirteenth, the day you gave me this,
there's a record of a sale, either of this ring or one that
sounds just like it, to a Señora Lopez-Figueroa in Caracas."

"That's right," he said brightly.

"You mean Smitty was carrying two rings like this in
her inventory? If so—"

"No, no," he said.

"If so, where's the record for the sale of this one? If
both rings were sold the same day, that department
would have had a record day."

"No, no. You don't understand," he said. "Señora
Lopez-Figueroa is just a bookkeeping entry code we use.
It's a gimmick, really. You see, I didn't know whether
you'd like the ring. I didn't know whether you'd accept it
or not. We often do that, with clients we know who want
to take something out of the store on approval. We let
them try something for a few days, see how they like it.
Everybody does that for good clients. Cartier does it,
Winston does it, everybody does it."

"I see," she said, but she wasn't sure she really did
see.

"Certain special clients may even borrow a piece like
that—for a party or some sort of special occasion. When
the piece of merchandise leaves the store, it's written up
as a sale to Señora Lopez-Figueroa. It was your father's
idea. It makes good business sense. It builds goodwill."

"I see," she said again. "You mean that Señora Lopez-Figueroa doesn't exist?"

"Oh, she exists all right," he said. "She's a very good customer of ours. Her husband owns the Bank of Venezuela. Her brother-in-law is president of the country. Her father is the Venezuelan ambassador to the U.N."

"But it said Charge-Send," she said. "Does that mean she'll be charged for it?"

"How could she be charged for it when it wasn't sent?" he said. "How could it have been sent, when you're wearing it right now? Look," he said with a sudden grin, "why don't I tell you the real reason why I punched Lopez-Figueroa into the computer? Because I didn't want you to find out how much I'd paid for it. And of course I didn't pay retail. I got it at cost, just as I get everything I buy in the store at cost, just as you and your mother get things at cost, and your father got things at cost. So now you know my shameful secret. I'm an old-fashioned, orthodox cheapskate."

"Well, hardly," she said a little weakly. "But I guess, as you can see, I've still got a whole lot to learn about retailing."

"Look," he said, "sit down. We've got more important things to talk about than numbers." He patted the Victorian sofa, and she seated herself beside him, her drink in one hand. He lifted the hand that wore the ring and squeezed it gently. "I must say it looks beautiful on you," he said. He looked deeply into her eyes. "And you look beautiful tonight, Miranda. But then, you always do."

"Thank you, Tommy," she said, and he released her hand. "Anyway, I think I've figured out a way to get Mother to vote her shares against the takeover. It involves Smitty, believe it or not. I don't want to tell you what it is right now, because I'm not sure it's going to work, but I think it will, and if we have Mother's shares, and my shares, and your shares, and Aunt Simma's shares we'll have a clear majority. And Aunt Simma thinks she can get my grandmother to go along, and if that happens nobody can touch us! Moe Minskoff has sold his shares already—thank God! That puts him out of the picture."

"Not yet. Not quite. All he's done has been to trade

his shares for some Continental shares. If Continental wins, Moe will be part owner of Tarkington's all over again."

"But Continental's not *going* to win! We're not going to *let* Continental win. Mother's vote is essential, and I'm going to try my plan on her this weekend. Tomorrow, in fact. I'll have her all to myself."

"Okay, good," he said. "But enough talk about numbers, enough about the business. That can wait till Monday. Tonight, there's something much more important I want to talk to you about, Miranda."

"Our partnership, you mean?"

"Yes, that, and—"

"I did a tarot reading on myself the other night. The cards said I'd work well in partnership with a man. Not that I believe in tarot cards, but it did give me a little boost of self-assurance."

"That's fine—"

"I've been doing some thinking about this," she said, "and here's what I've come up with. You're a super salesman, Tommy, you really are. And so I thought that anything that had to do with selling the merchandise and dealing with the customers would come completely under your domain. Meanwhile, my bailiwick would be the buying end. I'd work with the buyers and the merchandise managers, and also with the vendors and designers. That was more or less Daddy's specialty—going out into the market. Granted, I don't have much experience at it, but the only way to get experience is to go out there and do it. Daddy didn't have any experience to speak of when he started out either, and look what a success he became! He used to talk about what a jungle it was out there, but I don't see why a woman couldn't deal with that jungle as well as a man—maybe even better. After all, most of the vendors and designers are men. So you'd be the umbrella over the store's entire selling effort and sales force, and I'd handle the buying aspect. Of course, we'd meet at least once a week to discuss overall merchandising strategy. Does that sound fair to you?"

"It sounds just fine, Miranda," he said. "But do we

really have to discuss business right now?" He reached out and took her hand again, twisting the ring on her finger. "Beautiful," he whispered. This time, it was she who withdrew the hand.

She thought: Is he going to try to seduce me? Is that the hidden agenda of this evening's little rendezvous? If so, he is not going to succeed. Drop your anchor, she told herself. Steady as she goes. Don't lose control of your ship. She had heard too much about Tommy Bonham's alleged sexual prowess. A business partnership was one thing, but a love affair was something else again, and the two things did not mix. She began to wish she had left the ring at home or, even better, had not accepted it at all. Did men still think they could buy women with expensive jewels? Maybe so, even in the Year of Our Lord 1991. And what had Smitty said to her the day she quit her job at the store? That it was *her* ring. What was Smitty's role in all this, anyway?

"As for the accounting end," she continued, "I mean —well, we do have this little problem with the pension fund, and the books seem to have been kept—well, somewhat casually, it seems to me. I really think we should bring in an outside accountant. I mean a real C.P.A. Neither of us is a C.P.A. . . ."

His hand had traveled to her knee, and while she wondered how to deal with this, divine intervention came. From behind the drawn curtains of his windows came a sudden pale flash. "Lightning!" she cried, and jumped to her feet. "We're going to have a storm. My convertible top is down!"

"Now, now," he said, reaching up and taking her hand and pulling her gently down to the sofa again. "Don't you know how to count out a thunderstorm? We count the seconds: one . . . two . . . three . . ." At the count of eleven, there was a smothered concussion of distant thunder. "You see?" he said. "The storm is eleven miles away and moving east, away from us."

Proving him right, there was another pale flash of lightning at the windows and a longer pause before the

fainter, faraway rumble of thunder. The deity had inter-
vened but was now abandoning her.

He was gazing deeply into her eyes again. "Don't you
understand what I'm trying to say to you?" he said. "I'm
trying to tell you that I love you, Miranda."

She was on her feet again. "Oh, for heaven's sake,"
she said. "Why do you want to complicate things? Aren't
things messed up enough already? You don't love me,
Tommy! You just want to get laid! If that's what you
asked me out here for, why can't you be honest enough to
come right out and say so? At least Mike Tyson was honest enough to say right away what he wanted—or so he
said. I don't want to be another one of your famous con-
quests, another notch on Tommy Bonham's belt. Let's
have some of Nino's Filipino chicken. I'm hungry, and it
smells done to me."

"Now wait a minute," he said quietly. "Please listen
to what I have to say. Please hear me out. It's something
I've wanted to tell you for a long time, Miranda. I've got
to tell it to you now. If you don't like what I have to say,
we'll have another drink and go in to dinner, and you can
go home, and that will be the end of it, and I'll never
mention it to you again, I promise. Will you please just
listen, Miranda? Will you please sit down and hear me
out?"

"Oh, all right," she said, and perched herself on the
far corner of the sofa. "We'll let the super salesman make
his pitch."

"Do you mind if I smoke?"

"Not at all. But I thought you quit."

"I did. But now and then a cigarette helps, in certain
situations." He reached for a pack in the left inside
pocket of his velvet smoking jacket. His too-handsome
face in the blue-green flare from the lighter looked determined, preoccupied. It was a finished face, she always
thought, a completed, sculpted, Michelangelo face. The
flame went out and he exhaled loudly, the smoke rising in
a long, thin stream. He shaped his cigarette ash along the
edge of a silver ashtray. He hunched his shoulders toward

her, not looking at her, now, but at the cigarette between his fingers. "How to begin?" he said.

"I'm listening," she said.

"Do you remember when you and I first met, Miranda?"

"Nope," she said, though in fact she did.

"It was in the early summer of nineteen-eighty. I can even give you the date. Saturday, May seventeenth. You were only thirteen, and you'd come down to the farm for the weekend from Ethel Walker. I was of course older—twenty years older. I'd been invited to the farm by your parents for the weekend too. It was before I bought this house. I was sitting by the pool, reading a Ngaio Marsh detective novel. I was on page twenty-six, and her detective had just discovered the second body. You appeared at the pool. You were wearing a blue swimsuit, a blue two-piece, and your hair was tied back with a piece of yellow yarn."

"I remember that swimsuit," she said.

"It had a red mermaid appliquéd on the right side of the panties, a red mermaid smiling at her tail."

"Yes, and you were wearing—"

"I don't remember what I was wearing."

"White."

"So you do remember."

The smoke spiraled upward from his cigarette. Somewhere in the distance on Heather Lane a motorist's automobile horn had stuck and was moaning plaintively across the night. Then, gradually, it faded away, like a loon's call across a lake, and the night was blanketed in silence again.

He stubbed his cigarette out fiercely in the ashtray, half smoked.

"What was your first impression of me?" he asked her.

"That you were very—good-looking," she said.

"We spoke. Not much, because you suddenly ran off, into the pool house, pretending you heard a phone ringing. There was no phone ringing. At first I thought I might have frightened you. Because I'd had an inappro-

priate response to a thirteen-year-old girl. Because I'd felt
something pass between us in that moment. It was like an
electric current, passing between us. It wasn't at all appropriate, I knew, and I suppose you knew it too. But I
know I felt it, and I think you felt it too. It was desire."

"I was only . . . a little girl," she said. Suddenly she
felt that she had dropped her anchor in the sand, that her
ship was being dragged by the tide, that she was drifting
inexorably toward the reefs and shoals of some dangerous and alien shoreline. "Only in my second year at
Walker," she said, struggling to adjust her course, to find
the channel, the safe passage through the rocks.

"A woman in a young girl's body. Your breasts—
your wonderful breasts—had already begun to bloom. I
thought you were the most beautiful creature I'd ever
seen. I never finished the Ngaio Marsh. I stopped caring
who the killer was because I'd fallen in love with you."

She was silent for a moment. Then she said, "Why
didn't you ever tell me any of this before?"

"It was out of the question. I couldn't."

"Why not?"

"Your father. He wouldn't have stood for it. I wasn't
good enough for his only daughter. Remember, I was
only a boy from an Indiana cornfield. He wanted someone out of the top drawer for his daughter, and that
wasn't me at all. He was always telling me I should get
married. He was always urging me to marry one of his
unattached rich Tarkington's ladies, who would turn me
into a kind of gigolo. 'Get married, get married,' he kept
telling me. 'It will be good for the store's image. People
are beginning to think you're gay.' Well, one day I'd had
enough of this, and I said, 'There's only one woman I've
ever wanted to marry, Si.' 'Who's that?' he asked me.
'Miranda,' I said. He flew into one of his white rages. He
said, 'If you ever lay a hand on my daughter, I'll ruin you.
I'll see to it that you never work in this town again, or in
any other town.' "

"Daddy said that?"

"Oh, yes. But he's dead now, so I can tell you. Let's
face it, I've been with a lot of women—too many, perhaps

—but none of them ever meant anything to me. They never meant to me what you do. Often, when I'm making love to a woman, I try to fantasize that I'm making love to you. Sometimes it works, sometimes it doesn't. Because you're the only woman I've ever loved or wanted to make love to. Miranda, let me put that ring on the third finger of your left hand. That's what I really bought it for. Marry me, Miranda. Ah, Miranda, I love you so!"

He reached out and drew her to him and kissed her on the lips, gently at first and then with a fiercer urgency, and she felt herself giving in to him—at first pleasantly, agreeably, and then with an urgency of her own which was quite unexpected as she returned his deep kisses, longingly, passionately, and finally with an abandon coupled with discipline and, oh, yes, determination.

"I nearly died when I thought you might marry David Belknap," he said.

"Oh, never . . . him. . . ."

"I've waited for this so long, Miranda. So long . so long . . . years and years." He drew her to him again, and one hand moved slowly, expertly, beneath the shoulder of her dress, and as she pressed against him she felt the thrilling shape of his erection.

"What about . . . Nino's chicken . . . pineapple rice?" she whispered.

"In the oven . . . on warm. That can wait. This can't."

"Oh, Tommy, I feel so—" she began.

"I want you so, Miranda. I want to marry you."

"Oh, yes. Let me quickly run into the bathroom." She leapt up.

She had had a wild idea for their lovemaking. She would dash to the medicine cabinet where he kept his condoms, snatch one from the packet, run back out to him, and toss it to him playfully, saying, "Let's see how you look in one of these!"

In the bathroom she pulled the medicine cabinet door open. Nino's housecleaning efforts had not extended to the medicine cabinet, but that hardly mattered now, and her hand flew out for the packet of condoms.

But then her hand stopped in midair. On a shelf in the cabinet was something she had never seen there before. It was a spray bottle of Equipage, Smitty's perfume.

She closed the cabinet door with a gasp.

Then she stood for several minutes at the sink, her fingers gripping the beveled rim of the countertop, her cheek pressed against the cool surface of the mirror, feeling ill—no, not ill, confused and exhausted.

From a distance, she heard him calling to her. "Miranda?"

"Coming." It was barely a whisper.

Returning, she detoured through his bedroom and picked up the largest of the boxes, the one he said contained everything that was important. It weighed easily twenty pounds, maybe more.

When she entered the room, she saw that he had removed his smoking jacket, rolled up his sleeves, and loosened his tie, ready for action. Seeing her with the heavy carton in her arms, his face looked stricken, and the right corner of his lip began to twitch violently.

"I thought we ought to start with you explaining Tarkington's bookkeeping system to me," she said.

"Take the box home with you," he said angrily. "Figure the system out for yourself."

Then he muttered something under his breath.

"What did you say?" she asked him.

He said nothing, but she had heard him: "*Cock teaser!*"

26

For the next few hours, with her convertible top still down, she drove randomly through the night neighborhoods of the North Shore, up one winding lane and down another, discovering pockets of civilization she never knew were there. Through picture windows, television sets flickered. In dining rooms, families sat at dinner. She passed what had to be a pair of lovers in a parked car. She paused to watch a touch football game in a lighted field behind a school. Everywhere the world seemed ordered, planned, sequential, and organized according to human rules as she struggled to compose her own cascading thoughts. At a McDonald's drive-through window she ordered a Big Mac and fries. Tommy's chicken adobo had gone uneaten, and she ate her burger in the parking lot, using the big carton on the passenger seat beside her as a table. Finally, she saw that her gas gauge was close to empty, and she headed homeward toward the farm.

At the entrance, she pressed the five-digit code, and the electric gate swung slowly open, then closed behind her, and she drove up the long gravel drive past the rhododendron hedges. The night had grown chilly, but she needed the fresh air to be able to think clearly, and her head was full of thoughts and plans. Thoughts had to match with plans. She looked at her watch. It was eleven o'clock.

The big house was dark, but the entrance lights had been left on for her, and she parked in the circle, turning off her headlights and ignition. Then she let herself out of the car, lifted the heavy box from the seat, lugged it up the front steps and across the terrace to the front door, and let herself in with her key. With the box in her arms, she tiptoed up the carpeted steps to her room, where Margaret, as promised, had turned down her bed for her. She placed the box in the bottom of one of the two walk-in closets and closed the door. She would go through its contents later.

There was a sliver of light under her mother's door, so she went down the hall and knocked.

"Is that you, Miranda? Come in, darling," her mother's voice said.

Connie was sitting up in bed propped by many pillows, reading a paperback. "I thought I heard your car in the drive," she said. She folded down the corner of a page to mark her place and laid the book aside. "Well, how was your dinner with Tommy?" she asked.

"Interesting," Miranda said. "Not a festive occasion, exactly, but interesting. Mostly we talked store business."

"The store, the store," her mother said wearily, reaching for a cigarette. "Your father was getting a little tired of Tommy, you know. I don't know what the matter was, but for the last six months of his life or so, he'd frown whenever Tommy's name came up. Your father had become less than satisfied with Tommy's performance. The blush was off the rose."

She sat at the foot of her mother's big canopy bed, her hand on one of the ribbon-twisted bedposts. There was something about her mother's appearance tonight that was different, and she couldn't immediately put her finger on what it was. Then suddenly she knew. "Why isn't your hair up in rollers?" she asked. "You don't even look as though you've creamed your face!"

"Oh, I've quit all that," she said with a smile. "It was such a bloody nuisance."

"Your Dead Sea mud pack? Your mask?"

"That damn mud pack! It stank, and the rollers meant I had to sleep in one position, on my back, all night long. I hated it. I'd wake up in the morning with a stiff neck. In order to sleep, I had to take a Seconal. Then it was two Seconals. I was afraid of becoming addicted to Seconal, so I decided to quit all that nonsense. It's much more pleasant to read myself to sleep."

Miranda had always regarded her mother's elaborate beauty routines with a queer mixture of amusement and derision. Then why was she all at once dismayed to hear they were being abandoned? "Mother, don't you want to stay looking beautiful?" she said.

"I've decided it's time I looked my age," she said. "Why not? When your father was alive, perhaps there was a reason for all that silly business. Now there just isn't any. I've also decided to let my hair go to its natural color. Look." She lifted a strand of hair. "You can already see where the gray's beginning to come in."

Miranda reached out and covered her mother's hand with her own. "Oh, Mother, I don't want you to get *old*!" she cried.

"It's a situation we all have to face, Miranda," she said. "Fortunately, you've got a long time before you have to deal with it."

"Let me just put some night cream on your face!"

"No!" she said with a laugh. "I threw most of the greasy stuff away. It got all over the bed linen. Please, Miranda, I'm quite content to let my face do whatever it decides to do."

Miranda felt tears standing in her eyes, and still she did not understand why these revelations of her mother's had managed to upset her so. Had she worshiped Connie's beauty too?

"I'll promise you one thing," her mother said. "I won't let myself get fat. I've got enough vanity left not to let that happen. Now let's talk about something more interesting than your mother's face and figure."

With that, a blue Persian cat leapt onto the bed and made its way purposefully across the bedclothes. "What in the world is *that*?" Miranda cried.

"Isn't he beautiful? His name is Bicha. I've always loved cats, and always wanted one, but your father was allergic to them. Bicha, meet Miranda. This is Miranda's house too, at least part of the time."

Miranda held out her fingertips to let the cat sniff them, which it proceeded to do, daintily, gingerly. Then she rubbed the cat's throat and felt its purr box come to life. "I think Bicha likes me," she said.

"Of course he does. Cats are marvelous. Sometimes I think cats hold the key to everything. All they need is a little stroking, and everything else they take care of for themselves."

Bicha spread himself out across the bedclothes, his forepaws folded beneath him. He looked first at her mother, then at Miranda, yawned, and blinked.

The two women sat in silence for a moment, admiring Bicha.

"Mother, I've been thinking," Miranda said.

"Yes?"

"About Smitty."

"Yes?" There was no change of tone in her voice.

"The other night you said you felt sorry for her."

"Yes. I do." In the same tone.

"I said I disagreed. I said I thought Smitty got exactly what she deserved. But I've been thinking about what you said, and I've decided you were right. I feel sorry for her too. I think we should both feel sorry for her. She's got no job. She's got no money. Obviously, the curatorship Daddy wanted for her isn't going to work out. She's got no family that she's close to. She's got no"—cautiously, now—"man in her life anymore."

"All this is true, Miranda." No change in tone.

"She hasn't got much of anything, has she? I feel we've sort of let her get washed overboard and left her to sink or swim."

"Yes, I feel the same way," her mother said.

"I wonder whether we shouldn't try to toss her some sort of life jacket."

Her mother sighed. "There are a lot of women out there like Smitty," she said. "She's got good looks, but not the best. She's got a good mind, but not the best. She was elected to the National Honor Society in high school, but just barely. Women like that—I pity them. If they don't find the right man by the time they're thirty, they're doomed. Doomed to revising the facts about themselves and blaming other people for their plight. Then, by the time they reach about age thirty-five, they panic. How old is Smitty now?"

"Thirty-four."

"Yes. You see? The onset of the panic age. You might want to remember this bit of motherly wisdom, Miranda, in contemplating the next decade of your own life. But what kind of life jacket could we toss to Smitty?"

"We could offer to give her back her old job at the store. She loved the job, and she was awfully good at what she did. She was a damned good buyer. The figures from her department were among the best in the store."

"But the store's going to be sold, Miranda," her mother said.

Miranda bit her lip. "It hasn't been sold yet," she said.

"What's Continental up to, anyway? Why do they keep extending their deadline?"

"Because they're having trouble collecting the voting shares necessary to buy us out," she said. "And our employee shareholders are turning out to be surprisingly loyal. They don't want to sell because they don't want the store to change."

"You mean they're afraid they'll lose their jobs."

"That too, of course. But I'd also hate to see them lose their jobs. Wouldn't you?"

"Oh, yes, of course, but—"

"I haven't agreed to sell my shares yet. And neither have you."

"No, but only because Jake Kohlberg hasn't given me the green light. He says he doesn't like the way this par-

ticular deal smells. He doesn't like the two-tiered aspect
of it, whatever that means. He thinks a better offer might
be coming down the road. Some Canadians. But where
are these better offers? Where are these Canadians? If we
hold off on the Continental offer for too long, the whole
deal could fall apart and we'd have to go out, hat in hand,
begging for another purchaser. That wouldn't be good for
us, would it? Still, I have to wait until Jake tells me what
to do." She stubbed out her cigarette in an ashtray.

"Why?"

"Because I've always taken Jake's advice. He's always advised your father and me very well, over the
years. Anyway, the store is going to have to be sold to
somebody, sooner or later."

"Why?"

"Jake says so."

"Why? Do we need the money, Mother?"

"We very well may! Jake says your father didn't leave
his affairs in quite as good shape as he might have. He's
still waiting for some figures."

Miranda thought, Jake says, Jake says, Jake says. It
was always the same. But she said, "I want to run the
store, Mother."

"Oh, Miranda! You're not still talking that foolishness, are you?"

"I can do it. I know I can. I want to keep Tarkington's in the family. Wouldn't Daddy have wanted that?"

"He wanted the store for Blazer, but Blazer didn't
want it. He didn't want it for you. He was very old-fashioned, very Old World, in his ideas about women. He
thought a woman's place was in the home."

Or at his feet, Miranda thought, but she didn't say it.
Instead she said, "Are you afraid I'd run the place into the
ground and land us both in the poorhouse?"

"No, it's not that, Miranda. I'm thinking of your future. I'd like to see you married, having children. I'd like
to have some grandchildren in my old age, and you're my
only chance for that!"

"I've already turned down one—no, two—proposals
of marriage, Mother. So I like to think I'm marriageable."

"Married to the right man, of course."

She thought, Not like the man you married, Mother. She said, "I have no intention of becoming a spinster."

"No, but—this is true, Miranda—men often don't feel comfortable marrying women who 'do things.' Who have a busy career. That probably sounds like a terribly old-fashioned thing for me to say, but I was raised in an old-fashioned way, in an old-fashioned city. But I still think it's true. And I still think marriage is important, terribly important. Marriage and children. Human beings weren't meant to live alone. Companionship is so important, some kind of companionship."

Miranda's eyes and her mother's eyes traveled simultaneously to the blue Persian cat that lay stretched across the coverlet. Her mother laughed her bell-like laugh and reached out and touched the cat's nose with a fingertip. "Yes, that is going to be one of Bicha's functions," she said. "Companionship to this old lady in her old age."

There were several things Miranda could have said to her mother at this point, and she chose her words carefully. "I think," she said, "that what I hear you saying is that you don't have sufficient faith in my ability to head the store and be a good wife and mother at the same time."

"It's a tall order for any woman."

"It's funny. Aunt Simma and Granny Rose have faith in my ability. They've agreed to withhold their shares as long as they possibly can to help me fight the Continental takeover. Why can't you have the same faith in me?"

Her mother blinked. "Aunt Simma? Granny Rose? I haven't heard those names in years. I've never met either one of them. Your father didn't want me to. But you, I gather, have."

Miranda nodded.

"Goodness, you really *do* want to do this, don't you!"

She nodded again.

"All I want is to see you happy, Miranda."

"This is what would make me happy."

"Then tell me exactly what you want me to do."

"Together, Aunt Simma and Granny Rose control about fifteen percent of the company's stock. You and I each own about twenty percent. Employees own small amounts. If you and I and Simma and Granny Rose were to issue a statement that none of us is willing to sell this stock to anyone, under any circumstances, for any price, we'd represent a majority. Continental would withdraw its offer, and Tarkington's would be ours."

"Yours, you mean. I'd want nothing to do with it."

"Mine, then." She leaned toward her mother and said with some urgency, "Mother, will you just let me try it for a year? Just one year, Mother, that's all I ask. *Please!* If I make a mess of it in one year's time, you'll be the first to know, and I'll concede that you were right, and we'll sell the store. But if I don't—if I succeed the way I want to, and I'm going to try, I'll try so hard—then will you give me another year? Can we do it that way, Mother, letting me take it year by year? All I'm asking for is a chance, a chance to fail and a chance to succeed. Is that too much to ask of you—a chance? It's what I want most in the world."

Her mother hesitated. Then she said quietly, "And of course you're right. It would give us an opportunity to do something to help Smitty."

"To be honest with you, Mother, I've always resented Smitty. But if you feel we owe her something, offering her her old job back would be better than offering her money. It would be a more human thing to do."

Her mother's eyes grew thoughtful. "I do feel badly about Smitty," she said. "Smitty's suffered a great deal through this . . . this little family situation of ours, which you and I both know about. She's still suffering, poor thing. I do feel we owe her something. I feel guilty, too. I suppose I could have done more to prevent what happened from happening. I could have worked harder to put an end to it, I suppose, but I didn't. Partly, it was the way I was brought up. It was a man's world, my father taught my sisters and me, and a wife's job was to do what her husband wanted, so I did what my husband wanted. But I suppose I could have talked to Smitty, and explained certain things to her about your father that she didn't understand. I could have prevented her from having such high expectations . . . such false dreams. Perhaps. But I didn't. Perhaps I could even have prevented—but never mind that. Was I just lazy? Or did I just know in my heart of hearts that it would end sometime?" Her mother's voice was growing drowsy. "She was deluded, and delusions can poison a woman's mind, and lead her to have . . . unrealistic expectations. . . . Is it all water over the dam . . . or under the bridge . . . or however the saying goes? Or . . . ? Never let yourself become deluded, Miranda . . . keep your eyes open . . . be sure your eyes take in everything there is to see. Take your old gray-haired mother's advice. . . ." Her voice trailed off.

"Then will you help me save the store, Mother? Will you give me at least a year?"

"Let me see what Jake Kohlberg thinks."

"For once, could you say yes or no without consulting Jake Kohlberg?"

Her mother yawned and covered the yawn with the back of her left hand. With her right hand, she reached out and stroked Bicha's thick slate-blue fur. "I haven't said no, and I haven't said yes, and I haven't said maybe," she said. She closed her eyes. "It's good you're going to be here the whole weekend," she said. "We'll talk some more tomorrow. Let me sleep on this one, darling. Let your old gray-haired mother sleep on this one."

Miranda winced. "I wish you wouldn't keep talking about getting old," she said a little crossly. "You're hardly dying on the vine, Mother." Then she said, "Maybe I'll stay here a few days longer. I don't feel like going back to the store right away. Maybe I'll take a couple of days off next week. Would that be all right with you?"

But she realized her mother had fallen asleep—as asleep as she had apparently been throughout her father's and Smitty's long love affair, never guessing how serious it had been about to become. Suddenly she felt a stab of pity for her sleeping, beautiful, innocent mother. *Darling, did you really believe it all would end on its own?* She sat for a moment longer on the bed, then rose, kissed her mother lightly on her pale forehead, and turned off her mother's bedside lamp.

Her mother slept. Bicha the cat, another innocent, slept. The house, a keeper of guilty secrets, slept. Miranda tiptoed down the dark hall to her own room, a route she could have traveled blindfolded, and fell across her bed, face forward, as though sleep had felled her with a truncheon from behind.

In his cottage, farther down Heather Lane, Tommy Bonham lay beside Nino, not sleeping.

"She not eat my chicken adobo," Nino said. "She not like."

"No. It was just that she had other things on her mind."

"You tried to make love with her."

"You were listening?"

"I stay in the cellar, like you say. I hear your voices."

He raised himself on one elbow. "You must have sneaked up the stairs then!"

Beside him in the darkness, Nino nodded. "You ask her to marry you."

"I don't like you spying on me, Nino!"

"I not know marrying her was part of plan. You not ever tell me that, Tommy."

"I've got to get control of her stock! Her stock!"

"But she not say yes."

"She will, damn it! I just have to work on her some more."

Nino's voice was far away. "So this is the way it ends for us, Tommy," he said. "You and me are ended now."

"Of course not! You and I would still be together. It's just that she'd be with us too!"

"You keep secrets from me, Tommy. You not tell me this part of plan."

"My plan is for whatever works, damn it! I was going to tell you as soon as I'd found a plan that worked.

Now go to sleep. I'm going to work things out. Leave everything to me."

Nino lay silently beside him. Then he said, "No, I don't think plan is going to work, Tommy."

"It is," he said, and then, "She took my big file box."

"I hear her do that."

"It has all the store's important records in it."

From beside him, in the darkness, there was a shrug.

"Do you think she'll be able to find anything in them, Nino?"

Another shrug. "Don't know. Don't know what is in your records, Tommy."

"I'm sure she won't be able to find anything. She knows nothing about how I've run the store. She won't find anything she can possibly understand—will she?"

Still another shrug. "God knows these things, Tommy," came the reply.

Now there was a long silence. "Nino?"

"Yes, Tommy."

"Have you ever killed a person?"

"No, Tommy."

"Neither have I. It would have to look like an accident, of course—like the other one."

Nino said nothing for a moment or two. Then he said, "I am thinking, Tommy."

"What are you thinking, Nino?"

"I am thinking we will never go to Paracale, you and I. It was only dreaming, you and I."

And, beside him, staring up at the dark ceiling, Tommy Bonham now said nothing.

Part Three

DIANA'S DREAM

27

It is a rainy Saturday morning in October, and Peter Turner—freelance journalist, would-be biographer, one-day well-known name (according to Miranda's tarot reading)—is sitting in his apartment, high in one of the Gothic dormers of the Dakota, listening again to the tapes he has made thus far of those who have variously loved and hated Silas Rogers Tarkington. The chilly rain streaks his windowpanes, which could do with a washing, in the squiggly patterns of a river delta. Inside the building, a collective belch and rattle of steam pipes indicates that the Dakota's radiators have just been turned on for the first time this winter and, from the street below, a quickening sound of traffic, auto horns, and doormen's whistles provides an annual alert to the coming holiday season. As he listens to his tapes, Peter Turner continues to make notes in the ring-bound steno pad on his lap.

In *The Times* this morning was the news that Continental Stores, Inc., has again extended the time period for its two-tiered takeover offer for Tarkington's. Originally, it was ten days. Then it was extended to thirty days. Now it has been extended again, to ninety days. This means that Continental is having difficulty acquiring the majority of shares it needs, though it now stands in an eighteen-percent-ownership position. And this means that Miranda is having some success dissuading shareholders from parting with their shares, though the battle is by no means over. Who said, "It ain't over till it's over?" Yogi Berra, Peter thinks. Someone like that.

It has been two months since Silas Tarkington's sudden death and Peter's involvement in this particular project, and this morning he is feeling frustrated on two separate fronts. One is personal. It is frustrating that Miranda Tarkington must spend so much of her time closeted in meetings with Tommy Bonham as they plot defenses against the takeover. Right now they are considering a "poison pill" defense—a stock split, for instance, or the floating of a new issue of Tarkington's stock to the public. Both tactics, of course, involve enormous risk and could end up ruining the company. His other frustration is professional. Peter has still had no success in his efforts to locate the elusive Mr. Moses Minskoff, who, Peter is increasingly certain, is pivotal to the Silas Tarkington story and who also may hold the key to what actually happened that tragic Saturday morning in August at Flying Horse Farm in Old Westbury.

No Moses Minskoff is listed in the Manhattan telephone directory, nor does it appear that he has ever been. When Peter telephoned Jacob Kohlberg to see if Kohlberg could help him locate Minskoff, the lawyer's tone became almost testy. "Look, Turner," he said to him, "this is your project, not mine. It's you who's supposed to be the investigative reporter. So investigate! I want to have as little to do with that man as possible. Find out his phone number some other way, and leave me out of this. . . . No, I don't have an address for him."

Despite Blazer's promise, Jake Kohlberg is turning out to be less than cooperative. Beyond the expected guarded and lawyerly platitudes ("Si Tarkington was a great man, and a great friend, and you may quote me"),

Jake Kohlberg has offered very little, probably because he is acting in the interests of Consuelo Tarkington.

Her help so far has also been minimal.

"Tell me about Moses Minskoff," he said to her that night when she had invited him, Miranda, and David Hockaday to dinner at the farm.

"Moses Minskoff? He was an early business associate of my late husband's. They had very little to do with each other in recent years, though the Minskoffs did show up—uninvited—at the farm the night Si died. Much to my surprise—and displeasure, I might add."

"Displeasure?"

"He is an unattractive man. Miranda, tell Mr. Turner about the first time the Duchess of Windsor came into the store, how she made the Duke carry all her packages." And the subject was changed and effectively closed.

The other members of the family, it seems, knew Moses Minskoff only slightly, if at all. Alice Tarkington had only a few brief conversations with him, just enough to be impressed by his garlic breath. Blazer and Miranda each met him only once, the night he and his wife appeared at the farm, though both children had heard his name mentioned often during their growing-up years. Miranda remembered a fat man wearing a yellow Ultrasuede vest and chewing an unlighted cigar, with a fiftyish peroxide-blond wife wearing platform wedgies with ankle straps. Silas Tarkington's mother and sister had also each had one meeting with Moses Minskoff, and that was more than thirty years ago.

Peter Turner does not even have a clear picture of what Moses Minskoff looks like. The prison records from Hillsdale list his date of birth (Nov. 27, 1913), his height (5'11"), and his weight (280 lbs.) but do not include a photograph. "Prisoner is mug-shot on admission," Peter was told. "But if his picture was took, it's been lost at this point in time." And even if such a photograph were found it would not tell much, since it would have been taken in 1948, and a man's appearance can change greatly in more than forty years.

Listening to his tapes and hearing Moe Minskoff's

name repeated again and again, Peter ponders the conun-
drum of this man.

He looks at his notes.

> How did M.M. learn of Si's death the after-
> noon it happened? Obit did not appear until two
> days later.
>
> Alice thinks M.M. had a hand in Si's death.
> But why would murderer appear at victim's
> home the night of death to pay a condolence call
> and stay approx. three hrs uninvited?
>
> Would condolence call be designed to deflect
> suspicion? Murderer would have to have nerves
> of steel to revisit scene of crime seven hrs later,
> and then just hang around.
>
> What is Consuelo Tarkington hiding?

Now his telephone rings, and Peter reaches to pick it
up.

"Mr. Turner?" a woman's voice says. "Is this the Mr.
Peter Turner who's writing the story about Silas Tarkington?"

"Yes, it is," he says.

"Mr. Turner, this is Honeychile Minskoff," the
woman says. "Mrs. Moses Minskoff."

"Well, hello!" he says in disbelief.

"Mr. Turner," she says, "I'm calling you because I've
heard you're going to be talking to a certain Miss Smith."

"Who?"

"Diana Smith. The one they call Smitty. She was jewelry buyer at the store and a friend of Si's."

"That's right," he says carefully. "In fact I just made
an appointment with her, Mrs. Minskoff."

"That's what I heard," she says. "And I just want to
warn you not to believe a word that little tramp says."

"Oh?" he says. "Why is that, Mrs. Minskoff?"

"I guess you know she quit her job at the store. And I
guess you know she didn't get the job she was supposed
to at the museum. She's real mad about the way she's

been treated, and she's going to try to tell you bad things
about my husband and I."

"Oh? What sort of bad things?"

There is a moment of hesitation. Then she says,
"Well, I used to work for my husband. Just part-time.
And I sold some things, some jewelry, to Smitty that she
said weren't bought quite right."

"What do you mean, not bought quite right?"

There is another brief hesitation. "Well," she says finally, "there was some things Smitty bought from me that
she said was bought with bad credit cards. She accused
me of selling her stuff that was bought with bad credit
cards. She called me a fence for my husband. That's all a
lie. Nothing my husband or I ever sold her was bought
from bad credit cards. There's a lot I could tell you about
my husband and Si Tarkington, but that wasn't one of
them."

"I'd very much like to talk to you, Mrs. Minskoff,"
he says. "And I'd also like to talk to your husband."

"Oh, that won't be possible. Except—unless—"

"Unless what, Mrs. Minskoff?"

Another silence. Then she says, "I might be able to
arrange for something. But I'd need you to do me a little
favor first."

"Oh?" he says. "What's that?"

"It's a big favor. It's a favor of a more personal nature."

"Please tell me what it is."

"I want you to scare him."

"Scare him? You mean your husband?"

"Yes," she says, and a note of panic has suddenly
crept into her voice. "I'm scared, Mr. Turner," she says.
"That's the thing of it with me. Daddy—my husband—he
just won't scare. He just laughs it all off and tells me not
to worry. But you—you're a member of the legitimate
press, and maybe you could scare him for me. God knows
I've tried, Mr. Turner. You don't know what it's been like
these past few weeks for me, Mr. Turner. There's people
my husband owes money to. Not *really* owes, but they're
saying he owes it. And not just money, but they're saying

favors. It's all legitimate, because everybody owes something to somebody, don't they? These people are
shylocks. Do you know what that means? It means I've
been getting all these phone calls. They come all hours of
the day and night! They don't have any last names, these
people. One is Julius. Another calls himself Don from
Cleveland. Another is Ernie. One is Harry. They make
threats to me. They know I have a niece who's retarded,
who I take care of, and they make threats to her. They
make threats to my husband. He just laughs it all off and
changes the phone number. But last night, just after we'd
changed the number again, there were eighteen more
phone calls! Eighteen! Sometimes they just breathe hard
and hang up. I'm really scared now, Mr. Turner, and
maybe you could help me. I even think anti-Semitism
could be a part of it, y'know."

"Maybe you should report this to the F.B.I., Mrs.
Minskoff. After all, threatening phone calls—"

"The F.B.I.? Are you out of your gourd? We're in
enough trouble already without bringing the Feds in on
it! But you—you're a member of the legitimate press. You
could do it."

"But I really don't see how I—"

"Look. He's got some real money now. He could pay
off his debts, and there'd be plenty left over for he and I
to live on. Plenty. For years, he's been promising me he
was going to retire and we'd live in the Bahamas, free and
clear. Have you ever been to the Bahamas, Mr. Turner?
Neither have I, but I've got all the brochures. It's beautiful there. And in Freeport, there's gambling, and Daddy
likes a little action now and then. We could be happy
there, happy at last, the both of us—with no more pressures from the business. But with each new deal he
makes, he just . . . goes on to make another one! Deals
to Daddy are like drugs to an addict! But he's getting too
old for this, Mr. Turner, and so am I. He's got the money
now to retire and take the both of us to the Bahamas. Just
scare him into doing it, Mr. Turner. You can do it with
just one phone call, because he's terrified of the legitimate
press."

"Why is that, Mrs. Minskoff?"

"Look," she says, speaking rapidly now, "I haven't got all day. He could walk in on me at any minute. But let me put it to you this way. My husband is a very major man. He's an internationally respected mergers-and-acquisitions specialist, with clients all over the world, but some of his clients don't like their names to be all that well known, which is why they use Daddy as their behind-the-scenes man, which is what behind the scenes means, staying out of the limelight, staying out of the press, keeping the people he works for confidential, important people whose work is top secret, and confidential, like the C.I.A., and who don't like to see their pictures in the papers; these are private and powerful people, some of them even run whole countries, and there are other reasons, which I won't go into now, why he hates the legitimate press."

"Something in his past, perhaps?"

A pause. Then she says, "Maybe. Years ago. But we don't need to go into that. That's not the point. Everybody has something in his past he doesn't want everybody else to know about—even you, I bet. The point is, Mr. Turner, just one phone call from you would do it. If he knows the legitimate press is after him, he'll retire and move the both of us to the Bahamas, and we'll have what he always promised me—our second honeymoon, free and clear. I'm desperate, Mr. Turner. Will you do that for me—just one phone call from the legitimate press?"

"But if he hates the press so much, why would he talk to me?"

"Look. Do I have to draw you pictures? Of course he won't talk to you. He'll *never* talk to you. All I want you to do is *scare* him! I want you to make him crazy! But if you do that for me, *I'll* talk to you. I'll tell you everything you need to know about Silas Tarkington, and Moses Minskoff too. Is that a deal?"

"Can you tell me how Si Tarkington died?"

Another pause. "Maybe," she says. "I can tell you what my husband thinks. He was cheating on his wife, you know. He was going to run off with that tramp, Smitty."

"You mean you think that Connie—"

"That's all I'm saying for now. I can also tell you who killed President John F. Kennedy, and it wasn't Lee Harvey Oswald, who was a friend of Jack Ruby, who was a client of my husband's years ago. Are you going to make that phone call?"

"Well . . . all right," he says.

"Okay. Do it today. Right now, before he gets all the phone numbers changed again. Got a pencil? I'm going to give you two numbers. The first one's his office. He won't answer. His secretary will. Her name's Smyrna. Just tell her who you are and that you want to interview her boss. She won't put you through, but he'll get the message soon enough. Then call me back at the second number when you've done that, and I'll meet you anywhere you say this afternoon—your apartment might be best—and I'll tell you everything you want to know. Okay?"

She rattles off two telephone numbers. Then, abruptly, she says, "I've got to hang up now. He's calling me on the other line. Remember—don't believe anything that tramp Smitty tells you about Daddy and I. You'll get the truth from me."

Peter Turner puts down the receiver and sits at his desk, feeling slightly dizzy. All these weeks he has spent trying to get to Moses Minskoff, and now—suddenly, almost miraculously—Moses Minskoff, or at least his wife, has come to him.

He stares at the two telephone numbers he has written down, then picks up his telephone again and slowly presses the buttons for the first number.

A woman's voice answers. "Development Corporation, Limited."

"Mr. Moses Minskoff, please."

"Whom shall I say is calling, sir?"

"My name is Peter Turner. I'm a writer for *Fortune*. I'm writing the Silas Tarkington story."

"Mr. Minskoff is in conference, sir. May I take your number?"

•   •   •

But Moe Minskoff isn't in conference. In the office on West 23rd Street, Smyrna is working alone, answering crazy phone calls. She is very cross about this. She's not supposed to work on Saturdays. He never pays her extra when she does. But last night he told her to open the office up at 9 A.M., and of course when she got there, he was nowhere to be found, though from the looks of his old sofa he'd slept there. He's off somewhere this morning, doing God knows what. Now, about half past nine, he comes waddling in.

She hands him his messages. "Mr. Albert Martindale of Continental called three times," she says. "He's not happy. He says he doesn't like all these postponements of the deadline on the stock offer. He says it doesn't look good for his company. He's worried the whole deal is gonna come unstuck."

"Tell him to keep his shirt on, tell him to keep his pants on, tell him to keep his lid on. Tell him to keep everything he's got *on* on. Tell him I've got everything under control."

"He wants to know what's happening with that one stockholder, the woman in Florida whose shares you told him you had in your pocket. He wants to know what's happening with her."

"Did you tell him it was a woman in Florida?"

"Well, maybe. That's who it is, isn't it?"

"Goddamnit, Smyrna, you don't need to tell him things he doesn't need to know. Why'd you tell him it was a woman in Florida, for God's sake?"

"Sorry, Moe. I didn't know it was supposed to be a secret."

"Everything I tell you is supposed to be a secret. What the hell do you think the word 'secretary' comes from? Secret. The girl that's hired to keep the secrets."

"I didn't tell him what her name was."

"He'll figure it out soon enough, damn it! Anyway, Simma Belsky is giving me a hard time—can you believe it, after all I've done for her?—but don't tell Martindale

that, for God's sake! Just tell him I've got everything under control."

"He wants you to call him back right away."

"Well, I ain't gonna call him right away. Got that?"

"And now we got a whole bunch of those other calls
again today. Guys who won't give their last names: Don
from Cleveland, Ernie, Harry, and Julius. Another says
he's a friend of Herbie the Heeb, and that you'll know
what that means. Who are these guys, Moe? Where are
they getting our unlisted numbers? We just had 'em all
changed again last week. Are you sure everything's all
right?"

"Damn it, what did I just tell you? I just told you:
everything's under control!"

"Then there's a new call, on your private line, from a
man named Peter Turner. Says he's writing a book or
something about Silas Tarkington."

"Goddammit, Smyrna, where the hell did *he* get that
number from?"

"How the hell would I know? Where are all these
other jerks getting our numbers from? The heavy breath-
ers, Ernie and Julius and them, and the friend of Herbie
the Heeb? Maybe they've got a spy at the telephone company."

"Oh, no. Not this number, Smyrna. He called on my
super-private number, that is only known by you, Martindale, and me. *Did you give it to him, Smyrna?*"

"I did not! I never even heard of this jerk! Why
would I give out your super-private number to some jerk I
don't even know and never even heard of?"

"Maybe he paid you off. Is that what happened?
C'mon, Smyrna, 'fess up. You gave it to him, di'ncha? It
had to of been you. You been givin' out secrets lately,
Smyrna, so it had to of been you gave it to him. You're in
big trouble, Smyrna, if you did."

"Well, I fuckin' well didn't!" she says.

"Like I just said, nobody knows this number but me,
Mr. Albert Martindale, Esquire—and you!"

"Honeychile knows it too!" she screams.

He scowls and chomps down hard on his cigar.

"Yeah," he says between his teeth. "You got a point there. Honeychile knows it too."

"So quit tryin' to blame me!"

"Excuse me, Smyrna," he says, "but I got some very private phone calls to make," and he walks into his office and closes the door behind him.

First he dials the new combination on his wall safe and checks its contents. All seems to be in order there. Then he seats himself behind his desk and begins punching out telephone numbers.

"Bonham? Moe here. Listen, old buddy, when're you gonna stop draggin' your heels and come on board with what you promised? . . . You know what I'm talkin' about. Don't give me the dumb act, sonny boy, I want what you promised, and I want it now! . . . No, I can't wait a few more days. . . . I don't care what other side deal you're workin' on, things have reached the serious level. . . . Look what I done for you already, sonny boy. What more do you want? I got you promised an employment contract for five mil, where you won't even have to come into the office. That should be enough for you and your Jap boyfriend to retire in style, that, plus what you've already managed to stash away over the last twenty years, thanks to me. . . . No, I can't wait till Friday. I can't wait till tomorrow. *I want it now.* . . .

"Listen, you bastard, I'm not the threatening type. I never threaten people, which is the secret of my success. But if I was to threaten you, well, what about what happened to the Tarkington kid's trust fund? What if the kid found out what happened to the half a mil that was supposed to be his when he was twenty-one? You'd be in some pretty hot water, it seems like to me. Think about these items, pal; there's some others, too numerous to mention. So get your ass on the stick, Bonham! . . . You say I'm bluffing? *You'll find out!*"

He slams down the phone and immediately punches in another call.

"Eddie? Moe here. . . . Nah, I don't need any more credit card numbers right now, I got enough to last me at least another month. Those corporate account numbers

are the best. They're good for at least a coupla months.
. . . Yeah, that was good work you done for me on
them, so for that I got a special reward for you. For this
I'll pay you sixty bucks an hour—how's that?

"Eddie, I want you to put a tail on Honeychile. . . .
Yeah, you heard me right. My wife, Honeychile. I wanna
know every move she makes, and every move she makes I
wanna know about it as soon as she makes it by you
reporting it back to me. Understand? Okay, I'll go sixty-
five. . . . Let's see, we'll coordinate our watches. It's
now nine-forty-five A.M. Your meter has just started running, buddy."

He puts down the phone and smiles. But when he
looks down, he sees that the front of his shirt is drenched
with sweat, though the day is not a warm one.

28

Diana Smith (interview taped 10/19/91)

What can I say to you? He wanted to marry me, but his wife wouldn't give him a divorce. At least not without all sorts of nasty publicity. That broke his heart. That's what he died of, a broken heart. That's really all I have to say to you.

You're going to have to ask me some specific questions. I'm a private person. I can't just run off at the mouth about Si Tarkington and myself. It's too painful. Ask me some specifics, and I'll try to answer you. Except dates. I'm terrible on dates. Si used to tease me. And numbers. I've heard that some people have what amounts to dyslexia where numbers are concerned. If that's so, I'm one of them.

What do I think of Connie Tarkington? You really want to know what I think of her? Consuelo Tarkington is a bitch. How's that for a straight answer? When it comes to bitches, she wrote the book. She's also a liar. She's a patho—what's the word? That's it, a pathological liar. You can't believe a word she says. Take it from me.

I mean, what can you say for a woman who's only interested in clothes? She's not interested in her family. She has no interest in Miranda, who's really a mixed-up kid, always falling in love with the wrong kinds of men, and who could really have used some mothering when she was growing up. She has no interest in her stepson, whom she hardly ever sees. She had no interest in Si, either in his career or in him as a man. She has no interest in sex. Which was why Si—well, he was a normal, healthy male, after all, with the usual male appetites— always had to go looking for that elsewhere. If you ask me, she encouraged his extramarital affairs, because that meant he left her alone! The only thing she ever cared about was whether he had enough money to pay her bills. You should have seen her bills. He showed them to me once; it was a stack yea high! Just from *one month*. How could a woman spend so much on clothes? Especially since most of the designers who sold to Si gave her clothes for enormous discounts, and anything she wanted from Tony Delfino's salon she got for free.

No, I didn't know her before she married him. Before she broke up his first marriage—which was perfectly happy before she came along—before she got him to walk out on his first wife and little child. But I've heard stories. Someone told me that before she married Si, she went around asking everybody, "Are you coming to my fund-raiser?" Meaning the wedding. That's all she ever cared about. His money.

Nobody really likes Connie. She's a cold fish. I think she's got ice water running in her veins. No wonder she's a sexual refrigerator. That's what Si used to call her. I thought that was a pretty good description of Miss Consuelo Banning and her *Social Register* airs.

Oh, and here's another thing. This is important, and I almost forgot it. His mother. Did you know that Connie made Si sweep his very own mother under the rug? How about that? When Si started to get famous, and Connie started getting on the Best-Dressed List, she decided that Si's poor old mother wasn't good enough for the *image* she wanted for herself and Si and the store. She made him go around telling everyone he was an orphan. That both his parents had died years ago.

Well, his father may have been dead, but his mother sure as hell wasn't, and as far as I know she still isn't, though she must be well up in her nineties by now. But Connie forced Si to keep his mother in purdah, as he put it. She forced him to keep his mother like a damn prisoner because she didn't think his mother was socially good enough. Because his mother talked funny and liked to wear an apron around the house.

How did I find out about her? Quite by accident. I live in Morningside Heights, and there's a Gristede's at the corner of West End and Cathedral that I shop at. Two or three years ago, it was a Sunday and I'd gone out to get some things, and as I was walking home I suddenly saw Si standing on the stoop of a shabby old brownstone, with a briefcase, ringing a doorbell. I was so surprised to see him there that I ran up the steps. "Si!" I said. "What are you doing here?" He didn't look at all pleased to see me, I must say.

"Delivering something to a client," he said.

"In *this* neighborhood?" I said.

With that, this little fat old lady came to the door. "Right on time," she said.

He opened his briefcase, took out an envelope, and handed it to her. "Here's your envelope—Mother," he said.

"Mother?" she said. She gave me the once-over. "And who's this, your daughter?"

He was looking very uncomfortable. "Mother, this is Diana Smith," he said. "Diana Smith, I'd like you to meet my mother. Miss Smith just happened to be passing by."

She winked at him then. "Well, whoever she is she's a cute little trick," she said.

"Miss Smith may end up being my next wife, *Mother*," he said. There was a little note of warning in his voice.

"Whatever you say," she said. "But first you've got to get rid of the wife you've got, don't you?" And she winked at him again, as though they had a little private secret between them. "But you know how to get rid of women, don't you—sonny?"

He looked at his watch. "I've got to run now," he said.

"Sure," she said. "Nice to meet you, Miss Smith. Nice to see you, sonny." She tucked the envelope inside the front of her dress and closed the door.

Well, she may have thought she was making some sort of private joke, but he sure didn't think so. In fact, he was mad as hell. I was very sensitive to his mood changes. As we walked down the steps, I asked him, "What was that all about? I didn't know you had a mother!"

That was when he told me that his mother was a secret, that Connie didn't want anyone to know about her, and that even though his mother was often a royal pain in the ass he still took care of her and paid her rent. "I want you to promise not to mention this to anyone," he said.

"Of course not," I said. "Still, I think it's awfully sweet of you to take care of her like this."

"And she's getting senile," he said.

"What did she mean about getting rid of women?"

"My first wife was a woman you simply could not reason with," he said. He never liked to talk about his first wife, Alice.

He must have come up there by cab, because now he was looking up and down the street for a taxi. "I'd offer to walk you home with your groceries," he said, "but—"

"It's just a box of detergent and a carton of cigarettes," I said. "I can manage."

"I wish you wouldn't smoke," he said. Then he spotted a cab and raised his briefcase. "See you tomorrow at the store," he said, and waved goodbye.

We didn't kiss goodbye, as we usually did. Too public, I suppose, and besides his mother was probably watching us both from a window.

I never told another living soul about his mother, and I never mentioned it again because I knew how painful the whole situation was for him—what that bitch Connie had made him do. I'm only telling you now because—

well, now that Si is . . . gone, it doesn't matter, does it? And I think it says a lot about his character. He really owed a lot to his mother, you know. Oh, yes. She helped him get his start. His father was some kind of blue-collar worker, but his mother worked too, and she saved every dollar and every dime to help her only son get started in business. He told me that. And he never forgot his indebtedness to her, no matter how much of a pain in the ass she became later. Of course Connie forgot Si's mother long ago.

Now that he's gone, who'll take care of the little old lady, I wonder? Will Connie? Will Miss Icebox ever be caught dead on West End Avenue? Anyone who believes that will please stand on his head, as my own mother used to say. Will Miranda? I don't know if Miranda even knows she's got a living grandmother. I don't count on her for much of anything.

I'm sure Si's mother is still alive, because Si would have told me if she died, since I once actually met her. Every time I pass that shabby old brownstone on West End Avenue I wonder what's to become of her. I'd offer to help her myself, but I don't have any money. Right now, I don't even have a job. . . .

What's my beef with Miranda? Oh, nothing, I guess, except for the way she's always acted as though she owned the place—which I guess she does now, anyway. The day I left, for instance, she just borrowed a big diamond ring from my department without saying a word to anybody! What kind of a way is that to run a store? Well, of course by then it wasn't my department anymore, so there wasn't anything I could really say or do about it, except to think, What nerve! She'd never have got away with that sort of thing when her father was alive. Well, from what I read in the papers, Continental is about to buy the store, so she'll be out of a job. Like me. They'll all be out of their jobs, Tommy Bonham included. From the talk I hear on the street the store isn't in such great financial shape, and if that's the case the fault will be Tommy Bonham's. Si gave Tommy too much authority over the past few years, if you ask me. I tried to warn Si about

that. I think he was finally beginning to listen to me when
—well, when what happened happened.

Now I hear Tommy Bonham is making a big play for
Miranda. After her money, I suppose, or so my pals at the
store tell me. . . .

Why are you giving me that funny look? Don't tell
me you have a thing for Miss Miranda Tarkington! All I
can say is watch out. She's had a bad track record with
men. Emotionally insecure, I think. Like her mother. The
one Tommy should be making a play for is her mother.
She's closer to his age.

Oh-oh. You've just asked me for a date. I'm terrible
on dates. But let's see. It must have been in the spring of
eighty-five when I first went to work for Tarkington's.
Delafield & Du Bois's lease had run out, and Si didn't
want to renew it. He wanted to start his own jewelry
department. I answered an ad.

I'd had several other jobs before, and I'd just been
fired from my last one—as secretary for a building con-
tractor. But before that I'd worked as a saleswoman at
Cartier, I'd taken a course in gemology and got an A in it,
and I really knew my stones. I put all this in my résumé
and crossed my fingers. Would it be enough to qualify me
for a job as jewelry buyer for a store like Tarkington's? I
had no idea, but the pay was more than anything I'd
earned before, and so I thought what the hell.

My first interview was with Tommy Bonham. I certainly thought he was a handsome hunk, but that interview was really weird. He hardly asked me any questions
at all. Instead, he said to me things like, "Let me see you
sit down in that chair. Now stand up. Now walk across
the room. Now turn and walk the other way. Now reach
out and touch that picture frame and straighten it
slightly. Now pick up this pencil. Now pick up this telephone as though you were taking a call. Now let me see
your best smile. Now repeat after me, Papa . . . pota-
toes . . . poultry . . . prunes . . . and prisms." It was
like I was auditioning for a part in a high school play.
Then he asked me for a sample of my handwriting. He
was an amateur graphologist, he said. That really scared

me. I knew I'd be dealing with a lot of expensive jewelry, and he probably wanted to analyze my handwriting to see if I was honest or not.

Anyway, I left that interview feeling I hadn't done very well. And I thought, Oh, well, I still have four more months of unemployment coming, so I went back to the Help Wanted ads.

Then, a week later, I got a call from Bonham's office. They wanted me to come back for a second interview.

This time, he was a lot friendlier. "I like the way you move," he said. "I like the way you look, and I like the way you talk. You realize that this will be a fairly small department. In addition to dealing with the vendors, you're going to have to spend a certain amount of time on the selling floor with our clients. It's important to look just right when you're working for a store like Tarkington's."

I thanked him. It was nice to know that I looked right.

"You also have a sense of style," he said. "For instance, I notice that you're wearing the same white dress you wore when you came to see me last. But you've varied it with that black patent belt. Very smart."

"Thank you," I said.

"You have a sense of style without spending a lot of money on your clothes. That's unusual."

I thanked him again. I didn't tell him that at the time I had only three decent outfits to my name, and I had to hand-wash and iron that particular white linen job every time I wore it.

"For instance, the belt can't have cost you more than two dollars," he said.

"Woolworth's," I admitted.

"The buckle is beginning to chip," he said. "You might try patching it with a bit of black nail polish."

I made a mental note to throw that belt in the nearest Salvation Army collection bin the minute I left his office.

"There's only one thing that worries me, Miss Smith," he said.

I asked him what that was.

"You have a very quick, almost violent temper."

I thought, Oh, God. My Irish temper, my mother used to call it. That meant he'd been talking to my last boss. He'd blamed me for something one of the other girls had done, and I got so mad I trashed his office—threw his files all over the floor, dumped out his desk drawers, emptied his wastebasket into his IN box, really tore up the place. That's what got me fired. "It's true," I said. "It's something I'm trying to work on about myself. Whenever I lose my temper, I get into trouble. I think I've learned that it isn't worth it."

"Retailing can be a very stressful business," he said. "Particularly around the holiday season. There'll be long hours, tight delivery schedules, impatient and demanding customers. We can't have any outbursts of temper here, Miss Smith. Can you keep that pressure valve under control?"

"After the last experience, I think I know how to handle it," I said. "I guess you've been talking to the people at Shaughnessy Construction."

He smiled at me. "No," he said. "I saw it in your handwriting sample."

"Well," I said, "there's one other thing you should know about me. I'm really terrible at figures."

"I saw that in your sample too," he said. "But I assume you can read a price tag and tell a customer what an item costs."

"Oh, yes. I'm talking about long sheets of figures, computer printouts—"

"All that—daily sales figures, pricing, inventory keeping—is handled by my office. All you need in this job is good taste and a knowledge of fine jewelry—an 'eye,' as I call it—a winning, service-oriented personality, and an ability to sign a vendor's receipt. My office handles the rest. When can you come to work for us, Miss Smith?"

That was when I realized I had the job.

"I'm taking a big gamble on you, Miss Smith," he said. "A big gamble."

.   .   .

At first, I thought Tommy Bonham was my pal. I thought the little suggestions he made were his way of being helpful. Later, I was not so sure whether Tommy was my pal or not. There was something about the way he played his brand of office politics that I began not to like so much, not to really trust. Tommy is a manipulator, a conniver. He's very good at playing one person against another. Maybe he feels he can get the best work out of people by keeping things stirred up. But at other times he seems to just enjoy making mischief, causing trouble. Of course he was our liaison between the sales staff and department heads and Mr. Si, as everybody called him. He had Mr. Si's ear, and he was always making us aware of that fact. He'd say, "Mr. Si hasn't been too happy with your work lately," and things like that. Or, "Your department's figures weren't as good for May as they were for April, and Mr. Si wonders why." Who knew whether Mr. Si was really saying these things? Or Tommy would try to get one buyer to criticize another buyer's performance. Like, "Miss So-and-So in Lingerie has taken a lot of sick days lately. Do you think she's pregnant?" And you'd have to be careful what you said, or it could get back to Mr. Si.

In the beginning, I had very little to do with Mr. Si. Oh, I'd met him, of course. I'd been introduced to him when I joined the store. He was very polite, almost stiff and formal. "Welcome to our Tarkington's family," and all that. Whenever he passed my department he'd wave and smile, but he was rather aloof, really. The thought of a romantic relationship with him never entered my head because—well, he was at least twice my age, and he had this coldly beautiful white swan of a wife who wafted in and out of the store now and then, smelling of Shalimar and looking as though she'd been packaged by one of our window dressers. And I'd gathered that there was sort of an unwritten rule against employees socializing after hours. At the time I was dating two or three different guys, no one in particular and no one seriously. If there was anyone at the store I'd have liked to date, it would have been Tommy Bonham, just because he was such a

gorgeous hunk and because—well, you know, a girl can't
help but wonder what a guy like that, who's such a
smoothie, such a cool customer, would be like in the sack.
"Like a wild animal!" the other girls whispered, though
none of them could claim to have had firsthand experience.

But Tommy never showed any sexual interest in me,
except once, and I'm not even sure that was what it was.
I'd been working there about three months, and Tommy
came into my department. "Mr. Si is a little disappointed
in your figures, Smitty," he said. "We know this is a new
department, but we'd been hoping you'd do better. Do
you have any idea what might be wrong?"

"Well," I said, "this department is kind of tucked
into a corner of the store, where we don't get the traffic
they get on the center aisle, and I don't have that much
square footage or display space. Women like to browse
for jewelry, but they don't buy it on impulse, the way
they buy handbags, shoes, and apparel. I need space for
women to browse, spot a piece, remember it, and come
back and buy it."

"That's true," he said. "If they can't see it, they
won't want it."

"And I'll tell you something else," I said. "There's
this one vendor, Harriet Minskoff, who keeps insisting
that I call her Honeychile. Her stuff isn't very pretty and,
quite frankly, a lot of it isn't very good. And yet I gather
it's sort of store policy to take her things on consignment,
display them, and try to sell them. Just between you and
me, her things cheapen my department."

He frowned. "Mrs. Minskoff is something of a special case," he said.

Later, I found out what sort of "special case" this
Mrs. Minskoff was. At the time, I thought she might be a
girlfriend of Mr. Si's. Not at all. It was her husband, a
man named Moses Minskoff, a man I never actually met,
who had his hooks into Si somehow, some debt Si owed
him from years ago. I never did find out what it was. Si
wouldn't talk about it. But I knew Si had been trying to
get free of Minskoff for years, and Tommy was trying to

help. But Minskoff had stuck to Si like a leech, and I was stuck with trying to sell Mrs. Minskoff's crappy stuff, which had to be displayed front and center.

Anyway, Tommy said to me, "You know, Smitty, a lot of our jewelry customers are males, looking for gifts for their wives or girlfriends. I wonder whether you might try for a little sexier look. You have a wonderful body and great breasts. What if you were to try to display a little more of a cleavage? I don't want you to look cheap, of course, but try displaying a little more cleavage. And I want to suggest a scent for you. Try Equipage."

Well, at the time I didn't know whether this was a come-on or not, but I decided it was just an honest business tip. So I tried it. And believe it or not, sales improved. I could tell by just looking at the bottom line. A month later, Tommy came by again. "Mr. Si is very pleased with your last month's figures, Smitty," he said. He grinned and tapped his breastbone with his fingertip. "That's doing it. You look sexy but not cheap. You've got that Catherine Deneuve look."

Then, a couple of months later—I remember it was still summer—Tommy came by my department again and said, "Mr. Si is really happy with your department's figures, Smitty. In fact, he's looking into ways to give you more display space."

"That would be terrific," I said.

"He'd very much like to discuss this with you and get your input."

"Great," I said. "Does he want to see me now?"

"If you're free, he'd like to invite you to lunch next Saturday at his farm in Old Westbury. Can you make it?"

"That would be terrific," I said.

At the time, I thought to myself, If he wants to invite me to lunch, why doesn't he do it himself, instead of having his chief honcho do it for him? But I thought, What the hell? Maybe this is the way things work here. Everything goes through channels, through a chain of command.

"Mrs. Tarkington will be in Paris, for the *prêt-à-por-*

ter collections," he said. "So it will be just the two of you, lunching alone. Will you be comfortable with that?"

"Sure!" I said, in a kind of breezy way, trying not to show how excited I really was. Lunching alone with the Big Enchilada. Maybe he was going to offer me a raise! Maybe he was going to make me street floor merchandise manager! That's where you get into the real money in retailing, as a merchandise manager.

"You might want to bring up the Mrs. Minskoff problem when you talk to him," he said. "He's aware of it, of course. But hearing from you that there's a very serious problem here might have more impact on him."

"I'll do that," I said.

"Good," he said. "Mr. Si's car and driver will pick you up at your apartment at eleven-thirty next Saturday morning and drive you out to Long Island."

"Great," I said.

Great! That was hardly the word for it. I'd been invited to a private business lunch with the big boss himself, and I'd even been given an agenda, a business problem that needed solving. And I was going to be driven to Long Island in a chauffeur-driven Rolls! My only wish was that somehow my mother could be there to see me as I got into that car.

"Obviously, you won't mention this to anyone else in the store," he said.

"Absolutely not," I promised.

It was a tall order, keeping that promise. I wanted to squeal the news to everyone in sight. But I kept my promise, and I was so excited that I could hardly wait for next Saturday to come.

Of course I didn't find out till later that this had always been a part of Tommy's job, lining up women for his boss whenever the boss's wife was out of town.

With Tommy's looks and Si Tarkington's money, they had a winning combination.

Si Tarkington and Prettyboy Bonham. What a duo.

29

Diana Smith (interview taped 10/19/91, continued)

Billings, the chauffeur, picked me up in front of my building that Saturday morning at eleven-thirty sharp, and I was driven out to Old Westbury in the back seat of the Rolls, feeling like a queen. I'm sure Billings knew perfectly well what this mission was all about—he'd probably made this same run with a girl out to his boss's house a hundred times before—but I didn't know that yet.

I'd dressed for this meeting very carefully. I wore my white linen—it was still my best outfit—though naturally I'd thrown out the damn patent leather belt. I dressed it up with a scarf this time. I wore what I thought a girl should wear for a business lunch with her boss in the country. Very little jewelry, just gold earrings and a gold bracelet.

Flying Horse Farm was the most beautiful place I'd ever seen—the circular gravel driveway, the white Georgian columns—and Si was standing on the front steps to meet us. I'd never been in a house like that before, and Si took me on a little tour: the white living room overflowing with chairs and sofas in red and green English chintz, with a Lautrec, a Gauguin, and a Cézanne on the walls; the dining room draped in green faille swags at the chair rail and, above that, the most beautifully delicate green-and-white striped wallpaper, with tiny roses trailing between the stripes. Upstairs, his wife's pale yellow bedroom had a canopy bed of white tambour trimmed with red satin ribbon, and his bedroom walls were covered with hunter-green felt, with matching draperies, and a Dufy watercolor over the fireplace. His bathroom was all green marble and bronze-tinted mirroring, and his bedroom even had its own kitchenette and wet bar. But you've been to Flying Horse. I don't need to describe it to you. Everything about it was perfection. Every beautiful, tiny object was perfectly in place.

Later, I found out that Connie's perfectionism was one of the things that irritated him about her. He liked to make a bit of a mess now and then. But that wouldn't do for Miss Perfect. With her, everything had to be *just so,* right down to the arrangement of the Shalimar bottles on her bathroom shelves: big bottles on one shelf, smaller ones on the next, and so on.

Lunch was very polite and rather formal, served by Milliken, in white gloves, on green-and-white Meissen china that matched the wallpaper. I noticed the little touches. For instance, the roses and baby's breath in the centerpiece had been misted, so they looked as though they were covered with dew. I made one gaffe. When I unfolded my napkin, a small dinner roll flew out of the center and bounced across the carpet. Milliken scooped it up without comment and immediately replaced it with a fresh one. Si pretended not to notice.

Our conversation at lunch was rather formal too. "We're very pleased with the figures in your department, Miss Smith," he said to me.

"Please call me Smitty," I said. "Everybody does."

"Then you must call me Si," he said.

"It will be hard not to call you Mr. Si," I said, "the way everyone else in the store does."

"That will also do," he said with a little smile.

I mentioned the problem of Mrs. Minskoff's line of jewelry.

He frowned. "I know what you mean," he said. "The Minskoffs are old family friends, and I was trying to do Mrs. Minskoff a little favor. But I agree with you. I'm trying to get Mrs. Minskoff into the luggage business." He smiled again. "You may have noticed that Tarkington's does *not* have a luggage department," he said.

Lunch had started with a wonderful cold fennel soup. Now we were into the next course: a fluffy omelet, filled with crabmeat, and fresh baby asparagus.

"We've only had one other saleswoman at the store who could sell as well as you do," he said at one point. "Her name was Alice Markham."

"I don't believe I know her," I said.

"No, she left a long time ago," he said.

Later, I found out that Alice Markham had also been his first wife. Sometimes I got the impression that he missed her. Well, after a few years of living with Miss Perfect Connie, who wouldn't! Sometimes I wondered whether I reminded him of her—or at least of the way she was when she was my age.

"When Delafield and Du Bois moved out, I thought we might have a little difficulty establishing our own jewelry department," he said. "But you've done wonders for us, Smitty."

"Sometimes, when Tommy shows me my weekly figures, they even surprise me!" I said.

After lunch, he said, "I've got some work to do at my desk, and Billings has to run a few errands before he can drive you back to the city. Would you like to have a swim in the pool?"

"I'd love that," I said.

"There are suits in all sizes in the pool house dressing room," he said. "I may join you a little later." And he showed me where the pool and pool house were.

I guess I've always dreamed of a life of luxury—a big house like that, a pool and pool house, lawns, terraces, gardens with raked-gravel walks, a private lake—and I found myself very quickly feeling right at home at Flying Horse Farm. It was what I'd always dreamed of.

I think that was something else Si and I had in common. We were both born poor. Oh, I don't come from abject poverty, the way he did. My father is a podiatrist in Eastchester, but he's always been a very disappointed man. He hates his life. He wanted to be a real doctor, but there wasn't enough money for medical school, so he had to settle for podiatry. My mother works as his receptionist, and there were too many of us kids—I have four sisters and three brothers—and there was never enough money for any of the finer things in life.

As a kid, I used to ride my bike all the way out into the nicer part of Scarsdale, along those winding, wooded streets and lanes lined with big shade trees. I'd look at all the big houses—mansions, really—with their long drives and rhododendron hedges and big cars parked out front, and I'd wonder what it was like to live like that. I'd see maids in uniforms accepting deliveries, chauffeurs picking up and dropping off children from private school, and gardeners raking long gravel driveways. It was like another world.

Even as a kid, I decided the only way I could ever have any of those things was to find a man who would marry me and take care of me.

But Flying Horse Farm was grander than anything in Westchester. I decided that afternoon that the only place I really wanted to live was *there*. And I could have, too, if it hadn't been for Connie.

Anyway, I found a suit that fit me in the pool house, and changed into it, and went out to the pool to practice my dives—I was a champion diver in high school, did I tell you that?—thinking all these thoughts.

There was a particularly tricky dive I'd been working on at the gym I was going to, a back jackknife with a full twist, and I'd been having trouble with my heels flipping backward as I entered the water. I decided to work on that one.

So there I was, practicing my back jackknifes, and I pulled myself up out of the water and was squeezing the water out of my hair when I looked up and saw him standing there on the pool house steps in a red robe, with a big black dog wagging its tail beside him. I had no idea how long he'd been standing there. He came down the steps to where I was sitting on the edge of the pool.

He was smiling a rather strange smile. "I've been enjoying watching you dive," he said. "You're a beautiful diver, Smitty."

"Thanks," I said. "But I still haven't got that damned back jackknife quite right."

"Another talent I didn't know you had," he said. "My son's a diver too. On the Yale team." This was the first time I knew he had a son. "You have a beautiful body," he said.

"Thank you," I said. My body is one of the few things I'm really proud of, because I do think I'm in pretty good shape and I'm always exercising. I scrambled up the ladder again to the board, walked out to the end, turned, stood on my tiptoes, and tried the dive again. I made one of my better entries into the water.

When I came to the surface, he had moved closer to the pool's edge. "How was that?" I asked. "Did that look better? It felt better to me."

"Beautiful," he said. Then he said, "I was going to swim some laps."

"Then you don't want me working on the board at the same time," I said, and started to pull myself out of the water again.

"Maybe you'd like to swim laps with me," he said.

"Well, I'm not a real fast swimmer," I said.

"I'll let you set the pace."

"Okay," I said.

He was still smiling. "There's only one thing," he said.

"What's that?"

"I swim in the nude."

"Then I'll just go back into the house and wait for—"

"Don't go," he said, and he stepped toward me, and

that was when he dropped his robe. It fell in a heap around his ankles.

Now picture this. From where I was sitting at the edge of the pool, his—you know, his *thing*—was right at the level of my face, and I must say I had never seen anything quite like it. He had a thing like a—well, I don't want to sound common, but he was hung like a horse. I never knew they came as big as that. "It wants to kiss you," he said, and pressed it against my face.

Then he whispered something that was—well, you know, kind of sweet and kind of dirty at the same time, and pulled me to my feet, and the next thing I knew he was carrying me—he was very strong—carrying me, with my legs wrapped around his hips, his thing pressing hard against me through my swimsuit, up the steps and into the pool house and into one of the bedrooms there, onto a big big water bed, and I was being made love to in a way—in a way I'd never thought possible before, literally seeing stars. I don't know if you'll want this for your book, but among his other talents, the late Silas Tarkington was a superb sexual athlete, despite his age. Perhaps, I thought, that first time he was extra randy because he'd spent so many long years having to endure Connie's frigidity. But I soon discovered that he was always like that. Being older than me, he had learned from experience how to please a woman—to the utmost. "Diana," he whispered. "Diana, goddess of the hunt!"

Why am I telling you all this? I'm telling you things I've never told another living soul. Perhaps because it gives me so much pleasure to remember the pleasure he and I had together. . . .

When it was over, I was in tears. Partly they were tears of joy, but they were also tears of guilt. "We shouldn't have done this," I said. "I don't want to be a home-wrecker."

"My home is already wrecked," he said.

I giggled. "I feel like I've just lost my virginity," I said.

"I feel like I've just lost mine too," he said. Then he said, "Will you spend the weekend?"

"What about the servants?" During lunch, the place had seemed to be swarming with them.

"I've given them all the weekend off."

So Billings wasn't just out running a few little errands. He was gone for the weekend. All this had been planned in advance, but I didn't care. Already, I think, I had fallen in love with him. Head over heels in love. It didn't matter at all that he was a much older man.

"I didn't bring any clothes," I said.

He laughed. "You won't be wearing many clothes."

"I didn't even bring my toothbrush."

"All the guest bedrooms are stocked with new toothbrushes."

"Should I?"

"I want you all to myself," he said. "Diana—goddess of the hunt!"

"I love you," I sobbed, and we were in each other's arms once more, making love all over again, and that second time was when I felt that sudden explosion inside me and knew I had finally, and for the first time in my life —at age twenty-six—had what my girlfriends and I had talked about and were never quite sure we knew what it was, and what I'd read about—an orgasm!

For the next day and a half, it seemed as though we did nothing but make love. We swam in the pool and made love in the pool house. We walked in the gardens and made love on a garden bench. We played tennis on the grass court—we played naked; there was no one to see us for miles!—and then made love on the grass. That night, we sent out for pizza and then made love on Connie's big canopy bed with the red ribbons on it.

That was the best place for me, making love in her bed, though I turned all the fashion photos of her that were on her dresser against the wall, so I wouldn't feel she was watching us.

After that last lovemaking of the day, he went down the hall to his own room to sleep. He said he felt more comfortable sleeping there, and I didn't mind. I was too happy to mind. I liked being all alone in Connie's bedroom, pretending that I was the famous Mrs. Consuelo Tarkington and that everything she had was mine.

I wasn't sleepy. I tried on her rings and bracelets and necklaces. I tried on her nighties and underwear. I tried on her shoes and her dresses. She had this big refrigerated closet, just for her furs, and I tried them all on too. I splashed myself with her Shalimar perfume. Why shouldn't I make believe that everything she owned belonged to me? I asked myself. I'd given her husband more pleasure than she'd ever given him in her lifetime. I deserved her possessions more than she did.

And of course the next morning Si came into my room—it was my room by then—and we made love again.

Around six o'clock that Sunday afternoon Si became terribly nervous. She was due in on a flight to Kennedy at nine o'clock that night. He was going to drive me back to town, drop me off at my place, and spend the night at the apartment over the store. But she was going to go directly to the farm—to unload all her Paris purchases, I suppose —and he was terribly nervous that she might find some scrap of evidence that I'd been there. He began going through the house, room by room, seeing that everything was in the same perfect order that she'd left it in, and I helped him.

We put all the sheets and towels that we'd used through the washer and the drier and saw that they were ironed and folded and stacked just so. We put fresh linen on her bed. She liked a deep reverse on her top sheet, he explained, so that the fold occurred at *exactly one and a half inches* above the top of her big "cTb" embroidered monogram. That had to be measured with a ruler, because if it was off by so much as a fraction of an inch she would have a fit. The swimsuit I had borrowed had to be dried and folded and put back in the pool house exactly where I had found it, or she would smell a rat. The box our pizza had been delivered in had to be burned in the incinerator. Even the toothbrush that I'd borrowed from one of the guest bathrooms had to be burned and replaced with one of the exact same color. Have you seen

Connie's collection of designer toothbrushes? She actually has them! As eight o'clock approached, he was in an absolute panic that some tiny detail we'd overlooked might catch her eye and strike her as the least bit off.

All this frenzied activity in preparation for Miss Refrigerator's homecoming annoyed me. It was beginning to make me mad. It upset me to see my lover polishing the bathroom fixtures and emptying wastebaskets. He seemed actually terrified of this woman. What kind of basis was that for a marriage? I asked myself. Terror? I could feel my Irish temper coming on, but I managed to hold my tongue.

Finally, at about eight-fifteen, he announced that everything we needed to do was done. We turned out all the proper lights, and left the proper ones on for her, and we went out to get into the car. He was taking the station wagon because the Rolls was too conspicuous and he didn't want any of his neighbors—Tommy Bonham was one, incidentally, though he lived four miles away—to see us driving away together and recognize us.

I was about to get into the car when I said, "Let me go back, darling, and give the place a final once-over, just to make sure there's nothing out of place," and he said okay.

Now I'm not exactly proud of what I did next, but I promised to be honest with you, so I'll tell you.

I went back into the house and upstairs to her bedroom. I stepped out of the panties I was wearing, turned back the coverlet of her bed, and stuffed the panties deep down between the sheets. Then I sprayed her pillowcases with a good, heavy spritz of my Equipage before folding the coverlet back in place. Then I went into her bathroom and wiped my lipstick on a couple of her white, perfectly ironed, monogrammed Porthault hand towels. Then I went downstairs again and joined him in the car.

"Everything in perfect order?" he asked me.

"Perfect," I said, and we drove off into the night.

Don't ask me why I did those awful things. It wasn't a temper tantrum, exactly. It was more like a fit of jealous rage. They were crazy things to do. But when you're in love you do crazy things.

Driving down Heather Lane, he was still nervous, and he made me scrunch way down in the seat so I wouldn't be seen in case we passed anyone he knew. But when we got out onto the Long Island Expressway, he relaxed and let me sit up. He put his arm around me and pulled me close to him. "I've loved being with you this weekend, Smitty," he said. "I hope we can do this again very soon."

"So do I, darling," I said.

Enough for today? I'm exhausted—emotionally exhausted—remembering it all.

At this very moment, just a few dozen blocks to the south, Moe Minskoff is on the telephone. "Yeah, Eddie," he says. "You got any news for me? . . . Okay, shoot. . . . She left the apartment at ten-thirty A.M. this morning and got into a cab. . . . You tailed her in another cab to the Dakota, One West Seventy-second. . . . Yeah, I know the building, creepy old place. . . . She got out and went inside. . . . In there about two hours. . . . Came out, got in another cab, and went home. . . . That was her total today's activity.

"Okay, now, Eddie, did it occur to you to slip the doorman a fin and find out who she was going to see in there? . . . Good boy! . . . His name's Peter Turner, huh? . . . Yeah, just as I suspected. You find out anything more about this guy from the doorman? . . . Middle to late twenties, single, lives alone, some kind of writer, carries a tape recorder around a lot of the time. . . . Yeah, that's the guy. You done a good job, pal. This assignment's completed. I'll call you when I got another for you. . . .

"You figure eight hours on the tail, total? Okay, that works out to four hundred and eighty bucks, right? . . . Well, maybe I did say sixty-five an hour. That makes it five hundred and twenty I owe you. . . . Yeah, plus two cab fares and a fin for the doorman. . . . No, I ain't payin' for your lunch. Lunch is on you. When I hire a tail, I don't pay for its lunch. . . .

"I'll have the money for you Friday. . . . No, I ain't got it right now. . . . Look, don't give me a hard time, pal. I said I'll have it for you Friday. You can wait till Friday. . . . Look, I had a really lousy day at the track today, Eddie. Fuckin' jockey double-crossed me. I had a deal with this jock. He was supposed to slow his horse in the stretch and let mine win, but he double-crossed me and came in first in a photo. Can you believe that? Anyway, it's getting so you can't trust nobody! . . . Eddie, I said I'll have the full money for you *Friday*. Have I ever broke a promise to you? . . . Okay, that's more like it. See you Friday. Have a nice day."

He hangs up the phone and stares thoughtfully into space.

30

Diana Smith (interview taped 10/20/91)

So that was how it started, our love affair. I spent many weekends at the farm after that, whenever Connie went out of town. Fortunately for us, she traveled a lot. She went to all the collections—in London, Paris, Rome, Milan, even to Tokyo, where there were a couple of Japanese designers she admired. Her Tokyo trips were longer, and that meant Si and I could often spend two consecutive weekends together. And the store paid for all this glamorous travel of hers, I happen to know. Because she was considered an international fashion figure, her trips could be written off by calling her a fashion scout.

I'll say one thing about the man I loved. He may have had a lot of other women before me, but after he met me I was the only one. I know that, because he swore it to me, and I believed him.

We did take a couple of trips together, while she was away. We spent one weekend in Las Vegas and another in Atlantic City. He chose touristy places like that because there was less chance of him running into any of his fancy

Tarkington's ladies there, and being recognized. We even talked of a weekend at Disneyland, but we never got around to it. He was always nervous traveling with me. We had to sit in separate sections of the plane. In a hotel, he always wanted separate bedrooms for us. Partly it was fear of us being discovered. But also, when the lovemaking was over, he always liked to go to his own room to sleep. I didn't mind that. Two people sleeping in the same bed together isn't always all that great, you know. People snore. They fart. Separate bedrooms are more romantic, it seems to me, and, besides, I think Si liked tapping on my bedroom door in the morning and having me let him in, all showered, shaved, and smelling nice.

I do remember one bad moment at Las Vegas, when he *was* recognized. We'd registered under phony names, of course, and we were sitting by the pool at Caesar's Palace, just minding our business and reading our paperbacks, and a waiter came over and said, "Excuse me, sir, but aren't you Mr. Silas Tarkington? I used to be a room service waiter at the Ritz-Carlton in Boston, and I remember serving breakfast to you and Mrs. Tarkington. It was June of nineteen-seventy. I never forget a face, and I never forget a date."

Si jumped to his feet. *"You . . . are . . . mistaken!"* he shouted. When Si got angry, he had a temper almost as bad as mine. He picked up one of the poolside chairs, and I thought he was going to brain the poor guy with it. "Get the hell away from here, or I'll report you to the manager for annoying the guests!" he said. Then he threw the chair into the pool.

The poor waiter backed away. "Sorry, sir," he mumbled.

Then Si grabbed my arm and said, "C'mon," and we went back up to our rooms where we could have some privacy.

But on the whole those little weekend trips were happy times. I dug out some photographs to show you, and these are pretty rare, you know, because he didn't like to have his picture taken. This was taken in Las Vegas, in the dining room of the hotel, the two of us having dinner. Don't we look happy? It was taken by a couple we'd met earlier in the day. The wife came over to our table, and handed this to me, and said, "The two of you look so much in love that we decided to take your picture." Si started to get angry and asked to have the negative. But when the woman explained that the picture was taken with a Polaroid so there wasn't any negative, he simmered down.

This is just a silly picture of the two of us taken on the Boardwalk at Atlantic City, with our heads poked through cardboard cutouts that make us look like a couple of tramps. He wasn't too worried about anybody recognizing him in *that* picture. . . .

This is Atlantic City again, the same trip, some pictures of me he took on the beach, and these are some pictures I took of him. . . .

This is my favorite picture of him, I think. Even though he's got his hand across his eyes to shade them from the sun, you can see what a handsome man he was. And look at that physique. Isn't that the body of a much younger man? Look how well he fills out a bikini. I bought him that bikini, mostly as a joke, because I was always teasing him about how well endowed he was. I think this was the only time he ever wore it, but I think he looks pretty sexy in it, and I told him so. Of course I can't expect you to call another man sexy, but to me that's a pretty damned sexy man. That's why the difference in our ages never mattered.

Of course he never worried about these photos. They were all taken with my camera. He trusted me. He knew I'd never show them to anyone. But now that he's dead, it doesn't matter, does it? And it's nice to have these to help remember some of our happy times.

Still, he was always most relaxed at the farm—eighty-two acres of total seclusion and privacy, with the entrance gate closed and locked, the servants let go for the weekend, nobody to disturb us. Of course I wondered how much the servants, especially Milliken, knew about what was going on. But I imagine he paid them well enough so they'd keep their lips well buttoned.

During our weekends at the farm, he told me I was to treat the place as though I owned it. It was at the farm that he first mentioned marriage to me.

"I'd love to be married to you, Smitty," he said. "So we could go out in public, wherever we wanted, and not be hiding all the time."

"I'd love that too," I said. "Would Connie ever give you a divorce?"

"I don't know," he said. "I just don't know."

"Could you ever get anything on her that would give us a little leverage with her?" I asked him.

"Like catch her in bed with one of her fag designers? I doubt that," he said.

"What about her denying you your—you know, your attentions? Your rights as her husband?" You see, I was already working on a plan of my own that might give us a little leverage with Connie.

"That's been more or less mutual for some time now," he said.

He was always comparing me with Connie. He told me I was the best thing that had ever happened to him. He told me I was the first woman who really understood him, including his mother. He told me I was the first woman who'd really shown an interest in his business.

You see, the thing he liked about me was that I was more his kind of woman. I'm a down-to-earth person. I was brought up always to tell the truth, to be completely honest, and not to try to pretend that I'm something I'm not, like that bitch he married. Connie was, and is, nothing but a decorative detail, like one of the red ribbons on her canopy bed. He never really felt at ease with Connie and her so-called friends in the so-called International Set. But he felt comfortable with me. He could be himself with me: warm, humorous, spirited, down-to-earth, no pretense.

"Do you know what I love about you?" he said to me once. "You're common."

"Common?"

"Yeah, like me. I may run a fancy store, but deep down I'm as common as dirt."

"Well, I guess that's a compliment," I said with a laugh.

"Hell, yes! You call a man's cock his cock, which is what it is. You don't mince words and call it a wee-wee. When you go to the toilet, you go to the toilet, not the powder room."

"Like—*she* does?"

"Yeah. And speaking of cocks, I've got a stiff one. Let's fuck."

"Right here in the Japanese garden?"

She had a garden she called her Dell Garden, landscaped in a Japanese style, with an artificial lake and an arched bridge, and we were walking there. Like everything else she did, it was perfect. Too perfect.

"Yeah, let's muss up all these carefully raked little Japanese pebbles of hers. The gardener will think the dog did it."

"Those little pebbles do look temptingly smooth," I said. American pebbles wouldn't do for Connie, of course. Her pebbles had to be imported from Kyoto.

"Whaddaya say?" he said.

"I say okay!" I said.

You see, when he talked with me, he even spoke differently—more down-to-earth, more direct. People always talked and wrote about Si's *courtly* manners, his *polished* poise, his *impeccable* tailoring, his *suave* bearing, his *dignified* appearance. That was just his corporate pose, his boardroom manner. With me, he was uncourtly, unpolished, non-impeccable, non-suave, and downright undignified. With me, he could loosen up and be himself. With me, he was just the overgrown kid from the Bronx that he really was at heart. He could let his hair down. He didn't have to put on an act.

I hope you can get that across in your story—the other side to his personality that he showed to me. He was really like two different people, the public figure that everyone else saw and the private man he was with me.

Love letters? No, I never wrote him any love letters, and he never wrote any letters to me. Are you kidding? That would have been much too dangerous. Letters can be found, lying around. We had to be very careful, particularly at the store, so no one would suspect what was going on. At the store, it was no more than a wave and a "Good morning, Mr. Si." If I had any business with Si, I was careful to route it through Tommy Bonham, who was more and more beginning to run things for him.

Meanwhile, the person at the store I began to dislike more and more was Tommy Bonham. I decided Tommy Bonham was a hagfish. Do you know what a hagfish is? It's a particularly nasty little marine creature of the South Pacific. When it gets swallowed by a bigger fish, it doesn't get digested and it doesn't die. Instead, it starts feeding on the innards of the bigger fish until the bigger fish dies. Then the hagfish swims away, looking for its next meal, which will be some other poor fish's mouthful. To me, that describes Tommy to a T. To me, that's what Tommy's doing right now, sucking up to Miranda, looking for his next meal. I just hope she's not foolish enough to swallow his bait.

A year or so ago, I even began to suspect that Tommy was plotting something against Si. I had a question to ask Tommy about some merchandise I'd ordered, and I went up to his office. Linda, his secretary, was away from her desk, and I started to go in when I saw he was with somebody—a fat man—so I stepped away without their seeing me.

I heard Tommy say, "Si isn't going to like this little scheme, you know."

"But that's the beauty part of this particular proposition," I heard the fat man say. "Si ain't gonna know whether he likes it or not likes it, because Si ain't gonna know about it!"

Later, I ran into Linda, who'd become sort of a pal of mine, in the ladies' room. "Who was that fat man in Tommy's office this morning?" I asked her casually, as though I really didn't care.

"That," she said with a wink, "was the famous Mr. Moses Minskoff. Watch out for him. He's a fanny-pincher. And also a tit-grabber."

"I thought he hardly ever came into the store."

"Son-of-a-bitch hardly ever does. Today, we had a rare treat. My left nipple is still sore."

So that was the other half of Harriet Minskoff, who liked to be called Honeychile, formerly of the funny jewelry, more recently in the luggage business. I saw the Minskoffs again, that night when people gathered at the farm after Si . . . died. But I didn't speak to them. In fact, I gave them both a wide berth. I was only there for a few minutes, to pay my respects. I didn't want to go at all, but Connie begged me to come. She said I *deserved* to be there, which I thought was a funny way of putting it. Like it was my . . . punishment, or something.

Anyway, neither of the Minskoffs looked like the kind of people who would have been old family friends of Si's. And the scrap of conversation I'd overheard certainly didn't sound at all friendly. I debated whether to tell Si about it but decided against it at the time. After all, Tommy might have struck me as a hagfish, but he was still Si's second in command, and Si relied on him for a lot of things, and I didn't want to stir up trouble. One troublemaker in the organization was enough.

But then last year, after the two suburban stores folded—which had been Tommy's idea, and which I'd argued against—I ran into Tommy in the corridor and said, "I'm really sorry about White Plains and Morristown, Tommy. I know you put a lot of work into those stores, even though I questioned their feasibility at the time."

He gave me a really evil look and said, "Are you implying that Si should have listened to *you* and not to *me*?"

Now, mind you, I didn't want to get into it with Tommy. I didn't want to lay my job, or maybe my career, on the line by getting into it with him. I didn't like him, but I didn't want to make him my enemy. He could have been a very dangerous enemy to have. He was still the executive V.P. and general manager of the company, and I was just a buyer for one department. On the other hand, I had thought my position with Si was secure enough so I could speak to Tommy about the business as a peer. I realized I was mistaken, so I simply said, "Of course

I wasn't implying that, Tommy. I'm just sorry that the suburban stores didn't work out. We all are."

"Just because you're fucking the boss, don't get the idea that you're going to run the place," he said.

I thought, How does he know that, unless, with his hagfish way of thinking, Prettyboy Bonham just figured it was a good guess? But that remark really made me mad. My pressure valve blew. "I think you're the one who's fucking the boss!" I said.

He was smiling a really nasty smile. "Don't forget, I'm the one who lined the two of you up for your very first fuck," he said. "I do that for all his girls. And I'll be around here long after you're gone and forgotten, sweetheart."

"You really are a shit, aren't you?" I said.

"You're not stupid enough to think he'll ever marry you, are you?" he said.

"He's asked me to! He's even picked out a ring!"

It was true. There was a beautiful diamond ring I'd taken on consignment from an estate sale. Three point nine carats. He'd promised to buy it for me as soon as he was able to divorce Connie. It was the same ring, incidentally, that Miranda either pinched or borrowed from my department the day I quit my job.

"You stupid fool," he said. "You're even stupider than I thought you were. He's always got a ring picked out—for all his girls. He'll never leave Connie."

"He wants to!"

"He'll never leave her. She means too much to him. You mean nothing to him. To him, you're nothing more than a convenient weekend piece of ass."

"Liar!"

He was still smiling. "You'll see," he said. "And by the way, Smitty, stop in the ladies' room on the way back to your department. Your lipstick's on crooked." Then he walked away.

Well, after that little scene, I was so furious with him, and I hated him so much, I decided to tell Si about the little conversation I'd overheard between Tommy and Minskoff. Also, I was a little scared. Tommy could have tried to have me fired on the spot for the way I'd spoken to him that afternoon, and if push came to shove between Tommy and me—well, I just didn't know what might happen. Would Si let Tommy fire me? I suddenly didn't know. But I decided I'd better cover my tracks or else I'd be right in the middle of a very ticklish office situation.

So I told Si about Tommy and Minskoff. He didn't seem too surprised, but he seemed very interested. He kept nodding his head, and there was a grave expression on his face. Finally, he said, "Thank you for this information." And so I think I planted a little seed in Si's mind that Tommy was not to be trusted, that he was up to no good, that he and Minskoff were plotting something. Because right after that I know Si was starting to think of ways to ease Prettyboy out of the company. And I'm certain that if Si hadn't died when he did, he'd have figured out a way to get rid of Tommy—to vomit out the hagfish.

Oh-oh. Your tape's run out. . . .

They are sitting in the living room of Smitty's small apartment in Morningside Heights, not far from Columbia University. Winter is coming, the days are shortening, and though it is not yet five o'clock, the sky outside her windows is already growing dark. From the street below, there is a rattle of trash cans being emptied into the revolving maw of the collector's truck. She reaches out and turns on the bridge lamp beside her chair, and nervously twists the gold bracelet on her left wrist. The lamplight reveals tiny lines at the corners of her eyes and mouth, and suddenly Peter Turner feels intensely sorry for this woman.

"Never mind the tape recorder," he says. "There are only a few more questions I want to ask you."

She reaches for another Salem, and lights it with a match, and inhales and exhales noisily, like a man. "The only thing he didn't like about me was my smoking," she says. "Of course we couldn't smoke in the store, not even in the ladies' room."

"Connie smokes."

She nods. "You *are* going to write a fine and beautiful story about him, aren't you?" she asks. "Because he was such a fine and beautiful man. So bighearted. Maybe too bighearted. That may have been his only flaw."

"I'll try," he says. "Now let's talk for a minute about how he died."

She twists the gold bracelet, staring at the lighted cigarette in her hand. "How he died?" she says. "Everyone knows how he died. He died of a heart attack. That's what the newspapers said. That's what his doctor said."

"Did you have any idea that he had a bad heart, Smitty?"

"No . . . but these things can happen suddenly to a man that age, I guess."

"When was the last time you saw him alive?"

"Oh, dear. You're asking me for specific dates again."

"Can you remember?"

Her eyes shift focus, and she appears to be looking inward, at herself. "Let's see," she begins. "It must have been four, maybe five days before he died. Maybe a week. He came here. That was unusual in itself. He hardly ever came here. But he came here, and he sat right in that chair where you're sitting now."

"How did he seem?"

"He was . . . upset. He'd tried to have it out with Connie . . . told her he wanted a divorce, to marry me. But she'd refused. Told him that if he tried to divorce her, she'd create all sorts of nasty publicity. He kept saying, 'It's no use. It's no use.'

"I said . . . I said, 'Well, if she's going to threaten bad publicity, we can threaten some bad publicity of our own, can't we?' He said, 'How can we do that?' I said, 'What if we were to let it out that she made you sweep your own mother under the rug? That she made you pretend your mother was dead? When in fact she's alive and well and living on West End Avenue?' He just kept shaking his head and saying, 'No, no, that won't work. That would just make me look like a shit for letting her make me do a thing like that in the first place.'

"That had been my plan—to make her look like a shit. But I could see his point, that it could make him look like a shit as well, and his reputation was more important than hers."

"And then?" Peter asks.

"And then . . . and then . . . and then I think I said something like, 'Darling, let's just let the dust settle for a few days. Let's let things simmer down, and maybe in a few days we can both think more clearly.' And then I said something like, 'It doesn't matter, darling. No matter what happens we'll still have each other. No matter what happens, we'll always love each other.' But he kept shaking his head. 'No, no,' he said. 'She wants me to give you up.' Then he began to cry.

"Can you believe it, Peter? This great man, who'd met with heads of state, was actually . . . crying. He sat all hunched over in that chair, actually sobbing. That's what that wife of his had reduced him to . . . to tears . . . that great man. I went and sat on the arm of the chair and put my arms around him, cuddled him like a baby, and tried to comfort him." She stubs out her cigarette angrily in her overflowing ashtray and immediately lights another, and in the flare of the match he thinks he sees tears standing in her eyes.

"And then what happened?" he asks gently.

"And then . . . and then . . . I don't really remember. You see I still thought my plan to embarrass Connie might work, perhaps if I approached it from a different angle. And then . . . oh, yes, I remember. After he calmed down, he began talking about his will. He was rewriting his will, he said. Isn't that strange? It was almost as if he knew he was going to die, because he was rewriting his will. He told me he was leaving me five million dollars in it. 'You don't have to do that,' I said. 'I want to,' he said. He also told me that he was leaving his art collection to the Metropolitan Museum, along with funds enough to pay my salary as special curator of the collection so I'd always have a job, if they didn't want me at the store after he was gone. He wanted to be sure I was taken care of, he said. And he told me he'd also decided to reinstate a bequest to his son Blazer in the will, because he'd decided to forgive Blazer. But what happened to all those bequests?"

Suddenly she lets out a little shriek. The lighted cigarette in her ashtray has ignited several other filtered butts, and a column of acrid smoke is rising from the ashtray.

She jumps to her feet, carrying the smoldering ashtray, and runs into her bathroom. Peter hears the hiss of live ashes hitting water and the sound of the toilet flushing.

"I *do* smoke too much," she says, returning with the ashtray in one hand and her cigarette in the other. She stands in the doorway. "So," she says. "What happened to those bequests? Answer me that one, Peter. Obviously, Connie got him to change all that. There was nothing left to Blazer. There was no five million left to me. And the art collection? There's been nothing in the papers about that, and there surely would have been if it had been left to the Met. Look at all the ink Walter Annenberg's collection got. But the Tarkington Collection? Not a word about it. I've called the museum a couple of times, about that and about my alleged curatorship. All they'll say to me is, 'We suggest you take the matter up with Mrs. Tarkington.' Well, you know how far I'd get if I tried taking the matter up with *her*. Obviously she got him to change everything, so that everything was left to her and Miranda. I got zilch, Blazer got zilch, and the museum got zilch. That's Connie Tarkington for you." She returns to her chair and lights another Salem. From the street below, a police siren wails.

"Did Si say anything more to you that night, Smitty?"

"No. He had to leave. We kissed goodbye. Oh, yes . . . yes, he did say, 'I don't think I could ever live without you.' Something like that. I didn't take that too seriously. After all, maybe she could refuse to give him a divorce. But how could she prevent us from meeting on weekends at the farm when she was away, the way we'd always done? I didn't see how she could stop us from doing that."

"And so that was that," he says.

"Yes—the next time I saw him—no, I never saw him again."

He hesitates. "Do you have any idea what could have happened to his television set?"

Her eyes flash. "What television set? What do you mean?"

"There was a television set that was given to him by President Ford. He used to place it by the pool when he swam his laps."

"Oh, yes. I guess I do remember that. He never did it when we swam together, though. No, I loved him, you see, and so—"

"The TV set is missing."

"Well, I don't know anything about that," she says. "No, no."

"Milliken says there might have been a prowler on the estate that day."

"Prowler? How would a prowler get in? There's an electric gate that you have to know the code for. There are electrified fences all around the property. But yes—there could have been a prowler!"

"I guess what I'm trying to say, Smitty," he says carefully, "is, when he said 'I don't think I could ever live without you,' do you think he was planning *not* to go on living without you?"

"You mean did he—oh, no. But wait! Wait! There was something he said once, I remember it! It was about Miranda; she worried that the TV set might fall into the pool and electrocute him. And he said to me once, 'You know, if things ever get too much for me, that's what I'll do: I'll jump into the pool and pull the TV set in behind me and that will be it, fast and neat.' I thought he was only joking. But—but could that have been what happened? Was that why he was so upset the night he came here? Did he commit suicide—because of me? Oh, no, not because of me!"

"But why wasn't the TV set found in the water with him?"

"Connie! Connie did something with it—hid it—

something! But it wasn't because of me, it was because of Connie! Because she wouldn't give him the divorce. Because she was going to make him give up the only woman he'd ever loved, ever truly been happy with! Connie will try to put the blame on me, but she's the one who made him do it! Oh, God . . . poor Si. . . ." Suddenly her face drops into her hands, and she begins to sob. "Oh, I can't bear it," she cries. "I can't think . . . I can't bear to think that. . . ." The ash falls from her cigarette and lands on the carpet.

Peter rises from his chair, steps to her, and puts his hand on her shoulder. "I didn't mean to upset you, Smitty," he says.

She looks straight up at him through streaming eyes, her face streaked with tears. "Oh, no," she sobs. "You don't understand. That's not what I'm thinking. I'm thinking that Tommy was right, that he'd never leave her for me. Tommy was right! He knew all along! Tommy called me a stupid fool for believing anything Si said to me. He said I was a stupid fool for falling in love with him, for believing that he was in love with me, for believing that he'd ever marry me. Is that what I was, Peter, a stupid fool? Was that what I was all along? Just a *stupid, stupid* fool?"

It is early morning, and Moses Minskoff, still in his office on West 23rd Street, has been busy for most of the night on the telephone.

"Jesus H. Christ, Moe!" Smyrna's voice is yelling in his ear. "Do you know what time it is? It's three o'clock in the morning!"

"Yeah, but I got some important things for you to do. You writing this down? Okay. First, I want you to call Vince, the insurance agent, and take out a ten-million-dollar accident policy on Honeychile. . . . That's right. Ten mil. On Honeychile. Accident policy, with me the beneficiary. Then tell him I want another ten-million accident policy on me, with Honeychile the beneficiary. Tell him it's something Honeychile and I have worked out together, in case anything should happen to either of us, so he won't think anything funny is going on.

"Next get over here and I'm gonna give you a bunch of Visa cards, with their access codes, and I want you to go to as many automatic teller machines as you need to and cash out each of those accounts to the max. Got that? To the max, till the red light comes on and says 'No more cash' or whatever the hell it says. Okay?

"Now, using some of that cash, I want you to go to the Bahama Airlines ticket office and buy two tickets to Nassau for Honeychile and me. First class. One way. They got a flight goes out of Kennedy at seven-fifteen P.M. this coming Friday the fifteenth, that's day after tomorrow. Next, you're going to Argentine Airlines and buy a ticket for me to Buenos Aires. They got a seven o'clock flight, same date. Get me on that. One way, economy. . . . Whaddaya mean the airlines will think it's funny me going two places the same night? I'm talkin' two different airlines, dummy! Two different airlines don't talk to each other! Does Macy's tell Gimbels? Stop askin' a lotta dumb questions and do like you're told. You got all that? . . . Okay, I'll see you back here in the office when you got all that done."

He hangs up the phone and immediately places another call.

"Eddie? . . . Moe here. Sorry to call you so late at night, but I got a really big job for you this time, buddy. You did so great on that tail job that I'm gonna reward you with a big one. . . . How big? Well, how's ten grand sound to ya, okay? Now listen carefully. You're gonna take Honeychile for a ride, only she's not comin' back, if you receive my meaning. . . . Yeah, I know you don't like to do jobs like that. That's why I'm offering you ten big ones. . . . Yeah, I know it's too bad, but my mother warned me I'd have trouble when I married so much a younger woman. She told me I'd have trouble with her sooner or later, and now I got it. . . . Yeah, you guessed it. She's been gettin' it off with this Turner guy. . . .

"Okay, listen carefully. Friday afternoon, around

four o'clock, you're to come to my office. . . . Yeah, I'll have your tail fee for you. I'll be giving you two tickets to Nassau. . . . Not Nassau, Queens. Nassau, the Bahamas. Then you go up to the apartment and pick up Honeychile. She'll be ready. She'll be expecting you. You're gonna hand her the two tickets. You're gonna drive her out to Kennedy, and tell her I'm gonna meet her there at the gate for the plane. But she ain't gonna get to the airport, right? . . . Naw, I don't care how you do it. I don't even want to know. You figure that part out. . . .

"Yeah, I know you don't like these jobs, but somebody's gotta do it. Here's the deal. I'm gonna give you two grand in advance, plus your tail money, when you get the tickets. Then eight grand more when the job is done, which I should have proof of by Monday morning, right? You stop by my office Monday morning, and I'll have the rest of your dough for you. . . .

"Oh, I almost forgot. When it's over, save those airplane tickets. Get them off her, after it's done, and bring 'em back to my office on Monday. If I should happen not to be in, give 'em to Smyrna, 'cause there's a chance I may not be in the office by Monday. . . . Yeah, Smyrna will also have the rest of your dough for you. You can trust Smyrna. Have I ever broke a promise to you? . . . Okay. And remember, whatever you're gonna do, you're gonna make it look like an accident. Thanks, Eddie, and you have a nice day till I see you on Friday."

Now he makes one final phone call. "Honeychile? Yeah, workin' late at the office again. But listen, I got news, great news for ya. You know like I said we was always gonna retire and live in the Bahamas? Well, we're finally gonna do it, Babycakes. I got two tickets, first class, for the both of us on a flight to Nassau this coming Friday night. Whaddaya think of that, Babycakes? . . . Yeah, your daddy thought you'd be real pleased. . . .

"Now, listen, lover, here's the deal. I'm gonna be pretty tied up down here between now and then, winding up the business and all that. So what I'm gonna do is have Eddie—you know, Eddie who does the occasional odd job for me—pick you up at the apartment about four-thirty Friday afternoon. Think you can be packed by then? . . . Good. Don't pack too much, 'cause remember we're gonna be livin' in the tropics. Don't bring no fur coats. . . . Never mind about the furniture. We can send back for what we need later, and we're not gonna need much 'cause what I got for us down there is a completely furnished villa by the sea. Just for Daddy and you.

"Think of it, Babycakes. A tropical paradise . . . us basking in the tropic sun, the breezes rustling the palm fronds, miles of sandy beaches, the blue crystalline waters of the sea, a furnished villa with a pool. I'll show ya the brochures when we're on the plane. Sound like heaven? It's gonna *be,* Honeychile. It's gonna *be.*

"Anyway, Eddie will give you the first class tickets for the both of us, and he'll drive you to Kennedy. I'll take a cab from here, and I'll meet you at the Bahama Airlines gate for our seven-fifteen P.M. flight to Nassau. . . .

"Yeah, I know that's allowing a lot of time. But you could hit traffic at that time of day, it being a Friday and all, and Eddie's a pretty cautious driver. He wants to make sure you don't miss that plane.

"Listen, Babycakes, there's just one more thing I wanna tell you while I got you on the line. I wanna say thank you, Honeychile, for being such a wonderful wife. You've been the best wife a guy could have, Honeychile. No, I don't mean to sound like I'm sayin' goodbye. I just wanna say thank you for waitin' so long for this, which is gonna be your reward. I just wanna tell you this before we start out our whole new life together. Our new and beautiful retired life in the Bahamas. Good night, Angel Face . . . sweet dreams . . . bon voyage."

31

"I've heard Tarkington's described as a unique store," she is saying to him. "And it certainly has a unique book-keeping system." Miranda and Peter are seated on the long white sofa in the living room of her apartment at 11 East 66th Street, with the big open carton on the cushion between them. A pencil perches in Miranda's hair. "I spent an hour and a half on the telephone with Tommy Bonham this afternoon, while he tried to explain his so-called system to me, and he still insists that everything that pertains to the store's business is right here in this box."

"What a mess!"

"Since you've already got your M.B.A., and it'll be years before I get mine, I thought maybe you could help me make some sense out of all this," she says. "But let me tell you what I've figured out so far. To begin with, there are lots of different bank accounts; I've counted seven-teen. There are a lot of checks that Tommy seems to have written to himself, marked *Expenses* or *Operating Cash*. These aren't for large amounts—a hundred dollars here, two hundred there—so I don't know if there's any point in questioning him on those. But here's another thing. The store apparently gave discounts to certain customers if they paid for merchandise in cash, or in checks written out to Thomas E. Bonham or to Silas R. Tarkington, and these checks were deposited in separate banks. But what happened to the cash is hard to tell.

"Certain other customers were offered rebates if they paid for merchandise in cash—just another form of discounting, I suppose. If, for instance, Mrs. X bought a three-thousand-dollar dress and paid for it in cash, she'd get a rebate of ten to fifteen percent. The rebate checks were paid from one or the other of two accounts, one called SPECIAL ACCOUNT and the other called GENERAL OPERATING ACCOUNT. I don't know whether there was anything shady about these deals, except they make us sound like we're in the used-car business."

"That would depend on what happened to the cash," he says.

"Again, I can't seem to find out. Incidentally, most of these rebate checks were signed by Tommy, but a lot were signed by Daddy, and a lot of *those* were not in his handwriting. Tommy signed them."

"Faking signatures is called forgery, I believe," he says.

"I know, but apparently Daddy had authorized Tommy to sign his name on certain accounts. Is it still illegal then?"

"I don't know. You'd have to ask a lawyer, Miranda."

"But I've also discovered something that went on that I *know* was illegal. Quite often, on purchases of expensive items—from Smitty's department, for instance—customers were allowed to take the items from the store. But the sales were written up to indicate that the items were being sent outside the city, to save the customer the state and city sales taxes. A customer would have an article sent to friends in Connecticut or New Jersey, and all these friends would actually receive would be empty boxes."

"Wasn't that one of the things they caught Leona Helmsley on?"

"Tommy says that sort of thing is done all the time. He says it's a routine favor for a good customer, that stores all over town do it all the time."

"Hmm," he says.

"Anyway, to get back to the discount-rebate business. One thing that doesn't seem quite right is that all these sales were written up as having been made for the full retail price. That made our figures look much better than they really were, and this was evidently useful when the store went to the banks for loans."

"That doesn't sound kosher to me," he says.

"Nor to me. Now here's where it begins to get a little complicated. I'm not sure I understand, but this is the way Tommy explained it to me. The store tries to keep a kind of rolling inventory in every department: for example, so many sweaters, in so many styles, sizes, and colors, at all times. To finance this inventory there's something called the Retail Credit Corporation in Atlanta—R.C.C., he calls it. R.C.C. pays our major vendors direct and gets paid whenever we sell an item of merchandise, and whenever we order new merchandise, R.C.C. adds to our credit account. But on certain months, Tommy would report fewer sales to R.C.C. than there actually were, so R.C.C. would roll over the indebtedness on this merchandise, and Tommy would deposit the proceeds in a separate bank account."

"It sounds to me," he says, "as though, if this sort of thing were kept up, you'd end up with no merchandise at all and an enormous debt."

"That's what I said to Tommy! I said it sounds like taking out a mortgage without telling the bank you've sold the house! But he assured me this is standard business practice. He calls it 'a form of borrowing against future profits.' He says the store obviously can't afford to do that sort of thing all the time; only in months when there are, as he puts it, 'certain cash flow problems.' He says that as long as the store is paying the interest to R.C.C. on this debt, which the store appears to have been doing, R.C.C. doesn't mind the arrangement. The only trouble is, for the last two or three years the debt has been growing, and so—naturally—has the interest cost."

"Naturally."

"The more questions I asked, the more annoyed he got. In explaining all this to me, Tommy kept saying that the most important thing a retail store has to do is to see that its vendors are paid on time. I agree. If the vendors aren't paid, they won't ship more merchandise, and without new merchandise you don't have a store. Most vendors want payment within ten days of delivery. But here's another thing I discovered, going through all these papers. Tommy has worked out different payment schedules with different vendors, depending on the size of the store's orders. For a larger order than usual, Vendor X will agree to wait fifteen or twenty days for payment. A few of the big French fashion houses—Dior, Chanel, Le Croix—where we place large orders for very expensive merchandise, will even give us thirty to sixty days to pay, even ninety. Tommy seems to have persuaded these people that the prestige of their presence at Tarkington's makes it worth it to them to wait for their money.

"Of course it doesn't seem fair to make some vendors wait to be paid longer than others, but since they've agreed, I guess it's not illegal. But it throws the value of our inventory way off kilter on the books. We're listing hundreds of thousands of dollars' worth of merchandise in our inventory that we haven't even paid for! But, again, that huge inventory figure seems to impress the banks when we go to them to borrow money—which we seem to have to do every six months or so."

Peter Turner runs his fingers through his curly dark hair and mutters, "Good Lord!"

"Here's another thing I discovered," she says. "I didn't realize how much of our merchandise is being sold on consignment. We're just acting as the seller's agent on this stuff. If the goods are sold, the store takes a commission. If they're not, they just go back to the consigner, and the store doesn't make a penny. But, again, Tommy lists all these consigned goods under INVENTORY at full price—a mink coat listed at ten thousand dollars, for example, when it's actually on consignment. Most of the garments in the fur department are on consignment. Those aren't Tarkington's assets at all, but listing them as assets—well, it impresses the banks.

"Which brings us to the store's Accounts Receivable, another item in the assets column: what our customers owe us. With Tarkington's famous liberal credit policy, we really show an *imposing* Accounts Receivable figure on the plus side—over eighteen million dollars! The banks seem to practically lick their lips with glee when they see this non-asset asset of ours! If they could figure out a way for us to collect these Accounts Receivable, it would be more helpful than handing us another loan, it seems to me!

"And now I'd like to introduce you to a mystery woman, Peter: Señora Lopez-Figueroa of Caracas. Every store should have a customer like Carmelita Lopez-Figueroa. She spends hundreds of thousands of dollars annually in the store—forty-two thousand in April, for example, seventy-three thousand in May. She shops in all departments, always by phone, but she seems particularly fond of precious stones, and she's given Smitty's department an enormous amount of business. No wonder Smitty's figures looked so great!

"There really is such a person. I checked Carmelita out. Her husband isn't just the president of the Banco de Venezuela, he owns it. And other Lopez-Figueroa relatives seem to own the rest of the country. I even found a letter from Carmelita's husband, authorizing her to charge as much merchandise at Tarkington's as she wanted. I think I sort of get the picture. Her husband probably has a mistress, maybe several. To keep Carmelita off his back and out of his hair, he gives her absolutely unlimited spending. Her bills are always promptly paid, with international money orders drawn on her husband's bank. Any store would kill to have a customer like Carmelita.

"But here's the thing that worries me about Carmelita. Her purchases are always marked 'Phone Order /

Charge/Send/Signature on File.' But when I went through the shipping orders in these records here, I couldn't find anywhere near enough shipping orders to match these sales slips. I began to wonder how many of these orders were actually shipped to her, how many were actual orders, and, if the merchandise was never shipped, what happened to it."

He rises from the sofa and walks to the window, his hands thrust deep in his jeans' pockets, and stands there, looking out.

"Did Bonham have any explanation?" he asks her.

"He said that unfortunately a lot of the computer disks that the shipping department kept its records on had been accidentally erased," she says.

He nods. "The Rose Mary Woods defense," he says.

"He was vague on other questions that I asked him, too. He kept changing the subject. He'd interrupt to tell me how the strong yen was hurting us. About how the South Koreans and the Vietnamese, with their cheap pelts, along with the animal rights activists, were killing the American fur business. How the downturn in the economy was hurting retailers all over. How interest rates had to come down before we'd see a real turnaround. When I asked him why we had to do so much borrowing —or 'leveraging,' as he calls it—he launched into a long lecture on how the Gulf War had affected our first-quarter profits."

"When in doubt, blame the Japanese. Or George Bush."

"The thing I didn't ask him was this: Peter, do you think that—with so many of the Lopez-Figueroa purchases coming from Smitty's department—Tommy and Smitty were somehow in collusion to cheat my father? If it's true, I'm in a terrible spot. I promised my mother that if she'd vote her shares with mine, I'd hire Smitty back. But if Smitty's a cheat, I can't possibly do that."

He turns and faces her. "I don't think that's true," he says. "I think Smitty is basically an honest woman. And I don't think she's really clever enough—or good enough with figures—to get involved in a rip-off scheme like that one. Besides, I think she and Bonham actively disliked each other."

"I thought so too. But suppose that was just an act, to throw everybody off?"

"No, I tend to believe her. I also think she was genuinely in love with your dad. I don't think she'd knowingly take part in a plan to cook the store's books and skim profits from your dad's store. But I think she was naïve enough to let Tommy Bonham use her department to post false sales."

Then what was a bottle of her perfume doing in his bathroom medicine cabinet? she almost asks him, but stops herself, the next question being, *What were you looking for in that medicine cabinet, Miss Miranda?* Instead, she says, "I did get Tommy to concede that the store might need some—financial restructuring, as he put it."

"Financial restructuring! My God, Miranda, that's what banana republics are always doing. That's what they're doing with the Texas S&L's. Financial restructuring is just a polite term for bankruptcy."

"Bankruptcy! Don't say that awful word, Peter!"

"Well, things don't look that great, do they?"

She nods and studies the backs of her hands, now ringless. "No," she admits. "And I haven't even mentioned the employees' retirement pension fund."

"Tell me about that," he says.

"As of the first of June, there was about three and a half million dollars in the pension fund account. But then there was another of these little cash-flow problems, as Tommy calls them. Some vendors were demanding to be paid and were refusing to make fall shipments until they were. And so it was decided—and Tommy insists that all these decisions were made jointly, between him and Daddy—that the pension fund should be subsumed— Tommy's word—temporarily into the store's general operating account. No one expected anybody to be retiring soon, least of all Pauline O'Malley, our oldest employee, who everybody assumed would be staying with the store forever, so I suppose it seemed like a practical move at the time. But now Pauline's very upset. Her brother-in-law, who's a C.P.A., wants her to hire a lawyer."

"And what does our friend Tommy Bonham propose to do about that?" he asks her.

She sighs, discouragedly. "He says we just may have to do some more leveraging," she says. "But I've saved my biggest shocker for the last. The two ill-fated suburban stores. I found out that the contract to build the Morristown store was given to something called the Peterloon Construction Company of Paramus, New Jersey. I thought: Peterloon—that's a strange name. I decided to find out what I could about them. Well, I didn't find out much, except that Peterloon Construction declared bankruptcy in nineteen eighty-nine. But I did find out that the C.E.O. of Peterloon was a man named Saturnino Salas. I also discovered that the land on which the store was built was leased from an outfit called Wellington Partners. Wellington Partners is still in business, and guess who owns Wellington Partners? Saturnino Salas."

"Same guy!"

"Apparently. And how many people do you know named Saturnino Salas?"

"Nobody."

"Saturnino Salas is the name of Tommy Bonham's Filipino houseboy, Nino. Funny coincidence?"

"My God, you mean he's the brains behind—"

"Hardly. The boy can barely speak English, much less work out a deal like this one. The land lease was for ten years. Our company is still paying rent to Wellington Partners—to the tune of a million dollars a year."

"Dummy corporations. . . ."

"Exactly. And now we can see why Tommy was so eager to open those suburban outlets."

"And it didn't matter to him whether they succeeded or not. Either way, he'd collect his money on the lease."

"That's right," she says. "And this only involves the New Jersey store. What do you suppose we'll find when we look into what happened in White Plains?"

"Probably the same damned thing!"

"That's what I'm assuming," she says.

"Damn it, Miranda, you've got enough evidence already to send this guy to jail!"

"I thought of that," she says. "But is that what we want at this point? The publicity alone could kill us."

"Okay, so let's talk about assets for a minute. What are the store's tangible assets?"

"Well, we do own the Fifth Avenue building. It's prime business property, on one of the most desirable street corners in Manhattan. Unfortunately, we seem to have taken out another million-and-a-half-dollar mortgage in January."

"Oh, me, oh my." He shakes his head.

"Oh, and I almost forgot one other minor mystery, the E.K. bonus. With Tommy's accounts and Daddy's accounts and the store's accounts all mixed up in here, I began to notice deposit tickets—to Tommy's account—with monthly items marked *E.K. bonus,* always for five hundred dollars and always in cash. Tommy got really testy when I asked him what that was all about. At first he said it was a private arrangement he had with my father and he couldn't discuss it. When I pressed him, he said that E.K. stood for Extra Kindness. He said that whenever a Tarkington's employee demonstrated a little extra kindness to a customer, he or she was rewarded with an E.K. bonus at the end of the month, always in cash, prorated according to salary. He said it was a little system my father had worked out to improve employee relations and keep the unions from trying to move in on us. I must say I didn't find any evidence of any other employees getting E.K. bonuses, but Tommy seems to have gotten his every month for years—from the summer of 1970, not long after he joined the store, through the end of 1986. I know five hundred dollars a month isn't much, but over more than fifteen years it adds up to quite a bit. *I* never got any E.K. bonus, but then of course I never worked directly with the customers."

He frowns. "Look," he says quickly, "why don't you let me go through all these figures and papers you've got here and see if I can find a bottom line to all of this."

"Oh, that would be a big help, Peter," she says. "Maybe you can uncover some assets I couldn't find. And while you're doing that, I'll fix us a pot of coffee. No, wait. I've got an even better idea. Why don't I fix some dinner for us? Can you stay for dinner?"

"Hey, I'd love that!"

"Good. I make a mean lasagna."

"I don't want you cooking for me, Miranda. Why don't we just send out for pizza or Chinese, like the yuppies we are?"

"I'd rather cook," she says. "My head's so full of figures. I need to do something that will really drain my brain. For me, that's lasagna." She stands up. "If you need me, I'll be in the kitchen."

And Peter tackles the big box of records, out of which, he quickly sees, Miranda has already managed to create some sense of order and design.

Cats, when they are in doubt about what to do next, wash themselves. Women like Miranda Tarkington, when they are in doubt, cook. In her kitchen, she lines up her ingredients from her refrigerator and pantry shelves in the order in which they will be needed: Ground beef, olive oil, tomato sauce, pasta sheets, ricotta, mozzarella, Parmesan. She is a very orderly cook. As soon as she finishes using a utensil or a pot, she washes it and puts it away. There is never any mess when Miranda cooks. Orderliness makes the act of cooking seem that much more brainless, comforting, relaxing. System is the opposite of despair. A man, a plan, a canal: Panama.

It is very kind of Peter, she thinks, to offer to make some sense out of a boxful of loose papers, numbers and cryptic notations on file cards of different sizes and colors, and all the rest of it, the sorry detritus of her father's dream. But then Peter seems to her a very kind man, a very nice man. If you were looking for a nicer, kinder man than Peter Turner, that nicer, kinder man would be hard to find. She likes that healthy, curly, dark head of hair of his, and the fine brain beneath it. Yes, you are a fine fellow, suh!

She shapes the meat into balls the size of marbles, ready to brown them in the heated olive oil. Her pasta water has come to a boil.

Ten minutes later her baking dish is ready, its bottom covered lightly with tomato sauce. Now it is time for the layering to begin—first the pasta, then the cheeses, then more sauce, then the tiny meat balls, then another layer of lasagna—and I am doing all this for this fine, kind man whose name is Peter . . . a layer of pasta, then a layer of Peter, then . . .

She stands, a potholder in her hand, ready to place the completed masterpiece of Peter pasta into her preheated Thermidor when she realizes he is standing at the kitchen door and watching her. His expression is difficult to read.

"Could you come into the living room for a minute?" he says.

She puts the dish on the countertop and follows him wordlessly into the next room, the potholder still in her hand.

"I've done some figuring," he says. "It's worse than we thought. It looks as though the store is in the hole for at least twenty-seven million dollars—if this one box is really all there is."

She sits down hard on the white sofa. "In the hole . . ."

"In the red."

"Twenty-seven million . . ."

"At least."

"Well," she says with a little shudder. "That's that."

"I'm afraid so, Miranda."

"Tell me something," she says. "How much of this do you suppose my father knew about?"

"That's hard to say, isn't it? But toward the end I imagine he knew quite a bit, if not everything. But by then he was trapped. He was in a corner. He was between a rock and a hard place, with no place to move. He was trapped by those two."

"Two?"

"Tommy Bonham and Moses Minskoff."

She gestures vaguely toward the cardboard carton. "I didn't see Moses Minskoff's name on any of those papers."

"Neither did I. I didn't expect to. Moses Minskoff kept a very low profile in his dealings with your father."

"The two of them."

"Not that they were working as a team. Just the opposite, in fact. Each of those two men was out to get whatever he could from your father, each on his own, each guy out for himself. Minskoff started years ago. Bonham started later, but they were both bleeding your father, each in his own way. You see, what seems to have happened is that about four or five years ago your father began turning full control of the store's finances over to Bonham. He let himself look the other way while Bonham handled things. That's when the shenanigans started with the R.C.C., and the banks, and the phony sales to South American ladies. Then, six or eight months ago, something—it may have been something Smitty told him —made your father suspicious, and he started looking into things. But by the time he found out what was going on, it was too late. He was trapped. The debt was too big. When he died, I imagine he was looking for some way out —some honorable way out."

"Tell me something else," she says. "Do you think that all the trouble he was in, and that the store was in, would have caused him to—to take his own life?"

"I don't know," he says. "Smitty thinks so."

She nods.

"No wonder Tommy Bonham wants to marry you." Dully: "Why?"

"Until he died, your father was in his pocket. Now Tommy wants you in his pocket."

She nods again. "Partners." Then she says, "I think I need a drink."

"Lillet?"

"Something stronger. A real drink. Whiskey."

"Where?"

She points to the liquor cabinet.

He goes to the cabinet, where he finds whiskey, glasses, an ice bucket. He fixes strong, dark drinks for them both. Then he returns and hands her drink to her. She takes a quick sip and makes a small, wry face. "My mother used to say that the first sip of Scotch always tasted to her like dirty socks," she says. Then she says, "Well, that's it. I quit."

"Quit?"

"Yes, quit. I'm out of this. I'm not going to fight this takeover any longer."

He sits beside her on the sofa. "You can't quit now, Miranda!"

"I can't drag my mother into this mess. I can't drag Aunt Simma into this. And my grandmother, who's ninety-six! Let Continental Stores inherit this whole can of worms."

"There are things you can do, Miranda, legal things."

"And destroy Tarkington's reputation? No, thanks."

"Don't quit now," he says. "You've gone too far to quit now."

"There's no point in going any farther."

"There is! Now you know what you're dealing with. The cards are all on the table now. You can't quit now."

"The card game's over, Peter."

"Please don't quit now—for my sake."

"Your sake?"

"I don't want you to be a quitter. Damn it, I'm not going to *let* you quit. I want to help you."

She looks up at him. She is still clutching the pot-holder in one hand. "But you've got a book to write."

"To hell with that. This is more important."

"To *you*?"

"Did you really remember me from Yale?" he says. "In a red shirt?"

"Certainly."

"I'm in love with you, Miranda."

She is still looking at him. "Funny," she says quietly.

"You're the second man this week who's said that to me."

"And one of them's a crook."

She begins to laugh, and her laughter makes him start to laugh, and all at once they are both laughing, laughing like children, giggling uncontrollably in each other's arms.

In his office on West 23rd Street, Smyrna is saying to her boss, "Listen, Moe. It seems like you're either flying to Buenos Aires or to Nassau in the Bahamas, one of those two places, on Friday night. Not that it matters to me which one. But would it be out of place for me to ask when you're planning to come back from whichever place it is? Or is that one of those secrets which a secretary isn't supposed to know?"

"Ah, Smyrna," he says. "I neglected to tell you that this office will be closing on Friday, and I shall not be needing your good services after that date."

"What?" she shrieks. "You mean you're firing me?"

"I believe 'terminated' is the word they're using at this point in time."

"What about severance pay? What about that?"

"Smyrna, ours has been a wonderful relationship. Let's not end it on an unpleasant note."

"You mean you're firing me without severance pay?"

"I didn't say that, did I? Let me take you to lunch at Harold's across the street around twelve-thirty, and we can discuss these various matters. Right now, I have some important calls to make."

"I'm not going to lunch at that greasy spoon!" she says, and flounces out of his office, slamming the door hard behind her. "Cheapskate!" she yells through the door.

In the anteroom, one of her phones is ringing. "Development Corporation, Limited," she says, her tone still angry. "Whom is calling? . . . No, I'm afraid Mr. Minskoff is in conference right now. . . . No, I do not know when would be a good time to reach him." Then she says,

"Listen, I don't know who the hell you guys are, but I'll tell you this much. This office is going to be closed after Friday, so you can lay off with these calls. . . . No, I know nothing of the bum's future plans." Then she says, almost sweetly, "Why don't you try Mrs. Minskoff? I believe you have her private number."

Farther uptown, it is Honeychile Minskoff's telephone that is ringing. She answers it and then gasps when she hears the voice on the other end of the line. "You can stop trying to frighten me!" she cries. "I don't care whether you're Julius or a friend of Harry the Heeb's or Don from Cleveland or Joe Blow from Kokomo! You can just stop trying to frighten me, 'cause my husband and I'll be leaving the country—permanently—Friday night! So there!" And she slams the receiver down into its cradle.

THE SCENE: *The interior of Moses Minskoff's inner office.*
THE TIME: *Ten o'clock Friday morning. Moses Minskoff is talking on the telephone.*

MINSKOFF: Yes, Mrs. Van Degan, I received your check in this morning's mail. Thank you very much. You have made a very wise investment, Mrs. Van Degan, very wise indeed. Your late husband would be very proud of you, I'm sure. He was a fine man, Truxton Van Degan, a fine man of high caliber, with whom it was always a great pleasure to do business. *(pause)* Yes, Mrs. Van Degan, I will be sending you the promissory notes you purchased by Federal Express today, and you should have them in your good hands by tomorrow morning. I just have to get the necessary documents out of my safe. *(He eyes the safe.)* By the way, Mrs. Van Degan, could I trouble you to give me your Federal Express account number, since I seem to have momentarily misplaced mine? . . . Mrs. Van Degan? Hello? Mrs. Van Degan, are you there? Hello?

He begins jiggling the buttons of the receiver up and down, then furiously pushes buttons for other lines.

MINSKOFF *(yelling):*   Smyrna! What the hell is going on here?

The lights come up in Smyrna's outer office. She is at her desk.

SMYRNA *(crossly):*   All right, all right. Hold your water.

She rises, with her pad, and enters his office.

MINSKOFF: All our phone lines just suddenly went dead. We paid the phone bill, didn't we?

SMYRNA *(sarcastically):*   So far as I know, Moe.

MINSKOFF: Run down to the corner to the pay phone and call Repair Service. Damn it, we pay for business service so we oughta get it.

Smyrna returns to her office and reaches for her coat and bag. The lights in both offices fade.

Cut to: Outside Moe Minskoff's building. It is a gray fall day. A sheet of newspaper blows in the wind. From right, a brightly painted panel truck appears and parks in front of Moe's building, next to a sign that reads, NO PARKING ANY TIME TOWAWAY ZONE. On the side of the panel truck is the legend "SIR PRIZE PARTIES, INC. Weddings. Banquets. Bar Mitzvahs. Corporate Meetings. Theme Parties. Special Events. Picnics. Conventions. Birthday Parties For All Ages. Hablamos Español." The panels of the truck are painted with colored balloons and grinning clown faces. Bunched Mylar balloons float from the truck's rooftop.

Inside the truck sit two clowns in whiteface with rouged cheeks and lips. One has an apple for a nose, the other a carrot. Both wear jesters' caps with bells.

Another vehicle appears, a dark blue Chevrolet Caprice, and pulls in just behind the party truck. Its driver wears a dark fedora and a black trenchcoat.

The two in clown costume wait in their truck, the ignition turned off. The driver of the Caprice waits in his car, slouched in his seat, his coat collar turned up, his hat brim turned down, his motor running.

Presently Smyrna emerges from the building, wearing a down-filled parka, and goes running off down the street.

Immediately, the two clowns step out of the truck and head for the door. One clown has his hands deep in the pockets of his red-and-white striped pantaloons. The other carries a suitcase.

A woman leading a little girl by the hand comes down the street.

WOMAN: Look, Robin. Some lucky child is going to have a nice birthday party.

CHILD: What's in that one clown's suitcase, Mommy?

WOMAN: Why, his bag of tricks, of course!

The two clowns disappear into the building, and the woman and child stroll off.

Silence. Then we hear the muffled sound of gunshots, nine in all.

Silence again. The two clowns emerge from the building, moving quickly. The suitcase carried by the second clown appears to be noticeably heavier. They jump into the back seat of the Caprice, and the driver pulls quickly away. The street is empty except for the abandoned party truck, its Mylar balloons tugging in the wind.

Presently Smyrna reappears, looking agitated. She enters the building.

The lights come up again on Moe's pair of offices. Smyrna enters the outer room.

SMYRNA *(yelling):*   They think somebody musta cut our phone lines, Moe! They won't be able to fix 'em till Monday.

She enters her boss's office. The first thing she sees is the wall safe, open, empty, its steel door hanging crazily on one hinge. Then she turns to her boss's desk.

He is tilted steeply backward in his big swivel

chair, and his yellow Ultrasuede vest is drenched
with blood. From the impossible angle that his head
hangs backward over the back of his chair, and from
the look of horror on Smyrna's face, it is clear that
his face has been completely blown away. Where his
head was, he wears a bib of blood.

SMYRNA *(A piercing scream. A pause. She sobs.):* Oh,
Moe . . . Moe . . . don't go away. Oh, please
don't leave me, Moe. They won't be able to fix the
phones till Monday, Moe. . . . But you won't be
here on Monday, will you, Moe? You're going to
Nassau, or else to Argentina. The tickets are in the
safe. . . .

> She sinks to her knees on the floor.
> *Curtain*

Part Four

CONSUELO'S GARDEN

32

"Moe Minskoff's death leaves us with some advantages, as well as some disadvantages," Jacob Kohlberg is saying to Consuelo Tarkington on the telephone. "On the plus side, Moe claimed to have some promissory notes of Si's that he was trying to peddle. If they ever existed, no evidence of them has turned up since the murder. The police have thoroughly searched his office and his apartment, and nothing of the sort has been found. The murderer or murderers emptied Moe's office safe at the time, and considering the—uh—nature of the decedent's demise, it seems unlikely that anyone will be coming forth to demand payment from Si's estate. So I think we're safely off the hook on that one, Connie."

"Good!"

"But on the down side, I'm sorry to say that Continental Stores has withdrawn its offer for your company. I've just had a long talk with Mr. Albert Martindale of Continental in Chicago. It seems that Minskoff was trying to act as broker in their acquisition. Martindale feels that, owing to the—uh—notoriety surrounding the murder case, he must ask his board of directors to bow out of the picture altogether, at least for the foreseeable future. Martindale doesn't rule out the possibility that his group might come back into the bidding at some future point, but, frankly, he doesn't sound sanguine about it."

"Bidding? Is there bidding, Jake?"

"Well, that's the other thing, of course. There really aren't any other offers at the moment—none, at least, that could be taken seriously."

"What about the Canadians? You mentioned a Canadian group."

"There was a Canadian consortium, yes, that was interested in talking to us. But considering the situation in Canada right now, that group has been unable to get the bank financing it hoped for."

"Just what I was afraid of," she says. "We've got a store for sale, but nobody who wants to buy us. We're going to have to go out and start begging for a purchaser."

"Well, I wouldn't say begging, Connie. Meanwhile, there've been a couple of meetings of the store's employees, and talk of the employees trying to buy Tarkington's. I don't know how far any of that talk has gotten. It seems to me a little bit like letting the lunatics run the asylum, but I've made it clear that we'll listen to any serious offer."

She sighs. "Well, let me talk all this over with Miranda," she says.

"Miranda?"

"She's taking a few days off from the store, staying here with me, and we've been talking about lots and lots of things." She hesitates, and then says, "Jake, what would you think of letting Miranda run the store?"

There is a silence. Then he chuckles. "All I can say is that if Si were here he'd hit the ceiling at that idea."

"But Si isn't here," she says quietly. "Is he?"

"How do *you* feel about it, Connie? Do you want to give the kid a chance?"

"That's what I'm thinking," she says. "Why not give the kid a chance?"

· · ·

"How did your meeting with Peter Turner go?" Her mother asks. They are seated at opposite sides of the candlelit dining table at the farm.

"Very well," she says noncommittally. "He's being very helpful, going over the store's books with me and so forth."

"He seems like such a nice young man."

"Yes."

"He'd be perfect for—"

She glances at her mother. "You were going to say perfect for *me,* weren't you, Mother?" she says.

Her mother smiles. "But I didn't, did I? I stopped just in time. Anyway," she says, changing the subject, "I'm glad you came back to the farm for a few more days. You've had the store's problems on your mind so much these past weeks. You deserve a little vacation. And I do enjoy your company, Miranda. Somehow, when your father was alive, there was never enough time—"

"For us to get to know each other."

"Yes."

She studies her mother's face across the table. "Tell me something, Mother," she says. "That afternoon at Jake Kohlberg's office, when he read Daddy's will and when Blazer blew up and said all those terrible things, he referred to Smitty as Daddy's mistress, which of course she was. You know it, and I know it. But you didn't bat an eyelash. It's as though you accepted it. And now you talk of wanting to help Smitty in some way. I don't quite understand. If I'd been in your shoes, I'd have resented Smitty terribly. I'd be delighted to see Smitty fall by the wayside."

She sighs. "I didn't accept it, exactly," she says. "But I understood your father. There were always other women in his life. There were other women long before he met me, and I knew there would be afterward. There's been a lot written lately about people who are sexual addicts. More men are addicted to sex than women, and I think your father was one of them. He simply had to have other women. He craved them. He got high on them, the way an alcoholic gets high on alcohol. He got a thrill from them, from the danger of them. They were like a narcotic to him. He was addicted to them, the way I'm addicted to—these." She reaches for another cigarette and lights it with a silver table lighter. "That's why he never criticized my smoking, though he disapproved of it. He knew he had his own, more dangerous addiction. When I married him, I knew I was going to have to live with that. It wasn't always easy, but I did. His first wife, Blazer's mother, couldn't live with it. Not all women can. But I knew I was going to have to. I knew it was useless to try to change him. He was never going to change. People don't change, Miranda. They just grow older, and a little tougher, if they're lucky. If all the psychiatrists in the world accepted this, they'd be out of business by this time tomorrow night. All of them. Remember you heard it here."

"But Smitty was different. He was going to marry her."

She shakes her head and fans the smoke away from her face with the long fingers of one hand. "No," she says. "He was never going to marry her. Oh, he may have led her to believe he was. He often did that, particularly as he grew older, and younger women became—harder to find. He'd lead them on. That wasn't very nice of him, of course. But then your father was not a perfect lover, just as he was not a perfect husband."

"I think you're wrong, Mother. I think he and Smitty had definite plans."

"No, no. I knew him too well. You see, there were things I could do for your father that no other woman could do. These weren't things I knew I could do in the beginning. But I discovered I could do them, and he discovered I could do them too."

"What sort of things?"

"For instance, of all the women that he—we can't say slept with, because he didn't sleep with them. But after each meeting, tryst, whatever you call it—Blazer would use the F-word, I suppose—he always came home to me. He never spent the night with any of them."

"Why was that?"

"He suffered from—well, let me start from the beginning. When he was nine years old, his baby sister was born, his sister Simma, who was always sickly. In those days, there was always a QUARANTINED sign on the family's front door. He had no idea what the sign meant, but he looked the word up in the dictionary and read the words 'disease,' 'pestilence,' 'plague,' 'isolation,' 'danger,' and 'death' in the definition. He began to believe he lived in a house that had a terrible curse on it, and he also began to be taunted by other children in the neighborhood about his baby sister. They were saying that Si's father wasn't the baby's real father, because she didn't look like anyone else in the family. She had bright red hair. They were saying that the baby's real father was another man, a friend of the family, who also had red hair. Si told me once that the only time his mother ever struck him was when he came home from school one day from the third grade and said, 'Are you a whore, Mama? Everybody says you're a whore.' He didn't even know what the word meant, but he'd looked it up. When she hit him, he took it to mean that what the other children said was true. After that, his relationship with his mother was never the same.

"That was when he began to have terrible nightmares and night sweats. He'd wake up in the night wringing wet. And yes, though this isn't very pleasant, he'd sometimes wet or soil his bed. He was too ashamed of these night terrors, as he called them, to ever let himself fall asleep at another woman's side. But I learned to cope with them. I could comfort him out of the terror, and I learned to deal with—the other matters. He trusted me with these secrets of his, which, as he grew older, became worse. Much worse, in fact. It wasn't easy, but I learned to cope. And it pleased me to think that I was the only woman he could trust to see him through his terrible nights, that I was the only woman he could lie down and try to sleep beside, that there were things I could do for him that no one else could do."

"You really loved him, didn't you, Mother."

"Oh, yes. There are so many things I could tell you about your father. I don't know why you and I have never talked like this before."

"You never seemed to want to."

"No, I suppose not. They seemed too private. But now it's as though he's finally released me, set me free to talk about these private things. And it's nice, isn't it? I've enjoyed this visit so, Miranda. It's nice to sit here in these quiet evenings on the farm, just you and I, and talk about love."

"Yes, it is. Nice."

"Yes. And now that I've told you that, I might as well tell you the rest. His doctor, Harry Arnstein, told me that these symptoms of his, the night terrors, might also be symptoms of tertiary syphilis—which is not transmittable at that stage, I hasten to assure you. But we don't know this for sure, because your father would never let Harry test his blood. So that's just a guess. But it was women, women, always women where your father was concerned."

Miranda's gaze at her mother is long and steady. "And so I suppose the little old lady on West End Avenue was just another one of Daddy's girlfriends that he was paying off," she says.

Consuelo Tarkington smiles faintly. "Oh, no," she says, putting out her cigarette. "Quite the opposite, in fact. Your poor father. So many troubles. At least he's at peace now. No, she was a night maid at the Ritz-Carlton in Boston, where he was staying years ago. . . ."

"Housekeeping, sir!"

At first he had not heard her. He stood at the open window, with the sheer curtains blowing inward, staring down at the sidewalk on Arlington Street below. The doorman had just discovered the horror that lay there and was frantically blowing his whistle, running out into the street, waving his arms to summon help.

"Housekeeping!"

This time he heard her, and he stepped back from the window so fast that he cracked his head, hard, against the sash.

"Do you want turn-down service for your bed tonight, Mr. Tarkington?" she said.

"No, goddammit! Get the hell out of here!" he shouted.

"Sorry, sir." She retreated hastily, pulling the door closed behind her, and he slammed the window shut.

He ran to the telephone. "Moe?" he said when he reached him. "There's been a terrible accident. A girl's dead," and he told him what had happened. "But, damn it, Moe, the girl's things are all over the room—shoes, underwear, nightgown, pocketbook. There's gonna be police all over the place in a few minutes! What'm I gonna do with her *things*? They're gonna be searching rooms. Where'm I gonna hide her *things*? You gotta help me, Moe!"

"What floor're you on?"

"Seven."

"Bonham's with you, right?"

"Right."

"What floor's he on?"

"Four."

"Which side of the building?"

"Other side. Newberry Street."

"The hotel know you two are together?"

"No. I checked in yesterday. He checked in this afternoon."

"Okay. Now listen carefully. The cops'll probably start at the top of the building and work down." Already, from outside on the street, the sounds of police and ambulance sirens could be heard. "Call Bonham and get him up there as fast as you can with a suitcase. Throw all the girl's shit into the suitcase and have Bonham take it down to his room and hang it all up real neat in his closet. Tell him to use the elevator, not the stairs. If I know cops, the cops'll be using the stairs. Then straighten up your room the best you can. You dressed?"

"Yeah."

"Good. Turn on the TV set. And one other thing. Call Room Service and order a sandwich or some damned thing. By the time the cops get to your room, you'll be sitting there, watching TV and eating a sandwich. You got all that? Okay. Meanwhile, I'll do what I can from this end in terms of damage control. Now get moving!"

And so that was what happened, more or less. In fact, while the police were searching Si Tarkington's room, going through Si's closets and dresser drawers, his luggage, the medicine chest, looking under the bed and even stripping the bed itself, and while Si was politely asking what might be the object of this sudden search, this unexpected intrusion, and while the hotel's assistant manager stood anxiously by, apologizing to his guest for the necessity of all this, the Room Service waiter arrived with Si's chicken salad sandwich and glass of iced tea on a silver tray with a single, long-stemmed rose.

Later that evening, after the police had completed their search and relative peace and quiet had been restored to the Ritz-Carlton, Silas Tarkington's telephone rang. Assuming it to be Moe calling from New York, Si answered it.

"My name is Ernestine Kolowrat," a woman's voice said. "You don't know me, but I am the night maid who came in to turn down your bed earlier this evening. Your window was open, and you were leaning out of it, looking down at the street. There were quite a few women's things lying around the room. I couldn't help but notice. I know who you are, Mr. Tarkington. And I think you and I ought to have a little talk, Mr. Tarkington, before I take what I know to the police."

"What am I going to *do*, Tommy?" he moaned, his head in his hands. He had gone immediately down to Tommy's room, where he sat in Tommy's armchair while Tommy, in his pajama bottoms, sat on the unmade bed opposite him. "She's going to blackmail me!"

"Were you able to stall her a little, Si?"

"I told her I'd meet her in my room tomorrow morning at eleven and we'd talk about it."

"Good," he said. "Now let's think about this, Si. Let's think very hard. First of all, I've shipped my suitcase with the girl's things in it back to my apartment in New York. When I get home, I'll put everything in the incinerator, and there'll be no more evidence."

"Thanks, Tommy," he whispered. "But what about what this maid *saw*? She saw it all there!"

"I'm thinking," he said. "What about Moe? Could Moe help us?"

"I don't want to get Moe involved in this any more than he already is! I know what Moe's solution would be!"

Tommy nodded. "I know what you mean," he said.

"My God, I've already got one woman's blood on my hands! I don't want another!"

"You didn't push the girl—"

"But she was in my room!"

"You'd invited her in."

He nodded.

"And you had sex with her."

He nodded again.

"And on a number of previous occasions."

"I didn't know how crazy she was!"

"Have you talked to Connie?"

"My God, no!"

"I think you should, Si. I really think you should. I think in a situation as serious as this one, you should bring Connie in on it. You need all the support you can get. You've got my support already, but I think you need your wife's support even more. I think we should all meet with this woman in the morning—you, Connie, and I— and perhaps when she sees you've got our united support—"

"I can't drag Connie into this, Tommy! I just can't!"

"I think you must, Si. I think if you make a clean breast of it, she'll stand behind you. If she finds out about it later, as she certainly may, she may not be so sympathetic."

"How would she ever find out about it?"

"This maid, this Ernestine, could threaten to tell her. And she *could* tell her. You and Connie are in this together, Si."

"Oh, God . . . oh, God. . . ."

"Remember Hillsdale, Si."

"How did you know about Hillsdale?"

"Moe Minskoff—mentioned it. This could be much, much worse. Call Connie, Si. Have her get on the first shuttle to Logan in the morning."

"When my phone rang at three A.M. that morning," Connie says to Miranda, "I knew—at that hour—that it had to be bad news. He told me he was in trouble and needed me in Boston as soon as possible. So I got on the eight o'clock shuttle from La Guardia in the morning. When I arrived at the hotel, the two of them told me what the trouble was. We met with the maid, Ernestine Kolowrat, a woman from Poland, who struck me at first as very ignorant. 'How much do you want?' I asked her.

" 'Five hundred dollars a month,' she said. 'In cash. Hand delivered. By Mr. Tarkington.'

" 'I am not a lawyer,' I told her. 'But my father was a well-known attorney in Philadelphia. What you are talking about is deliberately withholding evidence in a case of suspicious homicide. That in itself is a felony. You could go to prison.'

" 'I could say I forgot!' she said. 'I could say I didn't remember about the clothes in the room until later.'

" 'You are also talking about extortion, blackmail,' I said. 'That is also a federally punishable crime.'

"She looked at me narrowly. 'I might get a coupla years for that,' she said. 'But he could go up the river for life for what he done. I could say I seen him push her. In fact, I've just changed my mind. I think what I know is worth five *thousand* a month!'

"At that point, Tommy took over. He said, 'I think

Miss Kolowrat and I should talk in private for a moment.' The two of them left the room, and Si and I were alone.

"I couldn't bear to look at him, and he couldn't bear to look at me. Your father and I just sat there like two dummies, saying nothing, staring at our hands in our laps. Suddenly I felt terribly sorry for him. He was like a little boy who'd been caught doing something naughty on the playground and was terribly ashamed of what he'd done. I thought, Well, he's been in trouble before, but this is the worst trouble he's ever been in, and I thought—remember, this was more than twenty years ago, and I was younger and much more naïve—I thought, Well, maybe this will teach our bad boy a valuable lesson. Of course I was wrong. It didn't.

"Pretty soon, Tommy and the woman came back into the room. Tommy said, 'I've got her to agree to fifteen hundred a month.' The woman interrupted to say, 'Cash! Hand delivered! In person!' And Tommy said, 'That's as low as I can get her to go. I think we'd better accept that, Si. I don't see what else we can do.' He looked at us. I nodded, and Si nodded, and that was that.

"And so that was our friend Ernestine," Consuelo Tarkington says. "She moved to New York, where she could keep closer tabs on him, and he paid her off for the rest of her life."

"And the girl who died?"

"She was a little model named Christine something."

"Wandrous."

"Something like that. Si had been seeing her, and she began claiming that she was pregnant with Si's child. That couldn't have been true, because by then Si and I both knew that he was sterile. After you were born, your father and I tried desperately to have another child. He wanted a son, to help him run the store, and he was sure that Blazer's mother was poisoning Blazer's mind against him. But I couldn't seem to conceive. Tests were made. Something, perhaps those years of night sweats and chills, had made him sterile—not impotent, but his sperm count was zero. That was another terrible blow to him, of course. But if the girl was pregnant—"

"The autopsy reported that she was."

"Then it couldn't have been by your father, Miranda, and he knew it. He knew she was trying to trap him into marrying her. Anyway, Moe Minskoff could be useful for damage control, as your father used to say. The girl had a sister—"

"Mrs. Helen McCullogh of South Braintree, Massachusetts."

"Moe got to her and paid her off, got her to change her story and to say that the girl had been depressed and probably suicidal, and after that the newspapers left the story alone."

"But what do you suppose actually did happen, Mother—to the girl, I mean?"

"She wanted to marry him. Si refused to believe her story. They quarreled in the hotel room. She told him she'd kill herself if he wouldn't marry her. She threw open the window and threatened to jump. Si struggled with her, but she was too much for him. In the struggle, she fell."

"The newspaper stories said jumped—or was pushed."

"Oh, no. Don't think that, Miranda. I knew your father too well. He could never have taken another human life. It just wasn't in him. He was too—abject. He was always the victim, never the victimizer. That was the story of your father's life."

With a little hissing noise, one of the lighted candles on the dining room table sputters out, and Connie Tarkington looks at her watch. "Goodness, it's after midnight," she says. "We'd better be getting to bed, you and I."

"But there's just one thing I don't understand," Miranda says. "Why did Tommy want to get you involved in what had happened in Boston? Did you really need to be? Surely you didn't want to be. Why did he drag you into it?"

Her mother's smile now is distant and knowing. "That," she says, "is a very good question. Think about it. And think about whether, if you really do want to run the store, one of the first things you ought to do isn't to get rid of Mr. Tommy Bonham."

"But can I really do it without him? I know some of his methods have been—well, a little unorthodox, to say the least. And I don't trust him anymore. But he does have all that experience I don't have. He knows the vendors, knows the market, and all those special lady clients whom he waits on personally and who won't purchase anything without his advice. Won't I need his help, at least for a while?"

Her mother is still smiling. "No," she says. In the remaining candlelight, she lifts a pale, thin hand in an inquiring gesture, and, as Consuelo Tarkington fixes her eyes on her daughter, Miranda's eyes withdraw.

In Miranda's dream, she was in a vast open space, standing small in front of a tall Christmas tree, its branches spreading outward in gestures of embrace, covered with thousands of fairy lights, tinsel, shiny balls, and candy canes. Hundreds of brightly wrapped packages lay strewn, unopened, beneath the tree. The tree swayed, as if in a wind, and the branches lifted, and suddenly the branches of the tree became arms, and the tree became her father, standing tall before her. His arms seemed to beckon her to come closer, and she could see that what had been ornaments on the tree had become clusters of fruit that he was holding in his hands; and as she stepped even closer she could see that the fruit was overripe, dripping nectar, begging to be picked, and that in less than a day's time the fruit would be rotten and unfit to eat. "This is the tree of my life," the tree father told her. "This is the closest glimpse you will have of my heart. Pluck this fruit now, before it's too late." Then a finger of the arm branch of the tree father reached out and touched her eyelids. Its touch was dry and brittle and tickling, yet light and feathery, like beautifully arranged hemlock needles, and she woke, brushed at her face, and realized that the hemlock needles were only the whiskers of Bicha, the cat, curled on the pillow beside her. Still, the dream disturbed her, and it was a long time before she was able to sleep again.

It is Saturday morning and, with the exception of brief trips back to the city to consult with Peter Turner, Miranda has been at the farm for a week. Connie has risen at her usual hour, and now, in her bedroom, she is on the telephone. "Tommy, it's Connie Tarkington," she says. "I'm glad I found you home. I'm wondering if I could pop over to your place and talk to you for a minute. . . . Good, I'll be there in ten minutes."

She picks up her keys and purse, hurries down the stairs, and goes out the front door to where the station wagon, which she drives herself when in the country, is parked in the drive. The gate to Flying Horse Farm draws open at her battery-operated signal, and she turns out into Heather Lane, heading toward Tommy's place.

She parks the wagon in front of Tommy's cottage and moves quickly up the front walk. Nino, his houseboy, greets her at the door. "Mr. Bonham, he expect you, Missus," Nino says.

She steps into the living room, which is in its usual state of disarray, and Tommy springs to his feet with a smile. "Connie! How wonderful to see you," he says. He steps toward her to kiss her on the cheek, but she moves away and seats herself on the Victorian sofa. "Hello, Tommy," she says, and his face darkens. "What I have to say will only take a minute." She picks a speck of lint off her white slacks, and he seats himself slowly, facing her.

"I had a long talk with Miranda last night," she says. "In fact, we've had a number of long talks since she's been out here visiting me. I told her about Ernestine. I saw no reason not to, since all the principals involved in it are now dead. Except you and me, of course."

"Yes."

"She asked me an interesting question. She asked me, 'Why did Tommy drag you into it?' It's a question I've often asked myself. I certainly didn't enjoy being dragged into it. I'd have much preferred not to have been. Ignorance would have been bliss."

"I felt we all had to show a united front, Connie."

"Is that it? Well, showing a united front didn't help us much, did it? No, I've always thought that somehow you assumed that if I were exposed—at first hand, in the flesh, as it were—to one of the more disastrous results of Si's womanizing, I'd divorce him."

"That's ridiculous!"

"Is it? Well, if that was your assumption, it was wrong. If anything, sharing that awful secret brought us closer together. In retrospect, it strengthened Si's and my marriage immeasurably."

"That was exactly what I'd hoped! That it would strengthen the bond between the two of you."

"In an ordinary marriage, it wouldn't have done that, I suppose. But ours was not an ordinary marriage."

"As I knew all along, Connie!"

"But dragging me in on it also made the last twenty years of Si's life miserable. It was bad enough that Moe Minskoff knew what had happened. It was even worse for him, knowing that you also knew. But it was far, far worse for him knowing that I knew too. But for you, what happened that night in Boston presented a door of golden opportunity, didn't it? When you went up to Boston, you were an assistant buyer in the shoe department. That was what the trip to Boston was supposed to be about, if I recall—meetings with some footwear manufacturers. When you came back from Boston, you became street floor merchandise manager. Then it was vice president. Then it was executive vice president and general manager. Your 'meteoric rise at Tarkington's,' as I've seen it described in the press."

"Connie, if you're suggesting that I ever threatened—"

"Your very presence was a threat! He knew you had

the ability to expose him at any time. That was the secret of your power, of your ability to manipulate him. He lived in terror of what you might decide to reveal, and you made sure that he was continually frightened. You told him to have his face lifted, in case another hotel employee recognized him and placed him in that room that night with that girl. You told him to beware of photographers, for the same reason. And all the time, you were moving higher and higher up the corporate ladder, closer and closer to the king's throne. But you never quite made it to the throne itself, did you? And you're not going to."

His face is angry now. "So this is the thanks I get for keeping your husband's dirty little secret all these years!"

"I'm going to use my share votes to elect Miranda the store's new president."

"And I'm to be second in command—under *her*? Is that what you're saying, Connie?"

"Not exactly."

"Then what are you saying?"

"I don't want my daughter to live the way my husband did. I don't want her to have a second in command who can impose a reign of terror. I want you out. In fact, I'm going to make that a condition. If she gets my share votes, it will only be on the condition that she gets rid of you."

"Did she—did she tell you something, Connie? Something about me that's made you turn on me like this? Because—"

"She said nothing about you, except that she still thinks she needs you. I don't agree. But I'll tell you something about you that I've finally figured out. I used to think, If Tommy insisted that I come to Boston to get involved in all that, it had to be because he hoped what I'd find there would be enough to make me want to end my marriage. But then I'd ask myself, Why would he want to do that? Just to make mischief? Just for power? What would be the advantage to Tommy if I were to divorce Si? What would be in it for him? Now I think I know. I think it was because you were in love with Si and wanted to marry him yourself. That was it, wasn't it, Tommy? You were in love with him."

She stands up.

"Why is your lower lip trembling like that, Tommy?" she asks him.

33

The next day, Sunday, it is one of those autumn days when summer suddenly seems to return to the East. The sun is warm, though low and slanted, casting long shadows on the lawns, and Connie and her daughter are walking in the garden. Later this afternoon, Miranda will go back to New York, but to do what she has not yet completely decided. Bicha the cat, in his *dégagé* way, follows at a discreet distance behind them, wanting their company but not wanting to appear to want it too badly, seeming to find many more important items of interest along the path than two women strolling in a garden.

"There's one big thing I haven't told you, darling," Connie says. "And that's that I'm planning to marry again."

Miranda stops in her tracks. "Really, Mother? Who?"

"Jake Kohlberg. He's been a great help to me over the years, and I've always been very fond of him. And now he's asked me to marry him. What do you think of that? Pretty good for your old gray-haired mother, don't you think? Maybe there's life in the old girl yet. I'd like a husband for my old age."

"How funny," Miranda says. "Someone's asked me to marry him too."

Her mother laughs her bell-like laugh. "I'm not surprised," she says. "And I know who it is."

"How do you know?"

"I have eyes in my head, darling. It's perfectly obvious that Peter Turner's besotted with you. What did you tell him?"

"I told him I'd think about it. I really like him very much."

"So do I. He's quality goods, as your father used to say."

They continue along the gravel path toward the Dell Garden, with the blue Persian following them.

"He told me something about you that I didn't know," her mother says.

"What's that?"

"That you've been working on your M.B.A. at N.Y.U."

"Yes."

"Why didn't you tell me about that, Miranda?"

She hesitates. "I guess I was afraid you'd laugh at me," she says. "I was afraid you'd think it was a silly thing for me to do."

"Not at all! It just shows me how serious you are about preparing yourself to run the store. I think it's wonderful."

Miranda says nothing.

"Let's go up and sit on the bridge and feed the fish," Connie says. "I've brought a little bag of their food." She removes a plastic bag of pellets from the pocket of her slacks, and the two women climb the steps of the moongate bridge and seat themselves on the pair of wooden benches at the top. Connie begins tossing pellets into the water, aiming her tosses carefully so the clusters of smaller fish will not be outmaneuvered by the larger ones. Up from the depths of the pond comes the big blue-and-yellow koi that Miranda remembers from years ago, when she sat right here with Blazer. The koi is much bigger now, easily three feet long, his whiskered mouth the size of a silver dollar.

"Here comes Bucephalus," her mother says. "That's his name. Fish are lovely. So are cats. Husbands are even lovelier. I hope you're going to say yes to Peter."

"Mother," Miranda says quietly, "tell me how Daddy died."

"I was sure you were going to ask me that question again," she says, tossing a pellet, with perfect accuracy, into the gaping dollar-sized mouth. "There have been times, Miranda, when you and I haven't gotten along too well together, and I didn't think there was any reason why I should tell you. But lately—just these past few days —you and I seem to have become close, closer than we've ever been before. And so now I don't see any reason why I shouldn't tell you what happened. After all, I was there."

"You were—there?"

"Oh, yes. You see, your father and I had been having a lot of serious talks those last few days before he died." She tosses another pellet. "Talks like you and I've been having, talks about the future, the future of the store, and his and my future. There were troubles at the store he didn't like to talk about, but, more important, there were troubles with the marriage. The situation with Smitty was getting out of hand. She was very demanding—not that I blame her, because she was obviously very much in love with him, and when you're in love you do crazy, willful things.

"Si felt torn. He needed her at the store, but he'd grown tired of her as a lover. And of course I scolded, I nagged. I kept telling him that he had to take some sort of stand, that he had to make up his mind, that he was going to have to confront Smitty somehow or other and tell her how he felt. But in the meantime, he and I both agreed that we wanted to make a new start. After all, neither of us were getting any younger, and neither of us wanted a divorce. So we decided to go back to Bermuda, where we'd spent our honeymoon at the Princess Hotel. I even wrote your father a letter; I typed it myself. Your father used to complain that he could never read my handwriting. . . .

"I promised him not to be a boring, nagging old hag anymore. I told him I was going to be a whole new wife to him. I think I even signed it *the soon-to-be new Mrs. Silas Tarkington.*"

"I know about that letter," she says.

"Really? How?"

"That day I was helping Pauline clear out his office, I found it among his things. It reeked of Equipage, Smitty's perfume."

"How interesting. Well, I didn't put it there. I used to come home from travels to find my bed linen reeking of Equipage, which I didn't put there either."

"Anyway, go on."

"The thing he had to do, I told him, was to confront Smitty. He had to take a firm stand with her. But that was one thing your father always had trouble doing with any of his women, taking a firm stand. He kept begging me to do it for him. Well, I'd done it for him before, when I was too young to know any better, with his first wife, and that had been a terrible mistake. I told him he was going to have to take a stand with her *himself,* if it was going to have any meaning to her. Then he asked me whether we couldn't confront her together—so we could show a united front, as he put it, though I knew he really wanted me to be there as a sort of second in his duel. I agreed, reluctantly. It was a compromise, I knew, and a little cowardly, but that was your father. He called Smitty and asked her to meet him that Saturday morning at the farm.

"She came here that morning?"

"I met her at the door. I think she was a little surprised to see me. I said, 'Si's expecting you. He's down at the pool,' and we walked down together. I still think Si thought we women would have it out together, then and there, and he'd be spared this scene, and that was why he'd gone to the pool, hoping to avoid the confrontation by any possible means. But I didn't think he should be let off the hook that easily. I thought Smitty should hear his decision, whatever he had to say, straight from the horse's mouth. I was determined to keep my own trap shut. He was sitting by the pool, watching television, and Blackamoor was with him, and he looked horrified when he saw us walking toward him. For a moment, I thought he was going to jump up and run away. But he just turned off the TV set.

"Smitty spoke first. I stood a little distance away. She said, 'Well, I suppose you've brought me here so I can hear you tell Connie that you're leaving her and that you want to marry me.'

"At first he said nothing, looking at me. Then he just shook his head.

" 'Then what the hell is this all about?' she said.

" 'I'm not ready to leave Connie,' he said. 'And I'm not ready to marry you, Smitty.'

" 'What the hell does that mean—you're not ready?'

" 'Just what I said.'

" 'But you don't love her. You love me. Tell her so.'

" 'That's not really true, Smitty,' he said. 'I do love Connie.'

" 'But you told me you didn't love Connie! You told me you loved me.'

"His eyes searched mine for some assistance, which I wasn't quite prepared to give him. 'I do love Connie,' he said, 'but I loved you too.'

" 'You loved me *too*?' she repeated. She glared at me. 'What about some of the things you called her—Miss Sexual Refrigerator—all of that? You're just saying these things now because you're terrified of what she could do to you, aren't you?'

" 'Am I?' The question lacked conviction.

" 'Because she's blackmailing you. Because she knows how you've swept your mother under the rug, keeping her in a dreary little apartment on West End Avenue! She knows that dirty secret.'

"He was still looking anxiously at me. 'Tell her, Connie,' he said.

" 'Si's mother is in a nursing home in Florida and has

been for almost ten years,' I said. 'A very nice nursing home. The best Si and I could find.'

"She looked confused, disoriented. 'But you told me you never loved Connie!' she said. 'You told me you never loved her—ever.'

" 'Did I?'

" 'Of course you did. You know you did. Tell her you never loved her.'

" 'Never?'

" '*Tell her!*'

" 'Don't push me this way, Smitty,' he said. 'Don't crowd me. You know I don't like to be pushed or crowded. Don't force me to say things I don't really mean.'

" '*When?* When did you ever love her, just once for a single minute?' He was looking at me so desperately now, begging me for some suggestion as to how to answer this question and end all this, as though I was the only one who could rescue him now. I had to help him.

" 'When?' he asked me.

" 'Perhaps it was in Positano,' I said quietly. 'At the Hotel Sirenuse.'

" 'Yes, and the Villa Rufolo.'

" 'Where I sprained my ankle on the steps.'

" 'And I had to carry you—'

" 'Shut up, you bitch!' she screamed at me. 'He loves *me*!'

"Then I heard him say in a strong voice, 'I've always loved Connie. And I think I always will.'

"I was terribly pleased and proud of him, Miranda, when I heard him say those words—say them to her, in front of me. I suddenly couldn't think of any time in my life when anyone, your father or anyone else, had ever told me that he loved me in such a direct way. Certainly my father never told me he loved me. A great burden seemed to be lifted from my shoulders just then. All those troubled years"—she touches the corner of an eyelid with a fingertip and tosses a final pellet to the fish—"seemed to just drop away. I wanted to say, Thank you, darling, but I couldn't seem to find my voice. Smitty began calling me all sorts of names: a cold-blooded bitch, things like that. I've never seen anyone so angry. But Si just stood up and said, 'That's all I have to say to you, Smitty. That's what I asked you here to tell you. Now I'm going to swim my laps,' and he turned on the television set and dove into the pool.

"She went running toward him, and it was like déjà vu. All at once I knew what she was going to do. I screamed 'Stop!' and Blackamoor began to bark, and I heard her say, 'If I can't have you, nobody will!' And she picked up the television set and threw it at him, as though she wanted to hit him over the head with it, but she missed—and the set flew into the water with him. And then—but perhaps this was only my imagination working —it seemed as though the whole surface of the pool was lighted with a kind of blue flash. I saw Si's body flinch violently, then stiffen, and I knew it was all over."

"Then what did you do, Mother?"

"There were several things I had to do, and I had to do them quickly. First I had to deal with Blackamoor. He knew your father was in some kind of terrible trouble, and he started to leap into the pool after him. I grabbed him by the collar. Blackie's a big, strong dog, and he gave me quite a struggle. But how would it have looked if both Si *and* his dog had been found dead in the pool? Somehow I got Blackie back into his kennel, and I locked him there. Then I pulled all the circuit-breakers in the pool area. When I got back to the pool she was still standing there, looking stunned at the horrible thing she had done. I said, 'How did you get here?' 'A rental car,' she said. 'Did anyone see you come in?' She shook her head. 'Then no one will see you go,' I said. 'Get out of here. Get out of here as fast as you can. As far as I'm concerned, you were never here. Don't worry about me. I'll take care of everything.' She left then, without another word."

"And the TV set?"

"I knew I had to get rid of that. I pulled it out of the water by its cord, but then I couldn't think of what to do with it."

"What *did* you do with it?"

She points with her finger to the pond below, and the fish, seeing the shadow of this gesture, think they are about to be fed again and leap to the surface with open mouths. "I carried it out here and dropped it in the pond. It's down there somewhere, forty feet down. Then I remembered the Lucite case he'd had made for it, and I ran back to the pool house and got it, and dropped it in too, and watched it sink. It seemed to take forever to go down, and I knew I didn't have that much time. Blackie had set up such a howling I was afraid someone from the house would come out to see what the matter was. By then I was a mess. My slacks were sopping wet, and my shoes were covered with mud. I ran back to the pool house, and then I did a lot of crazy things. I took his wallet from his trousers pocket and that underwater chronometer you gave him. I thought, if there was any suspicion, I'd make it look as though there'd been a burglary. Those were quite unnecessary things to do, of course. Then I took off my dirty shoes, walked back to the house barefoot, and went upstairs, changed my clothes, rinsed off my shoes, and by then it was nearly noon. I rang for Milliken. I said, 'Mr. Tarkington's at the pool. Run down and tell him that it's nearly lunchtime.' When he came back to tell me that he'd found what I knew he'd find, I called Harry Arnstein in New York."

"Did you tell Dr. Arnstein what had happened?"

"No. I just said, 'No scandal, Harry—please, no scandal.' He understood what I meant. He took over from there. He called Campbell's for the hearse, made arrangements for the cremation. All this took several hours. Then I called you."

"Yes. . . ."

"At that point, I'd been running on energy I didn't even know I possessed. I thought, Now I'm going to collapse. But I didn't collapse. I just kept thinking of all the questions I might be asked, and of the answers I was going to have to give."

"But—Smitty. Shouldn't she be—?"

Her mother makes a little moue. "Be brought to justice? What possible reason would there be for that? For revenge? That's not a particularly attractive motive, revenge. What good would it do? It wouldn't bring your father or my husband back to life. It would just drag Smitty's and your father's names through the mud. It's not as though Smitty's any threat to society. She's not going to kill anybody else. She's like that poor Mrs. Harris who shot the Scarsdale diet doctor; it was something she did in the terrible heat of passion. What possible use is it to society to have that poor woman spend the last years of her life in a prison in Westchester, just spending the taxpayers' money, when there are so many useful things she could be doing instead? Smitty can still have a useful life, and it seems to me she deserves to have one. Besides, Smitty knows what she did, and she's going to have to live with that knowledge until she dies. Don't you think that's punishment enough? I do."

"Yes," Miranda says. "Yes, perhaps."

"I'm not even sure she meant to kill him. Perhaps she just wanted to throw something at him, and the TV set was the closest thing at hand. Perhaps it didn't even occur to her that the set was plugged in. That's why I wanted her to come to the house the night after your father died. I wanted her to see firsthand how I was going to handle it. 'You *deserve* to be here,' I told her. But in the weeks since it happened, I've been thinking. Tommy Bonham is a really evil man. He likes to pit people against each other and watch them squirm. He helped drive the final wedge between your father and Blazer. He was the one who first arranged to put your father and Smitty together, and that was what almost drove a final wedge between your father and me. He must have arranged for you to see my letter and think it was from Smitty."

Pauline needs help going through the things in your father's office, she remembers. *Someone in the family should be there when she does this. Can you give her a hand?* And there was the bottle of Equipage in Tommy's medicine cabinet. But Miranda says nothing.

"But then, carrying these thoughts one step further, I've been asking myself, Could Tommy, right from the beginning, from the moment he hired her, knowing the terribly violent temper Smitty had, have planned—or at least hoped—that Smitty would somehow be the instrument for your father's death?"

"Why would he have wanted that? So he could take over the store?"

"That, and out of jealousy. He was jealous of Smitty, and he was jealous of me. He was jealous of anyone who was closer to your father than he was. If your father's death looked like murder, I'd have been the prime suspect. The spouse nearly always is. Maybe Tommy was hoping to get rid of both your father and me. Or are these thoughts of mine too crazy, too farfetched?"

"Perhaps," Miranda says thoughtfully. "But then again, perhaps not."

"Tommy knew your father's mind so well. He knew every inch of it, inside and out, almost as well as I did. He knew all his faults and flaws, and he knew just when these faults and flaws were most likely to trip your father up. He knew all his Achilles' heels. He knew what a sad and disappointed man your father really was. It's a terrible thing, Miranda, for a man to be told—in the press and elsewhere—what a great success he is when in his heart of hearts he knows he is a failure, that his whole life has been a sham, a pretense."

Miranda nods.

"But that's where I came in, of course. That's where I found my mission, my calling. To bolster his morale, to stroke his poor ego, to try to force-feed his self-esteem. I don't know if I really succeeded, but I tried. I tried to be his nurse, to give him tender, loving care. That probably sounds self-serving, but it isn't meant to. It probably means there's something wrong with me. Why do I seem to be attracted to weak men?"

The question hangs in the air, unanswered. The fish, having decided that there is no more food for them, have descended to the deep water. The two women sit there on the garden bench, in the warm Indian-summer sunlight. The cat dozes.

"Jake Kohlberg doesn't strike me as a weak man," Miranda says at last.

"No. And we do have happier thoughts to think about, don't we?" her mother says. "Wedding plans: definitely for me, maybe for you. And for you—first things first—you're going to have a store to run."

"Oh, Mother, I don't think so. Not now."

"Now, Miranda. You know it's what you've always wanted."

"I still do. But it's hopeless. Peter's gone over the books, and things are in even worse shape than we thought. The best thing we can do is have a close-out sale and put the building on the market."

Her mother looks pensive. "I could help you," she says.

"How? How could you help?"

"If it's only money, I could help."

"How?"

She gestures around her. "I could sell this place," she says.

"Oh, Mother—not sell the farm!"

"Why not? This place is a white elephant. It's an anachronism. People don't live like this anymore. Think of it—eighty-two acres of prime Long Island real estate, including half a mile of shoreline on the Sound. Developers have been after us for years to buy it. It's what everyone else has done. We're the last of the dinosaurs—as they said of your father."

"And give up your beautiful Dell Garden? I wouldn't let you do that."

She looks out at the garden. "When I first saw this hollow in the land, this was what I wanted. This garden and this pond. Where did I get the vision for it, I wonder? When I started designing it, I had no idea what I was doing. I just said, 'Plant this tree here, plant that one there.' And it worked, didn't it? But it's finished now. It's done. I'm ready to move on to some other project. And these fish, too. They've bred well in this deep water. I had an ichthyologist here from Woods Hole the other day, and he tells me some of these hybrid specimens of koi are quite rare, worth thousands of dollars apiece as breeding stock."

"You wouldn't sell the fish too!"

"Wouldn't you want them to have a nice home, Miranda, where they'd be fed and cared for and have a lovely sex life? You wouldn't want to trust them to some real estate developer!"

"You're not serious, Mother!"

"I am. Absolutely. And of course I'd sell my furniture as well. Your father's art collection may not be worth much, but most of the furniture I researched and collected myself, and some of the pieces are very nice indeed. I'm going to call Mr. Grenfell at Sotheby's and have him come and take a look at it."

"But, Mother, where would you live?"

"I could live in the apartment over the store—that is, if you don't mind. Jake likes that idea. He doesn't want to keep his present apartment because it reminds him too much of his late wife. We'd promise not to interfere with anything you're doing. And I've already planned to sell the Lake Sunapee house. And I'd also sell the little apartment in Paris, which I have no need for at all now. And then there's the Palm Beach house, which I haven't set foot in for at least three years. And I haven't even thought about the china and the silver and the glassware and the furniture in all those places. And then there's my jewelry—"

"I will not let you sell your jewelry, Mother!"

"There are some pieces I just don't wear anymore. And let's not forget the racehorses we both own. The horse market is depressed right now, now that the Arabs have moved out of it, but there's a filly who's a granddaughter of Nashua, and two stallions are the sons of Flying Flame. I think that when you and I sell off some of this excess baggage we seem to have, we'll be able to reduce the store's debt considerably."

Miranda bites her lip. "You'd really do all this for me, Mother?"

"Absolutely."

"Peter's offered to help me," she says.

"Peter has an M.B.A. from Harvard. He should be a nice help. And Jake will help you too. I don't know how fond you are of Jake, but to do what you're going to do you'll need the services of a good lawyer, and Jacob Kohlberg is one of the best. There's only one thing."

"What's that?"

"Forgive me, but I tend to think of the two of you, you and Peter, as two children, trying to run this complicated store. I keep wishing there were someone—someone with a solid background in retailing—who could help advise you. These courses you're taking at N.Y.U.—is there someone there, an instructor perhaps, who could work with you, at least at the beginning?"

"As a matter of fact there is," Miranda says. "His name is Mark Horowitz. Before he retired and went into teaching, he was the comptroller at Bonwit's for thirty years."

"That's the sort of person I mean. Would he do it?"

"For me, I bet he would! He calls me his star pupil."

"Good. Then ask him. You see how simple it is to find solutions once you put your mind to it?"

"Mother, I don't know what to say."

"There's nothing you need to say."

"I may fail, you know."

"You won't fail. You're a Tarkington woman, and we Tarkington women are not put together with flour-and-water paste."

She reaches out and touches her mother's hand, and her mother squeezes her hand in return. "I'll say this much," Miranda says. "I love you, Mother."

"I love you too. And don't forget I also loved your father, and your father is a part of you." Connie Tarkington stands, and her hand rests lightly on her daughter's shoulder as she looks out across the pond. "I'm glad I had them dig this pond as deep as I did," she says. "Creatures need depth to love and procreate. I sometimes think there is nothing but a deep pond between life and death, and the bridge is love. Love is the bridge between where we are today and wherever we'll find ourselves tomorrow. Between the night terrors and—" She shivers suddenly. "It's getting chilly, isn't it," she says. "The days are getting shorter. Let's go inside. We both have so much to do.

We'd better get started, if we're going to have the store in shape for the Christmas season. Come, Miranda. Come, Bicha. Come, kitty."

Her eyes seem to come to rest on a line of evergreens just along the ridge, and she raises one hand in the attitude of a priest bestowing a blessing, and realizing her mother is saying goodbye to the Dell Garden, Miranda looks away.

34

"Well, hello, stranger!" he says cheerfully as she steps into his office the next morning. "We've missed you around here. How was your vacation?"

"Just fine," she says. "Tommy, we need to talk."

"Sure," he says, and he rises, steps quickly past her, and closes the office door behind them. "Sit down, Miranda, and tell me what's on your mind. Have you given any more thought to that little proposal of mine?"

She remains standing. "That's not what I came to talk about, Tommy," she says.

He frowns. "Something's bothering you, I can tell. The other night at my house. One minute you were so warm, so passionate. And the next minute you were cold as ice. What happened? And last week you stayed away from the store, as though you were trying to avoid me, and when you called on the phone it was only to discuss figures. Obviously, I've said or done something to upset or offend you, Miranda. Please tell me what it is."

She looks him squarely in the eye and forces the words out. "We've decided to let you go, Tommy," she says. "I'm sorry."

"What do you mean, let me go?"

"We don't want you working at the store anymore."

His eyes narrow slightly. "*We?* Who is we?"

"A majority of Tarkington's stockholders."

"What majority? Where do you get your majority?"

"My mother, my grandmother, my Aunt Simma— and myself."

"You—*women?*"

"I can get you executed proxies if you'd like. But that shouldn't be necessary, should it? I think you and I understand each other."

"Your *grand*mother? But your grandmother is senile, for God's sake!"

"As a matter of fact, she's not. But that's neither here nor there. We still represent fifty-five percent of the voting shares of this company."

"You mean you women are *firing* me? You can't do that!"

"Why not? I believe I just did," she says.

"Who in God's name is going to run the store?"

"I am," she says.

He laughs softly. "You can't run it without me."

"Oh, yes, I can."

"Now, Miranda, be sensible," he says. "You know you don't have the experience to run an operation like this one. Oh, maybe some day you could, but not yet. The Christmas season is coming up. Do you know what that means? Of all times of the year to—"

"Our Christmas orders are all in. Merchandise is being shipped."

"But you yourself admitted—just the other night, to me—that you had a lot to learn about retailing. And the only person who can teach you anything about this store is me."

"I've learned a lot just in the past few days," she says. "I'm a fast learner. Always have been. Smitty will help me, too."

"Smitty? What's Smitty got to do with it?"

"Smitty's agreed to rejoin us."

"Now wait a minute," he says, running his fingers

through his thick blond hair. "Just calm down a minute. Just settle down and try to talk sensibly, Miranda."

"I am calm. Do I seem agitated?"

"Just a minute. Hear me out. Do I have a right to know why you—you *women*—have made this very unwise, financially dangerous decision? Can you tell me that?"

"For several reasons," she says. "Funny business with the Retail Credit Corporation in Atlanta. Sales records that don't match up with shipping records. Discounts and rebates. Too much consignment selling. The disappearance of the employees' pension fund. These things have been going on too long."

"I can explain all that," he says.

"The only thing I'd like explained," she says, "is what you managed to do with all the money you seem to have skimmed from us. You never struck me as a particularly high liver. Where did the money go? I wonder, is it in some numbered account in Switzerland? Is it in some bank in the Cayman Islands? But I don't ever expect to get to the bottom of that."

"Now wait a minute," he says. "Just wait a minute. You're making a very serious allegation there, Miranda. I can explain."

"Then please do," she says.

"To begin with, your father and I were very close. He was my closest friend. I loved him like a brother, Miranda. We were even closer than that. We were like—like one *soul*. He often told me that he could never have had the success he had without me. We were *that close*," and he presses the two forefingers of his right hand together in demonstration. "Now your father was a great merchandising genius, as you know, a true retailing innovator in every sense of the word. But every genius has his shortcomings, and your father was no exception. I used to refer to your father's shortcomings as his little blind spots. He was a man with great merchandising ideas, but he was not a financial wizard. Covering his little blind spots was where I came in, and I handled nearly all the store's financial matters for him, increasingly so, over the years, as he placed more and more trust in me. But there were times when, in your father's enthusiasm for his ideas and innovations, he let himself get carried away, and he'd overextend himself, and that's when I'd have to step in to try to rescue him financially. And sometimes, in order to do that, I'd have to resort to certain fiscal practices which —to an outsider, at least—might seem a little bit . . . unorthodox. That was what happened with the pension fund, when Pauline caught us short by unexpectedly announcing her retirement. But I assure you that I have careful plans in the works right now—the details of which I can't go into yet—to have that fund fully restored by the end of the year. And I can promise you, Miranda, that every red cent of the money you see as missing was plowed back into helping your father run this store. If you'll let me go over the books again with you, I can show you exactly where and how. If it hadn't been for me, your father would have been a ruined man, and this store would have been bankrupt years ago. I did it because I loved and believed in this store. I did it because I loved and believed in your father. And I did it for your mother's sake, and of course for your sake too, because I loved you so. Do you believe me, Miranda?"

"Perhaps," she says, feeling her resolve beginning to waver. "But still—"

"I love you, Miranda," he says. "Whatever it is you think I've done that's made you decide to ruin me now, I'll always love you. Remember that." He reaches out to take her by the shoulders.

"Please, no," she says, stepping away.

"Remember those feelings you had for me years ago, when we first met? By the pool? The blue swimsuit with the red mermaid? You still have those feelings, don't you?"

"I was just a child," she says. "And somehow I feel we've been over this ground before."

"My child love. Face it, Miranda, you need me and I need you. It was to be you and me, from the moment we met." His gaze at her is steady and hypnotic. "Now, why don't you calm yourself down? You've let the store's little

problems worry you far more than those little problems
are worth. Relax, and we'll talk some more later." He
glances at his watch. "In fact, why don't we have lunch?
Let me book a table for the two of us at Le Cirque, and
we'll talk over a nice relaxed lunch."

"Damn it, I am calmed down! I am relaxed!"

"See? You're all on edge. You're a bundle of nerves."

"If I am, it's because of things that were done here at
the store—illegal things."

"Now, Miranda, nothing was done that was illegal, I
promise you. Sure, sometimes I was forced to do things
that were a little bit—creative—with the books to bail
your father out, but nothing was done that was in any
way illegal."

"I don't know whether it's illegal to shift funds
around within a company—the pension fund into the
general operating fund, for instance—but for a trustee to
steal from someone else's trust fund is definitely against
the law."

His face goes suddenly pale, his eyes flash, and his lip
begins twitching violently. "Trust fund? What trust fund?
I don't know what you're talking about."

"Blazer's trust fund. The half-million-dollar trust
fund that Daddy set up for Blazer, that was to be his
when he was twenty-one."

"I had nothing to do with that!"

"In 1979, you somehow got the Connecticut Bank
and Trust Company to turn over its trusteeship to you,
and you and Alice Tarkington were supposed to adminis-
ter it together. For the next five years, you and Alice authorized systematic withdrawals from it, and we've found
matching deposits to the store's general operating account for all of these withdrawals. By 1984, the trust
fund was depleted."

"Who 'found'? Who's 'we'? Did Blazer tell you this?
Blazer is a stupid jerk."

"No."

"Was it Alice? Alice is a lush."

"No."

"Was it Jake Kohlberg? Kohlberg is a cheap shyster

who's always hated my guts because I was closer to your father than he was."

"No, it wasn't Jake."

"Then who? Who's 'we'?"

"A friend of mine and I, a friend who's been helping me go over the books."

"That writer you've been screwing, I suppose. Your mother told me about him. He's a lightweight, you know. He may have got an M.B.A. at Harvard, but it took him an extra year to get it."

"He was ill with hepatitis for most of one school year."

"Hepatitis? Is that what he told you? It was more likely AIDS!"

She smiles, because she sees a light, however dimly, beginning to glow at the end of this long and murky tunnel. "And so," she says carefully, "it looks as though you, with Alice's unwitting aid, managed to raid my brother's trust fund."

"What do you care? He's not even your real brother!"

"Nonetheless, I think of him as my brother," she says.

"Your father hated Blazer. He never intended Blazer to get any of that money."

"But he didn't intend you to get it, did he?"

"It all went back into running the store! It was done to help save the store!"

"That may be true, but it was still illegal."

"It was all done with your father's full approval. Everything I did was done with his full approval. Are you going to try to have me fired for doing what the president of the company ordered me to do?"

"Somehow, I don't believe that, Tommy," she says.

"Have you told Blazer any of this? Are you going to try to get him to make trouble for me?"

"I haven't decided," she says. "I'm actually a little afraid to, because I really think Blazer might try to kill you if he knew. He has such a quick temper. It's not so much that Blazer wants the money. I really don't think the money means that much to him at this point. But if he knew you'd stolen it from his poor mother while Alice was—physically incapacitated—I think he might really try to kill you. And much as I distrust you, Tommy, I really don't want your blood on my hands. So maybe I won't tell Blazer. But," she says, "I could always report what I know to the state Attorney General's office."

He hesitates, staring hard at her. Then he says, "Your mother put you up to this, didn't she?"

"No," she says. "She approves of what I'm doing, but she didn't put me up to it. I'm telling you this entirely on my own."

"You know why she's turned against me, don't you?"

"I don't think there's any particular reason."

He sighs, spreading the palms of his hands. "I was hoping not to have to tell you about this, Miranda. But I guess I'm going to have to."

"Tell me about what?"

"Did she tell you she came to see me Saturday morning at my house on Heather Lane?"

"No, she didn't."

"I thought not. Well, she telephoned me Saturday morning and said she wanted to see me. I had no idea what it was about, but I asked her to stop by. She drove over in her car. I let her in. She was wearing a light raincoat, one of our Selancy rainwear line, though it wasn't raining. I offered to take her coat, but she said no, she was a little chilly, she'd rather keep the raincoat on. I gave her a cup of coffee, the way she likes it, with a little yogurt spooned in instead of cream. She sat on the sofa.

"She began telling me how lonely she was with your father gone—'desperately lonely' was the way she put it— how terribly she missed him, how she wasn't sure she could ever adjust to life without a man around the house. She talked for quite a while about her loneliness, so I suggested things she might do to keep busy, instead of working for the hospital ball, which she never really enjoyed. Join the local garden club, I said. Work for that little symphony they're trying to start in Manhasset. How about travel? She kept saying no, that there was no real substitute for male companionship.

"I got up to get her another cup of coffee, and she lay back against the sofa and opened up her raincoat, and—Miranda, this is very difficult for me to say to you—and she had nothing on underneath it. She was naked."

Miranda stares at him in disbelief, with the unlikely picture of her fastidious mother sprawled naked on Tommy's sofa suddenly flash-frozen in her mind. "No," she gasps.

"Oh, yes. She said something like, 'I want you, Tommy,' and I couldn't believe my eyes myself. She looked so pathetic there . . . the aging beauty. I said to her very sharply, 'Pull yourself together, Connie! You're making a fool of yourself. I have no interest in you. I don't love you, I love Miranda.' She jumped to her feet. She was very angry. She ran at me, and for a minute I thought she was going to try to scratch my eyes out. But instead she just called me a few choice names, buttoned her coat, and dashed out of the house.

"So that's why she's turned against me. That's why she's turned *you* against me. That's why she wants to get rid of me. That's why you're firing me—because of a jealous woman's anger. She'll deny it, of course, but that's the truth. I never planned to tell you any of this, but now you know. You're dismissing an executive with more than twenty years of loyal service because of a woman's jealous rage."

She is still staring at him. Finally she says, "I know when you first came to New York from Indiana, you wanted to be an actor. I'd just like to say, Tommy, that I think the English-speaking stage lost a great performer when you went into retailing. And I've just figured something else out. Those E.K. bonuses you paid yourself all those years, those bonuses that were supposed to be for *extra kindness*. Those bonuses came from Ernestine Kolowrat, didn't they? Your share of Daddy's blackmail money, from the little deal you worked out with Ernestine on the side. Very clever, Tommy, I must say. You didn't blackmail Daddy directly. You just collected a third of the money Ernestine got. I suppose, the way you figured it, that meant your hands were clean."

He jumps to his feet. "That's ridiculous!" he shouts.

"Is it? Why is your mouth twitching like that, Tommy? Is it something that happens to your face when you tell a lie? Like Pinocchio's nose?"

His hand flies to his mouth, and his look is one of purest hatred now, his eyes narrowed to tiny slits. "Listen, you little bitch," he says, "I've spent the last twenty years bailing your father out of his messes, doing everything but wipe his ass for him. If it hadn't been for me, this store would still be a two-bit operation backed by a handful of two-bit crooks. You think your father was a merchandising genius? He was a merchandising *moron,* was what he was, with his stupid policy of letting customers take years to pay their bills, just for the publicity! *I* was the one who was the genius, trying to make his stupid policies look like they made economic sense. Who figured out ways to bail him out whenever the store was short of cash? *I* did! Who helped him buy his fancy houses and his racehorses and kept your mother and you in designer dresses, and you in fancy boarding schools and colleges? Who sat back and let him grab all the glory? *I* did. Your father would have been *nothing* without me—nothing but a washed-up ex-con piece of shit, which was all he ever was from the beginning!"

"And this is the man who was closer to you than a brother? Oh, my, oh, my," she says.

His words come pouring out now, rapid-fire, the sentences tumbling on top of one another. "Shut up, you stinking bitch! Listen to me! If you try to make trouble for me over this Blazer business, you'll see the shit really hit the fan! All his dirty little secrets that I helped him keep! His real name! His prison record! The girl in Boston! The Van Degan swindle! I could go on and on. You think you can run this store without me? Well, let me tell you what you're going to find! You're going to find I've dug a hole for you so deep you're never going to climb out of it! The walls of that hole are going to cave in on you and bury you in shit! And you know why you'll never be able to dig yourself out of that shithole? Because you're too *stupid*, that's why!

"You know what your father really thought of you? He thought you were a stupid, oversexed, round-heeled slut with popcorn for brains—popcorn soaked in piss! And he was right! I never should have talked him into giving you that stupid little job in the advertising department. He knew you were too stupid even for that, and he told me so. It was me, *me*, who begged him to give you that job, remember? And this is the thanks I get for it— fired—because you think you can be just like him, Mr. High and Mighty! You'd be nowhere if it weren't for me! Neither would your mother! Everything you've both got you owe to me! I've done everything for the two of you but wipe the cum out of your cunts! That's all you are, ass-wipes!"

"Oh, my, oh, my," she says again. "And this is the woman you said you wanted to make your full partner?"

"Shut up! I offered you that because I knew if I gave you enough rope you'd hang yourself! And when that happened—and it wouldn't have taken long—I'd have taken over, and I'd have what should rightfully have been mine all along, right from the very beginning. This store always should have been mine to run, and I'll tell you what's going to happen if you try to run it without me. In six months' time, you're going to find yourself dead in the water! This store is going to kill you, Miranda, just the way it killed your father. And I'm going to enjoy watching you die. I can't wait for you to die. I hope you die very soon. And meanwhile, if you try to cause me any legal trouble over the trust fund thing, you're going to find out what trouble really is!"

"Are you finished?" she says. She wants to smile, but resists the impulse. "Okay. Then listen to me. There isn't going to be any trouble if you do exactly what I say. I want you to clear out your desk and be out of here by the time the doors close at five o'clock. If you need help packing your things, I'll send a boy up from the stockroom. Between now and when you are ready to leave, you are not to set foot outside this office. Is that clear? Oh, and one other thing." She reaches in the pocket of her skirt. "This ring. The accounting department tells me Mrs. Lopez-Figueroa has already paid for it. True to form, her husband's bank always pays her bills on time. Oh, to have a husband like Señor Lopez-Figueroa! It didn't seem quite right to put this back into Smitty's stock and try to sell it again, even though that sort of thing's been done often enough before. It's an excellent stone. I thought you might like to have it, in lieu of severance pay." She places the ring on the top of his desk.

With one hand, he sweeps the ring off his desk. It flies through the air and falls, sparkling, on the carpet. Then he raises his hand as if to strike her, and instinctively she lifts her knee slightly into what might be called the firing position. But his hand falls to his side again.

"Goodbye, Tommy. Don't forget to turn in your passkey to Oliver. He'll be expecting it." And she turns and leaves him standing there.

"I did it!" she cries when she meets him at the Cafe Pierre bar. "I did it! I did it!"

"Was it pretty bad?"

"It was worse! No, it was better! I told him everything you said to tell him, and a few more things of my own!"

"Thank God we've got the box of records. If we didn't, they'd be in the incinerator by now."

"I can do it!" she says. "I know I can do it. Up till now, I've been whistling in the dark and *hoping* I could do it. But now I *know* I can do it, Peter! I've never felt so sure of anything in my life. I can run it! *I can run the store!"*

"Of course you can do it," he says. "I've always known you could."

"But I should say *we* can do it, shouldn't I? Because we're going to do it together, my darling, aren't we? We're going to do it together, you and I."

"What did you say?"

"I said I should say *we*. Because we're going to do it together."

"Funny. I thought I heard you call me 'my darling.'"

"Did I?" She laughs. "Yes, I guess I did. Yes, I did, my darling. Yes, my darling. Yes, my love. Yes, yes, yes."

He kisses her, and his kiss is so sudden that some of the sip of wine she has just taken spills into his mouth, and now they are both laughing, laughing at nothing at all, laughing at everything in the world, wine dribbling down their chins.

"We'll have to learn to do that better, won't we?" she says, laughing and sputtering. "We'll learn to do that next. So many things to do next . . . and next . . . and next . . ."

He scoops his hand around her waist and pulls her to her feet.

"Why is that couple dancing?" someone murmurs from the bar. "There isn't any music."

Epilogue

From *The New York Times*, March 11, 1992:

GROUND BROKEN FOR
FLYING HORSE ESTATES

OLD WESTBURY, N.Y.—One of the last great estates on Long Island's North Shore disappeared today as the Allen B. Sirkin Company of Manhattan broke ground for an ambitious new development. The estate, known as Flying Horse Farm, belonged to the late Silas R. Tarkington, the retailing tycoon. The Sirkin development will divide the 82-acre property into building lots of up to one acre each, where some 75 "personalized" luxury homes will be built to sell in the $1 million to $1.5 million range. The development will be known as Flying Horse Estates.

The Tarkington estate had included a small manmade lake. In the process of draining and filling this lake, an amusing relic of Silas Tarkington's era was discovered by workmen. It is a television set affixed with a brass plaque reading *For Silas Tarkington, a great merchant, with warmest thanks from President and Mrs. Gerald R. Ford, 1976.* "We have no idea what the TV set was doing at the bottom of the lake," Mr. Sirkin said. "But since it has some historic significance, it will be preserved and displayed in our new clubhouse, though the set is obviously no longer in working order."

Rumors Denied

Meanwhile, members of the Tarkington family denied rumors to the effect that Flying Horse Farm had been sold in an effort to raise cash for Tarkington's, the fashionable Fifth Avenue specialty store that has been reported troubled with management uncertainties since the founder's sudden death last August. "The farm was simply too much for my mother to handle," said Miranda Tarkington, 25, the store's new president and the daughter of the founder. "Also, it harbored unhappy memories for her," Ms. Tarkington added, "since my father died there." Silas Tarkington's widow, now Mrs. Jacob Kohlberg, is in the process of selling other of the former couple's properties, Ms. Tarkington confirmed. "My mother has a new husband and a whole new life now," Ms. Tarkington said. "That keeps her very busy."

Ms. Tarkington also denied rumors that the store has experienced fiscal upheavals since her father's death, noting that the store had a "better than average" Christmas season and that this year's first-quarter figures are expected to surpass last year's. She also stressed the store's "new and more youthful" management team, in which Peter Turner, 29, an M.B.A. graduate of Harvard and a former journalist, serves as the store's executive vice president and general manager. Turner replaced Thomas E. Bonham III, 45, who retired in October of last year and who had been serving as the store's interim chief executive.

Ms. Tarkington preferred not to comment on whether Mr. Bonham's retirement had been forced or voluntary. "You really should ask him that question," she said. Mr. Bonham could not be reached for comment, however, and *The Times* was told he was on his honeymoon. Bonham recently married the former Harriet Minskoff, the widow of the mysterious financier who, just days before his still-unsolved murder last fall, took out a $10 million accident-insurance policy on his life. The newlyweds, accompanied by a manservant, were said to be cruising aboard the Minskoff yacht, somewhere in the Philippine Sea.

Acknowledgments

My own career in retailing was youthful and brief, but memorable nonetheless. During the course of it I was able to meet, and get to know, a number of the great merchandising giants of their day, including Bernard F. Gimbel, Bruce Gimbel, Adam and Sophie Gimbel, Andrew and Nena Goodman, Jack Straus, Mildred Custin, Dorothy Shaver, Jo Hughes, and of course my boss, the late, legendary Bernice FitzGibbon. These people, and the perfumed jungle of department and specialty stores they inhabited were in no small part the inspiration—if that's not too pompous a word—for this novel, and I have even given a few of them small cameo (and fictional) roles in the story. I'd like to thank each of them now for this privilege.

More recently, I am also indebted to Mr. and Mrs. Fred Lazarus III, of the Federated Department Stores family, both of whom took time off from a busy schedule to read this book in manuscript, and to point out details where I hadn't got it quite right. Thank you both, Fred and Irma. Similarly, Mrs. Phyllis Sewell of Cincinnati, a former Federated executive, read the manuscript with a keen and finicky eye, and made many helpful suggestions. Even before a word of this book was written, Mrs. Sewell gave me an invaluable "update" course on retailing in the 1980s and 90s. Thank you, Phyllis.

My favorite editor, Genevieve Young, was, as always, endlessly helpful and supportive of the project, as well as endlessly demanding and hard to please. But who would want an editor who was any other way? My friend, Dr. Edward Lahniers, who understands more about the workings of the human mind than most people, read the novel chapter by chapter as it emerged from my typewriter, and offered acute and valuable psychological observations about my characters' motivations and behaviors. "Now why would she react like that?" was his favorite question, and he was usually right. She just *wouldn't* react like that.

I'd also like to thank my friend and agent, Carl D. Brandt, for his cool, smooth, and professional guidance of this project from the beginning.

And, last but not least, I'd like to thank the woman to whom this book is dedicated and who, in ways she may not realize, became this novel's heroine.

Stephen Birmingham

About the Author

STEPHEN BIRMINGHAM wrote advertising copy for a famous New York department store early in his career. Since then he has chronicled the lives of the wealthy and powerful in numerous bestselling books, both fiction and nonfiction.

BESTSELLING BANTAM AUTHORS
NOW IN PAPERBACK!

TREAT YOURSELF TO
DOMINICK DUNNE

A SEASON IN PURGATORY
❑ 29076-2 $6.50/$7.99 in Canada
THE *NEW YORK TIMES* BESTSELLER
"Highly entertaining."—*Entertainment Weekly*
"Mesmerizing."—*The New York Times*

AN INCONVENIENT WOMAN
❑ 28906-3 $6.50/$7.99 in Canada
"His best novel."—*The New York Times Book Review*
"Irresistible."—*The Philadelphia Inquirer*

THE TWO MRS. GRENVILLES
❑ 25891-5 $6.99/$8.50 in Canada
"A luscious novel."—*Cosmopolitan*

PEOPLE LIKE US
❑ 27891-6 $6.50/$8.50 in Canada
"Wickedly sharp."—*The Philadelphia Inquirer*
"Scandalous."—*Los Angeles Herald-Examiner*

FATAL CHARMS and Other Tales of Today
❑ 26936-4 $5.99/$7.50 in Canada
An unvarnished look at the gilded world of the real-life
rich and famous. "Powerful and personal...Dunne is at
his brisk, acerbic best."—*Chicago Tribune*

THE MANSIONS OF LIMBO
❑ 29075-4 $5.99/$6.99 in Canada
"A fascinating collection by *Vanity Fair*'s most high-profile
chronicler of the high-profile."—*The Washington Post*